DRIVEN INTO THE TUMULT OF BATTLE BY
FEROCIOUS DESERT KINGS . . .
THEY FOUGHT FOR THEIR FREEDOM,
THEIR HERITAGE, AND THEIR HEARTS.

SHOBAI—Noble keeper of the secret of the Children of the Lion, his mighty strength made him a legend, his unique talent made him sought by kings, but his blindness made him vulnerable to a woman's betrayal and an enemy's treachery.

MEREET—Gloriously beautiful wife of Shobai, she is torn from her husband's arms and carried into slavery . . . where in the glittering court of a Pharaoh she will face the ultimate test of her love.

JOSEPH—Young Israelite, blessed with a prophetic gift, he is destined to become adviser to the mightiest kings . . . while his soul is divided between his heritage and the sweet temptations of the Pharaoh's land.

TUYA—Sensual woman, once a wild orphan of the streets, she has been tamed by a gentle husband, but unable to forget the excitement of the past or to resist a future in a bold warrior's forbidden arms.

BALINIRI—Courageous soldier-of-fortune whose skill in battle makes him feared by his enemies and whose masculine charm makes him loved by many women . . . even one who is another man's wife.

# FAMILY TREES
## BIBLICAL CHARACTERS

HAGAR (2) = ABRAM = (1) SARAI
(ABRAHAM)   (SARAH)

ISHMAEL    ISAAC = REBEKAH

ESAU

LEAH (1) =    = (2) RACHEL

JACOB
(ISRAEL)

ZILPAH (3) =    = (4) BILHAH
(LEAH'S MAID)       (RACHEL'S MAID)
(CONCUBINE)         (CONCUBINE)

REUBEN                          JOSEPH
SIMEON                          BENJAMIN
LEVI
JUDAH       GAD      DAN
ISSACHAR    ASHER    NAPHTALI
ZEBULUN
DINAH

---

## THE CHILDREN OF THE LION
BELSUNU

AHUNI = SHEPSET

KIRTA = TALLAY

ANAT (1) = SHOBAI = (2) MEREET

KETAN
YETI

HADAD (1) = DANATAYA = (2) HASHUM
BEN-HADAD = TUYA        SHAMIR

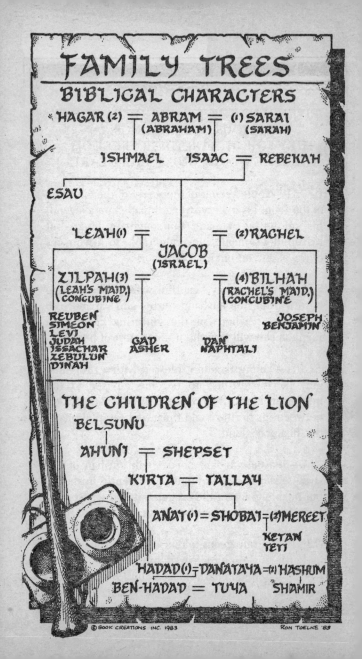

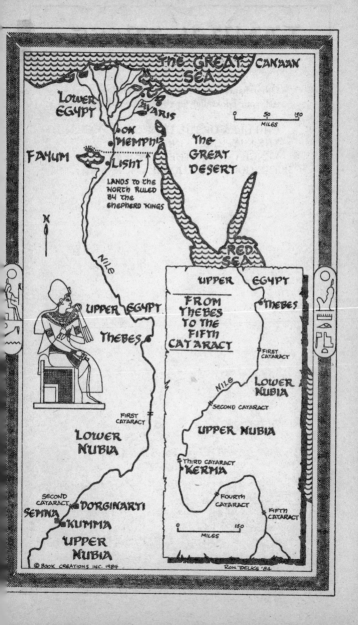

# Volume V

## THE GOLDEN PHARAOH

### PETER DANIELSON

Created by the producers of
Wagons West, White Indian,
Saga of the Southwest, and
The Kent Family Chronicles.

*Chairman of the Board: Lyle Kenyon Engel*

**BANTAM BOOKS**
TORONTO • NEW YORK • LONDON • SYDNEY • AUCKLAND

THE GOLDEN PHARAOH
A Bantam Book / published by arrangement with
Book Creations, Inc.
Bantam edition / March 1986

Produced by Book Creations, Inc.
Chairman of the Board: Lyle Kenyon Engel.

ISBN 0-553-25285-2

Published simultaneously in the United States and Canada

PRINTED IN THE UNITED STATES OF AMERICA

O    0 9 8 7 6 5 4 3 2 1

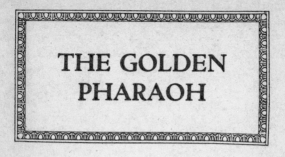

# THE GOLDEN
# PHARAOH

# Prologue

━━━━━━━━━━━━━━━━━━━━━━━━━━━━━━━━━━━━━━━━━━

The tall, hooded figure had stood silent, brooding, just beyond the campfire as the last rays of sunlight died before him on the western horizon. Despite his great age he had ignored the damp chill in the autumnal air and the biting wind that had swept down the mountainside behind him. Now, as the last light faded, he threw back the hood on his rough cloak and turned his white-haired, majestic old head into the wind, noting the slow coming of winter. And when he turned back to his audience on the far side of the guttering fire, his face was lit from below, dramatically, by the flames. His piercing eyes seemed to glow and fix each one of them with their prophetic glare. . . .

And now the Teller of Tales spoke, in that powerful, ageless voice of his: "In the name of God, the merciful, the compassionate . . ."

The wind sang and almost blew away his words. The people beyond the fire shivered, and strained to hear, cradled the children close to their chests. The old man raised his voice even higher and it carried above the wind: "Hear now the tales of the Children of the Lion . . . hear of the men and women of no people, and of their ceaseless wanderings among all nations. . . ."

He stopped for a moment and again sniffed the air. Was

1

*that a hint of the first rains? Were the chill hands of winter upon them so soon? But he shook off the thought and spoke, his voice reaching out, the people listening to his every word:* "You have heard how the Sons of the Lion—Shobai, the blind armorer, and his brother's son, Ben-Hadad—came to Egypt by two paths; and of how they fought to help the Egyptian king, Dedmose, hold back the invading tide of the fierce Shepherd Kings, who had seized the mouths of the Nile. . . ."

There was an almost audible sigh from the listeners beyond the fire. "You have heard," the old man continued, "of the valiant women of Shobai and Ben-Hadad, Mereet and Tuya: Rich man's daughter and pauper's orphan, they fought bravely beside the Sons of the Lion. Mereet bore Shobai twins, boy-child and girl-child, but fell captive to the Shepherd invaders as mighty Memphis, once capital of the pharaohs, was lost to the usurper, Salitis, who now ruled over Shepherd and native alike in his palace in Avaris, city of the delta overlords.

"I spoke, too," the storyteller said, his voice rising even higher, "of Joseph, once the favorite son of an uncrowned king in Canaan, now a slave to the Shepherd Kings, and of how the gift of prophecy came upon him in his captivity; and of how he met the lovely Mereet as their captors carried them into bondage; and of how he promised her reunion with her loved ones someday. . . ."

And now the Teller of Tales spread his hands wide, reaching out dramatically. "Hear me," he said. "Hear me, now. . . .

"Two years have passed since the fall of Memphis, and an uneasy peace lay on the divided land. In Avaris, Salitis's riches built a glittering empire, and men began to call him by flattering names——the 'Golden Pharaoh' among them. And as his power grew, a kind of madness began to come upon him little by little, as upon a man bewitched.

"And upriver in Lisht, Dedmose, rightful king of the Egyptian lands, landlocked and cut off from trade by sea, struggled to feed and arm his people. The king reached out to all peoples, seeking help. . . .

"And from across the seas in Moab, across the desert sands in Dilmun, others answered his call, and caravans from far lands once again brought food and trade goods to the beleaguered Egyptians."

But now an ominous note was heard in the storyteller's

strong old voice: "Only one nation was silent, and sent nothing, and even turned their caravans back—rich Nubia, to the south, where civil war, which pitted brother against brother, father against son, still rent the land asunder. And now word came of a mysterious third force men called the Black Wind, which fought loyalist and rebel alike in Nubia.

"War lay on all lands," he said, his voice quivering with emotion. "Only on the great lands of the Valley of the Two Rivers, many leagues to the northeast, lay the hand of peace, as Hammurabi of Babylon completed the building of his great empire. And as peace came to those far lands, men who had once been soldiers in Hammurabi's wars came drifting into the other nations still torn by war, looking for employment, as killers, conquerors, mercenaries—to Crete, to the Hittite lands of the North . . . and, in time, to the war-torn remnants of what had once been the greatest kingdom in the known world."

His listeners leaned forward eagerly, trying to hear, as the last words were blotted out by a low rumble of distant thunder from the hills beyond. Again the Teller of Tales raised his voice: "Such a one, my friends, was Baliniri of Babylon, greatest of Hammurabi's generals despite his youth, who worked his way slowly down the coast, drawn by rumors of a new pharaoh, rich beyond all imagining and powerful as a god—the man called the Golden Pharaoh, Salitis of Avaris, first among the great Shepherd Kings, ruler of rulers, Emperor of the Black Lands, once a nomad chieftain's son and now lord of all the southern coast of the Great Sea, yes, and of the mighty Nile itself. . . ."

Now in the night behind him a great lightning bolt split the sky, and it was some moments before the answering clap of thunder followed it. The speaker's eyes blazed. "Hear now," he said, "of divided Egypt, and of how the curse of God came upon all the lands beside the Great Sea, bringing famine and want. Hear now of the uneasy peace that came before the bleak days, and of what fortune it brought to the Children of the Lion. . . ."

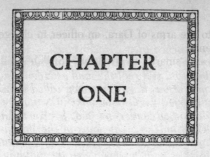

# CHAPTER ONE

## Nubia

### I

Below the battlements, below the high walls of the fortress of Dorginarti, the Nile's thousand voices spoke to the darkness. Close by the island's fortifications, where the river's only navigable channel cut close to the bank, the sighing of the water was soft and regretful; but a few leagues downriver the great second cataract continued its fall, and the water roared over the invisible black rocks, its voice powerful, dangerous.

High on the walls, Bek, the sentry, shivered in the reduced heat of evening and leaned out to peer down anxiously into the gloom. He had arrived with the new draft of replacements at Dorginarti only a day before and wanted to do a good job as lookout. For a moment the huge, baleful full moon came out from behind the drifting clouds and showed him the ghostly vision of the cataract below: a maze of rocky islets, bare and forbidding, stretching before him for miles and miles, and the great river threading its way among them.

But wait! What was that moving down there? There, by the shore— Did the moon's rays gleam on—?

Bek leaned forward, far over the wall's edge, but the moon went behind a cloud again, and darkness blotted out whatever it was that he thought he had seen.

Blinking, he cursed and stepped back from the wall,

4

almost into the arms of Dara, an officer in charge of the new replacements.

Bek came smartly to attention. "Sir!" he said. "I thought I saw—"

The moon, though, came out from behind the cloud again, and he could suddenly see Dara's florid face, the unfocused eyes. Palm wine? Bek gulped, tried to speak but found he could not. "S-sir . . ." he croaked. "I . . ."

"Rest easy," Dara said, not harshly. "You were just doing your job. Now, you say you saw something? Where? Show me." He leaned out over the edge.

Bek pointed. "There, sir. Where the moon glints on the rocks. I'd swear I saw . . . well, *something*, sir. Something moving."

"Crocodiles?" Dara suggested. "No, I'm jesting with you. Keep your eyes open." He moved back from the wall's edge. "There's a chance—just the outside chance, no more—of a raid." Seeing the alarm in the young man's eyes, he let his voice take on a more reassuring tone. "It's probably a false alarm, but there's always the chance these people aren't bluffing."

"What people, sir?" Bek said.

Dara looked around him, severeness and mild inebriation oddly mixed on his hawk's face. Then he spoke, keeping his voice low. "It's this rebellion thing." He went on to explain, his words few and quick.

Dorginarti, a few miles downriver from the giant twin strongholds of Semna and Kumma on opposite sides of the Nile, marked the farthest reaches of the Nubian lands and had been an outpost of the Egyptian pharaoh Dedmose within the living memory of even so young a man as Bek. The pharaoh now had pressing problems on his mind, besieged as he was by the invading Shepherd Kings, who now controlled the Nile delta and all of Dedmose's outlets to the Great Sea. A few years before, his sentries had been pulled back, abandoning the forts that had once commanded access to Nubia.

These—Dorginarti, Semna, Kumma, and various other smaller forts in the maze of islands that was the cataract—had been taken over by Taharqa of Nubia in his days of strength and manned by such as Dara. The forts had provided Taharqa with a small income, levying taxes on the few vessels bound downriver to engage in trade with the once-mighty Egyptian king.

But then, a year or two before, Taharqa's rebellious cousin Kashta had raised an army of his own: malcontents, younger sons, mercenaries drifting downriver, anyone he could press into rebellion. Kashta had declared war on Taharqa, pitting family against family, splitting the entire Nubian land. As his successes multiplied, so did his followers. Now many parts of Nubia lay entirely under Kashta's control. Thus far the war had had little impact on outposts as remote as Dorginarti, but . . .

"A week ago," Dara said, "the crew sent down to the river's edge for water one evening found, at the ford, a little ceremonial boat, only so long"—he held his hands out, just so—"the sort of thing one might find in a royal burial or in a rich child's playroom. In it was a papyrus. There was writing on it, in the language of the Egyptians, but in a strange hand, as if a foreigner's. It said, quite simply, 'Surrender by the full moon—or die at the hands of the Black Wind.' "

The moon shone full on Bek's startled expression.

"What's the matter, young man?" Dara asked. "What do you know of this?"

"The B-black Wind, sir?" Bek said. And just as he said it, the wind howled above them, like the keening of a damned soul, heard from far away. "You—you haven't heard of the Black Wind, sir?"

"No," Dara said. "I guessed that it is some idiotic name Kashta has given himself. I mean, who else would—" Something in the young man's expression stopped him.

"The . . . the Black Wind, sir, isn't Kashta. That much I do know. It's somebody else, but nobody seems to know who. They come out of the desert, suddenly, and strike, and retreat into the desert again as if they had never been. And—sir, they strike at Kashta's people *and* ours. Do you know a man named Beket, sir? One of Kashta's captains?"

"Yes. I served with him years ago. I was disgusted to hear he'd gone over to Kashta."

"Yes. Well, sir, he's dead. So is his entire detachment. Beket had captured the fort at Sai Island, at the third cataract. One night, sir . . ." He gulped again. "Well, we don't know what happened. They don't tell people on my level much in the way of details, anyhow, sir. The day following the attack I was part of a detachment sent to lay siege to the fort. We found it in flames, sir. Everyone in it was dead."

"The Black Wind?" Dara asked, his voice tense.

"Yes, sir." Bek shivered, despite the evening's warmth. "And not a man left alive to tell who they were, what they wanted, or where they came from."

Dara cursed softly. "And of course nobody bothers to keep us officers informed. They just send me a draft of you over from Semna, with no messages for the man in charge." He leaned out over the wall again to look down. "One of these days, young man, they'll—"

His words broke off suddenly as something near the rocks caught his eye. "There *is* something out there!" he said in a hoarse whisper. He turned to Bek and put a hand on the younger man's shoulder. "Don't make a fuss. Give me your spear, then go down to the barracks and get me the captain of the guard up here. As quickly and quietly as you can—I don't want any damned panic among all these green troops," he said, his voice losing none of its urgency in its half whisper. "Get going, now!"

The wind had begun to pick up, and the moon came out of the clouds. For scarcely more than a heartbeat it gleamed on shining, naked black bodies that slipped silently out of the river and moved quickly to the fortress's base, and glinted on the worn handle of a razor-sharp knife, painted as black as the ebony body of the silent warrior who bore it. Unseen black fingers and toes felt for holds on the sun-dried brick walls of the stronghold, and slowly the black tide rose up the rough wall, silently, with deadly efficiency.

Yuti, the sentry whose sector of the wall met the one Dara had taken over from Bek, hurried down the passageway that ran atop the wall toward the next post. Dara had told him that it was all-important just now to alert the other sentries without raising an alarm; but speed was also important, and Yuti cursed the clouds that obscured the moon and forced prudence on his steps. If only they could light this pathway on nights like this! Of course that was impossible: If one's eyes got used to the torchlight, one could not see into the surrounding darkness at all.

Up ahead, motion. Yuti stopped. "Iritisen?" he said, calling the name of the next sentry.

There was no answer. But even in the near-total darkness his sharp eyes could make out another movement. Why did Iritisen not answer? Then the moon came out and shone full on the naked body of the intruder, on the darkened blade

in the invader's long-fingered hand. Yuti's hand froze on his
spear hilt. He looked down the intruder's hard, bare body
and saw, crumpled on the stone flooring, the body of a
soldier in Nubian colors. Iritisen!

Yuti brought his spear up to the ready, just as the
intruder's knife lunged at him. But the knife never landed; it
did not need to. From behind, a strong black arm clamped
over Yuti's neck, and a powerful black hand drove a second,
unseen knife into Yuti's back. The spear fell from Yuti's hands
with a faint clatter, but by then he was beyond hearing or
seeing.

In the darkness of the moon's next retreat behind a
cloud, the black tide flowed silently, invisibly, down the walls
and inside the fortifications. The attackers dropped silently
on bare feet into the darkness; they fanned out to surround
the barracks. When the moon came out, they were invisible,
flattened against walls in deep shadow, waiting patiently for
the clouds.

Atop the wall, Dara was furious. Where was Bek? Where
was Neb-amun, captain of the guard? And Yuti . . . by now
he should have come to the end of his sector of the wall and
returned. Why was there no activity down below, in the
barracks? Why was there no sound but the sighing of the
wind above, and the ceaseless murmuring of the river outside?

Wait! What was that tiny *clank* over there in the darkness along the wall? Dara gripped the spear he had taken
from Bek and peered down the long corridor atop the wall.
"Yuti?" he said in a loud whisper. "Yuti?"

But now, from below, there came a shrill scream of pain,
and as he looked down into the interior courtyard, a barracks
door flew open and a shaft of light shot out, a long stripe of
light that blinded him for a moment. And from the interior
there was the sound of fighting!

*"Captain of the guard!"* Dara called out, casting aside all
caution. As he looked across the courtyard, he could see black
shadows moving just beyond the reach of the light. Shadows . . .
black, naked bodies . . . he could hardly make them out.

Now there was a sound up on top of the wall near him!
He gripped the spear more tightly and held it ready. "You
there!" he said in a voice that was forceful with false bravado.
"Show yourself! Advance and be—"

From behind him two powerful pairs of hands clamped

down on his arms. Other hands tore the spear from his grasp. He struggled, but to no avail. "Let me go!" he said in a tight voice. "Who are you?"

The screams from the courtyard drowned out his words. Turning his head, Dara could see the victorious black warriors pouring out of the barracks, some bearing torches torn from the interior walls, all carrying the ubiquitous black-painted knives. Dara gasped. They had come to the battle naked, the better to remain invisible in the blackness of night. They were lean, almost giants: a head taller than his own troops at least, and every last one of them was a woman! High-breasted, regal, with the strong out-thrust buttocks of the gigantic hill women of the South!

"Wh-what's going on here?" Dara said, his voice breaking. In the firelight he could see the women who held him: tall, small-bosomed, with the strong features of the Nilotic women of the high mountains. He struggled, but the huge black hands held him fast. His eye fell on the sharp knife in the hands of the woman before him. "Who are you?" Dara asked.

"The Black Wind," one of the women said in a heavily accented voice.

But then another, even more queenly figure, mature, powerful, sharp-eyed, pushed her aside and faced him.

"No," the newcomer said. "I'll give him a name. Where he's going there'll be no living person to tell it to." Her voice was almost gentle as she spoke to Dara. "Make your peace with your gods, my friend," she said in the voice of a native-born Nubian. "My name is Ebana."

She nodded gravely, and the knives fell.

## II

For several weeks now, rebel Nubian troops loyal to Kashta, leader of the insurgents challenging Taharqa, had held the west bank of the Nile between the great second cataract and the massive twin fortresses of Semna and Kumma. Quartered at the fortress of Kor, they had for a time harassed the smaller Tahárqa stronghold of Dorginarti until the relatively even balance between the two opposing units had forced a reluctant cessation of hostilities.

However, as dawn broke and the warm Egyptian sun rose slowly over the great river, the rebel sentry on the west bank surmounted the Rock of Abusir to look down at the virtually featureless expanse of the cataract, with its three hundred black-rock islets creating a six-mile-long maze. His partner, grumbling at the earliness of the hour, followed him to the top of the rock. When he arrived, the first sentry, shading his eyes, was looking across the river toward Dorginarti.

"What's that?" the second man, Upuat, asked. "Smoke? But there's nothing over there to burn. The rock is as bare as an egg."

"You're right, my friend," his partner, Menkh, said. "There's nothing to burn—nothing but the fort itself."

"The fort? Dorginarti? But—"

Menkh ignored him. "I know: We're the only detachment this far north right now, unless Kashta has someone doing something we don't know about." He frowned, squinting against the morning sun. "We'd better get over there and investigate."

Upuat stared wide-eyed at him, incredulous. "Do you want us to get captured or killed? Have you lost your mind? I've got a better idea. Let's go for help. Let's get back to Kor and tell the lord Amenatu about this. Then he can send an armed detachment."

Menkh made a thoughtful face. "Perhaps you're right. On the other hand, anyone with news like this will be taken before the lord Sita, not Amenatu. And you know what *that*'ll be like. Tell you what, my friend: I'll take a closer look myself, over there. Don't worry, I'll be careful. Meanwhile, you go back to Kor for help."

"All right," his partner said, and took off. Menkh watched him go, then clambered down the rock himself, wondering if he had done the right thing. It was not until he was in his little coracle, battling the current below Dorginarti, that he managed to come to the conclusion that whatever terrors Dorginarti held, they were little beside the greater peril of facing Sita, commander of the Kor detachment, in one of his rages.

Still, as he neared the island he scanned the towering fort, expecting at any moment to be hailed with a rain of arrows from the high walls. But the arrows never came, and the plume of smoke he had seen earlier from the Rock of Abusir drifted slowly downstream. And even when he landed on the island itself, there was no resistance. *Curious,* he thought. *It's as if the whole place has been abandoned.*

But the thought was scarcely formed when he found the first of Taharqa's Loyalist soldiers, at the foot of the great wall, throat cut, eyes staring. Stunned, Menkh made his way cautiously around the walls, where the great gate, ordinarily staunchly defended and virtually impassable, stood wide open.

Inside, not a soul was left alive. And there was no sign of any attacker, other than the silent bodies of the slain defenders.

Upuat had worked fast. By the time Menkh found his way back to the shore of the rebel-held west bank, a troop of soldiers had followed Upuat back to the foot of Abusir. Menkh looked—and gulped. Leading the group was Sita himself, commander of the fortress of Kor!

Menkh shivered in his sandals but forced himself to come smartly to attention and salute. "Menkh, sir, reporting. I've been to Dorginarti, sir. They're all dead. Every last man. And no sign of who did it."

Sita fixed Menkh with his raven's eye, then dismissed him. He turned to his second in command, Amenatu. "Have it investigated. A raw sentry can't be expected to find the right signs. The attackers must have left some clues as to who they were." He took note of the knowing look on his subordinate's face. "Ah," he said sarcastically. "You look like a man who *thinks* he knows something I don't."

"Well, sir," Amenatu said, no trace of servility in his voice, "I've been trying to tell you about—"

"Oh, yes," Sita said sourly. "This Black Wind thing. A bunch of phantoms who appear out of the night. And nobody knows who they are."

Amenatu's smile was thin and remote. "I beg your pardon, sir. That's not quite accurate. We have physical descriptions of the ones who raided our outpost at the desert's edge. Nilotic types, from south of the Sudd. But, sir, there's increasing evidence that their numbers now include some of Taharqa's own, who have deserted his forces to join them."

"Ah!" Sita said triumphantly. "That's good news! Anything that weakens Taharqa—"

"Unfortunately," Amenatu went on, "the same is true of our own side."

Sita stared, incredulous. "Eh? Are you trying to tell me there are turncoats from our army? People who left Kashta for Taharqa's side?"

Amenatu's eyes narrowed, but he said nothing for a moment. "No, sir," he said, keeping his tone carefully deferential. "I'm talking about people among us who . . . ah . . . have thought it better to join the Black Wind."

Sita threw a hot glare at him. Then he turned to his troop. "You!" he said to a seasoned subaltern. "Take ten men and investigate. Join us back at the fort. The rest of you, come with me." He turned to his second in command. "Ride with me in the chariot, Amenatu," he said. "You can tell me all about this swinish conspiracy as we ride."

An aide brought the chariot up and held the horses for their mounting. Sita took the reins of the light model, acquired by trade by Kashta before Nubian relations with the Shepherd Kings had broken down. "Now, Captain," he said coldly, "tell me about this apostasy business. Members of our own organization are going over to this—this bunch of ragtags? What justification could they adduce for such treason?"

The rattle of the high wheels cut off part of Amenatu's reply. Sita turned, watching his subordinate's lips as he spoke. ". . . captured one of the, uh, turncoats and questioned him. The man said that he was tired of the civil war and wanted to see peace again in Nubia, and apparently the only way to find this was to get out from in the middle between Taharqa and Kashta. If this meant going outside their quarrel and enforcing peace on them by whatever means—"

"Hah!" Sita said savagely, his eyes back on the road before him, his hands gripping the reins hard. "Typical self-serving drivel! Treason, I say! And the chap who captured this traitor? Did he hang him?"

Amenatu's habitual half smile was a sad one this time. "The punishment was the usual one, sir. Impalement."

Sita's eyes blazed. His first rejoinder would have been violent, but the chariot lurched crazily as a wheel hit a rock, and he fought to recover balance. When he regained his composure, he asked, "And you, Captain? Have the seductive importunities of the, uh, Black Wind made their inroads with you, too, perhaps?"

There was no answer for a moment. Their route lay

along a ridge above the shore. Below them reeds grew in the shallows, and in a sandy patch, palms, tamarisks, and mimosas grew on soil watered by periodic overflows of the river. Amenatu's expression was thoughtful, but at length he shook his head. "If you mean am I beginning to doubt our cause, sir, I'm a soldier. I follow my leader."

"Huh." Sita's mouth curved in a cynical sneer. "A properly soldierlike, diplomatic answer." He slowed the horses as the path climbed, and the two were silent until their chariot reached the top of the ridge, where Sita halted the horses for a moment to look up at the suddenly visible walls of the fortress of Kor.

The fortification was by no means the size of the massive twin forts of Semna and Kumma, upriver a matter of a few miles, but the builder had drawn upon the principles of their construction. The fortress of Kor, thick-walled and imposing, stood atop a rocky prominence; besides the two heavily guarded main gates, there were a small postern gate and a covered, totally enclosed stone stairway leading down to the Nile, to permit the safe drawing of water from the river during times of siege. This innovation dated from the time of Sesostris III, the great builder of river forts, and had been copied directly from the plan that that masterful architect had adapted for the fort built at Semna by Amenemhet I.

There the resemblance stopped. Kor, unlike Semna, held only a small garrison. The larger fort, still held by Taharqa's Loyalists, carried a permanent garrison of over three hundred soldiers, who lived with their families in a specially built town within the walls, complete with its own houses and temples. Kor, by comparison, sheltered an all-male garrison a third the size of the larger one. The difference reflected two opposing views of military discipline.

"Looks like a prison, doesn't it?" Sita said, deep irony in his voice.

Amenatu respectfully inclined his head, but did not answer. Instead, he looked to the top of the wall, to the tower that reared high above the northern gate, where his friend and messmate Pasab manned the lookout. On the side away from Sita he raised his hand discreetly at shoulder height and signaled. Pasab nodded. Amenatu turned to his superior. "Prison, sir?" he asked. "We're all free men, aren't we, sir? I mean, we've chosen to be here, haven't we? The better to oppose Taharqa's tyranny and create a free Nubia?"

"I see you have the litany down," Sita said, sneering. "Well, I don't care how mealymouthed my subordinates are when it comes to articulating their loyalty to the cause, as long as they *are* loyal to the cause." He flipped the reins at the horses, and they moved slowly out along the causeway to the gate. As they approached the great northern entrance, it swung open slowly. The guards did not wait to challenge the men approaching the fort, but saluted Sita with deference and motioned him inside. "Damn them," Sita said as he guided the horses inside. "They're getting lax. They're supposed to challenge me every time. I'll have to see to it that next—"

He never finished the sentence. The reins fell from his hand, and his mouth hung open as he looked around. The chariot was surrounded by rows and rows of gigantic, fierce-looking Nilotic warriors, all fearsomely armed, many with faces cicatrized grotesquely after the customs of the savage tribes of the far South. And with them, shoulder to shoulder, stood Nubians, similarly armed, subject—if Sita could believe his eyes—to the same discipline.

"Wh-what's going on here?" Sita demanded. "Guards! *Guards!*"

No one moved. Then Amenatu slowly picked up the reins Sita had dropped. "They, too, are loyal to their leader, sir," he said. "Only their leader isn't Kashta anymore." He stepped lightly to the ground and held up a hand to help Sita down beside him.

Sita did not take the proffered hand. He looked around him with eyes that blinked incredulously. He looked at the orderly ranks of the massed troops, white and black, Semitic and Hamitic. And now he could see the remainder of the little detachment that had followed him back from Dorginarti, marching in through the great gate, in step, unperturbed by the differences they could see around them. As Sita looked on, they came to a halt and stood to smartly.

Sita looked down at his sometime subordinate, and a bit of the old harshness and cynicism crept back into his choked voice. "And just when did all *this* take place, Captain?" he asked.

Amenatu held his hand out again, and this time, reluctantly, Sita took it, stepping down beside him. "We were approached some days ago, sir, when you were back at headquarters conferring with Kashta. The leader of the Black

Wind appealed to reason. This war has gone on long enough, and as long as Taharqa and Kashta are in charge, there'll be nothing but fratricide. Families and households are split, brother warring against brother. We thought about it, sir, and took a vote. We decided the war had to come to an end."

"Oh, you did, did you?" Sita said. His hand went to his sword, and a dozen spears around him came instantly to the ready. Up on the walls, bowmen stood poised, their arrow tips glinting in the sun. Sita sighed and took off his sword belt to hand to Amenatu with an air of disgusted resignation. "All right," he said wearily. "Where is this leader of theirs? Isn't he the one I should be handing this to?"

Amenatu bowed and took the belt from him. "That's just the point, sir," he said. "We're not following the usual rules of war anymore. We will fight only to end the war. But you asked about their—our—leader. From the look of the sentries atop the wall, I'd say he was preparing to enter just now, sir."

Sita looked back toward the huge gate, which still stood open. As he did, one of the black warriors barked out an order in a language Sita had never heard before, and the detachment sprang rigidly to attention. Drums beat high on the walls, and horns blared. A procession made its way slowly into the fort: first, foot soldiers, half of them Nilotic, the rest Nubian; then mounted troops bearing banners of black; then . . .

Sita's eyes narrowed. The leader, mounted on a gigantic charger, was the largest man he had ever seen: a handspan taller even than the tallest of his own black troops, massive, heavy-chested. He was as black as they, but age had turned his hair and beard gray in places. The effect was not of age so much as of authority. His eyes were piercing, his expression one of amused curiosity and—what?—a certain acceptance of all that his steady gaze lit upon. The posture, the stance, were those of a man half the graybeard's age, and there was still great power, focused and controlled, in that gigantic body.

Amenatu waited until the procession had come to a halt, and then bowed with respect to Sita. "Sir," he said, "I'm honored to present the leader of the Black Wind." His voice rose to carry to the entire garrison. "*Akhilleus!*" The massed troops, Nubian and otherwise, instantly echoed him; the Nilotic's troops's tongues altered the name to "Akillu."

The giant smiled, heard out their cries of enthusiasm, and then held up his hand. Silence fell immediately upon them. *Gods!* Sita thought. *He's got them in the palm of his hand!*

"Peace," Akhilleus said. "I bring news of Dorginarti. The fortress chose to resist. Its garrison is no more. And now, Ebana's unit moves on Semna. We will meet them there tonight. Our brothers and sisters in arms surround Kumma, across the river, as I speak. By noon tomorrow, the lower reaches of the river will be ours. And peace will once again reign on the lands of the cataract."

The cheer was rousing, causing the ground of the fortress to vibrate. Sita stood shaking his head slowly from side to side. His expression was that of a man who had gone mad.

# CHAPTER
# TWO

## Avaris

### I

"Really, my friend," said the noble Ersu, craning his neck to look around at the sizable crowd that had begun to gather in the marketplace. "Can this be the Bazaar of the Olive Tree? I can't recognize the place at all."

His friend Ameni shrugged and held out his hands, palms up, to indicate his own perplexity. "It's the times," he said. "Every day new buildings go up here in Avaris. In order for new buildings to go up, room must be made for them." He made way as the chair of a court noble went past, the slave bearers groaning under the weight. "I know what you mean, though. Even in the comparatively short time I've been in the delta, things have changed so much in this quarter that I can hardly recognize them." His tone remained delicately deferential as he continued. "As commander of the elite guards, don't your duties take you down this way sometimes?"

"Oh, come, my friend," Ersu said. "Surely you haven't remained ignorant of the way things are here under the noble, uh, pharaoh Salitis? I bought the title, and a pretty sum it cost me, too. I know nothing of police matters. My subordinates handle everything and hand me papyri to sign afterward to make it legal." He frowned at two men who jostled him as they passed. The area around the slave auction

17

block was getting very crowded. "Wasn't there an inn over there last year? I distinctly remember coming down here, oh, a year ago, maybe two or three, to watch the senet matches. They held them right there, where the auction block is now. Khensu, I think it was, played a match and lost to some foreign urchin from Canaan. Ben-something or other . . ."

"I have no idea," Ameni said. "I was still at the court of Dedmose then."

Ersu put a consoling hand on his friend's arm. "There, there. No use crying over one's losses. You made the right move, crossing the border and coming here. So what if you were once cupbearer to Dedmose? His time has passed. He's king of no more than Lisht and the Fayum and the southern nomes now, and they don't really amount to much. One of these days our armies will push him back into Nubia, and that'll be the last of the people who did you such an ill turn. Think of the future you have here, my friend."

"Thanks to your own generosity and help," Ameni said with a surge of genuine gratitude. "If you hadn't interceded for me—"

"What are friends for, anyway?" Ersu asked. His hand tightened on Ameni's arm. "Well, look *there*," he said, pointing to the rooftop opposite the slave market. "Now *there's* a rare sight for slave auction." He managed somehow to point without attracting attention. "See? The lord Kirakos himself!"

Ameni looked up at the old soldier's still-fierce figure, the hooded eyes, the beaked nose, and severe mouth, and nodded. "That *is* odd. Besides, I thought he was in mourning. He hasn't been seen at court for days."

"Yes," Ersu said. "Lost his wife. Seems to have shaken the old bear up. I suppose he has no one left now. He lost a son at the same siege of Melid that made him famous, up in the western marches of Padan-aram, and another son at Saïs, Who are those two chaps with him, I wonder? They don't seem to fit into his company now that he's virtually assured to fill the vacancy of grand vizier at court."

Ameni narrowed his eyes at Kirakos's burly companions. "Well, Kirakos is still a soldier," he said. "They could be soldiers. The bigger one has that look about him."

Ersu smiled. "Observant of you," he said, pleased. He looked up at the towering, strikingly handsome young warrior with the foreign-cut beard. "Yes, that has to be the fellow my officer told me about. In the Babylonian getup. His name's

Baliniri. The other man is probably a comrade he brought along for company. Rumor has it this Baliniri distinguished himself in the army of Hammurabi, by conquering the northern tribes and bringing them under one rule for the first time." His smile vanished. "So *that's* the way the wind's blowing."

"I don't understand," Ameni said.

"You'll soon get the hang of politics here," Ersu replied, a little patronizingly. "Kirakos is said to feel that in making that last climb up the ladder to Salitis's side, he's giving up too much—giving up control of the army, in fact. He obviously still wants to keep a finger on everything. And what better way than to install his own man as chief of the army, answerable only to himself?" He made a face. "Although he'll have a hard time of it trying to foist an outsider on the troops." He held up a hand as if weighing things. "On the other hand, he can't trust any of the old leaders anymore, with Vahan dead these two years."

"It's a sticky business, making it at court, isn't it?" Ameni asked, deferential again.

Ersu, as always, welcomed the chance to show off his superior knowledge. "Oh, quite, dear fellow," he said. "But if you can make it past all the traps, past the pits and the quicksand and the adders in your path, the rewards are great. And you'll make it, fear not. I'll help you. And when you do make it, you'll think your days in Memphis under a provincial kinglet like Dedmose ill-spent. You simply have no idea of the money there is to be made here, with Salitis spending like a drunken sailor"—here his voice lowered to a whisper—"and throwing gold around as if it were base metal."

The two made way now for a pair of competent-looking servants wearing a familiar livery. "Ah," Ersu said. "Look. There are Kirakos's men. They will bid in his behalf. I wonder for what." A sudden thought struck him, and he turned to his companion. "Are you bidding today?"

Ameni blushed. "I—I've no money for that," he muttered. "But . . ."

"Oh, come now," Ersu said. "You need a manservant. If anything becomes available here, I'll not let you pass it up."

"No, please, I—"

"I insist. Any sum within reason. I'll guarantee your credit on the purchase."

Ameni half smiled; there was something in him that

resisted going deeper into Ersu's debt. "I—I thank you," he
said. "But—"

"No buts. I won't have it. It's settled," Ersu said. "But
choose well. I won't let you waste good money on a bad
purchase." He nudged his companion. "Here comes the good
Abushed now. Things are about to begin." And he pulled
Ameni aside to make room for the auctioneer and his party.
Behind Abushed, guards trailed a long string of slaves, male
and female.

Ameni watched them pass. "*Clothed* slaves?" he asked.
"Is this some sort of strange local custom?"

"No—it's a special auction," Ersu explained. "The estate
of a well-to-do court official who died owing a bundle in
taxes. He'd disputed the official valuation of his assets and
held off paying, pending final settlement before a magistrate;
but before the thing could come to trial, he died intestate.
They're auctioning off his slaves and chattels to pay the
disputed amount."

"The slaves seem superior on the surface of it," Ameni
said. "This bunch of them would appear to be administrative
personnel. The dead chap must have been very well fixed.
There are quite a lot of them."

"Oh, yes," Ersu said. "I may wind up bidding on one or
two of them myself." He looked upward at the roof, and his
brows went up a trifle. "Kirakos seems to be alone now. I
wonder where those two Mesopotamians have gone to. . . ."

On the rooftop, Mekim—shorter, bright-eyed, thick-
bearded—had pulled his companion aside as their host leaned
forward to look into the street below. He spoke in the common speech of the Babylonian streets. "Look, Baliniri, I'm
not picking up this tongue of theirs as fast as you are. I didn't
understand half the words the old man said. What's going
on?"

Baliniri, a head taller, big-boned, grinned disarmingly
down at his comrade. "We're being wooed, as if we were a
couple of princesses. Our reputation has preceded us, and
our friend Kirakos is in the market not only for slaves, but for
a couple of good, seasoned mercenary soldiers, as well." His
grin widened. "Good, seasoned, *loyal* mercenary soldiers."

Mekim's smile was cynical, knowing. "I see. Hatchet
men for some old boy who's got ambition. Well, it isn't the
way I'd hoped to end my days."

"We came here to fight," Baliniri said, giving him a friendly cuff, "not to play bodyguard. And from the looks of things, this old fellow's boss, Salitis, seems to be more interested in putting on a show these days than in continuing the fight against the Egyptians. We'd wind up going to seed here."

"Then why waste our time—"

"Who's wasting time? He's picking my brain about conditions under Hammurabi, and about any new methods of warfare we may have learned. He's paying us for that privilege. He was a great cavalry leader in his own time, and his questions are intelligent. What's the matter, Mekim? Didn't you like the bed you slept in last night? Or the food you ate so much of, or the wine you drank? Or the servant girls . . ."

Mekim made a thoughtful face, reminiscing. "True, true. I have to admit, the little flutist was a bit out of the ordinary. And the tall one with the mole on her . . ."

Baliniri ignored him. "Meanwhile, I'm picking *his* brain. When I think I have enough information, we'll move on. All right? In the meantime, enjoy our host's bounty." His tone changed, though. "Here, I'd better get back to him."

With that, he walked to the rooftop's edge to stand beside Kirakos. "Have they begun yet?" he asked over the noise of the crowd below.

Kirakos turned to him, eyes distant and friendly at the same time. "Nothing important. A scribe or two have been sold. A sculptor. A gardener. The late Paheri was a man interested in the arts. There'll be a painter or two up for sale in a moment. Nothing that I'm interested in." He looked around him at the fine view of the city from the rooftop: temples, broad avenues, blocks of houses. "I haven't asked you yet: How do you like our city, what you've seen of it?"

Baliniri's handsome smile was formal but ingratiating. "It is all so new," he said. "I'm used to cities with all the sharp edges worn off." He shrugged. "You'll remember, sir, I'm not in the business of building cities or evaluating them. I'm more in the business of destroying them." He chuckled. "I think this town of yours might be a challenge to destroy. You could use a nice thick wall here, though. How vulnerable do *you* think Avaris would be to siege?"

"Not very," Kirakos said, smiling, his eyes unreadable slits. "A well comes in here at only a few feet down. Our granaries are well stocked. But you're observant."

"I'm paid to be, sir."

"So you are." The smile stayed the same, but the eyes opened a bit, grew friendlier. "I've decided I rather like you." A certain resignation came into his voice. "But I do have the feeling we won't become, ah, master and servant, that you'll be moving on."

"I haven't made up my mind, sir. But—that inspection of your army yesterday, at the encampment . . . well, sir, can I be frank with you?"

"Certainly, my young friend. Speak freely."

"Well, sir, I found myself thinking, can *this* be the army of the mighty Hai, the Shepherd Kings who conquered half the known world on the way here? The men are slack, out of condition, effete—" He paused, wondering if he had said too much.

"Go on, my friend. Your thoughts echo my own. You know I was a soldier myself once. And a rather renowned one, if I do say so. I look at the court, at myself— Look at me now: an aging and rather oily courtier. . . ."

"You do yourself wrong, sir."

"No, I don't. The court's gone soft, decadent. We have it too easy here. If your king Hammurabi wanted to take us and could solve the purely logistical problem of getting an army here . . ." He left the sentence hanging. "Don't bother arguing with me, young man—if your reputation is well founded, you could take the delta from us with an army half the size of ours."

Baliniri's eyes widened, then he smiled. He responded to this kind of honesty. "Why, yes, sir. I could."

"Very well. Salitis, our, ah, pharaoh, is the son of the wisest, craftiest leader the Hai ever had—a man named Manouk. His son, however, seems bent on proving that administrative genius does not run in the family." He waved away all thought of caution. "Yes, I know: treasonous talk. But I'm almost too old to care any more." He steered back to the subject deftly. "Salitis is a lightweight. Worse, he's beginning to show signs of instability: terrible headaches, wild dreams. He's convinced that one of the Egyptian gods is speaking to him through his dreams, and he's offered staggering rewards to anyone who can divine the meaning of them."

"Not a good situation, sir."

"No, it isn't. Everyone knows it, but no one dares to do anything about it. He's taken to calling himself the Golden

Pharaoh and insists that all official documents refer to him this way. He spends like a madman. If this country we now rule were not so limitlessly rich in gold and grain and other precious commodities . . ." He spread his palms wide in a gesture of helplessness. "You see, he—"

But something in the bidding below caught his attention, and he held up his hand, ending this string of confidences. "Here," he said, "I think they're about to start auctioning off the better sort of slave. I may make a purchase or two from this lot of them. Watch the bidding with me, eh?"

In the street below, Ameni suddenly caught his friend Ersu by the arm, gripping it tightly. "Gods!" he said. "I can't believe it. I can't believe my eyes! Ersu, you're quite serious about that loan?" Ersu nodded. "Oh, thank heaven," Ameni said, his eyes riveted on the auction block before them. "I won't forget this, really I won't."

"You've seen something you want, then?" Ersu asked.

But Ameni could hardly hear him. He was listening to the excited voices in his own mind. He kept muttering over and over again, "My fortune's made. Gods! My fortune's made!"

## II

Ersu looked at the slaves on the stand, one by one. "These are all young, too young. For a proper manservant, you'd want a mature man, one who's done this sort of thing before."

"I'll explain later," Ameni said excitedly. "Just stand by your promise about the credit. I'll be eternally grateful." He squeezed Ersu's arm again. "You'll be glad you did."

Ersu smiled beneficently. "Oh, to be sure, dear friend. Just keep the cost down to thirty gold rings or so."

"So many? Ersu, you're a true friend. I'll make it worth your while, I will. I tell you, my fortune's made, and perhaps yours, as well."

Ersu once again looked quizzically at him, but Ameni

waved away further questions as the bidding began. There were two other slaves to be auctioned, and then . . . Joseph!

There was no doubt in Ameni's mind that this was who the third man was: a little older, a bit more mature, but indisputably the same young man he had met in prison back in Memphis, during that terrible time some years ago when he, Ameni, had been falsely accused of conspiring against the lives of the pharaoh Dedmose and his all-powerful vizier, Madir. For days he had lain under sentence of death, accused of poisoning the wine of the king and the vizier. The red-tinged beard and hair, the upright carriage, the fair Canaanite complexion—these gave Joseph away already, but the eyes decided things in the end. The eyes were those of a man who, however young, had seen too much, suffered too much, yes, both in this world and in the strange world in which his prophetic visions took place. . . . The young man was an authentic seer.

Ameni's few conversations with Joseph had established that he was the son of a tribal chieftain, a man named Jacob, of some note up in Canaan. Jacob was also a priest of some tribal god as well, and from all available signs, the boy had been groomed to follow in his father's footsteps. But his father's favoritism, directed at him, the penultimate of many sons, had aroused his older brothers' ire, and they had planned to sell him into slavery. Before their plan could be completed, Joseph was kidnapped by traders. Thus by stages he had found his melancholy way, in chains, to Egypt, to his present low status.

But the gift, that amazing gift . . .

Ameni knew he would never forget that day in the Memphis dungeons when he had told Joseph his dream: He had seen a vine with three branches that had begun to bud and blossom as he had watched; soon there had been clusters of grapes, which he had squeezed into Dedmose's royal cup to make wine. The king had drunk deeply.

When forced to describe his dream to the chief jailer, Ameni knew he'd probably be condemned to impalement. His dream, after all, sounded like an admission of the blackest guilt. But then he had told it to Joseph, who had brooded upon the matter for a day, prophesied, then intervened with the chief jailer on Ameni's behalf. "It's good news," he had said at last. "It means that in three days you'll be out of prison, and you'll have your old job back, a bonus for good and faithful service, and the everlasting goodwill of your master, the king." And it had all come to pass, just as the boy had said it would.

More impressive, Joseph had also prophesied about the dream of Yusni, the chief baker, who had been imprisoned at the same time. Yusni had dreamed of three baskets of pastries on his head; the top basket had borne the precise kind of pastry Dedmose preferred most, but the birds had come down and devoured them before they could be taken before the king. Joseph, pleading weariness, had begged off, but Yusni had pestered him into interpreting the dream, to his own eventual horror. For what the dream had meant, Joseph had said, was that in three days Yusni would be dead, mere carrion, and the birds would eat his flesh. He had said this with an air of such pain and exhaustion that Ameni, overhearing, had shuddered.

And, horror of horrors, it had all come true.

Ameni wiped his sweaty hands on his loincloth. The first slave had been sold. Only one more remained. And then there was Joseph.

There was, of course, more to remember. After Joseph had made the prophecy about Ameni's future, the lad had looked him in the eye and caught his arm. "When you're back in your old position, cleared of charges of wrongdoing," he'd said, "you'll be a man of standing, of position, in the kingdom. You could do worse than to remember me—and, perhaps, put in a good word for me? I'm a stranger here, in a land far from the one I was born in, friendless and alone."

Ameni sighed. Of course he had promised to remember. But he had been so glad to be released from prison that he had let the whole matter slip his mind. And then he had learned that the king's friendship was no good without the friendship of Madir, the omniscient and powerful vizier. And for some reason Madir had continued to distrust Ameni, as if the mere fact of ever having been accused of a crime made him forever a prime suspect in any subsequent wrongdoing.

In the end Ameni had taken the first opportunity to convert his belongings into gold and smuggle it across the lines to Shepherd-occupied Egypt. It would have been a flawless plan except for the thieves who had fallen on him on the way to Avaris. He had arrived in the Shepherd city penniless, friendless; only his own good fortune in having met Ersu and been taken under his wing had saved him from a grubby life of helpless poverty and exploitation.

And now? Now, if he played his cards right, he would finally be back on the road to riches and power. If he bought Joseph—

Yes! There was talk at court about Salitis, the self-styled Golden Pharaoh, his strange dreams, and the failure of all the seers who had thus far come to court to interpret these dreams. Salitis had not only come to believe strongly in the prophetic quality of his dreams but had grown scornful and angry at all the inadequate readings the diviners at court had given him. He had even put the word out along the trade routes that true diviners of any country, any philosophical persuasion, would find welcome at the court of Salitis, and that the sage who correctly interpreted his dreams would be rewarded instantly with riches and power.

Emboldened by his own enthusiasm and by Ersu's offer of credit, Ameni pushed forward through the crowd to the front row, his eyes still on the slim young man at the auctioneer's side. Joseph's eyes scanned the crowd coolly; he seemed indifferent as to who purchased him. Briefly his eyes met Ameni's and held for a moment; a puzzled expression came over the young man's face, then passed. He looked away. Then he looked back.

Ameni smiled nervously. *He remembers! He remembers me, but isn't quite sure from where.* He nodded at the young man, smiling more broadly now. *Careful, now; try to look reassuring.*

The auctioneer stepped forward and indicated Joseph with a wave of his hand. "Next, my friends, an unusual purchase, this ablebodied, extremely intelligent young Canaanite of good birth. He is warranted sound in every limb, virile, healthy, and strong. He knows several languages and speaks Egyptian and Hai with precision and a good accent. He can keep accounts and knows all the many and complex skills needed to administer a large estate. He was, in fact, second in command to the chief administrator of Paheri's estate and would have moved into that position within the year if his late master had not passed over to the Netherworld before he could take over the running of the estate. An exceptional bargain, my friends, at eight golden rings. Who'll start the bidding at eight golden rings? Do I hear eight?"

Ameni was on the verge of bidding when a voice near

him cried out, "Eight!" He whirled and saw Kirakos's servant nodding at the auctioneer. Kirakos! His heart sank. He looked up at the rooftop, at the figure of the Shepherd noble. What a bad stroke of luck! Trading on the kindness of Ersu, he could hardly hope to compete with the immense wealth of Kirakos if the old man were determined to bid seriously against him.

"I have eight," the auctioneer said. "Eight golden rings, a paltry sum indeed for this superb young slave from the northland. Who'll say ten? Do I have ten?"

Ameni tried to speak, but his throat was dry, and nothing but a hoarse croak came out. He raised his hand and opened his mouth again, trying to swallow, but another voice, from the other side, said, "Ten!"

Ameni's heart was in his throat. He turned, looked for the bidder, and saw, to his horror, the chief administrator of the rich nobleman Mesdjer. A flash of anger went through him. Mesdjer was a notorious boy-lover given to exotic entertainments, like having slaves tortured for the amusement and delectation of his decadent friends. The thought of Joseph, turned loose among that horde of worthless scum, sickened him and gave him voice at last. "T-twelve!" he cried.

Mesdjer's man looked his way and smiled patronizingly, the smile of a rich man's slave who looked down on freemen. Ameni flushed with anger and turned back toward the stand. The auctioneer looked at Ameni's modest garb, raised one eyebrow, but accepted the bid. "I have twelve," he said. "Who'll say—"

"Thirteen," said Kirakos's man.

"Fourteen!" came the immediate reply from Mesdjer's slave.

"*Fifteen!*" said Kirakos's man after a hasty glance upward.

Ameni gulped and looked quickly from one buyer to the other. Then he shut his eyes and tried desperately to calm himself. *Think*, he told himself. *Think*. If he backed away from this great opportunity, his whole life would sicken and die on him.

"Sixteen!" said Mesdjer's slave.

"*Twenty!*" said Kirakos's man, in a voice strong and authoritative, a voice intended to strike terror into anyone bidding against his powerful and influential master.

Another danger worked its way into Ameni's mind: What if bidding against Kirakos were to draw *his* ire? Kirakos was known to be a ruthless and unforgiving man with people who had dared to oppose him in any way. But something surged up in him just then, some strange, inexplicable source of courage, and he lunged forward to grip the edge of the auctioneer's platform with both hands, look the auctioneer firmly in the eye, and say in a voice he could not even recognize: "Thirty! Thirty golden rings for the slave!"

There was a brief moment of stunned silence. Ameni, horrified at what he had just said, looked frantically from face to face, from Mesdjer's slave to Kirakos's servant. They'll outbid me, he thought.

Mesdjer's man, however, shook his head. And Kirakos's servant looked up at his master and got another small, solemn shake of the head. Ameni's heart was pounding as the auctioneer said, "Sold! Sold for thirty golden rings!"

On the rooftop Baliniri said, "Hmm . . . thirty rings." He laughed, scratching his head. "That's a great deal of money! You people play for high stakes."

But Kirakos was not listening. Instead he looked down at the woman who had just stepped onto the stand, demure and cool-looking in her white robes. She was slim, statuesque, graceful. Her neck was long and slender, her posture dignified and regal. And yet a slave! he thought. She was the most beautiful woman he had ever seen. Not since he and his wife were young had he felt such a longing.

## III

But Kirakos mastered himself and broke his reverie. He forced himself to look away. "Yes, indeed, my young friend," he said. "Thirty rings is a small fortune here. More money, I'd wager, than the fellow who bid that amount has seen in some time."

"I don't know what the customs are here, sir," Baliniri said, "but back where we come from, it's considered a very serious offense to bid money you don't have."

"It is here, too," Kirakos said. "I didn't say he couldn't

*raise* the money. Matter of fact, the chap for whom he's an agent is quite well-to-do and won't even miss the sum." He pointed discreetly downward. "That one over there, now."

"He's acting for this man?"

"I assume so, just as my man down there is acting for me. You've seen the signal I make now and then. Like this." The small wave of the hand was duly noted by his servant in the market below. The servant turned to the auctioneer, raised his hand, and called out a bid for the young woman on the stand, and looked back up at Kirakos for further instructions. Kirakos said affably, "If I were to wave my hand from side to side"—he did not demonstrate, with the servant watching him—"it would mean for him to continue bidding until I gave the signal to quit, as I did just a moment ago when that fellow down there bid thirty rings for a slave perhaps worth twenty-two. But if I signal to him like *this*, holding my hand palms up, my man knows to win the bidding whatever the cost." This time he did demonstrate, and his servant in the street below nodded.

Mekim, behind Kirakos's back, made appreciative signs with his two hands—a woman's ample, curving hips—and rolled his eyes; Baliniri dug him angrily in the ribs. In the street below the auctioneer called out during a lull in the crowd noises: "Twenty-eight! Twenty-eight golden rings!"

Kirakos turned to Baliniri, his manner benign and friendly. "I think you may have heard," he said, "that I, ah, lost my wife of many years a little while back. She had outlived all our children, all my other close relatives, everyone I cared for in the world. She was, besides, the chief administrator of my estates." He sighed, a deep, resigned sigh. "I am now, like this poor fellow whose estate they are auctioning off below, a man without heirs. The only sons I had who lived to adulthood died in battle."

"I'm sorry, sir."

"Don't be. One learns to live with disappointment. We are—perhaps I should say were—a warlike people. Our lives were arranged around losses such as these." He looked down into the crowd below, at Egyptian and Shepherd alike, and for a heartbeat his lips curved in an expression of distaste. Then, his expression once more detached, he waved the whole thing away. "I should learn to control my dislike for the direction things have taken since we came here. There are, after all, good aspects of the move. After years of great droughts, we live at last in a land of plenty. But we have grown weak; we have lost the sense of purpose. Manouk warned of this. He also warned that there was little else we could do about it, other than go back north. It is useless to try to escape one's destiny."

"Is it, sir?" Baliniri asked thoughtfully. "I like to think I have some control over the course my life takes."

"Yes. One has that illusion when young. When you grow old, as I have, you will look at life and see patterns, as in the ornate rugs of Elam. And some, even older, claim to see the hand of the weaver." Again he waved the thought away. "Listen to me. I prattle on like an old fool."

"Not at all, sir," Baliniri said. There was more than just politeness in his tone. "Don't say that of yourself."

"Well, be that as it may," Kirakos said, "I was about to say that I now need a chief administrator for my house, and I'm rather used to having a woman do the job. There are many servants and slaves to oversee, and I prefer to hear the orders being given in the soft voice of a woman. Having some man in my house, barking out orders like a brash young subaltern—"

"I understand, sir."

"Perhaps you do. At any rate, you'll be seeing how I live while you're here. I've given orders to have your gear brought to my house."

"The place you had us put up in last night was quite adequate, sir."

"I know. But I have questions to ask you, if you don't mind, and they'll be the easier asked, and answered, at my villa. I won't take no for an answer. I've a large and pleasant place, with gardens and fountains, slaves to wait on you hand and foot." He smiled. "You'll also find the food more to your liking than the sort of thing one finds at a tavern. I recently purchased a fine cook. Makes food more to the taste of a man from your part of the world. He's butchering a fine lamb even as I speak."

Baliniri smiled broadly at Mekim and addressed his friend in their native tongue. "Lamb!" he said. "How long has it been, Mekim?"

"Too long! I'm so sick of salt fish and boiled ox and figs and dates and—"

"We accept your invitation," Baliniri said to Kirakos.

"Very well," the older man said. "Then it's arranged.

And tomorrow, after we've dined and talked tonight, we'll go to court, if you like. You can have a closer look at things at the divan of our, ah, Golden Pharaoh. I think you'll find it all vulgar and . . . well, interesting."

"I'm sure I will, sir."

And, in the street below, the auctioneer said, "*Sold! Sold, for fifty golden rings!*"

Baliniri did not look down, nor did he look at Kirakos's face. But he took note of what he had seen and heard. Fifty golden rings! In a place where thirty was a fortune! He remembered the expression on Kirakos's face, when the old soldier had looked down at the young woman. Curiously, it had not been a look of lust. It had been a look filled with a longing much deeper than lust, the longing of a man lonelier, perhaps, than anyone he had ever seen in his young life.

"I hope you know what you're doing," Ersu said.

"Don't worry," Ameni said. "This is the best purchase I've ever made. It'll be the making of me. You'll not have to worry about your investment, my friend."

"Oh, I'm not worried about that." Ersu's smile was benign, even a little smug. "Now go attend to your purchase. Have dinner at my place tonight. Bring your new slave. Perhaps he has an interesting background and will amuse the other guests. Don't worry about clothing him. We'll find something suitable, I'm sure, in the wardrobes of my own servants." With that he handed Ameni a small purse, clapped his friend familiarly on the shoulder, and went away through the crowd.

At the end of the corridor between the two buildings Ameni could see the newly sold slaves conversing. *They probably know each other well*, he thought. But of course: They were from a single lot of slaves, drawn from the same household. They would have farewells to take of one another.

He walked toward them, watching Joseph, tall and straight as a young hart, converse with the lovely young woman Kirakos's man had purchased at such incredible cost. For a moment he thought: *I wonder whether she and Joseph . . .* But no. The woman, for all her startlingly statuesque beauty, was a decade older than Joseph. She would see him as hardly more than a stripling. From the look of them, they were friends, perhaps, but nothing more.

He stopped before them, hardly knowing what to say.

Then, after a moment of embarrassment he could scarcely
have explained even to himself, he spoke, almost timidly.
"Joseph? Joseph, son of Jacob?"

The young man turned to him, but not before exchang-
ing sad smiles with the young woman. "Yes, sir," he said. He
bowed formally, deferentially. The woman looked once at
Ameni and turned away. Her eyes were haunting, large,
dark, the eyes of a person who had suffered.

"Joseph," Ameni said. "I've concluded the agreement.
We can go now. Have they fed you?"

"Yes, sir."

"Good. Joseph, you may not remember me—"

"On the contrary, sir, I remember you quite well. You
are Ameni, formerly cupbearer to the Lord of Two Lands.
You were falsely accused of attempted murder and treason."
The young man managed at one and the same time to maintain a deferential look and to speak as an equal. It was a trifle
disconcerting, but for now Ameni had decided to tolerate
anything short of outright abuse from the young man. Better
to implant in him the memory of kind and gracious treatment.

"Why, that's right. And—I've never forgotten you, either, Joseph. I—"

"I'm honored," the young man said politely, his tone
belying the impoliteness of breaking into his new owner's
speech. "And, sir, I apologize for the uncharitable thoughts I
had about you after you were freed. I realize, sir, that after
your release you could hardly be said to have had the power
or influence to secure *my* freedom."

"Diplomatically put, my young friend." He noted how
the slave's eyebrow went up a bit at the word "friend," but
went on as if he had not seen it. "I had the best of intentions
of putting in a good word for you, but unfortunately the hand
of suspicion lay heavily on me all the time, and I was followed
around constantly by agents of the lord Madir. Eventually I
had to convert what property I had to gold and bring it over
to this side."

Joseph's eyes seemed to take in instantly, and his mind
to assimilate, Ameni's present unpretentious garb and lowly
state, compare it with the healthy sum he had managed
somehow to pay for a new slave, and come up with some sort
of conclusion. He waited expectantly for Ameni's next words.

"Now I am in a better position to help you," Ameni said.
"In the meantime you'll find me a kind master."

"I'm sure I will, sir. I've generally been fortunate in that regard, sir, with the unhappy exception of my lord Potiphar."

Ameni made a face. "Oh, yes, that silly wife of his. Well, those days are over, Joseph. Your fortunes are about to change."

He waited for some expression of pleasure or gratitude, but none was forthcoming. Instead, Joseph's face bore an expression of complete equanimity. Ameni frowned. After a brief pause, he said petulantly, "I suppose that your, ah, voices, or whatever they are, have told you this already. I mean, about the coming change of fortune."

Joseph did not react to the tone in his voice. He said in that unruffled voice, "The God of my fathers has revealed to me that my circumstances were due for a change for the better. He did not inform me that you, sir, would be the instrument of that change. I'm happy to see you again, sir, and I hope that I may be of service in the furthering of your own fortunes."

The smooth flattery was just the right balm for Ameni's deflated ego. "There, now, Joseph. I'm sure that we are well met today. Come, we have to get ready to go to dinner tonight with a friend and patron of mine."

Joseph bowed once again, a slight and barely deferential motion. "Sir," he said, "may I have your leave to say farewell to my friend here?" His nod indicated the beautiful woman slave nearby, who stood patiently, awaiting her own buyer with dignity.

"Certainly," Ameni said. "Who is she? I have the vague feeling that I've seen her somewhere before."

"You may have seen her at Memphis, sir. Her name is Mereet, and she is the wife of the blind armorer Shobai, who makes weaponry and armor for the Egyptian army. She was not active in court circles, but she was known there through her husband."

"Ah. I may have seen her at some court function."

"Quite so, sir. Then I have your leave? For a moment only?"

"Yes. But make it short, please."

Joseph ordinarily didn't like to touch or be touched. But now, taking leave of Mereet after their two years of service together under Paheri, he took her slim, cool hands in his and looked her in the eye. "Mereet," he said gently, "I must go, but I know we'll see each other again. Be of good cheer.

I've heard talk about the man who bought you. He's said to be uncommonly gentle and humane for a Shepherd. You won't be mistreated."

Mereet seldom smiled these days or showed any other emotion before strangers. Now she forced a grave smile to her lips and squeezed his hands briefly. "Thank you, Joseph. Luck be with you."

"I'll do well. I . . . I had another of my dreams. The great change in my life is about to occur. And, Mereet—"

"Yes, Joseph?"

"You *will* see your loved ones again. Don't give up hope. Never."

## IV

Everywhere in the magnificent villa Kirakos had built outside Avaris, the immense wealth of the Shepherd Kings and of gold-rich Egypt itself was evident. The friezes above the doors of the outstanding house testified to the great victories Kirakos had achieved in his years as a leader of Shepherd cavalry. The carved, painted columns in his banquet hall bore the same ornate, Egyptian-style pattern of date frond and lotus, and the embroidered linens on the dinner table picked up the pattern in vivid colors made from dyes from lands far away, lands that had paid tribute to the pyramid-builders in ages past but now paid tribute to the Golden Pharaoh, Salitis.

Ordinarily dinner would be celebrated with great pomp, even for only two guests. But Kirakos, among soldiers like Baliniri and Mekim, reverted to the plain, simple habits of his soldier days. Dinner proceeded at a leisurely oriental pace, with the minimum of servants attending. As a concession to Mekim's elemental tastes, the entertainment, which Baliniri would have foregone altogether for the sake of talk, took place on the far side of the room: Girls in transparent robes played pipes and kitharas softly, and two slim, high-breasted slave girls, wearing only strands of earthenware beads that hung low on their slender hips and rolled volup-

tuously on their hard, bare buttocks, danced slowly, undula-
tory, like sleepwalkers.

After the obligatory course of cool delta melons, the
dinner had proceeded along decidedly un-Egyptian lines. In
friendly deference to his foreign guests, Kirakos had ordered
his new cook, a man of Haran, to prepare a modest version of
a dinner as his homeland might prepare it in a *mahrajan*,
the traditional outdoor festival. The only things Egyptian
were the jeweled, inlaid armchairs in which they sat while
they ate, the soft cushions that lined these seats, the golden
bowls, the lotus cups of blue glaze, and the delicate ivory
spoons, carved by a master's hand.

The food was simple, hearty country stuff: *lahum mishwi*,
lamb broiled on skewers; *fatayer laban* and *sfeeha*, delicious crusty turnovers made with yogurt and meat stuffings;
kibbe, tabbouleh, flat bread. The lamb was fragrant with
garlic, sage, ginger, thyme, marjoram, bay leaf. After dinner
Mekim excused himself and moved to the far side of the room
to watch the nude dancers, while Kirakos and Baliniri sipped
wine from golden goblets inlaid with emeralds.

"Your hospitality, sir, is only exceeded by your generosity and sensitivity," Baliniri said. "How could you possibly
know how homesick a pair of old soldiers are, just now, for
the food of the hills above Mari?"

"I was a soldier once myself—I had the tastes and habits
of an honest horseman of the Hai." He sighed and looked
pensively down into his wine. "I'm almost ashamed to take
you to court tomorrow to see what we've become. I can
hardly believe our Salitis, this Golden Pharaoh, was born the
son of Manouk, a fierce commander of the armies of Hayastan.
If his father could see him now!" He stared morosely into his
cup.

"This food," Baliniri said, thinking to change the subject,
"you say it's the food of . . . Carchemish?"

"Of Haran. Carchemish no longer exists in any form its
former inhabitants would recognize. Our armies, under the
great commander Karakin, besieged Carchemish, and in the
final battle, in which I had the honor to serve, we leveled
the city and rebuilt it along our own characteristic pattern.

"No, my cook comes from the only city we never conquered: Haran. It still stands and has retained its independence, although our own cities now surround it."

"I don't understand why, sir," Baliniri said, holding his

cup up for the silent slave behind him to refill. "What could have stayed the hand of your leader?"

"It was a surpassingly strange story," Kirakos said, "one you might enjoy."

In the thoughtful voice of a man who had pondered the story for many years, he began to tell the tale: When the Shepherd Kings, fleeing great droughts, had come down from the high mountains above Lake Van, the poorly armed cities in the Shepherds' path had had little chance of withstanding their superior might. The nomads numbered well over a million and had developed body armor, war chariots, and superior methods of handling cavalry and infantry. One city after another had fallen, before the Shepherds turned south toward Haran and Carchemish.

The warrior-king of Carchemish had armed his people and declared his brave intention to defend his city to the death. Haran, dominated by cowards and appeasers, fired its military commander and replaced him with traitors loyal to a pro-Shepherd turncoat named Reshef.

As the Shepherds prepared to march south and level Carchemish and Haran, a strange thing had happened: A gentle, crippled young man named Hadad, disguised as a madman, went alone into the Shepherd camp and rescued his brother, Shobai, a slave of the Hai. Hadad also tricked the Shepherd commander into thinking Haran in the throes of a plague epidemic, thus saving the city from destruction. Reshef, the turncoat who had tortured and then blinded Shobai, killed the gentle cripple in a brutal duel.

"Ah," Baliniri said appreciatively. "The stuff of which legends are made."

"Exactly," Kirakos said. "And the people of Haran, whose city we abandoned without destroying it, now celebrate little Hadad the cripple in story and song, and the bards tell his melancholy tale as far west as the Greek islands."

"I can understand why. It's a good story. The weak defeating the strong."

"Yes. At any rate, alone among the cities of the north, Haran has no occupying force of the Hai within its walls. Haran pays a token tribute to us but is otherwise left alone."

"How did the Shepherds settle this far south?"

"It was decided by Salitis's father, Manouk, when he became the new leader of the Hai. In his wisdom, he pushed us across the waterless wilderness where nine of our ten beasts died of thirst, until we had reached the rich, fertile—and, by now, lightly defended—Nile delta.

"Manouk realized what we did not," Kirakos continued, shaking his head. "That we had to change, to give up the nomadic life. And with the strength of his personality he brought us here. I think he deliberately pushed us across the wilderness in order to kill off the livestock on which we had lived for so many generations, to force us into a position of living in the new manner, as settled people in a land of plenty. But he died—alas!—before he could carry his whole plan through, and it fell to his son to execute the last segment of it." His sigh was deep and regretful.

"Then . . . things haven't followed Manouk's plan, sir? Your people have strayed off the path?"

"I think so. With Manouk in charge, we'd have kept our strength, our manhood. There wouldn't have been the emphasis on gold, on show, on pomp and meaningless ceremony. You'll see what I mean tomorrow, my young friend."

"Perhaps, sir. But may I ask why you are telling me this? Me, a stranger, a foreigner?"

Kirakos's gaze into his eyes was straightforward, sincere. "Because I think you, alone of the men I've met in recent years, might be able to put some spirit back into our armies, help put us back on the right path. You could retrain the young men, teach them discipline, the ways of war—"

"I came here to fight," Baliniri said, "not to train reserves. And there's no fighting here. Perhaps on the Egyptian side—"

"No—you'll not find fighting there, either. Nubia, now: There's another matter. There's a civil war going on, and our spies report that a third faction, the Black Wind, has arisen to oppose both sides. That'll be desert warfare, though, except along the Nile."

"Ah," Baliniri said. "I've fought that way. Some of Elam is like that."

Kirakos smiled at his young friend, feeling some of the excitement. "Look at you! I see your eyes light up. This civil war excites you, as the thought of staying here does not. Very well: Go your way. But remember that you have a friend in Avaris, an old soldier who will continue to hold the door open for you in case you change your mind. In the meantime I'll show you a bit of the city. Who knows? You may be tempted by how easily an able man like you could rise to the seats of power here, in the absence of comparably capable people of my own blood. . . ."

After a time Kirakos went off to an early bed, and slaves showed Baliniri to his own quarters in a wing of the new building whose windows looked down on an interior court. Mekim was nowhere to be found: Baliniri grinned to himself, wondering which of the dancers his comrade had gone off with. *Likely both,* he thought.

When he himself had stripped to his loincloth and sought out the narrow Egyptian-style bed allotted to him, he found he could not sleep. After a time he rose and, barefoot, padded silently to the window to look down at a single source of candlelight below in the small inside court. To his surprise, he saw Kirakos standing in the window opposite, looking down. Baliniri stepped back into shadow but quickly realized Kirakos could not see him and was, at any rate, intent on the scene below. He went back to the window and looked down.

At one end of the little court, a tiny pool lay, framed by dwarf palms and other ornamental shrubs. In the pool, ankle-deep in the water, stood the lovely slave Kirakos had purchased that afternoon. She was naked in the soft light of the candles and was attended by two young woman-slaves in flimsy shifts. They were bathing her by candlelight. Her hair, pinned up this afternoon, was down now, soft and silky; it hung on her perfect shoulders, cascading down their alabaster loveliness like the water that gleamed on her slim and graceful body; a single lock hung down between her dark-tipped breasts, still high and haughty despite the luxuriant maturity of her flawless body.

Now, at the slaves' soft request, she turned, and Baliniri could see the soft curve of her back, and the finely turned buttocks, and the long, straight legs. The slaves' dark hands laved her light skin with plump sponges from the Great Sea; she leaned her head back in a half-voluptuous gesture, abandoning herself for a moment to the tactile pleasure of their handling. He could not see her face, but as the girls washed her long body he saw her take one slim foot out of the water and place it on the edge of the pool; the long and delicate toes gripped the raised edge.

A shudder of desire went through Baliniri—and was as quickly quashed. Suddenly he felt a spasm of shame, staring down, unobserved, at the vulnerable nakedness of a woman of such dignity and beauty. So what if she *was* a slave? She had the presence, the carriage, of a queen. It was a shameful and dishonorable thing to look at her this way as if she were some tavern slut or hired dancer.

He blinked and tried to make himself turn away. But his eyes would not leave her. He thought: *Who is she? Where does she come from?* He had paid little attention to the auctioneer's words, being more intent upon Kirakos's conversation during the auction. Slaves could come from any land, any station of life. She might well be a queen, a princess, the wife of a great man in some other land—all the more reason not to profane her with his lustful eyes, to insult both her and himself by gaping.

Finally he forced himself to look away. And as he did, his gaze went to the gallery opposite, where Kirakos still stood, looking down. He took note of the old man's face. *Ah, there's a spark left in the old boy still,* he thought. There was desire written plainly on the old soldier's face, but there was something else. There was that same deep longing Baliniri had seen earlier that day.

As he watched, Kirakos covered his eyes suddenly and wept. Baliniri could see the old man's shoulders shaking with great sobs that seemed to come from his innermost being. He wept silently, but deeply, uncontrollably. But in a moment or two he managed to master himself and straighten up and wipe his eyes, all self-control, severity, and dignity now. For an instant his mouth contorted once more in pain and smothered longing. He gave the young woman at pool's edge one final brief look and turned his head, stepped back into the darkness, and was gone.

In the patio below, the slaves dried the woman tenderly and held out a soft robe for her to step into. She walked back into the house with them, but somehow the ghost of her presence lingered in the candlelit space beside the little pool, like the hint of an exotic perfume, and Baliniri lingered at his window, looking down at the wet print of a slim naked foot, gleaming in the dim light, for a long while, until the candle at last guttered and died.

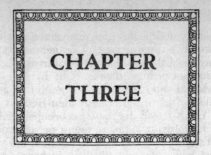

# CHAPTER THREE

## Lisht

### I

Tuya timidly poked her bewigged head out from behind a column and looked across the great hall, past the gathered nobles and their retainers and companions who stood awaiting the arrival of the god-king Dedmose. All were dwarfed by the mighty size of the audience hall and the great spreading friezes on the walls beyond.

The most immediate source of Tuya's terror sat complacently at the feet of the towering guard. The lion opened its great yellow-fanged mouth to yawn at the guests. And as Tuya peered fearfully across the hall, the great beast turned slowly and seemed to look contemptuously at the crowd, then at her in particular.

"Oh, I can't go out there," she moaned, retreating behind the painted column, into the arms of her husband. "Please, Ben-Hadad. Don't make me."

Ben-Hadad hugged her, ignoring the gooseflesh on her bare arms and the trembling of her thin, small body. "Tuya," he said gently, "it's just a tired, tame, old pet lion. He won't hurt you. I've walked right up to him and petted him a dozen times. He just sits there and looks bored." Ben-Hadad chuckled and squeezed her shoulders. "I'm sure he's bored, as a matter of fact. You would be, in his place, too. Palace life isn't the most fascinating thing in the world. When I come

40

here"—he looked around to make certain no one was within earshot—"I usually can't wait to get out. Everything that happens around here seems to be intrigue and backbiting."

"But we'll have to pass right by him. Look, they've hardly left any room at all."

"It's part of the protocol," Ben-Hadad explained to his wife. "You honor the king by honoring all things that belong to the king. And the lion's been a pet of his since he was a boy. It's quite old, you know." He held her at arm's length. "Let me look at you, now." He straightened her wig with an affectionate hand. "Why, Tuya, you look wonderful. You'll be the envy of every woman in the crowd. I can't think why you let this place get on your nerves. You look like someone who was born to high rank."

Tuya stiffened. "But I *wasn't*. I was born in the gutter and raised in the street. You know that. I'm out of place here, and putting expensive clothes on me doesn't disguise the fact. And the court women you talk about—the royal cousins, the courtiers' wives—they don't envy me; they look down their noses at me. If only—"

"There, now," her young husband said. "Enough of that. We'll have to go up in a moment. The king's coming in now." His words were almost drowned out by the blare of the trumpets announcing the arrival of the so-called Lord of Two Lands, who was, these days, at best the uneasy lord over only one land, the weaker and poorer of the two at that. "There. I see Shobai; he just came in on General Baka's arm. We'll be joining them on the dais. I understand the king has something to say to us."

"I'm so proud of you," Tuya said. "But—oh, Ben-Hadad, I think I'm more afraid of going up there before the king, before all those people, than I am of walking so close to the lion."

He took her tiny hand in his broad, square fist and squeezed it reassuringly. "Could this be my brave Tuya, who feared no man? Who'd stand up to a dozen armed thugs and dare them to come within reach of her knife?" He smiled. "Look, I'll be standing next to you," he said. "You won't have to do anything but bow. You know by court custom how little attention Dedmose usually pays to women. If you can't think of joining me on the dais as an honor, think of it as . . . oh, a chore you have to do, one that'll be over in a few minutes."

Tuya tried to answer but found her voice suddenly grown

hoarse. She looked up at the painted ceiling high above, at the gigantic and highly romanticized depictions of Sesostris I scattering his foes, and all it did was to make her feel even smaller than she was. She closed her eyes, swallowed hard, and tried to compose herself.

*I don't belong here*, she thought, *particularly at his moment of triumph*. She would just embarrass him, let him down, the way she had done ever since they had first come together.

*Yes, from the first.* The moment he had openly acknowledged her and registered their marriage before the authorities, she had begun to let him down even then. He had rushed their marriage through in response to what she had been sure was her first pregnancy. But it had turned out to be nothing more than the first in a series of false pregnancies, and she had yet to conceive, despite his often-expressed wishes for a child of his blood who could carry forward the heritage of his line.

Ben-Hadad, of course, with his uncle Shobai, was a member of a legendary caste of armorers dating back to dimmest antiquity in Ur, mother of cities. The Children of the Lion, as they were called, supposedly descendants of Cain, ranked among the greatest weapon makers of history, and bore, as Ben-Hadad did, a curious red-wine colored birthmark halfway down the lower back, shaped like the paw print of a lion. For centuries it had bred true in the males of the line, until Shobai's twins, boy and girl alike, had been born with the mark. So strong was the family tradition that Shobai had resolved to raise both little Ketan and his sister, Teti, to the family trade once it had been learned that the girl, too, bore the birthmark.

This tradition had been old when Belsunu, the greatest of the Sons of the Lion and a man trained in Ur itself, had lost his son, Ahuni, to kidnappers and begun his decades of wanderings in search of the boy. He settled for a time in Canaan, where he armed the patriarch Abraham, who was taking over the land he claimed had been forever bequeathed to him and his descendants by the nameless God he followed.

By some quirk of fate, Belsunu's son, Ahuni, had been trained as a metalworker in Mari and had also wandered into Canaan—but too late to meet his deceased father. Abraham told Ahuni about the Children of the Lion and their strange destiny—to travel ceaselessly, to forge the world's finest weapons.

Ahuni married an Egyptian girl, Shepset, and they had a son, Kirta. He grew to adulthood and abandoned his wife and his sons, Shobai and Hadad, to begin a relentless search for the secret of making iron. Before Kirta could return home to Haran, the Shepherd Kings, nomadic herdsmen, fierce and skilled in the ways of war, had come, conquering every city in their path. The invaders were looking for respite from a terrible drought in the north.

When Kirta had returned with the secret of making iron, he found one son, Hadad, dead, and the other, Shobai, blind. He took Shobai south, and together the two armed the great city Ebla against the Shepherds' siege; but to no avail; Ebla fell, and the two, father and son, continued their melancholy wanderings. Hadad's widow, Danataya, had escaped to Canaan with Hadad's friend Jacob. There, under the protection of Jacob's people, she gave birth to Ben-Hadad. But the boy was mistreated by Danataya's second husband. Ben-Hadad was saved from a life of servitude by his grandfather Kirta, who had stumbled into Canaan—lost, amnesiac, unaware of the fate of his blind son, Shobai, who had been separated from him in their escape from Ebla.

Shobai, crippled as much by his own regrets as by his blindness, had found his way to Egypt in the company of the gigantic black ex-slave Akhilleus, who had become a rich and powerful trader. The two stayed out of Egypt's seemingly fruitless war against the invading Shepherd Kings. But both fell in love: Shobai with Mereet, the beautiful, noble wife of an Egyptian general lost in battle; Akhilleus with a well-to-do Nubian widow named Ebana. Mereet gently nursed Shobai out of his bitter, self-imposed solitude, and the two married. She gave birth to the twins Ketan and Teti, and life was kind to them for a time.

Then Mereet's first husband, Baka, freed from Shepherd prisons, reappeared, consumed with rage at the man who had stolen his wife. Baka swore to kill Shobai, but when the two met, it was to share their grief: Mereet had been kidnapped and never found, despite Shobai's and Baka's best efforts. The two men surprisingly became firm friends, united in their love for the woman they had both lost.

And Ben-Hadad . . .

Tuya sighed, thinking about it. He had never known his

father. And only after Ben-Hadad had been freed from the cruel domination of his stepfather and bullying stepbrother had he begun his apprenticeship in the craft of his forefathers.

Even this had been cut short. Fast friends with Jacob's favorite son, Joseph, Ben-Hadad had quit his own dreams and gone off in search of his friend, who had been sold to slave traders, all the way to a land whose language he could not speak, a land fiercely divided by the war against the invading Shepherd Kings. There he had met her, Tuya.

She let out a little sob, remembering. For her, it had been love at first sight. She had been enthralled by his artless charm, as he made his living in the streets of Avaris, playing the national game of senet. He had hardly noticed her at first. Small wonder! She was just another skinny guttersnipe in rags, an orphan with no marriage-portion, fatherless, and without family. Everything about her had betrayed her plebeian origins: her stubby, short-legged body, her thin, snub-nosed face. While Ben-Hadad, curly-haired and handsome with a round face and ready smile, broad-shouldered and powerfully built, had looked from the first like a rich man's son temporarily fallen on lean days.

Tuya and Ben-Hadad had been caught up in the rebellion against the invader, and their adventures had thrown them together. Tuya had hardly been able to contain her joy. She had never in her wildest dreams been able to imagine so happy a set of circumstances for herself. They had settled down as a young married couple, in quiet domesticity, to await the birth of the child she had thought she was carrying.

But then the pregnancy had proven false. And Ben-Hadad's disappointment had been acute; he had not been able to hide it. And she had not been able to feel at home among the court society or adjust to the affluent city life in Lisht. She had no women friends. With her rough-and-ready street-child manners and her raffish background, what was there for her to say, after all? She had no children to talk about, and she had little interest in elegant clothing or jewelry, however easy it might be these days to afford such luxuries—for Ben-Hadad was now a journeyman armorer working under the guidance of his uncle Shobai, and a man clearly marked for great things.

There was another false pregnancy. And another. And Ben-Hadad knew none of the social graces that might have helped him hide his chagrin. Often, when she saw him coming home, she had wanted to hide somewhere, anywhere, to avoid facing his glum expression and perpetual air of barely concealed disappointment. She wanted to cry out, let the bitter tears come, and bury her face in his chest while he comforted her. But this was the one thing she could not do.

"Tuya," Ben-Hadad said beside her. "It's time for us. Come on, now. Don't be afraid. I'll be right there beside you. It'll be all right." His hand under her elbow gently guided her forward. Petrified with fear, she let herself be led out into the great hall.

After an initial stumble, it was not so bad, really. She let herself be reassured by his touch, his own inner calm. He was used to the palace by now and had met Dedmose and his formidable vizier, Madir, a number of times. Tuya shut her eyes when passing the lion; she could not force herself to ignore those great contemptuous eyes on her. Going up the shallow steps to the dais, she would have stumbled again if Ben-Hadad's steady hand had not held down the pace of her nervous steps. And now, at last, she stood before the man-god.

She looked—and blinked. Was this the god-king whose very name she had been taught to fear as a child of the streets? This hollow-cheeked weakling with the straggly beard and watery eyes? She blinked again and blindly went through the curtsies she had been taught.

*Ben-Hadad was right!* she was thinking. He had said that the whole thing would be mainly a formality, that she was being honored by being asked to attend and would not be noticed unless she committed some breach of decorum. The king was not looking at her at all, and after Madir's eye had sized her up and found a cubbyhole for her in that capacious mind of his, he too paid her no mind. Both men were looking at Ben-Hadad or—more often—at the gray-bearded, towering Shobai beside him, his scars hidden by the immaculate white cloth that neatly covered his eyeless sockets.

What was the king saying?

". . . recall that we were promised aid by the black trader, eh? What was the name again? Aki . . . Akirri . . ."

Madir interjected calmly, "Akhilleus, I believe, sir."

"Yes, yes," the king continued. "Promised us aid. Soldiers. Ore. Tin from Kush, for your forges. More importantly, the black metal you said your father taught you to work. Iron? Yes, that was it. Whatever happened to this Akhilleus? I want to establish contact again with this fellow.

I've sent two couriers, and they've never returned. There's civil war going on up there in Nubia. Shobai?"

"Yes, my lord?"

"You're his oldest friend, I understand. He was a friend of your father's."

Shobai nodded. "Yes, sir. They were slaves together. Later I traveled with his merchantmen all over the Great Sea. I've no finer or more respected friend, sir."

"Good," the king said, well pleased. "Madir tells me your rearming of our army is complete, thanks in part to the aid of your young apprentice here—"

"I beg your pardon, sir," Shobai interrupted. "My partner, not my apprentice. Ben-Hadad is now a fully certified master of the craft."

The king nodded. This was good news; Shobai was not getting any younger. "All the better. My point, however, is that we don't need either of you too badly here just now. Shobai, I'd like you and your . . . partner to head an expedition up to Nubia and contact this Akhilleus—see if you can't get him to make good his promise. If he has ore and can send it, you'll need Ben-Hadad to grade it and supervise the shipping. I'll send troops with you for protection. You'll have full diplomatic privileges and powers, under the royal seal, as my personal representatives."

Tuya, horrified, stared at him, her heart sinking. She peeked at her husband, and to her intense chagrin, his face wore a proud and eager smile. *Oh, no!* she thought. *No, please.* The king and his vizier were sending Ben-Hadad away from her, leaving her alone in this terrible, frightening place where she did not belong. And, worst of all, he seemed to be looking forward to it.

She was not certain how long she had stood there, transfixed, unseeing, stunned. When Ben-Hadad, taking note of her strange impassivity, nudged her back to reality, she forced a small smile onto her face, but the smile did not reach her eyes. These brimmed with unshed tears. She tried to relax her stiff posture, but to no avail. Their words came through to her now, and out of context they seemed only to confuse her.

Eventually some sort of sense began to emerge from the disjointed words. Dedmose was saying, in what for him seemed to be almost a relaxed and friendly tone: ". . . understand you've more than the usual proficiency at senet, young man.

Are you the chap one of my subjects told me about, who defeated the renowned Khensu in a public match over in, uh, Avaris"—his lips almost refused to frame the alien name of Salitis's new capital—"a couple of years ago?"

"Why, yes, sir," Ben-Hadad said, pleased.

"Did you know, my young friend, that Khensu, while he worked for the noble Shashank, played at my father's court?"

Shashank of Sile, rich and wise, had adopted young Mereet after her father's death. Tuya stole a quick glance at Shobai's scarred face and saw pain cross his still-handsome visage. *Everything*, she thought, *everything reminds him of her*. But as quickly as it had come, the expression was gone.

Dedmose was saying, ". . . talked about nothing but that victory of yours. He said that even Khensu himself admitted that he'd finally met his master. And for a man so full of himself as Khensu to speak thus, young man, your victory must have been indeed an impressive one."

"Fortune favored me, sir, now and then. . . ."

Dedmose smiled his thin, nervous smile. "Fortune favors the competent, young man. I've some small proficiency at senet myself. It is acknowledged in *some* circles, at least, that I'm not bad at it, as kings go." He shot a significant glance at his Wife of Wives, who glared back at him and made a discreet moue. He ignored her. "When you return, we will play. You will let me win from time to time, unlike *some* people I could mention." Again the acrimonious exchange of glances.

"I'm at your service, sir." Ben-Hadad's bow was at once relaxed and practiced.

"Good." The king turned to the hulking Shobai. "And you, my friend. Is there any news of your wife?"

The giant was prepared, and only a quiver of his scarred cheeks betrayed the strong emotions that were tearing at him. "No, sir. The land has been scoured. I've hired spies to cross the border and see what they can find, but none has returned. Either the Shepherds have intercepted them and captured or killed them or . . ."

Dedmose, quicker than Tuya had thought him, finished Shobai's thought. "Or they have defected to the other side. I appreciate your discretion, my friend, but we've little need of dissimulation here. Nobody can hear us except my wives and our friend Madir here"—he indicated the vizier, who bowed infinitesimally, eyes hooded, his face expressionless, unreadable—"and, Shobai, the truth is that a number of people *are* finding it worth their while to join the invaders. Many have prospered. There's simply so very much money in Avaris now." He sighed wearily. "These are hard times for us here in Lisht."

Shobai did not answer.

The king went on in a more matter-of-fact tone of voice. "But that doesn't solve your problem, does it, my friend?" He turned to the vizier. "Madir, of all people, surely you won't fail us. Your spies are the best under the heavens, and your men cross the border as if it were manned by the mummified dead instead of elite guards of the Shepherd Kings."

While the king spoke, Ben-Hadad carefully regarded the vizier of the Lord of Two Lands. "Madir of the Thousand Ears," as the courtiers tended to speak of him behind his back, had the hawk nose of the Egyptian courtier and the thin lips of an aristocrat. It was his eyes that caught and held attention, though: They were a basilisk's, unblinking, mesmeric. For a moment they rested on Ben-Hadad's face, and the young armorer felt as if he were being graded, like fish fresh from the Nile. And now Madir acknowledged the king's flattery with the minutest of bows, as if it were no more than his due.

"My lord condescends to flatter my poor efforts," Madir said in a diplomat's voice—not deferential, not insolent, just polished and mellifluous.

Dedmose smiled cynically, turning for a moment to Shobai. "The illustrious Madir is wasted in my court," he said, "in a defeated and debased Egypt. Better if he had been vizier in happier days—at the court of Khufu, or one of the better Sesostrises or Amenemhets." He turned back to Madir. "Be so good," he said, "as to put one of your clandestine observers to work supplementing Shobai's efforts in this matter, will you? See what he can find out for us, eh?"

"My lord's wish," Madir said, "is my command. Shobai, consult with me before you leave for Nubia. I'll need more than the usual sort of description. The more information, the better." He paused, then continued carefully, "You'll be interested to know that Baka, general of our armies, has made the same request."

"I'm glad," Shobai said in a voice husky with emotion. "I can use all the prayers, good wishes, and help I can find."

## II

When the royal audience ended, there was nothing in the world that Tuya wanted more desperately than to be alone with her husband. But as they emerged from the cold stone halls of the palace into the warm Egyptian sunshine, Ben-Hadad hailed a free guardsman passing in the street. "You, there!" he said in that friendly voice of his.

"Yes, sir?" The guard looked from the young couple to towering Shobai and then back again, registering recognition as he approached.

"You're, uh, Smon, am I right?"

"Yes, sir. How can I serve you?"

"I have some unfinished business with Shobai. Would you be so kind as to take my wife home?" The guard nodded. Only then did Ben-Hadad turn to Tuya. "Tuya, I have to talk with Shobai about the trip. I don't want you out in the street by yourself. It isn't safe. I'll be along in a bit." He squeezed her hands affectionately, but his mind was already somewhere else. "Now, don't worry. I won't be long."

"But—"

He embraced her, and the sheer strength of the bear hug he gave her cut off her next words. And in a moment he was gone, off down the street on Shobai's arm. She thought for a moment of calling after him, but after that first hesitation it was too late.

In the narrow street, Shobai miraculously walked like a sighted man, requiring almost no help from Ben-Hadad despite the uneven ground underfoot. He held his head high, like a lion sniffing the wind; by some sense that others did not have he seemed to *feel* where he was.

As he walked, he spoke easily, yet with an underlying sadness that was by now habitual. "I'm afraid I'll have to leave most of the preparation to you. I never was much good dealing with the soldiery."

"That's all right," his nephew replied. "Do you really

think we'll find Akhilleus? That he'll have a source of ore for
us?"

"I have a feeling he's alive," Shobai said. "I think I'd
know if he weren't."

Again the melancholy was prevalent in his voice, and
Ben-Hadad looked at him apprehensively: *He's thinking about
Mereet. He knows she's alive somewhere, in the same way. . . .*

"I have the suspicion he's very involved in the civil war
in Nubia," Shobai continued, "and that he's going to come
out of it in a position of power. If he does, he'll definitely
provide us with whatever we want. And Nubia is rich in
minerals we need: copper and tin for making bronze, and
iron ore farther upriver, near Meroe."

"Iron ore? But that could make us—"

"I know. But keep it quiet, please. So far Salitis hasn't
sent war vessels into the Red Sea to take possession of the
upper desert and its seaports. You can imagine that the
moment he learns how rich that country is—"

"Ah," Ben-Hadad said, taking his arm to steer him around
a corner into a wider thoroughfare. "Gold, you mean. I hear
they're beginning to call him the Golden Pharaoh in the
delta."

"Gold, yes, and many other precious minerals: jasper
and feldspar, for instance, and porphyry and turquoise and
beryl and malachite. You've heard how Salitis is about jewelry. And better still, amethyst near the first cataract, emeralds southeast of Thebes near the seashore . . ."

"But the thing to really keep secret is iron."

"Yes, because the word's got out that my father—your
grandfather Kirta—learned how to work the black metal many
years ago and taught it to me before he died."

Ben-Hadad slowed his pace. His voice was pensive.
"Shobai, I haven't brought this up before, but sooner or
later—"

"I know, I know," Shobai said. "I promised to teach you.
And I'm getting older. Something could happen to me, and
the secret could die with me." He shook his head. "Well, the
Hittites know the process, of course, and their metalworkers
are better at it than my father was. But they guard the secret
jealously." Ben-Hadad could hear his uncle's sigh. "It's a
good thing the Hittites haven't any territorial ambitions for
now. There'd be no halting them, armed with iron weapons
like those."

"But if we had them ourselves—"

"Ourselves?" the blind giant echoed sadly. "An arms maker has no country, Nephew. You and I happen to live in Upper Egypt and find the cause of Dedmose and his Egyptians more congenial than that of Salitis and the Shepherd Kings—for now, at least." He held up one hand to underscore his point. "But what would happen if we shared the secret of working the black metal with Dedmose—and he died, and the kingdom fell into the hands of a worse man? Dedmose has no male heir. Some nobles are saying unpleasant things about this, about the, uh, lack of vigor in the loins of our god-king."

Ben-Hadad winced but said nothing. *That's what they're all saying about me, too, I'll wager.*

Shobai continued: "You see what I mean? We must be doubly careful about into whose hands we convey so dangerous and powerful a tool." His sigh this time was deep and regretful. "In my youth I had little sense of this. What a fool I was!"

"But your father wasn't there to teach you. You can't blame yourself—"

Shobai's huge hand went out to clasp the shoulder of his nephew. "Blame is one thing, responsibility another. I accept responsibility for my actions and regret them almost daily. I lost my sight because, like a fool, I thought an arms man could sell his wares to anyone: to the highest bidder. You forget I helped to arm the Shepherd Kings. They are at this moment using a war chariot I helped to perfect. A battering ram. Body armor. A thrusting spear. These are being used right now, to kill and maim my friends."

"But you learned better. You refused to make more."

"Too late, much too late. I am blind because of it. And your father is dead because of me, dead without ever having seen the fine son he sent into the world. . . ."

Ben-Hadad's face contorted in pain. "Shobai! You know I don't blame you for that!"

The blind man stopped abruptly in the middle of the street. People were forced to walk around him. He spoke in a much softer, quieter voice. "I know, Ben-Hadad," he said. "You have your father's forgiving heart. You know, of course, that at the end he, too, absolved me of all blame. It was as if I'd never done anything wrong at all. He thought it important to tell me that he loved me, that there was nothing to forgive.

He didn't want me going through life with a bad conscience for what I'd done in my foolishness—"

His voice broke. For a moment Ben-Hadad thought the towering blind giant was going to break down in helpless tears. But Shobai mastered himself: The great jaw firmed, and the huge head went back, held high on his battered neck. "I'm sorry," he said. "Sometimes it all gets to be too much for me. The important thing is that we understand each other. The secret of making iron weapons is a terrible one. You're the logical one for it to be passed on to. But I just wanted you to know in advance the awful burden of responsibility that would be yours when you've learned it." He mastered himself now and put his hand back on his nephew's arm. "Come now. Let's go talk to the captains."

# III

Tuya saw very little of Ben-Hadad in the next few days. He arose at dawn and, taking his newfound responsibilities very seriously, left every morning while the sun was still low in the east to go to the military encampment and supervise the arming and provisioning of the forces that would accompany him and Shobai on their perilous expedition into war-torn Nubia. He did not return until after dark, and when he came home, he was exhausted, drained by the constant work. His eagerness to please Shobai and impress the court made his task all the harder.

There was little left of him to console Tuya, who needed her husband's comfort more than ever. In the night her tiny body would nestle close to his large one, seeking warmth, tenderness; but Ben-Hadad was by then deep in healing sleep. In the morning the cycle would begin again, and the great wound in Tuya's heart festered untreated. Still she would not let herself speak to him of this. It would sound too much like complaining. Who was she to complain? A barren wife? One who did not fit in?

She tried once again to conform to the court's expectations. She paid unscheduled visits to the homes of Hanofer, wife to the assistant sutler to the army, and of Ankhes, wife of one of the priests of Bast. She rehearsed her speeches carefully beforehand until she knew precisely what she was going to say on virtually every topic, but her memorized store of manufactured opinions quickly ran dry, leaving Tuya with nothing of interest or importance to say. She had no talent for small talk—worthless phrases that carried no information or emotion—which fills the gaps in conversation. Tuya was spoiled for all this by her earlier life on the streets, spent dealing every moment with an all too evident and inevitable reality: finding shelter, food, protection from the ruthless and the dangerous street people. She excused herself twenty minutes into her visit at Hanofer's house and escaped, embarrassed beyond all endurance, from Ankhes's house after running out of the same prepared speeches almost before the door had been closed.

In desperation she sought out Shobai's house, hoping to strike up a more congenial conversation with Heket, Shobai's housekeeper. Heket, after all, was of a social caste not incompatible with her own doubtful beginnings. Surely she could talk to Heket—or, failing even that, she could spend some time with Shobai's adorable twins, Teti and Ketan.

But as she arrived, Heket was putting the children to bed for their afternoon nap. Shushing Tuya, Heket led her in to look at the twins after they had slipped off to sleep. "Look how alike they are," the housekeeper said, stepping forward to cover naked Ketan, who had kicked his coverlet off.

"And how different." Tuya picked up little Teti's dangling arm and put it on the bed.

"Yes," Heket said. "Strange how, of the two, it's the boy who's the quiet, pensive one, easily hurt, quick to cry. Teti isn't like that at all. I confess I don't understand her at all. She'll defy me even as I punish her. And if anyone harms her brother, she goes into a rage and fights until she can't stand up. Teti takes up for him as fiercely as if she were an older brother. Why, in my day, girls weren't like that. They acted—well, demure, modest."

Tuya nodded. *Perhaps she's like me*, she thought. Perhaps Teti had, even in her early childhood—the twins were barely five years old—the same sort of rebelliousness that she, Tuya, had always had in her.

After all, the odds were against Teti. Shobai, responding to the astonishing fact that for the first time a girl-child of his bloodline had been born with the distinctive birthmark that set the Children of the Lion apart from other mortals, had insisted that Teti, too, be trained as a smith right alongside her twin brother. This flew in the face of all convention, and Shobai's friends and associates—the sole exception was his nephew Ben-Hadad—had lectured him incessantly against it. Surely Teti had overheard them and had been affected by the constant assertion that "girls weren't supposed to do such things."

Tuya sighed, thinking of it. To be sure, forging weapons was a demanding trade. She had had her own taste of it, acting as Ben-Hadad's assistant in Baka's rebel camp when they had harassed the Shepherds; there were scars on her arms and legs from the forging fire, and she inwardly groaned now at the drudgery she had endured simply to be closer to Ben-Hadad.

But if it was Shobai's will that the girl be trained in the family trade, it was his business. Tuya looked at the two chunky, short-legged little bodies side by side on the bed, with the identical birthmarks clearly visible on their backs, and sighed. It was quite a destiny to wish on a child.

"Yes," Heket said, as if reading her thoughts. "I also have my doubts, although I don't share them with Shobai." Tuya looked at her and saw the concern on the housekeeper's face. "The poor man. He has had so much to bear. And he won't talk about it with anybody." Heket, who seldom revealed her feelings to others, gripped Tuya's arm and looked into her eyes. "Tuya, when Mereet was taken away she told me to take care of Shobai, almost as if he were one of the children. She even told me to share his bed. And I would have, too. What woman would not? But he isn't interested in anyone else. Since she went away . . ."

"Poor Heket," Tuya said, and embraced her for a moment. "It hasn't been easy on you, either, has it? You must be lonely. You need a man of your own to care for, someone to keep you company. You—"

But Heket drew away, stiffened. "Don't say such things," she said. "I'm all right. I have plenty to keep me busy. I have the children to care for, and Shobai . . . Well, a blind man does require some looking after, even though he's independent and has been taking care of himself for all these years. No, I'm all right. Don't worry about me." She firmly showed Tuya out of the children's room. "Now, if you'll be so kind as to excuse me, Tuya, I have some chores to do. Thank you for coming by."

Heket pressed her hands warmly, but the contact was broken. And as Tuya went out into the bright light of midday, she thought, *Why, there was a moment or two of intimacy with another human being. She opened up to me.* The realization brought with it another thought, more sobering—that had not happened with anybody in quite some time, including her own dear husband, who was more and more lost in his own thoughts, his own dreams, which seemed to exclude her. And it was all her own fault. She had let him down so many times now, in so many ways. . . .

When Tuya came to herself again she was not sure just how long she had been walking, thinking, paying no mind to the people, the shops, the animals in the streets. She stopped, looked around her. This was a quarter of the city that she had never wandered into before. The people were of a much lower caste than those in the quarter in which she now lived; they had the look of people living on the edge of poverty. Their clothing was shabby but clean, and the women wore their natural hair, not the court wigs she had hated from the first. She suddenly felt like a fool in her own wig and stepped back into an alley to take it off. Standing with the hateful item in her hand, she wondered what she could do with it; it was equally conspicuous for her to carry it.

She frowned. *What do I care?* she asked herself. She had twenty wigs. She could spare this one and never miss it. She was about to toss it on the ash heap behind one of the wretched dwellings in the alley when she spotted a grimy street urchin staring at her, his eyes large with wonderment.

The boy could not have been older than nine. If he had come from the upper castes, he would never have been here; if he had come from the middle classes, he would have been apprenticed to some trade by now. Since he was neither, it was obvious that he was one of the many street children who lived by their wits and had no permanent home. She looked at the boy's ribs, clearly visible in his narrow chest, and at his skinny but wiry arms and legs. He was probably strong and quick, for all his half-starved appearance.

"You're probably just like me," she said kindly. "At your age I did not have a place to sleep, either. How easy it is to forget, when one has a full belly." The boy did not speak, but his curiosity held him there. Tuya noticed that his feet were poised for running if she grew too familiar with him. "You're not afraid of me," she said with a grin. "But you don't trust me either, do you? That's good. You shouldn't. Ladies like me aren't worth wasting trust on. We never come to this part of town unless it's to gawk at the poor, or play Lady Bountiful on feast days, giving away old clothes or even older food. And you're curious, too, aren't you? That's another good sign— you don't let much get past you. Keep that up. Keep your eyes open. You never know what you'll learn."

The boy just stood there, poised and relaxed at the same time, ready to run or to listen. Tuya grinned. "Like as not," she said, "you don't understand more than half of what I'm saying. You'd know street talk, not court blather. I had to learn this smart-aleck court speech. I grew up speaking alley argot myself, but the kind they talk in the delta towns; you wouldn't understand three words of it, most likely." Tuya smiled, warming at the memories. "I could take care of myself, and in towns easily as tough as this one is. I'll bet you've got yourself a knife, haven't you? I always did. I didn't let anyone know where I carried it, either. I bet yours is . . . oh, behind your back, under your belt, where it doesn't show. Right? Am I right?" The boy didn't speak, but he patted his side significantly, his eyes still on her face.

"Good," she said. "I bet you'd die before you let anyone take it away, too. I was that way." She sighed, looking at him, feeling like a fool with her hair all mussed up like this, standing there with the expensive wig in her hand, a wig worth more money than the boy would see all year.

"What a fool I am," she said. "Here, kid, take this. I don't want it. You can sell or trade it in the back alleys and make enough money to eat for a month." The boy did not budge. "Take it. I won't bite, really. All right, I'll just put it down here, and you can pick it up when you want. It's a gift. I won't turn you in for stealing it." She put the wig down carefully on the stoop of the hovel they stood before.

She backed away a step or two, and when she spoke again, there was a strange tone to her voice, almost wistful. "I'm glad you've got a weapon," she said. "Otherwise you'd never be able to hold on to a thing like this long enough to sell it. Good luck, boy. I hope it brings you good fortune."

Good fortune? It was obvious he did not have the slight-est idea what she was talking about. Eyes still wary, he stooped in one quick movement and swept up the wig. Poised to take off at a dead run, he stopped, looked hard at her, with her cropped hair and her rich-lady's robes. For a moment, he looked as though he were on the verge of saying something. But the moment passed, and in the blink of an eye he had scurried away as fast as his little legs would take him.

*Now look what you've done,* Tuya said to herself. *You're even more out of place than you were before, dressed like a damned bored, idle society lady except for the wig, which you seem unaccountably to have misplaced.* All of a sudden she felt like a fool. Taking off the artificial-looking wig hadn't helped assuage her feelings of unease. She simply did not fit here anymore. *And yet . . . look around you. If there's anywhere in the world you ought to fit, it should be here, in the gutter where you belong.*

With a sound that was almost a sob, she stepped out into the street, into the nest of shops and stalls that lined the thoroughfare, and stood beside a potter's stall. Tuya looked down at its wares: bowls, saucers, flasks for oils and unguents, water jars. "Yes, ma'am?" the potter said, stepping forward. "What can I find for you today, ma'am? I have some fine imported work from Avaris, in the Black Land—this black design with the lime inlays, perhaps? Look, here's my best: eggshell pottery brought all the way downriver from Meroe in Nubia before the civil war broke out there."

*Civil war?* Suddenly it came home to her. *But that's where my husband's going!* She would be without him. What would she do with herself? With her irreversible inability to get on with the court ladies, to fit in, to find a place for herself in the upper-class world here in Lisht?

*If only . . . if only she could return to . . .*

But no! It was madness, madness! It was positively insane! *You must, you must put it out of your mind!*

But even as she tried to reject her ridiculous notion, she saw a familiar sight, working his way down the narrow space between the stalls: Ben-Hadad's sturdy little Canaanite dog, Lion, tail held proudly high. The perky gray dog stopped to sniff the wares of first one stall, then another. He dodged a vegetable vendor's cart and slipped under a second stall, deftly stealing a sausage from the butcher's crate. Wagging his little tail, he skipped nimbly down the passage to safety, the sausage in his teeth.

*Good for you, Lion!* Tuya thought. So this was where

Lion, now a rich man's dog, spent his afternoons! *Perhaps he has the right idea*, she thought. This was where the real life was. Here the problems were real, life and death, ones that mattered. Nobody around here worried about whether so-and-so's wife had lied about her age, or whether such-and-such a courtier was playing around with the errant spouse of his immediate superior, or—or whether the drab little wife of Ben-Hadad the armorer could have children or not. None of these things mattered down here. The things that mattered were survival, finding a place to sleep, getting enough food to live through the day, and perhaps, after a time, if you were very lucky, finding someone to love you. These things mattered. The rest was sham.

# IV

"How late is it?" Shobai asked, scrubbing his grimy hands. "I've lost all track of time. Is it dark yet?"

Ben-Hadad, beside him, splashed his face from the basin. "It's been dark an hour or so," he said. "Oh, I forgot. One of the soldiers said there's someone to see you. From the description it sounded like your servant." He dried his face and pressed the thick cloth into Shobai's hands.

"Show her in, please. It's funny. For a moment I thought you might say . . . Baka, perhaps. Silly of me. Why would the general interrupt his busy schedule for a minor matter like—"

"As a matter of fact," Ben-Hadad said, "he's been here off and on all day. I don't know why he hasn't been in to see you." He stuck his head out of the tent and beckoned to the guard; Heket moved out of shadow and headed his way. "Baka has supervised the whole assembling and provisioning of our little expedition, Shobai. He's put his best young commander in charge, a fine bright young fellow named Anup, whom the troops love like a brother. There isn't a man in the garrison who wouldn't die for Anup in a moment."

Ben-Hadad could see the slow, sad smile on Shobai's scarred face in the light of the candles. *Poor man*, he thought.

*He always expects the worst. Perhaps he's afraid of being disappointed.* . . . There was a noise at the tent flap; Ben-Hadad turned to see Shobai's servant, Heket, standing there. "Oh, come in, Heket. How are you?"

"Very well, thank you, sir. Shobai, sir, I wanted to say—"

"Ah! Heket! Are the children with you?"

"No, sir. I put them to bed early. Our neighbor is watching them. Sir, you'll be leaving first thing in the morning. . . ."

"Yes, yes. Are they all right? The children, I mean?"

"Yes, sir. But I wanted to ask, do you have any special instructions for—"

"No, no. You know what to do. Give them my love. Don't let them forget me."

"No, sir. General Baka came by to look in on them, and . . ."

Shobai smiled again, that same melancholy smile. "Good, good. They'll be his someday; he might as well get to know them and love them. I must have a talk with him soon. Make sure he understands about their training, their apprenticeship."

"Baka? The children? Sir, what do you mean?" Heket's eyes were wide with astonishment and horror.

"There, now." Shobai reached out with a sure instinct and laid his huge hand on hers. "It's all right. I've been having these dreams, you know. Evocative ones. They tell me I won't be around forever. After all, I've outlived rather too many ordinary opportunities for death so far; I'm long past my due."

"Shobai!" Ben-Hadad put a hand on the giant's broad back and felt the welts left by a long-ago lash. "You'll outlive all of us—"

"No, I won't," the giant said with fatalistic calm. "And someday Mereet will be reunited with her children. I know it. It isn't clear to me whether I'll be around when she does. But Baka has always loved her. And, Heket, if anything happens to me, if Mereet is back by then, please steer them together, will you? He's a good man, one of the best. She'll need him to stand by her in the hard times to come."

Ben-Hadad listened, thunderstruck. There was nothing to say. Such a deep undertone of conviction in the blind man's deep voice could hardly be ignored. Several times recently Shobai had told of his specific, prophetic dreams, and every time the prophecy had come true.

Then the thought struck Ben-Hadad: *This expedition of ours—is anything going to go wrong with it?* What would happen to him, Ben-Hadad? Did the same fate lie in wait for him as well? A wave of panic swept through him like a sudden chill. *Am I going to die?*

Suddenly he thought of Tuya. The wave of cold and fear was replaced by a desperate need of her, by love and longing. *Tuya!*

He had neglected her so, lately. He had been so wrapped up in his own concerns that he had hardly thought about her from one self-centered moment to the next. How she must be suffering from his thoughtlessness!

He stepped out into the night, eyes staring blankly into the darkness beyond the circle of light, his hand pressed to his mouth. *Tuya!* He blinked back sudden tears. She had devoted her heart and soul to him almost from the moment they had met, when he was eking out a meager living playing senet in the cafés and squares. She had adored him as if he were some sort of demigod, waited on him hand and foot, kept people away from him if she thought they meant him no good.

Scenes from their past came to him: Tuya, naked and soot-blackened, slaving beside him at his furnace when he had made arms for Baka's little band of patriots back in the delta; Tuya saving him after he had been wounded in the raid on Baka's camp; Tuya lying in his arms in the moonlight on their little island after their escape, her eyes brimming with tears of love . . .

His own eyes filled with tears of remorse and self-loathing. How could he have neglected her so, these last few months? Well, he would make it up to her. He would go home now and take her in his arms and . . .

*And what?* he asked himself. After all, he was leaving tomorrow on a trip that did not include her. Leaving her behind in Lisht, where she felt desperately, terribly out of place. Where she would be horribly lonely without him.

What a way to treat someone you love!

*I'll tell her I love her. No, I'll show her. I'll give her a wonderful night of love and make sure she knows how I feel about her. And while I'm gone, I'll write her every day.*

As quickly as these well-meaning thoughts had brought

on a rush of self-justifying, self-congratulatory emotions, so quickly did the first cold splash of reality dash his hopes of making up for his misdeeds and failings. *You? Write letters home? You have yet to write your first letter home to your mother, Danataya, in Canaan, after all the years you've been here in Egypt.*

Yes, and what of his resolve to come to Egypt in the first place and find Joseph, his childhood friend, and bring the lad back to his family, back to his aged and grieving father, Jacob? When was the last time he had given a moment's thought to finding Joseph? When was the last time he had even inquired about him?

What a disappointment he must be to everyone! To Tuya most of all! It was a wonder she even cared for him at all after the way he had neglected her.

He stiffened his spine and firmed his jaw. *Look*, he told himself, *this is no way to think. You'll just resolve to do better, and you'll do it. The first thing you'll do is go home and let Tuya know what you think of her. You'll get to those other things one by one.*

Yes, yes, he thought. *Tuya first. Then Mother. Then Joseph. I'll find him if he can be found, and somehow I'll get him back to Jacob if the old man is still alive.*

He would do it as soon as he got back from Nubia—*if* he got back.

The last cries of the water birds over the great river had long since faded. High on the walls of the city, above the great encampment of the army, the crier called out "All's well" and continued his appointed rounds. The smell of cooking fires hung over the city as the laborers trudged home, exhausted, to their meager hearths and their families. Traffic in the city streets, bustling only an hour or two before, had slowed to a few isolated souls making their cautious way through the dangerous, unpatrolled streets by little more than the light of torches. The city, mostly quiet, slowly prepared for sleep.

Now, however, the moon, two days short of full, came out from behind a cloud and shone down on the quiet streets. The broad, open expanse of the Bazaar of the Twin Palms, in the working-class quarter, lay bathed in bright moonlight for a moment. As it did, two dark figures separated themselves from the shadow of the market wall and hurried to the door of a nearby building. One of the figures knocked, first three times, then twice, then three times again.

From within a voice called out softly: "Who's there?"

"Hefget and Dede. Open up! There's a guardsman in the neighborhood."

The door opened. The room inside was unlit. Hefget and Dede slipped inside. Only then did a second, inner door open, admitting light into the vestibule. "Come in here," the door guard said. "Mereb's waiting for you. You're certain the guardsman didn't see you?"

"Yes," Hefget said. "But he would have if we'd stayed out a moment or two longer. I didn't recognize him—he must be new. Unusually thorough, checking doors, looking up every alley."

The guard showed them into the lit room. Behind a low table sat a burly man dressed in the coarse cloth of a trades-man. His face was scarred from an old knife fight, and he had lost one eye; a patch covered the empty socket. "Well, Hefget," he said in a curiously hoarse voice, "what have you to report?"

Hefget looked at his partner, Dede, and then turned back toward the table. "The armorer's party is ready to leave with the first light, Mereb. They're taking fifty of Baka's best men with them."

"I'd hoped for more," Mereb said. "The more men they take along, the more they weaken Baka's garrison and the better off we are. Have they chosen the commander yet?"

"Yes. I was saving the good news for last. It's Anup." He watched the smile contort the ugly face of the one-eyed man. "I *thought* you'd like that," he said with a chuckle. "Baka's best and most able man. When *he's* out of town—"

"This is good news indeed," Mereb said. "I'd been wor-rying about Anup. If there were anyone—besides Baka himself—who'd be likely to stumble on our conspiracy, it'd be Anup. With Baka and Anup here and in constant contact, I was going to press the council for a postponement of the assassinations. But now—"

"Now," Dede broke in suddenly, "we can strike by year's end. Perhaps sooner."

"Yes," Mereb said. "Now I've got the leverage to push for the implementation of the plan." His fist pounded trium-phantly on the tabletop. "Dedmose, Madir, all of them—they're as good as dead. It'll take a little time and planning, but once we have control of the army—"

Hefget frowned. "Mereb," he said. "I'd be a poor friend, indeed, if I didn't try to remind you of Harmin and what happened to him when he opposed Madir. . . ."

Mereb scowled, but the scowl turned to a cynical smile. "Madir's getting old, lax, and is no longer as involved as he used to be, leaving more and more of his own work to subordinates," he said. "Time was, he'd have spies everywhere, ears to the ground in every bazaar, every street. But now the ears he thinks he has—they're ours. Virtually his entire network has come over to our side. They're all double agents, reporting to Madir, but what they report is either a fraction of what he should know or deliberately falsified. And when they've finished giving Madir the inaccurate information, they come to us, and we hear everything, my friend. Everything." The smile had turned vicious. "Our turn is coming, my friend. Soon."

Hefget didn't speak, transfixed by the madness in Mereb's expression. Hefget's thoughts, which had seemed so clear only a moment before, now wavered between elation and subtle fear. There was something about Mereb's insanity that destroyed confidence. *Am I doing the right thing?* he asked himself for the first time. Madir and his regime had abandoned Memphis to the advancing Shepherds; hundreds of unsuspecting townspeople had died, victims as much of Madir's expediency and duplicity as of the Shepherds' barbarity. He, Hefget, had lost kinsmen in the fall of the city, and that had made him an easy mark for Mereb's special pleading. He had joined the conspiracy early and committed himself irrevocably the night they had kidnapped Madir's courier and tortured him until he revealed the entire network of Madir's spies. But now, now he began to wonder. *Is Mereb any better? Am I working to replace one heartless, conscienceless leader with another?*

He started to speak, but something made him hold his tongue. Caution? Fear? Hefget knew that because of his silence, his cowardice, his timidity, he was even more firmly committed to this questionable cause than before.

Dawn came bright and early, to the tune of war drums, as the expeditionary force mustered, saddled up, and began to make its way off into the western desert. From the high wall of Lisht, Tuya looked down, waving to Ben-Hadad until she could see him no more.

The party would go south, avoiding the river. Instead they would head for the desert oases that stretched southward for many miles, and only then would they cut back to the river. With any luck they would make contact with Akhilleus's desert army long before the turn westward; it was widely believed that the black giant's encampments were among the oases, but which one, nobody knew.

Tuya hugged herself against the morning chill, unwilling to go back down into the city streets as yet. It had been a strange night. Ben-Hadad had come home full of a forced charm and had wooed her as if the two were in the first stages of becoming lovers. But it had felt unreal, shallow, and Tuya, dissatisfied, had been unable to fool herself for a moment. It was obvious that his mind was many miles away. His lovemaking had been welcome; she would take it in any form she could get it. But in the end, when he had arisen in the predawn hours and prepared to leave, his actions had been brusque, hurried. He was eager to get on the road, away from her, however much he might try to conceal the fact.

She heaved a deep and dejected sigh and turned away from the world outside the city wall, looking down at the city streets below, at the life just beginning to stir. And as she did, she spotted Ben-Hadad's little dog, Lion, threading his way through the crowds of tradesmen working their way through the thoroughfares and to the bazaars where they would spend their day. Lion had a jaunty look; his head and tail were held high, and he slipped unnoticed between the legs of the city dwellers. Suddenly she envied him. Intent on his own purposes, nothing bothered him. He did not worry about whether anyone loved him or thought about him. He had a busy, full life, was independent, could go where he chose, when he chose, without fear, without shame. He was never bored or lonely, and there was no place in the little world he inhabited where he was out of place.

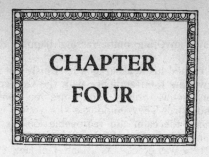

# CHAPTER FOUR

## Avaris

### I

"You're all right now?" Ameni said, hovering nervously over the young slave. "Joseph? Joseph? Answer me!"

Joseph sat where Ameni and Ersu had placed him when the seizure had come upon him, when his knees had buckled under him. He shivered for a moment and shook his head. "I . . . I *think* I'm all right, sir. Just a bit dizzy." They saw him close his eyes once again, and Ameni reached for him, fearful that another attack was coming. But Joseph opened his eyes again and held up one hand. "No, sir," he said. "You don't have to worry. It won't happen again. How—how long was I out this time?"

"Only a moment," Ameni said, flashing a worried look at Ersu. "Do you know where you are?"

Joseph looked around, blinked. "Y-yes, sir. This is the great hall of the palace. I couldn't forget this place—all that gold, all the precious stones. . . ." His eyes swept up the richly decorated walls to the inlays on the ceiling. Joseph, suddenly sober, asked, "It's almost time for our audience with the king, isn't it, sir? No wonder you were worried. But it won't be happening any—"

Ersu broke in, ignoring him. "Look, Ameni. Perhaps we can schedule it for some other time. I'll send my excuses in by the guard. If the lad isn't feeling well . . . we don't want to have anything embarrassing happen during our meeting. . . ."

Ameni craned his neck to look nervously out at the line of people awaiting their audience with the Golden Pharaoh. "I . . . I don't know. Joseph? You're sure you won't—"

"Oh, no, sir." They could see the young man's back straighten, and the calm and reasonable look return to his clear-eyed, handsome face. "It's quite over, sir." He stood up. His posture was erect. "As a matter of fact, I think I've had a sort of vision. It had to do with the king, with the dream he's been having lately. I think the God of my people has spoken to me." For a moment a look of pain flitted across his features, only to be hastily replaced by a reassuring smile. "I'm quite sure of it. It's all coming back to me now."

Ersu broke in once more. "Ameni, if he says something out of turn . . . Let me tell you what happened when the seer from Elam came to court. He'd hardly got his opening words out when—"

"Don't talk about it!" Ameni ordered in a hoarse whisper. "Look, Joseph, you realize what sort of position we're in. If you say something the king doesn't like—"

"It's all right, sir," Joseph replied, completely in control now. "I'm sure I have the answer to the king's problem. How strange it is! It all seems so simple, yet a moment or two ago, the whole thing was such an enigma."

"Don't let him go in," Ersu warned. "I have my position to think of—"

Ameni tried to speak but found he could not. His throat had suddenly closed up. Nervously he glanced from one face to the other, unable to make up his mind. A guard stepped forward and said, "You're next, sir. If you'll just step this way," thus taking the decision out of Ameni's hands.

Baliniri, looking into Egypt's Golden Pharaoh's strange, glittering eyes for the first time, thought: *There's something very wrong with him, something odd and alien.* Baliniri recalled Kirakos's words: The king had been having visions, odd prophetic dreams. These were the signs of the falling-sickness, in his own experience. Baliniri wondered idly just how good the doctors around here were.

Just then, however, Salitis spoke. "So you're the soldier who took the city of Mari," he said. "An impressive feat. My father chose to skirt Mari when the Hai marched across

Mesopotamia. We could have taken the city, he said, but at more cost than it would have been worth to us. We chose to take Carchemish instead."

"You mustn't forget, sir, that we took Mari nearly a generation after your father marched by it. It was much weaker in my time. And frankly, sir, I had no choice. When Hammurabi gives you a direct order, you either carry it out or they carry *you* out."

"Well put," Salitis said. "And diplomatically answered. You've a ready tongue on you for a soldier. I understand Kirakos has explained to you the advantages of working with our army?"

"Yes, sir. And I have respectfully declined. What your army needs just now, sir, is a man more garrison-minded than myself. I haven't the patience for the kind of work you've offered. Give me a pitched battle, sir, against a good, tough foe, and I'm totally at home. But retraining old troops and breaking in new recruits . . . well, sir, I'm out of my element there. I'm a field commander. I think I'll keep looking, sir, if you don't mind. But I'll remember your offer, and if I find my resolve wavering, I'll keep the court of Salitis in mind."

Kirakos broke in. "Baliniri has heard of the civil war in Nubia, sire," the old courtier said. "He has intention of looking into it. It occurred to me that if he did so, perhaps he could report back to us about the conditions there."

Salitis smiled, and the mad glint flashed in his eyes for a moment, only to be replaced by a more reasonable expression. "Yes, that would be very good." His attention was drawn over their heads. "The noble Ersu has just come in, and I think he has something for me. You're excused. And, Kirakos—"

"Yes, sire?"

"A purse of gold for young Baliniri here, and our royal commission to spy on the Nubians."

"Yes, sire." Kirakos backed away, head bowed; Baliniri, watching him, did the same. The long trumpets blew. There was a roll of drums and a flourish of more wind instruments.

Kirakos continued backing all the way to the curtains. His sharp hawk eyes scanned the great hall, the massed nobles and soldiers, the rich friezes and wall hangings. Once past the tall twin columns that stood at the far end of the huge chamber, Kirakos nudged Baliniri and motioned him to one side. Standing in the shadow of the easternmost column, Kirakos leaned close to the young soldier and said, "That went better than I had expected. As the king said, you've a diplomat's tongue in your head."

"You forget, sir," Baliniri said with a grin. "I've years of experience at the court of Hammurabi. Staying out of trouble there is a major achievement."

"I'm sure it is." Kirakos's eyes narrowed. "But I want to find out why Ersu's arrival was so important to our Golden Pharaoh," he said, peering down the length of the great room. "Ah, there he is, with his friend, oh, what's his name? Well, it doesn't matter. They seem to have a slave with them. Oh, yes, the one they purchased at the auction. Reddish hair. Northern stock, if I'm any judge. Hivite? Canaanite?" Kirakos's eyes narrowed. He took Baliniri's elbow. "I'm curious. Let's work our way closer. I'd like to hear what they're saying."

Baliniri shot him a sharp glance. There was something in the old man's countenance that Baliniri did not like. "Is something wrong?" he whispered.

"No, no," Kirakos said. "I just remembered—Mereet, my new slave, told me of a young man in the lot of slaves who had the powers of a seer or something. That must be it! I *wondered* why a pauper like Ameni—that's the name, Ameni—would borrow so much to buy the lad. They've heard of the king's dreams. Come, behind the wall hanging. . . ." As they moved forward along the wall, out of sight of the king and the massed nobles of the court, a guard saw them and started to stop them; but at a nod from Kirakos, he withdrew with a silent salute.

"Well?" Salitis said impatiently. "I'm waiting. What sort of blather is he going to tell me? What sort of mystical nostrums is he going to urge upon me?" The irony in his voice was heavy, scornful. "Speak up, my young friend. My time isn't lightly wasted. If you haven't anything to say—"

"The king has dreamed," Joseph said in a calm and distant voice, as if speaking from a deep trance, "of standing on the bank of the Nile and seeing seven healthy, well-fed cows come up to graze in the reeds. Then, in his dream, seven starveling cows, bony and emaciated, came up behind them and ate all seven of them. And when they had done so, the emaciated cows were as thin and underfed-looking as before."

"Yes, yes," Salitis said impatiently, in a harsh voice. "All men know that in this kingdom. Get to the point, young man—"

"Then on the same night, perhaps an hour later, the king had a second dream. He—"

"Wait!" Salitis said, standing up and looking down on the three of them from the raised dais. "A second dream? A *second?* I have told no one of this. Tell me more, young man."

Joseph continued as if the king had not spoken. "In the second dream, the king saw seven ears of grain, solid and healthy, growing from a single stalk—"

"Yes! Yes!" Salitis said.

"—but close behind them, there sprouted seven thin, blighted ears, shriveled and inedible. These seven thin ears consumed the healthy ones. Then the king awoke. . . ."

Salitis's eyes had the mad glint in them again. But there was anger in his face now, anger he directed not at the slave but at his master. "You! Whatever your name is—you've been bribing my attendants to spy on me!"

"No! No!" cried Ameni. To right and left, guards seemed to materialize out of thin air, knives flashing in their hands.

Joseph's voice broke in again. "The king," he continued calmly, "has not had two dreams, but only one. The two dreams are the same, and their meaning is the same. The God of my fathers speaks through me, to foretell the destiny that lies ahead for Egypt and all the world beside the Great Sea."

The guards had both Ameni and Ersu now, gripping their arms tightly. But Salitis raised his hand. "Hold!" he said in a voice that rang with authority. "Let's hear what the boy has to say."

The young slave took a step forward, away from the guards. "Ahead lie seven years of plenty, when the land of the delta will produce food in great abundance. But after that, seven years of the worst famine the lands of the Nile, or any other, have ever seen. It will wipe out all the years of plenty. Thousands will starve and die. Unless—"

"Yes? Yes? Unless what?"

Ameni, eyes wide, held his breath. This had gone much, much further than he had wanted it to. Joseph's prophecy was unwisely specific, exact, the sort of thing they caught you on. And what Salitis did to people whose prophecies did not work out . . .

"Joseph," Ameni said timidly. "Perhaps you'd better . . ."

"Let him speak!" Salitis said in a tight voice, waving Ameni to silence. "Young man—when is this going to happen? When will the period of plenty begin?"

"With the current crop. When the superintendents of your granaries give their reports, the king will find the harvest has been richer than any in recent history, and—"

"Sire," an aide whispered in the king's ear, "this is true. Our preliminary reports—"

"Silence! Later! The young man is still speaking!" The Golden Pharaoh's face was flushed; his eyes were full of dark fires. "The rich cycle has begun, then. I have seven years until the crops fail."

"Until the crops fail," Joseph said calmly, "and the locusts eat what little the fields do produce. Until torrential rains swell the Nile and flood the land, washing away the topsoil, and drought settles upon the world. Because, my lord, the famine will not just be in Egypt; it will lie on all the world, from Elam to the sea, on Canaan and Padanaram and the lands of the Hittites. Millions will die. Unless—"

"Yes, boy? Unless?"

But no sooner had Salitis said this last than a change came over him. He straightened, his eyes hardened, he looked with wary hostility right and left at his advisers and courtiers. "This audience is at an end," he announced coldly. "You, Ersu, you and your friend—I don't remember the name—come with me to my chambers. Bring the lad. Captain! Clear the hall. Escort us to my apartments. I would speak with these people in private, where no ears can hear." And with this, he turned abruptly on one heel and strode away.

As the captain of the guard barked out the orders to disperse, Baliniri's eyes sought Kirakos's, behind the wall hanging. "What do you suppose that was all about?" he said.

"I don't know," Kirakos said gravely. "But I will before nightfall."

# II

The surprising thing about the private dwelling of the Golden Pharaoh was its plainness. The furniture was sparse and, while crafted with great skill from imported woods, bore no trace of the golden inlays so prevalent in the public portions of the palace. The floors bore simple woven-reed carpets rather than the expensive Elamite rugs one might logically have expected. Through a side door they could see into the king's bedroom: the low bed with its carved ivory headrest, the plain bedside tables and cabinets, a simple chair whose seat was covered with leopard skin. Beyond they caught a glimpse of the royal bath, with its limestone bathing slab and screen. All were simple, plain. This, they realized, was a side of Salitis few saw, few suspected.

"Be seated," Salitis said. He turned and clapped his hands, once, twice. Three slaves materialized out of thin air: two slim young women, bare-breasted, in simple white loin-cloths; the third, a businesslike middle-aged man. Salitis dismissed the girls with a wave of his hand and spoke to the man. "Leave us," he said. "Make sure that no one disturbs us or hears us." His voice carried an extra emphasis when he added, "Not even you." The servant bowed and went out.

"Now," the king said. "You, Ersu, and—what's the name again? You, the boy's owner?"

"Ameni, sire."

"Yes. I want you to keep this very quiet. What goes on here is just among the four of us. If any of it leaks out, I'll hold the two of you to blame. Understand?"

"Yes, sire." Both men answered as with a single voice.

"All right. Now, Joseph. I heard you speak, and I believed you. I don't know why, but it was as if something were speaking to me, inside my head, telling me to take heed of your words, as if I'd thought about them myself beforehand. And yet I hadn't."

"The God of my fathers, sir, is no respecter of persons," Joseph said. "He will speak to whomever He wishes."

"Whatever." The king paced back and forth as he spoke in a nervous voice. His hand waved the statement away. "It doesn't matter." He wrung his hands. "Universal drought. Famine, with all lands lying fallow. Crops dying. People dying with them—"

"By the millions, sir." Joseph's clear young eyes followed the monarch as he paced. His voice remained calm and unshaken.

"Yes, yes. I believe you. That's what's going to happen. Let me tell you, we had a drought in my father's time in the lands north of the Two Rivers. It was what brought the Hai all these many miles to Egypt. Months, years went by without rain. My people lost all they had. My people, too, died by the thousands. It would have been worse, far worse, if my father, Manouk, had not prevailed upon Karakin, the leader of the Hai, and the chieftains to migrate when they did. And my father remembered the predictions of a seer much like yourself, Joseph. A seer who foretold the whole thing, the drought, the famine. But when the seer told this to Karakin, Karakin had him killed for spreading gloom. When the prediction came true, my father remembered. And although we acted on it too late to save everyone, we did act on it, and it was the saving of us."

Now Salitis stopped pacing and stared at Joseph with those piercing eyes of his. "You, young man. What does this God of yours tell you I should do?" He bit his lip and added, "He *did* tell you that, I suppose."

"Yes, sir," Joseph said. "Would you hear all of it?"

"All, all," Salitis said impatiently. "Now."

"Yes, sir," Joseph said. "The God of my fathers told me that the harvest of the fat years must be saved for the lean. You must . . . you must change the way these things are regulated."

"I must, eh? How?"

"Well, sir . . ." Joseph looked at Ersu and Ameni before he spoke. "The solution might seem radical. Some might think—"

"They'll think what I tell them to think!" Salitis snapped, the mad glint back in his eye. "Speak!"

"Yes, sir." Joseph cleared his throat. "The state must take over the entire business of food production. The whole thing. Otherwise, some people will be tempted to—"

"Yes, yes! I understand! Go on!"

"Yes, sir. The whole crop—*all* food in your realm—must be gathered up by your men and apportioned out to the people according to their need. But since the crops for seven years will bear far, far in advance of your foreseeable need, the surplus must not be sold to other countries, as would ordinarily be the case."

"Ah! Yes! We'll hoard the whole lot! Let the Hittites, the northerners go a-begging! Yes!"

"It must instead be stored for the entire seven years. You'll have to build great granaries capable of holding that much. A whole detachment of the army will have to be put in charge of guarding the stores, and another of rationing it to the people. And a third, of course, to supervise the harvesting of the crops in the first place. Otherwise there's bound to be resistance, unorganized at first, then—"

"Yes! I'll force it all down their throats! I'll hang the first man who resists! The first hundred! The first thousand!"

"As you will, sir. But you realize the implications. The army will be busy during these seven years administering all this. There will be no men to fight a war. The army will have to leave a standing force along the border and withdraw the rest to the agricultural lands. Then when the famine comes you'll be ready. Not only will you have the food with which to feed the people, you'll have the internal force ready to prevent revolution, seizing the food and—"

"Yes! I can see it now!"

"The whole rest of the world will go through the same cycle, but without forewarning. When the drought hits, they won't have food. Only you will. They'll have to come to you for food. And they'll pay whatever it takes to get it, whether in gold or precious metals or stones, power or subjection, or whatever currency the makers of your treaties can force upon them. Everyone, sir—including the leaders of the resistance in the south, at Lisht. Within one generation, you'll have become master of the world. It will be either submit to Egypt—or starve."

Salitis's eyes, wide, insane, shot from Ersu to Ameni. "You! Ameni! Sell me this slave! Right now! Name your price!"

Ameni gulped, tried to speak and failed, tried again. "Sire," he said. "Accept my humble gift, with my—"

"Done! I thank you. You'll have reason to thank yourself for this, mark my words. And you, Joseph. You're mine, body and soul. What shall I do with you?"

It was as if Joseph had been expecting this. He looked at the Golden Pharaoh with ingenious eyes and said in a matter-of-fact voice, "Sir, the administration of all this will require a man of discernment and wisdom who understands the need for taking and enforcing these radical steps. Not everyone will have the understanding or the complete loyalty to you that it requires."

Salitis's face changed. His eyes grew hard at first, wary. But then they softened, and a wide smile came over his face. "Ah, yes. And only a free man, with freedom of choice, can be loyal in precisely that way. Do I understand you?"

Joseph's expression was even more artless than before. "My lord?" he said. "I meant only—"

Salitis's smile grew. "I know what you meant," he said. "And I agree." He looked triumphantly at Ameni first, then Ersu. "Gentlemen," he said, "bear witness for me, of this young man's emancipation." The two inclined their heads respectfully. Salitis paused; his lip curled in a smile that was almost a sneer. "Hear me," he said to them. "Behold your new vizier."

Ameni and Ersu exchanged shocked glances. Everyone in the kingdom had expected Kirakos to get the appointment any day now. Ameni looked at Joseph, who had in one stroke gone from the lowly status of a slave to that of the highest placed man in all the lands subject to the Shepherd Kings, a man subordinate only to the king himself—a man to whom even the mighty Kirakos, or the commander of the Shepherd armies, would be subject, in the dark days to come.

*Oh, Joseph*, Ameni thought desperately, *remember me, please. Remember me as a kind and generous master who looked out for your welfare. Remember me as the man who made all this possible.*

In the street Baliniri shortened his usual long strides to match the steps of the much older Kirakos. The young soldier found the slower pace relaxing, conducive to observation. Usually, one city street was like another; cities didn't vary much between Hammurabi's realm and this one. But now Baliniri saw things that would ordinarily have escaped his notice: details of decorations on buildings, a sculpture at a well, the smell of ripe fruit in the market stalls, and—yes—

the curve of a woman's retreating haunch as she walked past him down the broad avenue.

More and more often as they negotiated their way through the working-class quarter, the expressions on people's faces came as a mild surprise. An overwhelming percentage of the faces bore expressions of hatred and resentment for him and Kirakos . . . despite the fact that Kirakos did not emphasize his differentness and not only dressed in the Egyptian manner but had trimmed his beard as the Egyptians did.

After a time Baliniri made a comment. "Sir," he said, "I'm coming to conclude that, as a member of the Shepherd hierarchy, you're not popular in these parts."

"You've noticed," Kirakos said wryly. "Well, we *are* an occupying force. I hope we'll eventually come to be considered Egyptian after a few more generations here. People still remember the days before the civil wars that preceded our arrival here, and they tell their children and grandchildren. The young are raised to hate us, despite the fact that, all in all, we've been a rather benevolent force here—I mean, compared to the way we treated the nations of the north once we had conquered them. Of course you treat the vanquished rather differently when you're going to settle down and live among them. But as strange as it may seem, the very people we've treated rather well continue to hate us. For a time Baka, who now commands the Egyptian forces at Lisht, hid out in the delta with a little band of rebels and malcontents, sabotaging our operations, assassinating a guardsman or soldier here and there, even staging full-scale raids on military outposts or on the big households where the owner of the house was judged by the rebellious element to have steered too close to our wind."

"I see," Baliniri said. "I have little direct experience with occupation forces myself. I was a commander of shock troops. What do you think would happen if your people clamped down and acted more like the despots these people apparently think you to be?"

"I have no idea. The Egyptians are strange people, and they've been used to domestic rule for thousands of years now. And for some reason even a bad native ruler is tolerated more than a lenient foreigner." He stopped at an alleyway and put a hand on Baliniri's arm. "I have to see someone here. Would you like to join me?" He did not wait for an answer, but steered Baliniri into a little court that led off the main thoroughfare.

It was a carpenter's shop. In dry weather the operation had moved outdoors; the busy master craftsman and apprentice, looking fit and bronzed in the sunshine, had spread their work out on the dry-packed earth and were now busy at work.

"We inhabit a nation incredibly rich in gold," Kirakos said. "What can we buy with it? Well, for one thing we can buy wood. Look what the locals have to make do with because only scrubby trees grow here: acacia, willow, sidder, tamarisk, sycamore fig. To produce a proper board, they have to piece smaller cuttings together and join them with tapered pegs. They've become quite adept at this of necessity; their joints are a marvel of precise fitting—dadoes, rabbets, overlapped miter joints, dovetails, pegged tenon joints. And despite this lack of good timber, we manage to make permanent resting places for ourselves in the end."

Baliniri started. The men at work were making a heavy, rectangular coffin! As he watched, one man chiseled chips out of the top, while another, on hands and knees, planed the inner surface with a lump of sandstone whose flat bottom had been cut into an abrading surface. The coffin was of a curious local design: The sides and back tapered in thickness from top to bottom so that the finished product, when completely assembled, would give the impression of using twice as much wood as actually had been used.

"Here," the young man said. "This is good Canaanite cedar. This will house the remains of a very rich man, I'd say."

Kirakos's unblinking eyes stared into his. "It's mine," he said flatly. "I grow old. I buried my wife this year. I have no heirs. Under the circumstances, I must make provisions for myself. I thought today I would look in and see how the work is progressing, but I see I have come too early. Come, let us continue." He nodded at the master craftsman and moved to the gateway of the little close.

But as he did so, a figure lunged out of deep shadow; Baliniri, behind him, saw sunlight flash on polished metal. "Kirakos!" he cried out, and, thanking the gods for his quick reflexes, bounded into the alleyway after the attacker.

Kirakos, up ahead, shrank against a wall; the attacker crouched and prepared to thrust again. Baliniri could see a red stain on the front of Kirakos's robe. Baliniri ferociously bellowed and charged, heedless of the fact that he had come out, uncharacteristically, weaponless. "*Haaaaaa!*" he cried in his piercing baritone, lurching forward on strong legs. But as he did so, two other figures moved toward them from the dark shadows behind the carpenter's shop, weapons in hand, silent as stalking wolves, deadly as adders.

# III

As Baliniri moved forward, seeing the two new figures moving toward him from one side, his hands reached down and snatched up from the street a scrap of wood from the carpenters' saws, roughly the thickness and length of a man's thighbone. The first attacker lunged toward him with a knife, so Baliniri whipped the club around and knocked the knife out of his opponent's suddenly inert fingers.

The attacker howled in pain. As he retreated, the other backed up into the little clearing formed by the convergence of two streets. Baliniri took him in and frowned; his opponent hefted a Shepherd battle-ax, stolen, no doubt, from the occupying army. This was a more formidable weapon than any Shepherd-made sword; and the man seemed to know how to use it.

Baliniri's wary eye swept the little clearing. To one side, Kirakos had produced a knife of his own from inside his voluminous court robes and with it held his attacker at arm's length, feinting from time to time with an old soldier's practiced skill. Good; this gave him, Baliniri, time to deal with his own two adversaries. Baliniri backed into the open space, keeping an eye on his opponents. The first man who had lunged at him was shaking his numbed arm, trying to get some feeling back into it after the blow he'd taken. But he had recovered his knife, and the blade shone evilly.

Baliniri grinned, tapping his stick softly against the palm of his free hand. "Come along," he said with mock friendliness. "You've got a knife and an ax. All I've got is this stick. Surely you can take a man armed only with a st—"

The speech was to lull them. In midword, without warning, he attacked. Baliniri feinted at the first man's kidneys, but arced the club high instead, swung back down, and chopped at the knife-bearer's neck. If it had landed as planned, the blow would have brought the man to his knees. But it landed hard on his collarbone, and Baliniri felt the bone break. The knife-bearer drew back for a counterstroke—and felt the pain. "*Ahhhh!*" he cried, and dropped his knife . . . just as the axman attacked!

Baliniri barely whirled out of the way of the first vicious swing of the heavy weapon. It cut through the cloth of his tuniclike outer garment, leaving a broad swath flapping across his arm. He ripped at the ruined garment and threw it off, leaving himself naked except for his narrow loincloth. Baliniri backed away just as the ax-bearer leveled a slicing blow at his midsection. He felt the *swoosh* of the ax going past him and chopped at the man's arm with his club.

But this was no ordinary assassin; he took the weight of Baliniri's blow on the much heavier hardwood handle of his ax, and Baliniri's hand stung from the force of his parry. As the ax came around on the backswing, Baliniri again spun out of danger.

The axman grunted with frustration and swung again. Baliniri felt the kiss of the sharp weapon along his ribs and looked down to see a thin line of blood along his chest. He stabbed with the blunt stick and caught his man in the gut, temporarily knocking the wind out of him, then hacked and clubbed with the stick. He aimed at the man's face with a last wild swing, but the assassin deftly ducked the blow.

The ax once again swung high, poised for a killing blow. Baliniri reached up, the club gripped in both hands, and took the blow in the middle of the stick before it had reached full impact. The stick split in two, and the ax blow swept down, harmlessly, past him.

Baliniri found himself hemmed into a corner. He could see only one way out. He dived forward and rammed his hard head into the ax-wielder's belly. He felt the man give way, fall back, and in the end recover and try to hack at Baliniri's unprotected back with the ax. The young Mesopotamian did not bother blocking the blow. Instead he bunched his fists and slammed them, as hard as he could, into the man's groin. The ax landed, but sideways. It fell from the wielder's hand and clattered on the packed earth and stones.

Baliniri's fists smashed into the man's face, belly, and neck. The man fell to one knee, trying to fend off the blows. But with the next punch to the carotid artery, his eyes rolled back into his head. He pitched forward onto his face, unconscious.

Baliniri picked up the ax. He looked right and left. The knife-bearer was on his hands and knees, trying to rise. Baliniri might have considered holding him or the axman for interrogation, but reflex took over, and the ax flashed in his hand, once, twice. The axman and the knife-bearer each died of a single stroke.

Now Baliniri turned back to Kirakos. The old man had managed to go on the attack. He feinted right and left and, in the backswing from a false cut at the assassin's belly, cut his attacker's throat. Baliniri blinked at the fresh gout of blood, watched the man fall on his face, and, without thinking, finished him quickly with the ax.

He frowned, looked at the bloody ax in his hand, and casually tossed it into the shadowed space from which the attackers had come. "Here," he called. "You're hurt. Let me have a look at—"

But Kirakos, panting hard, waved him away. "It's nothing," he said. "A flesh wound. My reflexes aren't what they were." He smiled. "I can see where you got your reputation. Swift reactions, young man. My confidence in you quite obviously hasn't been misplaced."

Baliniri grinned. "And mine in you, my lord. The guards searched both of us back at the palace. How did they manage to miss a knife the size of that one?"

Kirakos's knife disappeared as mysteriously as it had appeared. Watch as he might, Baliniri could not figure out precisely where, in the folds of that heavy robe, it had gone. "I'm neither magician nor sorcerer," he said. "At the first search I *was* weaponless. The second search was conducted by a guard who was one of my men. When he searched me, he *gave* me the knife." His smile was narrow-eyed and knowing. "There's no such thing as too many precautions, of course."

Baliniri looked down at his ruined garment, then kicked it into the gutter. "Well," he said. "It's a good thing nobody's much disturbed by informal dress around here. I won't have to feel too much out of place on the way home."

"This is Egypt, after all," Kirakos agreed. "Some of the

upriver tribes who used to come to market in the old days wore nothing at all, except perhaps for decoration. And nobody seemed to mind much, from all accounts." He shrugged. "Egyptians. They look at things differently than we, from colder climates, do." He put one hand on Baliniri's arm to steady himself, and Baliniri took note of the discreet wince as the unseen wound made its presence known.

Baliniri, supporting the older man's weight a bit, made off down the street at a deliberately slow pace. "I admired your performance. You've just dealt with a would-be assassin a handspan taller than yourself and a third your age. If there'd only been the one man there, sir, you wouldn't have needed me at all."

"As our Golden Pharaoh said, my friend, you've a civil tongue on you." Kirakos managed to increase the pace, as if nothing had happened. Only the touch of the old man's hand on Baliniri's arm betrayed the effort it cost him.

Baliniri took leave of Kirakos at the old man's villa, heading out into the streets to look for Mekim. Wearily, Kirakos put himself in the hands of his servants, who peeled away his bloody robe and bathed his wounds. As he sat on a couch, bent over with a pain he no longer bothered to disguise, he saw a new figure enter the room: a woman, dressed in the simple livery of his house. Under the hem of her robe, slim and graceful feet protruded, chastely together, awaiting his summons. At her waist, gentle hands held bandages and towels.

Startled, Kirakos looked up into the solemn brown eyes of the new slave, Mereet. Suddenly he felt embarrassed, sitting before her in his loincloth, his aged body fallen, covered with liver spots. He looked away irritably. "You," he said to her gruffly. "Hand me that clean robe there." But when he pointed to the garment that hung over the back of a wooden chair nearby, the stabbing pain caught him in the chest again, and he winced, in spite of himself.

"My lord!" the woman said. She rushed forward, putting the white cloths down and placing her hands on his shoulders. "Let me help you."

"No, no," he said. "I'll be all right. . . ." But his voice was hoarse with the effort, and he let her ease him down on the couch. Immediately he knew he had done the wrong thing; it would be almost impossible to get up now. And the moment his back touched the couch, he felt all the strength go out of him. He let out a disgusted sigh.

The woman pulled up a chair close beside him. She looked at the other servants. "I'll look after him now," she said in a voice that, gentle as ever, assumed command. "Would you ask the kitchen staff to prepare broth? And a cup of wine for my lord." She did not even wait to see if her requests were being granted, but turned back to Kirakos. "Where does it hurt, my lord?"

Kirakos scowled, but then relaxed and let out another sigh. "Right here," he said in a deflated voice, tapping his chest. "I know what you're going to tell me: The knife stopped on a rib, and I've got a fracture to contend with. Ah, if you knew how many broken ribs I've had over the years . . ."

"Yes, my lord." Her voice kept that same tone of calm confidence. "Then you know what you have to do: Lie still for now, and—"

"Yes, yes." He looked at her. The lovely face was framed by dark hair. The almond eyes, the patrician neck, the full lips . . . "Your name is Mereet, I believe. You haven't been properly presented to me by the staff."

"No, my lord. But my lord must know of me. He paid very dearly for me. I will tell him something of who I am, at least as much as my previous master knew."

He looked at her, frozen-faced. "You're a bold one. Perhaps I bought you for my bed. You're comely enough." He waited for a reaction. She did not react. Instead she sat calmly waiting for his next words, her eyes at once showing detachment and . . . tolerance. "If it weren't for this wound of mine, I could take you right here and now. You're mine, after all."

She looked at his wounded chest. "But you were not wounded yesterday, my lord, or the day before. You have owned me both days. You could have taken me at any time." Did those full lips curve for a heartbeat's duration in a sad smile? "I should feel fear, shame. But I do not, my lord. You have heard of Mereet, chief administrator of the estate of the noble Paheri until his death. You know me for a woman of honor, though a slave."

"I did inquire about you," he admitted. "Go on. You have something to say?"

She looked him directly in the eye now. "Yes, my lord. The circumstances of people's lives change, but the people themselves do not. Before I became a slave I was a married woman, with two children. My twins and my husband are alive. A master of mine could soil the sanctity of my marriage bed, dishonoring me and my children. Because my lord Paheri did not, I honor his memory."

"Paheri was a boy-lover."

"Paheri was a man of advanced age, who had outlived most of his habits of indulgence. In the time that I served him, he still surrounded himself with men of that persuasion, but my lord went to bed alone." She looked him straight in the eye now. "A woman to warm one's bed can be found anywhere: a woman more comely than I, more disposed to please in this fashion. This is as true of boys in the days of my lord Paheri."

"I see," Kirakos said with a smile that held little warmth. "And to serve me, to please me, what do you offer? A sharp tongue? A gift of argument, of disputation?" He immediately regretted his sarcasm, but he betrayed no sign of his regret.

She sat calmly looking at him, ignoring the accusations. "I, on the other hand, my lord, have heard of the lord Kirakos. My lord has a reputation of honor, of fairness and decency. My informant, my lord, told me that of all the Shepherd Kings, you alone, after the death of Manouk, would not take advantage of the conquered, the enslaved."

Kirakos, angry, tried to sit up suddenly. *"Ahh!"* he groaned with pain. "So my name is bandied about so easily among the subject class, is it? And who, pray tell, presumes to have such facile opinions about me, eh? Speak up!" Clutching the broken rib, he fought his way into a sitting position and glared at her with eyes grown hard. "Who speaks so lightly of Kirakos?"

She did not flinch. Her voice stayed calm and soft. "An old friend of yours, my lord, who saw you many years ago at the siege of Melid—who saw you show compassion to the people your soldiers were killing in hot blood. My own lord and husband, Shobai of Haran."

# IV

Kirakos's eyes narrowed, but he remained silent. Then a minute movement of his upper body brought a stab of pain, and his full lips contracted in a spasm of anger and hurt.

"My lord!" the woman cajoled. "Here, let me help you—"

"No!" Kirakos said, his voice tight and controlled. "I'm all right." He pushed her helping hand away, sat bolt upright, forced himself to ignore the repeated paroxysms of pain. "Now, could I ask you once again to hand me that robe I asked for?"

He did not look at her as she moved to the chair and retrieved the garment. He felt her draping it around his shoulders, felt the touch of her soft hands, suppressed a shudder of—of what? He closed his eyes and frowned. "Thank you," he grunted, aware of the irony of using court manners with a slave, a chattel he had bought body and soul in the marketplace.

*Body and soul?* he thought suddenly. *Are you so sure?* Now he did look at her, fussing with the jug of clear water, the white cloths. Her carriage was erect, her demeanor that of a free woman. Could a man own such a person? Own her, the way he owned a sword, a house, a pack animal? He doubted it. "Pardon me," he said, his voice low and thoughtful. "You said Shobai? Shobai of Haran?"

She turned and looked him straight in the eye. She was neither defiant nor resentful. "Yes, my lord," she replied. "The stories he told me of his days among the Shepherd Kings made me think you might remember him—the man who armed your army."

"He did work for me," Kirakos admitted. "Or rather, for Karakin, although his arms were used in my unit. But . . . that was long ago." He shook his head. "Shobai. I thought he was dead. As I remember, Karakin gave the order for his death—"

"He lives," she said. "Blind, thanks to the treachery of Reshef the Snake." Now defiance did indeed creep into her tone, defiance and pride. "Reshef, whom I killed." She waited for his reaction, but none came. "My lord does not believe me?"

"Go on," Kirakos said. "Shobai lives, then? And you—"

"I am the mother of his children. From whose arms I have been torn away, before the walls of Memphis." She smiled bitterly. "I'd been falsely imprisoned at the hands of a traitor named Harmin. I and the other prisoners were being moved when your men intervened. Joseph, a slave sold the same day you bought me, was another from that lot of prisoners."

"Oh ho," Kirakos said, his lips curving into a cold smile. "It might interest you to know that your friend Joseph may be on the way to becoming a man of great power and influence at the court."

Saying this, he kept his eyes on her face, expecting to see a look of shocked disbelief. Instead she smiled, and there was an intensity in her dark eyes. "Yes! Yes! That's what he said was going to happen. And when I saw him last, he even told me he knew it was going to happen soon. Quite soon."

Kirakos's eyes narrowed again. "He *knew* what was going to happen? Tell me more."

"Oh, he had his destiny worked out in considerable detail, my lord. He would be freed by the king and placed higher than any man in Egypt except the king himself."

"Higher than me? I expect to be named vizier!"

"That was the inference, my lord. He would successfully interpret the dreams of the pharaoh and be raised above all men. And when this occurred, he would, on the advice of the God of his fathers, recommend changes in the way Egypt was governed. Radical, revolutionary changes, which would reach deep into the lives of every man, woman, and child, not just in this land, but far beyond your shores, too. The king would hear his words and act upon them."

Kirakos forgot his wounds and gave a start; instantly the pain was upon him again. He gritted his teeth. "Act upon them?" he said. "What sort of changes? Are we to become a nation of believers in this god of his? Will we have to start sacrificing to—"

Her voice remained calm. "He did not share it all with me, my lord. But the changes had to do with the agricultural economy of the nation. In a generation, he said, the king would totally control all the means of food production, not only in Egypt but abroad. And—"

"Hmph!" Kirakos let out a snort of derision. "Nonsense. The ravings of a madman." He mused for a moment. "Still, it is the sort of thing Salitis takes to heart. He has delusions of grandeur now and then. He's shown signs of mental imbalance these days. If someone were to catch him when he's in this dream world of his and feed him on this sort of wild scheme . . ."

"I think, my lord, that 'wild scheme' is the very last phrase I would use to describe anything Joseph told me." Her voice was full of confidence. "Time and again I have

heard him make predictions. Always they have come true."
But now a touch of sadness came into her face. "All but once,
that is. He told me I would see my husband, my babies,
again before I died. . . ."

Kirakos heard her words and their undertone of sadness,
but something perverse in him made him ignore them. "How
was the lad going to talk the king into this?" he asked. "And
how was the king going to justify these radical measures
before his council? Before the likes of me, for instance? I still
have a voice in things, and so do the rest of the chieftains."

"That part I did not hear, sir. Only that the changes
would be made, and that the world we know would never be
the same again. 'The hand of the God is upon this land,' he
said again and again."

Kirakos waited, but there was no more. He thought for a
moment. *Why do I think all this is so plausible? When it
should sound like nonsense . . .*

"My lord?" she said now. "Shall I call the women to
attend you? It appears that I am not the person to get you to
lie down and rest. Perhaps another will succeed where I have
failed."

Kirakos looked at her. "I can't make up my mind whether
you're being insolent or candid," he said. "No, I don't want
the women. Get me . . . *hmmm.* Get me Cherheb. Get him
here as quickly as you can. And bring me the wine I heard
you order. Where are those women anyhow?"

"Just outside your door, my lord."

"Well, bring them in. Tell them to take back the broth.
Wine is the best thing for a broken rib. That much I do
remember of my vanished youth, here in my dotage in a
household full of insolent women and slaves who don't know
their place." His eyes flashed with annoyance. "Well, what
are you waiting for? Get me Cherheb, and be quick about it!"

She stood looking at him for a moment with those large,
serious eyes of hers. His anger passed . . . and he saw her
with the same eyes that had, that first night, wept over her
beauty and dignity. A great wave of tenderness and pity came
over him, and he wanted somehow to reach out to her. Then
the moment passed. She gave no sign of having noticed. She
turned away to do his bidding, and there was a moment when
he could have called her back, could have spoken to her
something of what was in his heart—*What is it? What?*—but
he let the moment pass.

He sighed, a long and deep sigh, and his shoulders drooped once again from the weight of his years and his fatigue. There came the stabbing chest pain again, and he cried out, and the women outside his door rushed in, clucking and chirping and fussing about him as all women tend to do. He corrected himself: all women but two. There had been his own Arpena, dead now after so many years at his side, and now this slave woman, who reminded him so of her.

Yes! That was it! Arpena, but thirty years younger! The same quiet dignity, the same calm beauty, with the fire, the intelligence, the understanding beneath. He closed his eyes now, gritting his teeth against the pain, and saw Mereet once again in his mind's eye, her long slim body luminously nude in the lamplight as the servants bathed her, and again the longing came upon him, and the great sadness, and the great loneliness.

In the guest rooms Mekim, wielding a sponge dipped in cold water, bathed Baliniri's wounds. "Here!" he said, grinning. "Stop moving. How do you expect me to do this without hurting you if you—"

Baliniri craned his neck to look at him. "If I could reach my own back, I'd do it myself. Stop complaining. When we're done, I'll buy you a drink and dinner."

"Throw in a wench or two and you're on," Mekim said, grinning. "Although . . . Look, you're not losing interest in the ladies, are you? Time was, you'd have had some slave girl tending your wounds, and you'd have bedded her long before she got this far! Come to think of it, the last two times I've suggested a bracing little trip to a bawdy house, you've begged off."

"Don't be an idiot," Baliniri said. "And stay away from the slave girls here at Kirakos's house. And keep your mouth shut around here. The old man has eyes and ears everywhere. I expect him to have the whole story of this Joseph chap before sundown."

Mekim made a small clucking sound. "All right. I get your point. Although there's one of the girl flutists who . . . But I agree to be careful. This Kirakos has more enemies than he knows. More than you know, either, for all that you had to do away with a few of them today. I hear things in the taverns. It pays to watch your step here."

"Yes," Baliniri said. "And I have a feeling about this Joseph business. A premonition or something. I have the feeling we'd really do well to move on."

Most slaves in Kirakos's household divided their time among various duties. Only one slave, Cherheb of Thebes, had no more than a single function. Cherheb had no household duties at all: His only responsibility was to act as go-between for Kirakos's spies—spies in the military encampment, on the army staff, in the court, in the streets.

He was well chosen for the role. Of all the men in Avaris, Cherheb was the least likely to stand out in a crowd. He was neither stout nor slim, neither tall nor short. His blandly average features were unmemorable, his expressions mild. He could move into a gathering of people and in moments completely disappear. The only impression he left behind was one of moderation. Yet no one among all the people on Kirakos's payroll was paid a higher stipend, or more richly earned it.

Thus he was able to get inside Salitis's household and bring away a fairly full account of the interview among Ersu, Ameni, Joseph, and the king in no more than a matter of hours, all without stirring up any undue interest in his own curiosity. Like any such courtier, he had a network of informants, men and women whom he kept on retainer. Some information he routinely passed along to Kirakos; some he kept for himself. He had learned this was the judicious way not only to rise but to survive.

In the present case it was immediately obvious that Kirakos had to know all, except the name of his informant. He found his way back to Kirakos's villa and spilled the entire story as he had heard it, with almost total recall. Kirakos sat up in bed, the neglected supper growing cold on the plate before him, listening.

When there was no more to tell, the old man looked at his informant. "Salitis is quite mad, you know."

"Yes, sir. But apparently coherent about it."

"I was sure he would be. And the worst thing is, he can probably pull it off. In the first place, there are quite a number of councillors who don't think the Egyptians should be allowed to own agricultural property. They were for expropriation the moment we moved in here. While Manouk was still alive, I was able to argue successfully against this, on the grounds that we'd have a permanent revolution on our hands. But now that Salitis has succeeded his father . . . It's obvious this Joseph has told him exactly what he wanted to hear, what he'd been waiting in vain for all the other seers to say. The older chiefs remember the drought in our home-land, which devastated Hayastan and all the lands of the high mountains. They'll see the wisdom of this action. What they won't see is the danger of it."

"Yes, my lord." Cherheb's tone was as neutral as ever. "Will that be all, my lord?"

"Yes, yes." Kirakos watched him bow his way out. He then sat for a long time, staring at the bare wall before him. A new, disquieting thought had occurred to him, and he cursed. If his spy's account of the matter were accurate, Joseph would now be over his, Kirakos's, head—but it would be Kirakos who would be charged with the responsibility of supervising and carrying out all of these radical changes. And it would be Kirakos whom the angry and rebellious Egyptians would blame for it all.

## V

From an upstairs window Mereet looked down as Cherheb went out. "So he's the one," she said.

The chambermaid Ayla came up, looked down, and nod-ded. "Yes, ma'am. He's the spy. My lord relies on him very heavily for information. Why?"

"I'd like to meet him if it can be arranged." She smiled wryly. "I'm not sure it can. I still haven't any idea of what my status here will be."

"Oh, that's been settled since earlier today, ma'am, when my lord came home," Ayla said in her friendly way. "After you left him, he gave the orders. You're to be in charge of all of us—the staff, the free servants, everyone, just as my lord's late wife was." But now she noticed the look on Mereet's face. "What's the matter, ma'am?"

"I—I had no idea," Mereet said. "I thought he was angry

with me. I was more forward with him than I should have been. Total charge?"

"Yes, ma'am. We're all to report to you. I'm sure he would have gotten around to telling you by tomorrow. My lord has his own ways of doing things. And he's still in some pain, you know."

"Yes. Well, this puts a different complexion on things. I'll have to work things out. There are some changes that ought to be made. I'll have to think about how to go about making them without causing undue discomfort among the lot of you."

"How kind of you to worry about us," Ayla said. Mereet looked at her: young, plain, but with a pleasing smile, cheerful and open. "I do hope you'll be happy here. And I'll leave word that Cherheb is to check in with you next time he's here."

"Thank you," Mereet said. "I have some questions to ask him; perhaps while he's running errands for Kirakos, I can get him to ask a question or two for me. If I could get through to Joseph, perhaps . . ." When she turned back to look at Ayla, there was such a look of open, unfeigned sympathy on the girl's face that she did not continue.

"Oh, ma'am," the girl cried. "You looked so sad, so—"

Mereet sighed. "I *am* sad," she admitted. "And lonely. But I thought I was doing a better job of hiding it." She leaned against the wall and folded her arms across her chest. "I've needed someone to talk to. I didn't have another woman friend around Paheri's household. Ayla, I like you, and I need a friend. If I've the autonomy around here that you imply I will, I can reduce your duties in order to keep you near me, just so I can have someone to talk with."

"Oh, ma'am! Thank you!"

Mereet smiled, took the girl's hand, and quickly squeezed it. "Tell me about yourself. Are you married? Do you have family?"

"No, ma'am. I thought I was going to be given to one of my lord's court retainers, but he was assassinated six months ago. Since then . . ." She sighed. "Well, that's neither here nor there. I had a father and mother, and two sisters. Our parents died during the civil wars, before the Shepherd—" She stopped and tried again. "Before the Hai came. I keep forgetting to call them the Hai. Anyway, my sisters, well, I never heard what happened to them."

"I see. You were born free. We have that in common. Well, I'm not going to let you forget that, just as I never let myself forget it. And one day I'll see you freed. I promise you that, Ayla. Freed and dowered and given in marriage to someone nice." The sad look came back into her face. "No one should be a slave. No one should own other people. . . ." The words trailed off, and Mereet's sad expression became one of utter desolation.

"Oh, my lady!" Ayla said, putting her hands on Mereet's arms. "You've family yourself, haven't you?"

Mereet managed not to cry. "A husband . . . twin babies . . ." She bit her lip and clenched her fists against the feelings that shook her now. "That anyone could stand between us like this! When my family needs me so!"

"Your twins," Ayla said, "a boy and a girl?"

"Yes." Mereet sank down onto the couch, where she sat with shoulders slumped. "My adorable little darlings . . . and poor Shobai. He needs me most of all. I lie awake nights and think of him going through life without—" The words became a sob, and again she suppressed it. "He—he's blind, you know. Large and strong and gentle—and blind. I was his eyes. He perceived so much of life through me. You have no idea how it is to be that much a part of a person's life." She swallowed and wiped the sudden, hot tears away with one slim hand. "He's been through so much. How he managed to live through it all, I'll never know. A lesser man would have become bitter, hate-filled. But not Shobai. The only person he never forgave—other than the man who blinded him and murdered his brother—was himself. I used to try so hard to get him to realize . . ."

"Oh, there, my lady," Ayla said, hugging her gently, soft hands rubbing her back. "Try not to think of—"

But Mereet stiffened and pulled away from her. "But that's exactly what I mustn't do," she said, quivering with emotion. "I mustn't ever forget them—Shobai, my babies—ever, so long as there's a breath left in me. As long as I can remember the look of them, the feel of their dear bodies, the sound of their voices, I can stay sane."

The servants were already beginning to close down Ersu's villa for the night when Ameni arrived, preceded by a servant lighting his way with a torch. The slave who tended the front door had his instructions in advance and let Ameni in. "My lord is waiting for you, sir. He'll be enjoying the evening breeze beside the pool."

Ameni nodded nervously and turned to his own servant. "Get yourself something to eat," he said. "I won't be long." Then he hurried out to the garden, not waiting to be shown the way.

Ersu, wearing only a loincloth in the warm evening, sat on the steps that led down to the reflecting pool, dabbling his bare feet in the tepid water. "Ah, Ameni, did you talk to him?"

"Well, yes," Ameni answered, coming to the pool's edge but making no move to sit down beside him. "B-but . . . I don't know what to think. This whole thing takes my breath away, I'll admit it does. One moment the lad's my slave, and the next—"

"Then Salitis is quite serious about this?" Ersu's face reflected his incredulity. "He's going through with it?"

"Yes." Now Ameni did sit down—but he did not relax. Ersu could see the tension in him, could almost feel it in the air between them. Ameni sighed, letting all the air out of him; he seemed to collapse like a puppet whose strings had been cut. "I'm frightened, Ersu. I had no idea it was going to go this way. This isn't just a matter of finding Joseph a better station in life and hanging on to his chariot as it goes on to greater things. If Salitis does the things he says he's going to do, and if the people find out Joseph—an ex-slave elevated suddenly to this high place—is to blame . . ."

"They could trace it to us, eh?" Ersu pulled his feet out of the water and rested them on a lower step. "I wouldn't worry about that, my friend. We'll still have the entire weight of the Shepherds between them and us. You and I are going to rise. Things are going to get suddenly better for you. And," he said, a sly smile on his face, "for me as well."

Ameni looked blank-faced at him. "What do you mean?"

"I have plans," Ersu said. "My wife's brother is a priest, over in On. Don't worry; he's not one of those scheming fanatics. He purchased his position, much as I did. He has this young and very comely daughter—a dear, sweet girl, actually. He's wanted to marry her off for quite some time, but I've talked him out of it until I can actually steer him to a match that will mean not just money but power. And believe me, my friend, in the years to come, power is going to be a lot more important in this kingdom than money."

"I don't understand," Ameni said.

Ersu smiled. "Just listen. Up till now land has been the most important form of currency. Land, and what one could grow on it. But what if the government seizes the land and its produce, and doles back only what it thinks the former land-owner should have?" He watched the expression on Ameni's face change slowly. "Yes, you begin to see. In time to come, ownership of land will mean nothing, and closeness to the pharaoh will mean everything. If you can keep your friend-ship with Joseph and if I can steer him successfully into the path of my brother-in-law Petephres and his fetching young daughter Asenath, why, we'll outlast all the people who are scheming to buy bottomland in the flood plains right now. They'll be wiped out, and we'll be sitting pretty."

Ameni gulped and stared wide-eyed at his friend. "But I thought *you* had been buying land! That island plot you purchased no more than a month ago, on a channel of the river—"

"Yes! But that was before we saw what we saw today. I've been giving the whole matter a lot of thought. And I called on my land agent. He tells me that everyone's on a buying binge just now, and I'll do extremely well if I begin selling, discreetly, so as to give no one any suspicion that I know something they don't. I'll drop the country property and buy city real estate: houses, apartments, anything to house the hordes of people who'll be forced off the land and will wander into the city looking for work. Then, when the days of plenty have come and gone, and drought and famine are upon us, if Joseph's prophecy holds true—and I think it will—"

"You do? Really?"

Ersu grinned and patted his friend's knee. "The truth is, my brother-in-law says the auguries have been running the same way for weeks now. He just doesn't bother to tell the king. The oracles, regardless of the source of their divina-tions, all seem to agree with this nameless god of Joseph's. But Petephres and his fellow priests have so far suppressed the information; Salitis has been giving the state religion a wide berth lately. Why then should his priests be supportive in return?"

"Ah. And meanwhile—"

"Meanwhile, Petephres and his colleagues, on the strength of their information, have been quietly buying up property in

On and in other cities north of the partition. He's been urging me to join him; if we pool our resources, we can virtually control all property within the city gates before those seven years of prosperity have come to an end."

"You've spoken to him today?"

Ersu smiled benignly. "The moment I left you, I hurried to his villa. He keeps a house here, as well as the one in On; it pays to maintain whatever political connections he can, given the king's neglect of the priesthood. Anyhow, he's in town now, and I conferred with him. Don't be alarmed, Ameni. I didn't tell him everything I knew, just enough to draw him out. We found ourselves in perfect agreement. Look: The king is sure to reward you handsomely for giving Joseph to him. Take the money and come in with us. We'll wind up the real power behind the throne."

Ameni looked up at the myriad stars above in the cloudless sky, then down at the moonlit reflecting pool. Everything was happening so fast, it made his head swim. He wrung his hands in agitation. How could he know what to do? It all sounded so plausible, so sensible, but there was no solid ground underfoot. It was like trying to walk across the river on lily pads, with the banks to both sides rimmed with hungry crocodiles.

Joseph suddenly sat up in bed, wide awake, terrified, covered with cold sweat. *Where am I?*

But then he looked through the open door at the far end of his room and saw the patio beyond, bathed in moonlight, and the tall pillars and the wide shuttered windows of the apartment on the far side of the garden. He breathed deeply and let the tension ease out of him. He was in the palace, in the rooms the king had assigned to him. It was all right. He was safe. He was—

But no. Now he remembered the dream, the vision that had come to him as he slept: The old man's hair had been white instead of red-tinged gray, and he was thin and weak and bent with age. Nonetheless, there had been no mistaking him in the dream. It was Jacob, also called Israel, Joseph's father, and the father of the nation that had already begun to be called Israel in honor of Jacob when Joseph had been spirited out of the country.

The dream showed the old man being carefully, tenderly helped down from a donkey by a slim young man in his twenties. Joseph had looked the lad in the face and recognized his brother Benjamin, now grown to manhood. As he watched, Benjamin settled Jacob down on a flat rock and went back to the pack animals. He led forth a tethered lamb, tying it to a nearby tree branch; then he unwrapped the sacrificial knife. It was clear that he was going to make the sacrifice to the God, to the nameless, all-powerful, all-knowing Being his fathers had called El-Shaddai.

And now Joseph remembered. He remembered his own shame and his own tears of remorse. It should be he, Joseph, there beside his father, readying the sacrifice. It should be he, not his younger brother, who assumed the duties of the priesthood of the God. It should be he there beside Jacob in his last years! He had looked at his father, thin and pale, his face lined as deeply by suffering as by his great age, and wept. He had wept at his own guilt and at his own loss. *Land of my fathers! Will I ever see it again? And Jacob . . . will you die before I can hear your voice once more?*

He wept again. But in a moment he stopped, and a new feeling came over him. Was not all life, all existence, in the hands of the God? Was not his own path laid before him by El-Shaddai? He had come here not of his own will, but by his brothers' wicked and envious actions. It was obvious that he was here for a purpose, and thus it was not his duty in life, just now, to be at Jacob's side. Instead it was his duty to be exactly where he was, at the side of the pharaoh. It had been perhaps given to him to fulfill a great destiny. One that would change the tide of human events, as the God directed. The changes he made would, in time, affect Jacob as well. He would do what the Voice within him told him. He would do El-Shaddai's bidding and perhaps change the world.

Mekim had chosen well: The tavern had an upstairs room, accessible only through a well-hidden alley entrance, which was bricked up at the other end. From the street no one could see who entered. Now, as the stranger left after delivering the information Baliniri had paid him so well to tell, Mekim looked at Baliniri, one eyebrow raised quizzically. "What did you say his name was?" he asked. "And where did you get him?"

"The name's Pentauert, as close as I can pronounce it," Baliniri said. "He's the boyfriend of a chap named Cherheb, who's the go-between for Kirakos's spy network here in Avaris.

And you wouldn't believe how much I had to pay, here and there, to get this much information this fast. Cherheb is very good at his job, a master. But he's vulnerable, like so many pederasts. You can get through to most by approaching them through their boy lovers. Usually there's a lot of anger and jealousy, and if you're lucky enough to touch off their resentment, they will spill their guts."

"Ah. And you patted his bottom for him?"

"I patted his palm. With a fat purse I had to hack a lot of heads to earn, back in the Land of the Two Rivers. What did you think of what he had to tell?"

"About this Joseph fellow? Salitis's plans? Unbelievable. He's going to have a full-scale rebellion on his hands."

"Maybe. In the meantime you and I, my friend, have just come by an extremely valuable piece of information."

Mekim grinned that insouciant boy's grin of his. "Information we can sell across the border? I think *so*."

Baliniri nodded. "Then let's get it across the border before our friend Kirakos finds out we have it. He can't afford to have anybody around who's penetrated his spy network. However firm our newfound friendship may seem, somehow I'll feel more able to sleep nights when we've moved on."

Mekim reached for the wine, drank deeply, belched loudly. Without comment he passed the goatskin over to his friend. When Baliniri declined it, Mekim drank again. "All right," he said. "We'll sleep this one off, and tomorrow morning when the sun's high—"

He was about to take another drink when Baliniri reached over and firmly pulled the skin away from him to toss it into a corner. "Enough of that," the larger man said. "We're leaving tonight. I took the liberty of getting our things out of Kirakos's house when nobody was looking. I've left a fat bribe with the city guard on the midnight watch; we can get out with no trouble. There's a full moon, so there'll be no difficulty seeing the road."

Mekim stared, blinked, belched again. "Aw," he said, "I'd had notions of looking up that little dancer at the Sign of the Pheasant, the one with the dimple on her . . . But maybe you're right. Yes. Better to get moving. Still, that little dancer—"

"There'll be dancers in Lisht," Baliniri said. "Now come along. The road beckons."

# CHAPTER FIVE

## Canaan

### I

A gentle breeze stirred the leaves of the ancient oaks of Mamre's Grove as Jacob sat taking his ease in the hour after the noon meal. The old man had sat there almost motionless for the better part of an hour, eyes squinted against the bright sunlight. Benjamin, his youngest son, had chores to attend to, but the old man's passivity had begun to worry him, and he had not let himself get out of earshot of his father since the late morning. Jacob had a way of slipping off to sleep in the sun's warmth, and there was always the chance that he could fall and hurt himself. *Perhaps I should have one of my nephews stay with him,* he thought.

But now Jacob came out of his reverie, and his sharp old eyes looked around. "Benjamin?" he said. "Is that you?"

"Yes, Father," the young man said. "Are you ready to go in?" *How very thin and old he looks,* he thought. *How long will we have him with us?* The fiery red of Jacob's hair and beard had turned first to gray, then to stark white since the move to Canaan from Haran in the north. Now the hair on his old head was sparse, and his arms, once the strongly muscled arms of a man who had wrestled with the angel of the Lord, were thin sticks.

"The sun's still high," his father said. "Is there no word of them yet?"

"No, Father. Any time now." Jacob was speaking of his friends from Succoth, in the valley of the Jordan. He had been looking forward to the visit for days now, ever since their letter had come. Other than members of his own family, he had no older surviving friends than these. Imlah of Succoth, patriarch of the ancient ironworkers' town, was the son of Machir, the first friend Jacob had made among the men of Canaan in the days of the coming of the mighty Shepherd Kings. Fourth of Machir's sons, Imlah had been the wisest in the ways of men, and his father's blessing had fallen upon him in violation of the laws of primogeniture; his three older brothers had willingly submitted to his influence and had given over to him the management of his father's estates, so confident were they of his wise stewardship.

Imlah's wife, Danataya, was an even older and dearer friend. Her first husband was the martyred Hadad of Haran. When Danataya was pregnant with their child, Hadad had asked his friend Jacob to take her to safety in Canaan in the last fateful days of the Shepherds' bloody advance on the north country. Jacob obeyed his young friend's wishes, while Hadad went north to save his city at the cost of his own life.

For many years, Jacob's fortunes had been intermeshed with Danataya's. Her son, Ben-Hadad, and his own son Joseph, the darling of his heart, had been born on the same day; Jacob was godfather to Danataya's child.

Benjamin, watching the old man, saw the shadow pass over his father's face. *Whenever he looks at me*, he mused, *he sees Mother—and remembers that she died giving birth to me.*

Danataya also had known heartache. Her second marriage, a disaster, to the wastrel Hashum, had separated her and her son from Jacob for years, but when they were reunited after Hashum's death, Joseph and Ben-Hadad had become the dearest of friends. And when Joseph was sold into slavery by his jealous older brothers, Ben-Hadad had gone off to Egypt in search of his missing friend. Neither of the two had ever been heard of again.

"Father," Benjamin said a little tentatively, "are you sure you're strong enough for this visit? You know how emotional you get when—"

"Emotional?" Jacob said, straightening his ancient back and staring at his youngest son. "And since when am I supposed to avoid the exercise of my emotions? They make the difference between humans and animals, boy. Danataya and I have gone through much together. If our memories make us weep, so much the better." He saw the hurt on his son's face and softened. Benjamin, after all, was the only one of Rachel's two sons that he had left, and there was a strong bond between them. He put out one gnarled hand and touched his son's powerful young forearm. "Forgive me," he said gently. "The past is all she and I have when it comes to Joseph and Ben-Hadad. We've hoped for so long to hear news of them, something to awaken hope. Now I'm coming to think I should resign myself to the will of El-Shaddai, the one God who lives in all things, and abandon hope of seeing my Joseph again in this life."

"No, Father!" Benjamin said. "Don't give up! There's always the chance that—"

Jacob patted his hand and made a shushing sound. "It is all in the hands of the Lord," he said. "No purpose is served by keeping false hopes alive. I do have my memories and old friends. Do not worry about me, Benjamin. The visit from my old friends will be pleasant, a consolation for me. Memory is a strange thing, my son. One can find in it all measure of bitterness or beauty. One finds what one brings to it." He squeezed his son's hand and then released it again. "Now, go see to the preparations. Everything must be in order. I made the proper sacrifices to the God last night—"

"Yes, Father. I helped you."

"Oh, yes. I remember now. I . . . I dreamed Joseph was here with me, helping prepare the sacrifice, as priest of his people." He sighed. "He would have made such a fine servant of the Lord. There was an intensity about him, a dedication. And there was the true prophetic gift—the true voice of El-Shaddai Himself spoke through Joseph's divinations."

"Yes, Father. Now come inside the tent and lie down. When your friends arrive, you'll be fresh and rested."

After leaving his father, Benjamin went out of the grove into the bright midday sunshine and looked at the broad Vale of Hebron. Down the road, a lone horseman made his way slowly across the treeless plain. Benjamin shaded his eyes, peered out across the arid land. *Reuben*, he thought, and frowned. It wouldn't do for his father to see Reuben, his oldest son, just now. The two had never got along; every meeting left the old man upset, angry, drained.

Benjamin strode down the winding path to meet his half brother. For some reason, while Reuben had always resented Jacob's favoring Joseph, his resentment never carried over to Benjamin, the youngest, despite Jacob's obvious affection for him. "Reuben," he said, holding up one hand in greeting.

"Greetings," his half brother said, wiping his sweaty brow. He did not dismount. "I won't ask to see Father. Please give him a message for me: There's going to be a delegation from Hebron to see him in a day or so, and they're mad. They want some action, and fast."

Benjamin nodded knowingly. "What has Shamir been up to this time?"

Reuben's face was weatherworn, his hair thinning. He looked years older than his real age. "Same old tactics—swindling. He took a couple of settlers for their savings, promising a double return on their investments in some land deal. It turned out he didn't even have clear title to the land and couldn't get it if he'd tried." Reuben shook his head. "I'm afraid he's cut from the same fabric as his father. You couldn't trust Hashum, either."

Benjamin sighed. "And the villagers will be up to ask justice of Father. I wish one of us could deal with Shamir for him. But no one will accept any of us as a magistrate while Father is still alive and competent."

"The best thing to do," Reuben said between clenched teeth, "would be for me and Simeon and Levi to, ah, have a little talk with Shamir." He rubbed his big fists, one after the other. "In Grandfather's time he'd have been driven out into the desert to die. A good thing, too."

Benjamin thought a moment. He reached up and patted the nose of Reuben's horse. "Look, I agree Father has to do something about this. But Danataya and Imlah are expected any time now. Can we keep this to ourselves until the guests are gone?"

"Danataya and Imlah," Reuben repeated, then whistled through his teeth. "Ach! Damn it. But you're right. She bears no blame for Shamir's behavior. I'll see what I can do to keep things under control in the village. But let me know the moment she and Imlah have left, will you?"

Without waiting for an answer, he wheeled his horse around and set off down the path at a brisk trot.

Imlah's party arrived as the shadows of the oaks were

growing long. Imlah, a well-to-do merchant, traveled with twenty servants, all heavily armed against the bandits that had taken to roaming the hills ever since the sudden thinning of the Shepherd occupation force. As Jacob's own household servants helped Danataya and her women move their baskets into the tents that had been prepared for them, Benjamin helped Imlah and his men hobble their animals.

"Was there any trouble along the way?" Benjamin asked.

"It was very quiet," Imlah said. "We didn't even see a Shepherd party."

"There are few of them between here and Ebla," Benjamin said. "Manouk's son has called most of them back to Egypt. Seems to be trouble there."

Imlah smiled thoughtfully. "One might have predicted that, eh? No one is going to hold Egypt in bondage forever. More luck to the Egyptians, I say. I've no particular love for the Shepherds."

"Nor I, sir. How are things up north?"

"Blooming. Blossoming. The harvest was splendid, as fine as it's ever been in my lifetime. But tell me: How has Jacob been?" There was real concern in his voice, and Benjamin warmed to him for the fact. How fortunate that Danataya could have found a man like him, in her sorrow!

"Actually, I wanted to talk to you about my father before we see him. If the lady Danataya could perhaps limit her reminiscences, especially where Joseph is concerned . . ."

Imlah nodded. "I understand. She's still grieving for Ben-Hadad and Joseph. She can't believe that either lad could go this long without getting a message of some kind back to her and Jacob. She's losing hope that the boys are alive."

"I suppose all we can do is hope that the memories stirred up when Jacob and Danataya get together won't prove too painful for either of them. Now, sir, come to the well. We can freshen up, then join my father and your wife."

Mamre's Grove held special significance for the tribe of Jacob, whom the angel of the Lord had renamed Israel. Abraham, patriarch of the tribe that had been the first to bring the worship of the God El-Shaddai from the Land of the Two Rivers to Canaan, had made friends from among the inhabitants of the region: Mamre, tribal lord of the land below Mount Hebron, and his brothers, the fierce Bedouin warriors Aner and Eshcol.

Next, Abraham and his son Isaac had settled here, and now the tribe had purchased the entire valley from Mamre and his kin, and Jacob's status in the area was that of an uncrowned king.

Thus it was that the welcome his people gave their visitors was lavish within the customs of the land, and Jacob, thin and stooped with age, greeted the guests with the traditional words: "Come in, blessed of God; why remain without when I have prepared a place for you and your stock?" The formality once complied with, Jacob and Danataya embraced like father and daughter, laughing and crying at the same time. Surrounded by retainers and servants alike, they went into the tent Jacob's people had prepared for the feast, where merry music played.

But Benjamin lingered outside. Something was bothering him. He knew himself to have a little of the premonitory gift his brother Joseph had, but the premonitions in his own case remained vague and he could never read them accurately.

Now, however, he heard a terrible cry from the hillside below, where the visitors' animals had been hobbled at dusk to graze. He rushed down the hill from the grove. "Here, now!" Benjamin said as he approached the open space, seeing that a small crowd had already gathered. "What's going on?"

Nahor, one of his father's herdsmen, was bent over the inert body of what was a beautiful horse. He recognized it, of course; Jacob had given it to Danataya two years before. From the animal's side protruded a slender arrow, driven deep into its body by a powerful bow. "Look, sir," Nahor said. "Someone has killed this fine horse. It belongs to one of my lord's guests, I think."

Benjamin knew instantly what had happened. "Double the guard!" he said in a loud voice. "Close off all paths of escape! Maybe we can catch him before he gets away!"

But as Nahor stood up beside him and the two exchanged glances, both knew it was hopeless. The man who had killed Danataya's horse would be well out of reach by now. This was not his first act of senseless violence, but thus far he had always gotten away. If he were caught, he would deny the deed, lying easily with a smile—for Shamir had no conscience to restrain him, either from crimes against livestock or those against people. And the deep resentment he had always borne Danataya had taken this form precisely because of the affection she had for the animal.

*Ah, Reuben*, Benjamin thought, *you were right. This ugly business has to be dealt with quickly, whether I like it or not. Father has to render judgment against him, and the sooner the better—*

"Sir," Nahor said, breaking in on his thoughts, "do you suspect who I—"

Benjamin looked down at the dead animal, and his face twisted in anger and shame. "Probably. Only one man can have been so cruel," he said. "It's the lady Danataya's stepson, Shamir ben-Hashum."

## II

In the excitement of the reunion Benjamin was able to keep the news of Shamir's deed from his father and his guests for the better part of a day. But at midday Benjamin met Imlah on the path that led to the animal pens. "Good day, sir," Benjamin said nervously.

"Good day, young man," the Northerner replied. "Perhaps you can help me. I am looking for my wife's mare."

Benjamin took a deep breath. "I was hoping to keep the news from you a little longer." Quickly he told of the killing and of his suspicions. "This fellow has been a problem since his childhood," he said. "He's already caused the lady Danataya so much grief. I wish there were some way to spare her this."

Imlah reflected, deliberate in his answers as always. "I understand your concern. But Jacob must judge Shamir. He's not a boy anymore. It's time he answered for his crimes like the adult he is." He sighed deeply. "There are times when I wonder if it wouldn't have been better if he'd come to the same end his father did, all those many years ago. It's no good to kill the wolf and leave the cubs behind. Danataya tells me the boy made Ben-Hadad's life miserable all the time they were together. And I understand that Shamir also fought with young Joseph, years ago."

"One day my brothers found Joseph unconscious. Near his body was Shamir's sling."

"Well, young man, you have to break it to your father. I'll tell Danataya. She'll be heartbroken, of course. She loved that animal, in part because it was a special gift from Jacob."

"Perhaps Father can break the news to her. . . ."

"Or I will. Whatever . . . You call your brothers together. Shamir has to be stopped. He's like a lion loose in the fields."

Danataya entered Jacob's tent without announcing herself, as he had encouraged her to do. "Jacob," she said, looking down at where the old man sat, a piece of brightly colored cloth in his hands. "What are you doing, dear friend? What's that?"

"This?" he said in a quavering voice. "I thought you'd have recognized this, even if it has been a number of years since—" His voice broke off, and his narrow shoulders rose and fell in resignation.

"It's Joseph's coat, isn't it?"

Jacob's once-powerful hands picked at the brilliant cloth. "Yes, yes. What a fine sight he was! I think the coat is what set his brothers off in the first place. That, and the dreams he'd been having." His hands shook for a moment, then he regained control of himself. "All the sons I had by women other than Rachel have been a disappointment to me."

Danataya sat down beside him. "You really loved her, didn't you?"

"More than life," Jacob said. "More than anything except the God of my fathers, I suppose." His sigh came from the heart. "Ah, Danataya, what makes a man love a woman? To take her to wife, I served two full indentures under her father, and I had to take her sister Leah in the bargain. And then Leah bore children, and Rachel did not, and in that hard northern country a man needs sons. I had more sons by Leah's handmaidens, Bilhah and Zilpah. But I never loved anyone but Rachel."

Danataya took his hand in hers. "Everyone knew that. But that was some of the problem, wasn't it? That you favored her over the others? And in time, you came to favor the sons she bore you over—"

"Yes. Yes. And it was no good telling myself how unfair it was, how unjust. . . ." There was a strange look in his eyes.

"Primogeniture. Why should the first son receive the father's blessing, rather than the best son? My family has never been too strongly attached to the custom anyway. My grandfather had a son before Isaac. His name was Ishmael; his mother was an Egyptian slave. Grandfather preferred Isaac over the claims of Ishmael, as Isaac preferred me over my twin brother, Esau. Why then should I respect a custom flouted by earlier generations of my own family?"

"It's all right," she said. "Don't blame yourself for the rift in your family. Your sons' behavior toward Joseph is not your responsibility."

But he was not so easily persuaded. "No, no. I created the situation because I loved Rachel, and I didn't love Leah or the two servant girls. I loved Rachel's sons, and I didn't love my sons by—"

He stopped dead, a shocked expression on his face. Danataya looked around, startled, and looked into the hollow, pained eyes of Reuben, Jacob's oldest son, his first son by Leah.

There was a moment of dazed silence, and then Reuben spoke, his voice tight. "Father," he said. "I apologize for interrupting, but there's a problem that requires your attention."

Jacob's manner was cold, brusque. "It so immediately requires my attention," he said, "that you barge in without announcing your presence?"

"I'm sorry," Reuben said, his manner distant. He bowed awkwardly to Danataya. "Pardon me, ma'am. But something's happened. We'd hoped to deal with it later, but . . ."

Jacob put his hands on his knees and stared impatiently up at his eldest son. "Fumble, fumble, fumble. As usual you seem incapable of coming right out and saying what you have to say." He turned to Danataya, annoyance registering in his voice. "Forgive me, my dear. Reuben is a father many times over, and a grandfather as well. But in many ways he remains a child, one who—"

"Father!" Reuben said, resentment giving an edge to his voice. "It's Shamir! He's back. And he's been causing—" He gulped, fumbling like an adolescent before his formidable father. He turned to Danataya again. "Ma'am, he came into the compound, and . . . I'm afraid he killed your horse, the one Father gave you. He'd have gotten clean away except that he couldn't resist one last—"

"Eh?" Jacob said, struggling to his feet. "You mean you've got him? Well, why didn't you say so?" Reuben tried to help him as he rose, but he brushed away his son's helping hand. Now he stood, weaving a little. Danataya rose, and he made a point of accepting the hand that she gave him, leaning on her slightly as they made their way out into the sunshine.

Jacob blinked at the strong light. "Well?" he said irritably. "Where is he?"

No answer was necessary. A gap in the grove created a pool of unshaded light from the early afternoon sun; in this, his arms pinned by Jacob's burly sons Simeon and Levi, the miscreant stood, an insolent smirk on his dark face. His robe was torn, and there were other signs of a scuffle: blood on Simeon's bare shoulder, and Levi's bruised knuckles. A discoloration under Shamir's right eye was beginning to swell.

Shamir barked an unpleasant laugh and shot Danataya an insultingly disrespectful look. "Hello, Mother dear," he said, derision in every syllable. "Don't bother looking concerned. I don't want you to waste the effort. But you can tell the old fool to look over here if he wants to know where I am. I assume he can still see this far."

"Shut up, you!" Simeon said, giving him a cuff to the side of the head. "Show a little respect—"

This provoked an outburst of ugly laughter from the captive. "Respect?" Shamir said. "For a couple of disreputable bastards like you? For a doddering, senile old fool like this one here? Or a reformed but weather-beaten tavern slut like Mother dear?" The grip tightened on his arm, but he turned to Reuben now. "Or shall I respect this failed whoremaster, who was passed over for an eleventh son for his father's blessing? Who cuckolded his own father with his half brothers' tart of a mother because he couldn't find anyone to bed down with but a slave?"

Reuben sprang forward and pounded him to the ground with a rain of heavy blows. Shamir would have struggled to his feet to come back at him, but he was caught and subdued by Levi. Simeon yanked Reuben to his feet and shoved him angrily backward. "You fool!" he shouted. "Don't pay any attention to his foul mouth. Just stay over there and keep out of this." He helped Levi haul Shamir erect and took the captive's other arm again. Shamir ran his tongue over his teeth, testing them for breaks. A thin line of blood ran down from his nose to his upper lip; he licked at it, almost hungrily. His eyes were the eyes of a rabid animal. Danataya, watching him, shivered, remembering.

"Father," Simeon said. "The villagers in Hebron have petitioned for a hearing. Shamir has swindled several of them out of their entire substance. They demand justice and reparation."

"Reparation?" Shamir said. "They'd better not hold their breath until they get anything out of me. I haven't got a thing left. I spent it all on the whores in Jericho, every last—"

But then he caught Jacob's eye, and something in Jacob's eye transfixed him. He could not finish the sentence. He swallowed, coughed, tried to speak again, and managed no more than a stammered, "J-Jacob, I . . ."

"You've said enough," said the old man, standing a little taller, the years seeming to fall away from him. His sons' eyes widened; they could see it, too—the power, the authority flowing back into Jacob's aged body even as they watched. "If your father had lived a day longer, I'd have banned him from all the lands where my name was known. Yes, and saved all of us a lot of trouble and pain." For a moment a bit of that pain was visible on his face. "You admit to the deeds my sons describe? You took the goods of these people in Hebron?" Shamir, his bravado recovered, nodded, an insolent grin on his now-puffy face. One of his eyes was beginning to close, and the grin was twisted out of shape by a swelling that was beginning to appear on one side of his mouth. "You killed an animal just to show your resentment of the woman who beggared herself raising you? To show your contempt for life?"

Shamir laughed. His captors shook him, hard. "I did what I felt like doing, old man. And I'll continue to do so."

"Not in Canaan, you won't," Jacob said.

Shamir, hearing Jacob's words, started to laugh again; but something in the old man's tone, sharp and purposeful, caught his attention. He stared, listened.

"The people of this land have suffered with your presence long enough," Jacob continued. "From this moment you are banned from all the lands my grandfather conquered and took from the great Chedorlaomer of Elam, from Lake Chinnereth in the north to Timna in the south, from the desert of Moab in the east to the shores of the Great Sea in the west."

"Banned?" Shamir said, recovering his insolence. "And how are you going to enforce that, you old fool? I come and go as I wish. I—"

But when Jacob spoke next, it was to his three sons, gathered before him, and to Benjamin, who had come up at the end. "He'll not come and go so easily in the future, not with a thief's mark on his forehead." His tone was chilling. "Brand him!"

# CHAPTER SIX

## Along the Trade Route

### I

Far into the desert west of the great Nile stretched a great curving line of oases, connected by trade routes that had been old when Imhotep had built the first stepped pyramid for the great Zosar, in the Third Dynasty period. In past years bandits had roamed the caravan routes, only to be defeated and scattered in the great days of the Amenemhets, who had established discipline and, sending punitive parties out after the miscreants, had brought their leaders back one by one for a series of shocking public executions.

Then, in the days of the civil wars that preceded the coming of the Shepherd invaders, the oases had become hideouts for men wanted by the authorities; banditry had flourished once again for a time, and caravans had stood little chance of reaching their destinations. Solving this problem had been one of Madir's triumphs, when he had finally prevailed upon Dedmose to give him the money to pay new patrols. Madir had successfully argued that, since the mouth of the Nile was now closed to Egyptian traffic, it was all-important to keep the inland trade routes open.

As Shobai's party pushed its way first westward and then southward, little sign of life remained along the desert route. At the large Bahariya oasis, first of the great watering places on the crescent-shaped route, only ruins and a wadi remained of the great days when the oasis had provided enough water for agriculture on a limited scale and whole villages had sprung up in a sink dotted with brackish lakes.

Shobai's party paused here for less than a day. While the soldiers watered the animals or swam in the lower of the two remaining pools, Shobai walked amid the ruins of the village nearby with Ben-Hadad, asking questions, answering others. "It's so dry here," he said. "There's something about the air—something threatening. I can feel it."

"I know what you mean," his nephew answered. "There are places like this in Canaan, where I was born. When the hot wind blows off the dry desert, you feel as though you were going mad. Some people actually do." He sighed. "I wonder if that was what was wrong with the man my mother married after my father died. Some people can't take the desert country and should stay away. Hashum was that way—and his son, Shamir, inherited the problem." He took Shobai's elbow and guided him around a rough place underfoot. "Watch your step there."

"Your voice changed when you mentioned Shamir," Shobai said. "You had a problem with him?"

Ben-Hadad led the two of them onto a higher path, which led above the pool where the soldiers, sun-browned and naked, were splashing themselves lustily in the tepid water. "Yes," he admitted. "He was older than I was and used to beat me terribly. I had a stammer then, from all the abuse. Even now it comes back for a moment or so, in times of stress."

"I understand. I remember your saying that Hashum died, that my father killed him, defending you. What happened to the boy, then?"

"He got into a fight with my friend Joseph, the son of Father's old friend Jacob. Joseph, defending himself against one of Shamir's attacks, hit Shamir on the head with a rock and apparently left him for dead. But Shamir recovered and went away when he found out his father was dead. I never saw him again, which pleased me very much. But I did hear of him once more, before I left Canaan. Shamir told somebody he was going to seek me out and kill me, to avenge Hashum."

"Kill you? That's strong language."

"That's the way he was. I never gave it any thought. It's

all behind me now, most likely. He has to be hundreds of leagues away."

Shobai slowed his pace. A thoughtful, brooding look came over his face. "That's what I thought about Reshef: Put it behind you, he's gone for good. . . . But he came back, and did a lot of damage before—" The dark cloud came over his face again, and Ben-Hadad could tell Shobai was thinking of Mereet.

He decided to change the subject. "Shobai, just what will we find up here, in the way of ore?"

"In Nubia?" the blind man asked. "Well, from all reports the area is uncommonly rich in copper and malachite. If this is so, we can continue your education to good purpose. You've never smelted copper directly from malachite. It's time you learned."

"I understand there's tin there, too—and iron."

"True," the blind man said, warming to his subject. "The one thing I'd most like to find there, though . . . well, it's highly unlikely, desirable though it might be."

Ben-Hadad guided him over a rise. "Here, let's sit for a moment. I've a rock in my sandal." He helped Shobai to a seat on a natural shelf above the path. "What is it you'd like to find?" he asked, shaking the rock out and knocking the dust from his shoe.

"Sometimes," Shobai said, waggling a finger, "you find iron ore in combination with manganese. When you do, it makes iron that's not just better, it's—well, harder. It's like the iron that sometimes falls from the sky. You know how wrought iron bends when you swing your sword at someone and hit a rock instead?" He laughed softly at himself. "Of course you don't. I forget myself, in my enthusiasm. Anyhow, wrought iron does that. This special kind of iron doesn't. It's heavier and holds its shape better. It'll hack right through any other weapon in the world."

"Iron that doesn't bend!" Ben-Hadad said in wonderment. "Did Grandfather learn how to make that?"

Shobai's great scarred head went back; it was a habit he had developed when thinking. "Not consistently. It happened twice, by accident. Once, when the ore happened to take on more carbon from the charcoal. It sometimes does that spontaneously. I was there. Father didn't have enough iron for a full sword, so he made a battle-ax head of it. It was a magical, rather frightening thing. I often wonder what happened to that weapon. We gave it to a captain in the army of Ebla. He must surely have fallen when the city was captured. Which, of course, would mean that some Shepherd has it now."

"Fascinating!" Ben-Hadad said. "I'd love to have seen it, or held it in my hand."

"It happened another time when the ore was naturally manganic, when there's salt containing manganese in it. But that is extremely rare, Father said. I've never seen it myself; Father only began to teach me after I'd lost my sight."

"If that's very rare, then we're not likely to find that type of manganese in the iron ore up here." Ben-Hadad was disappointed.

"I've never heard of it. And none of the reports I've gotten ever made me suspect I'd find it upriver. Of course, that doesn't prove anything. The people I talked to weren't knowledgeable about ores, and if you don't know what you're looking for, it's very unlikely that you'll find it. Most people who go prospecting up this way are looking for beryl and jasper and emeralds. Or gold. Worthless stuff like that."

Ben-Hadad chuckled along with him. How exciting it was to talk with Shobai like this! It was so much easier for them to chat out here in the middle of nowhere, away from the army, away from the court. Suddenly it struck him that this might be more than fortuitous. "Shobai," he said in a lower voice. "Were we in any danger back at court? You seem so much more relaxed out here."

Shobai scowled, and he did not speak for a moment. When he did answer, his voice was calmer, more thoughtful. "I suppose it's partly being away from that intense conspiratorial atmosphere around the palace. A blind man's hearing gets better, to compensate for the loss of his sight, and . . . I hear things. Madir isn't popular with some people at court. They think he has too much power. There are people who'd have him assassinated in a moment if he let them get a clean chance at him."

"Remember Harmin?"

"Yes. But there are others, smarter than Harmin was, more subtle, quieter. Yet as quiet as they are, I hear bits and pieces of conversation. There's this curious thing—because I can't see, some people take little note of me, as if they think I lost my mind along with my eyesight. Anyhow, I don't like the feel of the place. It's good to be away, particularly to someplace new, where there aren't any memories. . . ."

"I'm sorry. You're thinking about Mereet?"

"Constantly. I can feel her hand in mine right now. You've no idea. Before I met Mereet, I'd thought that love was a thing I'd left behind. But what she brought into my life . . ." He could not go on for a moment. When he spoke it was in a voice hoarser than before. "Back in Lisht, even at our house in the Fayum, everything reminds me of her, everything. I hate to say it, but I haven't been spending as much time as I used to with the children because they remind me of her. I can almost feel her there in the room. There are times when I can't stand it, not knowing if I'll ever have her back, ever hold her in my arms again. . . ."

Ben-Hadad put a comforting hand on Shobai's broad back and felt the scars through the giant's thin garment, the great welts, relics of the slavery he had known among the Shepherds. "There, now, Shobai," he began lamely. He felt like such a fool; he did not know what to say.

But now Shobai straightened, a full head's height above Ben-Hadad's. "You know," he said in a voice grown suddenly pensive, "I have this feeling that I'll meet her again, sometime before I die. I woke the other morning, remembering a dream." Now the blind man turned toward his nephew and put a huge, callused hand on Ben-Hadad's broad young shoulder. "I wish I remembered more. Maybe then I'd understand it. In my dream I had Mereet at my side. But I was dying. I felt myself slipping away, little by little." He swallowed. "After that, the memories grow confused, indistinct. They trouble me. I search my mind, lying sleepless in the night, trying to bring it back. But that's all I can remember."

## II

Shobai lapsed into silence. Something in the memories had disturbed him. In the morning the morosely silent caravan moved southward along the great route, negotiating the many leagues between the Bahariya oasis and the one at

Farafra. And on the narrow track the pack and passenger animals stretched out in single file, so that Ben-Hadad and his uncle could not carry on a conversation even if they were so inclined.

In the earlier days of the great empire the Dakhla oasis had been the administrative center for all of the southern lands under the control of the Twelfth Dynasty kings. Later it had become a place of exile for criminals whose offenses had merited punishment but not death. These had worked the irrigated fields or had been put to work maintaining the extraordinarily well-preserved mastabas of the Sixth Dynasty kings. Some criminals, working as forced labor, had built fine country residences for the overseers; now, with the oasis all but abandoned, these fine houses lay open, neglected, ghostly reminders of a greater age.

Ben-Hadad, under different circumstances, would have enjoyed poking around the abandoned tombs and buildings; but the urgency of their mission forced them to move on with no more than an overnight pause. As they rode out the next morning Ben-Hadad looked back to see the houses of the ghost town of Balat, white, in orderly rows, then headed eastward once more as the path curved around toward the Nile again en route to the Kharga oasis. His mind ran in unaccustomed channels, and he pondered the strange permanence of man-made things in this ancient land, which had seen so many thousands, so many millions of people like himself come and go without marking their passing, while the great tombs and monuments looked impassively down from their commanding heights. In time these, too, would die as had their owners, but slowly, slowly.

*And I?* he thought. *How many years have I left? And when I am gone, what will mark my passing? Who will remember me?* Indeed, what tracks had he made across the lives of others, that they would keep some small part of him alive in their minds once he had passed on to whatever next life there might be?

The thought turned his mind back to old guilts. *You've forgotten others,* he thought. *Why then should others remember you? Look how you've forgotten Mother all this time. How hurt must she be, thinking you dead.* And Jacob! Another name he had forgotten. He had come to Egypt in the first place to try to find Jacob's lost son Joseph and return him to his father. And here he had hardly given Joseph a second thought in months. Years. He frowned, shamed by the thought.

And then his mind turned as he had dreaded it would, to Tuya. *You've neglected her, too*.

His hands fidgeted on the reins of the animal he rode. Had it been because of her barrenness, her repeated false pregnancies, which had raised his hopes and then dashed them to a thousand pieces? Was it, perhaps, the feeling, way back in his mind, of being trapped? Of being weighed down by responsibilities? But he had always had responsibilities, had he not? He had to be the little man for his mother all those years, with no one but his own small and inadequate self to stand between her and the abuse she had got from Hashum.

So what was he doing now? Reacting against this? Rebelling against real responsibility, in response to memories of an earlier time when unreal responsibilities had weighed so heavily on him?

Why, if so, he had wronged her terribly. *Tuya!* The thought stabbed at his heart. If only he had her here, he could tell her what was in his heart, beg her forgiveness, swear to her to do better!

But he was many leagues away already, and getting farther away with every hour.

*Well, at least I can write to her*, he thought. *I promised her I'd do that*. Yes. He would start the first letter tonight and send it back with the first courier. He would . . .

Oh, what was the use? Come evening, when there would be time for writing letters, he would find some excuse not to do anything about it. He sighed. His shoulders slumped. He abandoned himself to the rhythmic sway of the animal beneath him and to glum thoughts that did him no credit at all.

The days passed, mostly without incident. Evenings, Ben-Hadad would try to engage Shobai in conversation, but the blind giant, lost in his own thoughts, answered in monosyllables whenever the subject strayed from neutral territory like metallurgy and the working of metal. Once or twice Ben-Hadad began letters, but destroyed them before they were finished.

At the Dakhla oasis they could see for the first time the real extent of the neglect the southern oases had suffered in recent years. Dakhla and Kharga had been famous for centuries for the quality of their wines; now, with no one to care for them, the vines lay dead. The few scattered inhabitants of the area, descendants, most likely, of exiles banished to the desert during the civil wars, withdrew into the hills above the green sink, fearful of the armed strangers. Dakhla had the feeling of a dead place, more fit for ghosts than for the living; Ben-Hadad consulted with the soldiers and directed the party to push on, eastward toward the Nile.

Midmorning the next day Shobai, who had ridden ahead of Ben-Hadad, leaving his mount to pick the path, allowed himself to fall back and called to his nephew. "From the sun," he said, "we'd be heading due east now. Is that right?"

"Yes." Ben-Hadad looked up ahead, squinting into the morning sun. "There's something up ahead. . . . Dunes. Tall sand dunes. They've drifted across the track. But the guides tell me that they know the way."

Now the giant was riding alongside him as the track widened, his mount lazily ambling down the worn path. "If I remember correctly, traveling far enough this way, crossing the Nile to approach the Red Sea, would lead us to the copper and tin mines. Strange that the Shepherds haven't sent an expedition to secure the ore and keep it from us."

"Perhaps they don't need to," Ben-Hadad said. "They're so rich in gold that they can buy anything they want from other parts of the world. Why should they fight us for Nubian ore? Ore that they'll then have to transport around us?"

Usually Shobai would have commented on this. Instead he fell silent, his head cocked first this way, then that, listening. "Ben-Hadad," he said after a time, "on the heights, on the hills beside us, can you see anybody? Watching us, perhaps? I have this strange feeling that . . ."

Ben-Hadad, looking at the high places above the road, could see nothing. "No, Shobai. What's the matter?"

"Oh, nothing. I suppose." His face took on an unreadable look. "I'd appreciate it if you kept an eye out, just in case. We're being watched. I've felt it for an hour or so. If you keep a close lookout on the hills up there, you'll eventually see someone."

"Who?"

"I have no idea. But this area was always near the southern edge of the domain of the Lord of Two Lands, and these oases were constantly raided by black warriors from the south, even in the days of Egypt's greatest strength. The

Nubians will eventually come to strike here, or at Kharga—they'll need the arable land the Kharga oasis can provide.

"Funny," he continued. "Egypt maintained its borders for centuries, using mainly mercenary soldiers from south of here—the light-skinned Medjai, who were the hereditary enemies of the black Nehsiu from the far south. But when we lost control of these lands, the Medjai mercenaries became available to the Medjai kings. United, they drove the Nehsiu far to the south, to the upper reaches of the Nile. Then, with peace established, the Medjai kings found their realm full of restless soldiers, out of work, with nothing to do."

"I see," Ben-Hadad said. "And the first family quarrel among the Medjai dynasties immediately led to war."

"Yes," Shobai said. "King Taharqa suddenly found himself fighting off a challenge from his cousin Kashta. The squabble split lower Nubia cleanly in two. A war between brother and brother. Then our couriers to Taharqa's court were turned back at the borders south of here, or in some cases disappeared altogether."

"This was about the time Akhilleus came back from the source of the Nile, wasn't it?"

"Yes. We expected to hear from him, but we never did. Rumors started coming back about raids by the Nehsiu on Medjai forts, emplacements. And I remembered that Ebana, Akhilleus's wife, was of the Nehsiu, of royal blood. And Akhilleus had always talked about establishing a kingdom in his wife's lands. After all, he'd given up a kingdom in his own homeland in order to come back here."

"But you don't know for sure that these Nehsiu who are raiding the Medjai are—"

"No. But I have my suspicions. My father knew Akhilleus; they were slaves together on the Great Sea. Father always said that the black giant was a man of infinite resources, that when he put his mind to something, there was nothing he couldn't do. And remember, he and I traveled together for years and years. I watched him build a small fleet of ships into a mighty empire, richer than that of any of the kings I served in the days before the Shepherds came." He smiled. "I see his hand in this. Dedmose may be right. If Akhilleus *is* the leader of the Nehsiu and can unify the Nehsiu and the Medjai—well, maybe he's the man to help us drive out the Shepherds."

He sighed, long and hard. "The problem," he said with

skepticism and resignation, "is in getting him to want to do so."

Ben-Hadad grunted his assent. Just then, he looked up at the hills to the south of the road. What was that? Did he for a moment see a single tall, lean figure silhouetted against the morning sky, looking down? He blinked. When he looked again, the figure was gone. He couldn't say whether the man he had seen was light of complexion—a Medjai—or dark—a Nehsiu. All he knew was that the watcher was tall, lean as a crane, and scantily dressed. And armed with a long and deadly looking spear, half again the warrior's own height.

# CHAPTER SEVEN

## Lisht

### I

"Look, Hefget!" Dede said. "There's Mereb." He pointed across the crowded square, to where the man with the scarred face and the eye patch stood buying Fayum lemons from a vendor at a stall.

Hefget, scowling, grabbed his companion's arm and dragged him behind the well. "Silence, you fool! We're to take no notice of him! Do you want to betray Mereb in front of all these people?" His voice was a harsh whisper.

"Oh. Sorry. I'm not used to—"

"It's all right. Just keep your mouth shut." Hefget released his arm, and Dede rubbed it ruefully. "You know what he told us when last we met: We're at a very dangerous stage in our plans. And whatever he may say about Madir, I don't think the old fox is losing his touch at all. Two people on the fringes of our operation were arrested yesterday." He paused while a shopper passed by.

"Arrested?" Dede asked. "But won't they betray us under torture?"

"No. They were supernumeraries, with nothing to betray. The only name they know is that of their supervisor, and he's been shifted upriver to keep him from being arrested."

Dede watched idly while a comely young matron, full-bosomed under her white dress, bent to draw water from the well. "I'm with you," he said, eyes on the woman's shapely rump. "Madir still scares me. Madir of the Thousand Ears . . . I'm afraid even to talk to my woman. If he got to her—"

"*Don't* talk to her!" Hefget said. "Don't talk to anyone!" As they walked back through the crowded market, Dede's hand strayed toward the corner of an orange-vendor's stall. Hefget slapped the hand hard. "Stop that!" Again he yanked his friend by the arm, pulling him away from temptation. "You idiot! What would happen if the guards saw you? And dragged you to the dungeons and took the hot irons to you?"

"Ugh!" Dede said. "Sorry." He shook his head in self-reproof. As he did, both of them took note of a curious sight: A little street urchin slipped into the crowd next to a pair of well-fed shoppers; her hand whipped out like the head of a striking snake and grabbed a handful of plump dried dates— and was gone almost faster than the eye could follow. Dede blinked; the urchin reappeared six steps down the path. She looked back, mouth full of dates. And now they could see: The front of the urchin's garment bulged ripely with the unmistakable shape of a woman's breasts. "Well, I'll be damned," Dede said. "I thought she was a child."

"Yes, I've watched that one before," Hefget said. "I don't know where she comes from. She seems to have just turned up a couple of weeks ago. Quite obviously she's born to this life; a quicker hand I've never seen. I've asked around, but even the people down in the Thieves Quarter don't know anything about her."

"Huh," Dede said. "Fetching little thing, in her own way. No ravishing beauty, but a good tumble in the—"

"You'd better get that idea out of your head," Hefget said, chuckling. "From what the street people say, that deft little hand is as quick with a knife as it is swiping fruit from a stand. Nobody touches her. At any rate, nobody seems to have tried twice."

"Ach!" Dede said with a sneer. "Women!" They watched the girl slip almost unnoticed around a corner.

At the end of the passage Tuya tucked the remaining dates into the bosom of her short dress and, looking around for guards and seeing none, quickly scaled the brick wall of the warehouse at the end of the cul-de-sac, fingers and toes easily finding holds in the broken caulking.

At the top she sat and, bare legs dangling over the edge,

looked down into the little marketplace. She fished a date out of her bosom and bit into it hungrily. But after chewing for a moment, she spat it out. How strange! Stolen fruit did not seem to taste the same when you knew you could afford to pay for it, when you knew that the vendor could not afford to lose it. Who knew whether or not the vendor might be beaten at day's end by a harsh master for losing a minuscule profit to thieves like herself?

She reached into her bosom again and retrieved the rest of the dates. She looked down at them in her hand. She could not return them: She would surely be caught in the attempt, and what would be the value in that? She frowned and, looking down, spied two street children in the next alley.

"Hey!" she called down to them. "You two!" Four wary eyes peered up at her. "Here! Take these! I can't eat any more!" She tossed the dates down; the urchins jumped nimbly out of the way, expecting rocks or slop, but when the fruit lay in the street, they picked it up and ran away.

Tuya shrugged and looked down into the street at the mostly shabbily dressed people passing by. For a moment she found herself musing over their imagined lives. *How vulnerable they are!* she thought. *How little defense they have against ruin, hunger, and want. The merchants, artisans, masons, barbers . . .*

She sighed and felt pity for them all, in their dreary lives of endless drudgery and little hope for better. What hard lives most people led! They worked like oxen all day under the blazing Egyptian sun, with little more to sustain them but a millet cake or two baked under the ashes, perhaps an onion or a morsel of dried fish. If they worked under overseers, they were beaten long and often; the highest praise a man might aspire to would be that he had lived out his years without once being beaten before a magistrate. So it had been in the great days, and so it was now.

How well she knew! This hard life in the city streets had been all she had known through all of her childhood. She had lived for nearly a year in the crawl space of a storage loft, her presence unsuspected by the owners. She had subsisted by slipping into an olive orchard at night and stripping the lower branches bare, coming back naked as a babe, her one garment shaped into a bag around her neck for carrying the stolen olives. Yes, she had starved and suffered—and in time had come to see that survival always had come first, before compassion and empathy and concern.

How had she not gone mad? She had seen newborn babies tossed onto an ash heap to die by mothers unable to care for them. Blind grandmothers pushed out into the street with a begging bowl, expected to find their own living and shelter however they might. Children of seven and eight, boy and girl alike, raped by soldiers or marauders during the last days of the civil wars, were tossed away, brains addled, to be gathered up by the owners of the child brothels. The many, many suicides. She had seen all of this and more, and her heart had gone out to one and all.

But somehow she had managed to find a way not to let it all hurt her, break her spirit. She had survived, aloof from it all.

How was it that now, when she had finally found a place in life where she no longer had to worry, where she could face those midnight attacks of fear as to what the coming day might bring, she could not look on the harsh life she had left behind her without the pain and fear once more coming back? Without wanting to scream? Without wanting to cry out in anger and indignation? Without wanting to weep like a child?

Desperately, she tried to sort out her feelings and to understand them. Had she not escaped from all this? Had she not at last found safety in her upper-class life, as the wife of a man well on his way to real riches and power?

Then why had she been irresistibly drawn, little by little, back into the fearful gutter life she had left behind? And, having slipped back into the streets in her old rags, why did she suddenly find that all her old hard-won defenses were gone? Did she not know how to protect herself against the suffering anymore?

Looking down on the passing parade of lower-class life, she suddenly knew the answer: *There's a part of you lost here, and you'll never be content again until you can find it.*

Yes! That was what she had been looking for, prowling the streets in her rags. No matter that she had grown up in a city that was hundreds of leagues away; the land of the poor was the same land everywhere. It did not vary from city to city; there was the same want, the same oppression, the same hopeless and dreamless life.

She remembered when a storyteller had come to town.

He had told the Tale of Sinuhe and the Tale of the Two
Brothers; enraptured, she had stolen fruit and nuts for him to
eat. Aged, unhappy, the storyteller had turned to her and
said, "I'm a man who creates dreams for people who don't
know how to dream for themselves."

It had been true. And in the first months of her marriage
she had thanked the apocryphal gods again and again that she
had a man who could sing, who knew the ballads, the great
story-songs. It was a tradition among the Children of the
Lion, and they had all been good musicians, men who could
play virtually any instrument. Shobai, who had supported
himself in the early years of his blindness as a wandering
bard, was even better than Ben-Hadad had been and knew
ballads from many lands, including the Land of the Two
Rivers, from which his earliest ancestors had come, and the
Isle of Crete, where his father had lived so long in exile.

But now both of them were gone. How she missed the
world of song, of story! Strange: The circumstances of her
present life called for dreams, just as poverty had done. As it
turned out, simply becoming a well-to-do young matron did
not solve all one's problems. The bloom was quite definitely
off the flower where her marriage was concerned; her husband's mind was, even when he was in town, many leagues
away from her bed. And unlike the other young wives of
court—some of whom had the same problem—she did not
have children for compensation, children to occupy her mind.
If only . . .

But now, as if in answer to her dream, there was some
commotion at the end of the street, where the market square
began; a crowd had begun to gather before the raised dais at
the well. A man of middle years, tall and robust but with gray
in his hair already, stood tuning his kithara. A singer! A
storyteller! She smiled in eager anticipation. And, agile as a
monkey, she turned and began clambering deftly down the
wall.

But as she did, two soldiers, seeming better than half-
drunk already at midday, lurched out the back door of a
tavern on the side street that ran into the cul-de-sac halfway
down the path. Weaving, they stood in the middle of the
narrow street, blocking her route. One of them blinked,
focused, and said, "Well, look, now! What do we have here?"
Grinning unevenly, showing broken teeth, he chuckled, looked
past her to see the end of the blind alley behind her. "Why,

scrub her off a bit and she'd be quite a little morsel! Come here, dearie. Give us a kiss. . . ."

## II

Instantly alert, Tuya crouched and backed away. Her hand went to her waist, where she kept the deadly little knife that accompanied her everywhere in her back-street ramblings. Sunlight glinted on the slim blade. "Now, get out of my way," she said. "Or I'll—"

But the soldier was not as inebriated as he had first appeared. A glint came into his eye, and from under his belt he produced a long driver's whip made of braided leather; in one quick movement he shook it out into the street, and with a light flipping motion it disappeared behind his back.

"Don't you dare try to—" Tuya began. But the lash, too quick to follow, whipped out, and its knotted tip knocked the dagger from her hand. The soldier jerked the lash back; the braided strands curled around Tuya's numbed wrist and yanked her forward, roughly, into the second soldier's outstretched hands.

"Let me go!" she said in a tense voice. Her tiny fists pounded into the big man's face, and he grabbed her in a bear hug that immobilized her hands. She bent forward and sank her sharp little teeth into his thick arm.

The soldier yelped and let go. His companion moved quickly to his side and closed his huge hand around Tuya's wrist just as she stooped to retrieve her knife. Scooping up the little weapon, she continued the long curve of her lunge and slashed at the soldier's legs with the sharp blade.

With any luck the motion would have cut into a tendon; but the soldier moved just as she slashed at him, and the knife struck bone instead. He howled with pain and rage and cuffed her alongside the head, driving her to her knees. As he did, his partner grabbed the hand with the knife and twisted it; once again the weapon fell to the hard-packed earth. Tuya yanked her other hand free and, balling her fist, punched her captor square in the groin. The blow jarred her hand, but it brought an answering howl of agony, and once again she was free.

Now, however, one of the soldiers was between her and her knife, while the other still barred her way to freedom. She looked around. If she could get to the wall, perhaps she could make it all the way up to—

But just then her luck ran out. Behind her a third soldier came barreling out of the side alley from the back door of the tavern and, quickly grasping the situation, he stepped up behind her to pin both her arms. With a lusty chuckle, he held her aloft as she struggled, legs kicking furiously at nothing. "Well, boys," the soldier said to his mates, "is this something you lost?"

"Just hand her over," the wounded soldier said in a gruff voice. "The little slut got her damned knife into me."

But then her captor recognized them. "Hey," he said, "you're from the Fourth Brigade! Far be it from me to steal anything belonging to a messmate. Here, we'll share the little tart." He put Tuya's feet down on the ground and, holding both her thin wrists in his huge paw in a viselike grip, stood back at arm's length to look her over. "She's pretty small," he said. "Maybe there's not enough to go around, with three of us."

Tuya looked in his eyes and tried to pull away, knowing what came next. But his grip was too powerful. She backed away; but he pulled her toward him and, with a single motion of his free hand, ripped her garment from seam to seam. A second motion yanked the rags from her body, and she was naked before them—naked and quivering with fear and rage.

"Well, now! There was more there than met the eye," her captor said with a chuckle. "She's quite an armful for all that she's no bigger than a kid." He grinned and looked around. The tavern's occupants had poured into the street, witnessing Tuya's distress. "Watch how an old trooper does it. You might pick up a pointer or two. . . ."

Tuya pulled vainly at his hand; bent forward once again to bite his wrist. But his free hand swept out and cuffed her on the side of the head, hard. For a split second her knees went weak, and she almost fell. Seeing his advantage, he forced her to her knees. "There, now!" he said. "First get her down on her knees, that's the best way. Make her beg for it. Here, now, sweetie. Make me happy, and maybe I'll give you a bauble or two. But you've got to earn it. . . ."

*   *   *

Baliniri and Mekim had come out of the tavern in the third wave, and the big man had stood watching the spectacle with growing disgust, pity for the girl, and anger at the three men. The unequal battle was too much for his stomach to take. And the girl, for all her ripe maturity of body, was so tiny, so incapable of fighting off the three soldiers, despite all her spunk and feistiness. An odd thought flashed through his mind: *Why isn't the girl screaming? Why isn't she calling out for help?*

For some reason he couldn't articulate, he was fed up, once and for all, with all such spectacles, fed up with rapists and spectators alike. He knew he could not stand by and watch, doing nothing, without serious damage to his self-esteem.

Mekim, weaving a bit from the wine they had drunk, wore both sword belts around his neck indecorously. When Baliniri reached for his weapon, the smaller man drew back. "Here! What are you up to? You're not going to—"

Baliniri pulled at the weapon, then threw up both hands in disgust. "All right," he said. "Be a spoilsport. Make me work harder." And, leaving the sword jammed in its scabbard, he turned back to the scene in the street.

As he did, Tuya attacked once again, bending forward to sink her sharp little teeth in the big man's thigh. He let out a howl of pain, but she held on. Baliniri could see blood flowing down the soldier's leg. The soldier reached for his own sword and pulled it free, drawing it back to swing.

Then Baliniri's reflexes and instincts took over. A growl of rage escaped from his throat as he leapt forward. His hand intercepted the arm with the descending sword and slowed the vicious downswing. His other fist smashed into the soldier's face. The sword fell to the ground, and the soldier staggered back into the arms of his companions. The girl fell forward onto hands and knees.

"Mekim!" Baliniri ordered in a voice of command. "Give her a hand!"

The soldier's friends had their swords out, and one of them had pushed his way out into the middle of the path. "You mind your own business, you—" he began.

Baliniri feinted with his fist again, and the sword hand parried with a move he had taught to hundreds of young recruits. And, with another feint, he bent and lashed out with a sandaled foot. His kick caught the swordsman squarely in the groin, bending him double. At the same moment the soldier's mate, also armed, dashed forward and hacked at Baliniri's neck just as Baliniri recovered from the motion.

The sword dealt him a glancing blow on the shoulder, bringing blood. Baliniri's hand flashed out and caught the soldier's sword arm just at the end of its arc, as it began a backswing. A quick twist, and bone grated against bone; the sword fell from the soldier's now-useless hand, and Baliniri, giving the matter a little extra, twisted the arm all the way. The soldier's scream of pain was high pitched, piercing, as well it might be.

He had been well trained, though. His other hand reached for the downed weapon. Baliniri's foot lashed out again and caught the sword squarely, kicking it down the dirt street. As he watched it bounce off a wall, he saw Mekim out of the corner of his eye, gently wrapping his cloak around the naked and frightened girl.

Now, however, the soldier who had been interrupted in the act of raping the girl charged at him, head lowered, like a battering ram. Baliniri stepped nimbly to one side, dodged the oncoming rush, and, grabbing the passing soldier by the clothing, propelled him even faster into the tavern wall at the end of the passage. The soldier's head struck the bricks with a sick sound, and he fell in a heap.

Baliniri turned. The man he had kicked in the groin now approached him warily, his sword circling slowly, his eyes on Baliniri's face. As he did, the man whose arm he had broken moved to the other side of him. He had retrieved the sword Baliniri had kicked away. There were two of them with swords, one on either side of Baliniri, who was unarmed.

"Mekim," Baliniri said, "I suppose I'll have to arm myself." Grinning, he caught the sword Mekim tossed him, glanced down at it. "Curse you, this one's yours! You mean I'm going to have to dispatch these two oafs with an inferior sword?" He shrugged and hefted the weapon appraisingly. "Well, so be it. I've given enough lessons with dummy weapons, back in camp. Perhaps I can give these chaps a bit of a workout with this dull blade."

To one side the soldier with the bad arm feinted high, hacked low. "Lesson one," Baliniri said, moving all the while to take the blade on his, forte against forte, and guide the stroke into the wall, where it struck sparks on the stone.

Flipping his own sword, he belted the attacker under the chin with its pommel, slamming him backward. "Keep your attack above the knee. A man attacking low is far too vulnerable."

As he spoke, the other man lunged. Baliniri parried, turned the blade in a complete circle twice as the man fumbled wide-eyed, trying to disengage. Then, as the man drew back, Baliniri leaned forward and delicately pinked the man on the arm with his point. "Lesson two," Baliniri said, "keep your balance. Don't get the weight on that front foot unless you're lunging to kill." He made agile motions with the borrowed sword as he spoke; it gave the didactic tone of his remarks an even more insulting edge. "Damn you, Mekim! If this thing had been a little sharper I could have written my name in blood on his arm by now!"

"I'll sharpen it tomorrow," Mekim called out from the crowd. "Some people are just too critical for—"

But now the one-armed man caught his partner's eye, and the two of them attacked together, from both sides. Baliniri parried the first cut, but the second man's lunge was too low for a second parry. Baliniri looked around, alarmed for the first time.

He saw something that gave him a start. The girl had thrown off the robe Mekim had given her, and stark naked, she attacked the lunging soldier from behind with nails and teeth! As he watched, she leapt on the man's back, encircled his throat with one slim arm, and sank her teeth into his shoulder over the collarbone as the nails of her other hand clawed with deadly accuracy at his face! One of her nails had caught him in the eye, and blood ran down his face.

The sound emanating from Baliniri's throat had begun as a low chuckle, but now became a hearty, full-throated laugh. He turned back to his other attacker, just in time. He parried a wild swing at his guts with the sword's blade, then disarmed the man with a single quick-wristed motion.

"Lesson three," he said solemnly. "Choose enemies who are your own size, and make sure you know beforehand who their friends are." With a serious expression, he ran the man through and, pulling his blade free, turned back to the one remaining soldier. The girl's bare legs were locked around his belly. She leaned way back, hanging from the firm grasp both her hands had on his hair. He staggered back and forth, top heavy. Somehow he had lost his weapon again.

Baliniri stood, hands on hips, the sword dangling from his fingers, looking at them, shaking his head. "For an *outnou* or two I'd let her finish you off," he said in genuine wonderment. "You deserve anything she can do to you. But I promised you the basic course in staying out of trouble, and I'd be cheating you if I didn't complete the last lesson."

They all shrank back in awed silence. Baliniri shrugged. "All right, miss, you can let him go." She unlocked her legs and jumped back; the soldier weaved drunkenly. "Lesson the last," Baliniri said gravely. "If there are any ladies in the next world—try treating them a bit more nicely."

And, with a smooth, easy motion, Baliniri lunged at the man's throat, struck home, and stepped nimbly back to avoid the gout of blood that followed when he withdrew his blade.

## III

Baliniri hardly bothered to watch him fall. Instead he looked to where Mekim was once again helping the girl into the robe he had given her. Then he scanned the thinning crowd again.

"Look at the lot of you," he said in a disgusted voice. "Disappointed? Hoping to watch three men rape a girl? What kind of people are you, who would stand by, doing nothing?" Under his angry gaze they began to drift off one by one, shamefaced. The rest he stared down. "What's the matter? Wasn't it as much fun watching three men get themselves killed for their foolishness as it might have been watching them rape a girl?" He sneered and spat into the gutter. "I started to say 'defenseless girl,' but that wouldn't have been accurate, would it? With any luck at all she would have taken the measure of all three of these cowards, and—"

But another glance at the two of them, Mekim and the girl, stopped him. He turned from the crowd in deep disdain. "Here, miss. Don't just leave. We'll see you home."

She still showed signs of wanting to leave, though, and he quickly stepped to her side. "Really," he said. "You wouldn't be safe. These rowdies have just come in from the front, and

they've been drinking too much. The town's full of them."
He stooped and found her knife at his feet; reversing it, he
handed it back to her; it disappeared under the robe, which
on her tiny frame hung all the way to her feet.

"Thank you," she said. "My clothing . . ."

"Not much left of it, ma'am," Mekim said. "Don't worry.
Baliniri, stay put for a moment or two, eh? I'll see what I can
come up with."

The girl looked after him, wide-eyed. "But—"

"Oh, don't worry," Baliniri said with a smile, guiding her
to the end of the cul-de-sac, away from the few stragglers and
gawkers that remained. "Mekim can steal the shadow out
from under a hippopotamus. He'll be back with something
halfway presentable in a moment. It won't be fit for wearing
to court, perhaps, but it'll get you home without embarrassment." He turned now to the stragglers. "*You!*" he bellowed
in that unmistakable voice of command. "Haven't you got
anything better to do? Go away! Yes, you!"

Then he turned back to the girl and noticed the clean
lines of her face, the pretty eyes, the pert nose, the perky
little chin. *Why, she's quite lovely,* he thought. "If you'll
pardon me for saying so, miss, you don't really seem to
belong down here, in this part of town. . . ."

The look she gave him, quizzical and a little pained, was
a bit unsettling. "Yes, you're right. I don't know what got into
me. I used to be able to take care of myself and know when
to stay away from certain areas. I grew up in city streets like
these. I suppose I lost the knack."

He listened, took a mental note. *So,* he thought. *She is
out of place. That means she belongs to another caste now.*
"Are you all right? I mean, are you hurt?" he said.

"N-no, thanks to you." Her face fell as she looked at
him. "But *you* are! You're bleeding. And it's all my fault."

"Don't worry about it for a moment," he said gallantly.
"I'm an old soldier. I heal quickly." He tried to turn the
subject back to her. "But you were saying you *used* to know
how to get by here? Then—"

"It's not important," she said, hardly bothering to conceal her haste in wanting to get off the topic. She turned her
head and was relieved to see Mekim strolling toward them, a
bundle in his hand. "Oh, here's your friend."

"All right," Mekim said with a wry smile. "Here's what I
could find on such short notice." Draping the rest over his

shoulder, he held up a freshly washed white robe, hardly bigger than a child's. "I had to guess at the size, ma'am." He handed it over, then shook out the other garment: a longer robe, the kind one wore over the basic garment. "In case you wanted to go to dinner with us, ma'am. That's where we're headed, isn't it, Baliniri? I mean, all this drinking on an empty stomach, with nothing in my innards but that dreadful bread these people make out of lotus plants. . . ." He looked down at the items in his hands. "Oh, I forgot, ma'am. I saw this quite serviceable pair of sandals on the lady's doorstep. I thought they'd at least get you home. Sorry they're only papyrus: I didn't see any leather ones your size lying around."

She smiled ruefully and let Baliniri screen her from the view of passersby behind his own outspread cloak while she slipped into the garments Mekim had given her. "Thank you," she said at last. "You can put your arms down."

He lowered the cloak and looked at her. His eyes widened. "Well!" he said. "You weren't jesting when you said you didn't belong down here. You look lovely."

"Right you are," Mekim said. "I was just going to take the first robe I could find, but then I thought to myself, 'Mekim, you can do better than that! She's a lady.' "

"Indeed she is," Baliniri said. "I think it's time we introduced ourselves." He made a small self-mocking bow. "Baliniri, miss, late of the army of Hammurabi, king of kings, now, uh, at liberty and looking for work. And this prince of dog-robbers and thieves is Mekim. Don't trust him for so much as a moment. He's the only person in the world who ever figured out how to cheat while playing senet."

She smiled and performed the same kind of tiny self-mocking curtsy. "Gentlemen, I'm in your debt. I might have known you weren't Egyptian. They don't make your kind of soldier in Egypt much anymore. Welcome to Upper Egypt. And my heartfelt thanks to both of you. You've restored my faith in human nature. But I'm afraid I cannot join you for dinner. I am expected to be somewhere. . . ."

"Very well," Baliniri said. "We'll escort you."

"No, no. Please. I can't explain, but I have to go home alone. I hope you won't think me ungrateful." She took their hands and pressed them warmly. "You've been both gallant and kind, far more so than a foolish woman like me deserves, bringing you, sir, into danger like that"—she looked Baliniri in the eye now, and there was great warmth and sincerity in her voice as she spoke—"and I'll never forget you. . . ."

She let the words trail off with an apologetic, sad smile. She turned to go, a little reluctantly. But Baliniri found he couldn't let her leave quite so easily as that. "Please, miss," he said. "Will I see you again?"

She shook her head, but then, closing her eyes, relented. "I . . . I'm often in the Market of the Four Winds, afternoons. But, please, I do have to go. Thank you, and good-bye."

Baliniri stood there like a man under a spell, looking after her tiny, graceful, retreating figure for some moments. Then she turned a corner and was gone. He blinked, came back to himself. "What a transformation," he said after a moment's hesitation. "In rags she looked like an urchin."

Mekim had a thoughtful look on his plebeian face. "And *out* of them, she looked—"

"Shut up," Baliniri said without real anger. "Barbarian! But when you brought her something decent to wear, she wore it like someone born to better things. What an enigma! She looked like a real patrician, taller, more dignified. . . ."

"He's in love!" Mekim said, rolling his eyes heavenward. "Gods defend me! Please, Marduk, Ishtar, Osiris, any one of you up there. Help me get him away from here to where there's some decent fighting to be done. If we stay in these damned cities much longer, he'll go domestic on me, start wanting to settle down with some little piece of fluff to raise petunias and snot-nosed brats."

He looked at Baliniri's face again, and grew more thoughtful. His voice was much quieter when he spoke. "Ahh . . . I see. I'd better go easy on that, hadn't I? Otherwise you'll get angry and start defending her, and then I'll never get you out of here. Damn!" He changed tack. "Look, Baliniri, I *am* hungry, just as I said. And if I know you, that exercise worked up a decent appetite for you by now. Let's go down to the little place by the river that we passed on the way here. There were some nice cooking smells coming out of there." He took the bigger man by the arm; Baliniri winced as Mekim's hand touched a wound from one of the dead men's swords. "Sorry, there, old man! Let's just walk that way, eh? We can talk about it on the way if you like. . . ."

Baliniri let himself be steered, because his mind was far

away. They passed through the marketplace now, oblivious of the hushed whispers that followed them:

"That's the one."

"Took on three soldiers at once!"

"They didn't have a chance against him."

Baliniri and Mekim also failed to notice the attention they attracted from a minor courtier named Aduna, a man reputedly close to Madir at court and, some said, one of the vizier's "thousand ears." Aduna separated himself from the people before the fruit-vendor's stall and approached one of the men who had spoken. "Pardon me," he said. "You said that tall man over there killed three soldiers? Three of *our* soldiers? When was this?"

Baliniri, however, was by this time far down the street, out of sight or earshot of the market, letting himself be guided by Mekim. They turned into a back alley. Mekim, always quick to learn new paths, new streets, in any city, regardless of what language the locals spoke, had already, in the two days they had been in Lisht, learned the best and fastest way from tavern to hostelry to bawdy house and back again. Finally they came to the last street before the river and mounted the steps to the rooftop patio. They sat down on seats overlooking the Nile, and Mekim whistled for the attendant. "Bring us some barley beer. And if I'm not mistaken, a while back I passed here and caught a sniff of something good. An ox on the spit, perhaps? Carve us a hunk of that. And fetch some olives. What's the best cheese you've got?"

Through all this, Baliniri had sat silently, looking out at the traffic on the river, where a cargo boat from Thebes was slowly making its way to the dock. The massive sail was down now; some deckhands struggled to fold it while rowers pulled heartily on the long oars. The helmsman, standing high above their heads behind the massive rudder post, tugged hard at the rudder oar.

But even this sight, fascinating as it was, faded. Baliniri sat up suddenly from his unsoldierly slouch. "Mekim," he said, "what a damned fool I am. Do you realize I didn't once think of asking her name?"

"What difference does that make?" Mekim asked, annoyed. "She said you could find her, afternoons, at—"

"The Market of the Four Winds. I'll check there tomorrow. And if I don't find her, then I'll go back the next day."

"Oh, for the love of— Look, Baliniri, we were just going

to pause here for a day or two, remember? We were going to—"

"That was then," Baliniri said. "Things have changed. For one thing, I'm going to court to see if I can sell some of the information we picked up back in Avaris. If I can, we can stick around here a bit longer before we have to get back to soldiering again."

Mekim sat back, slumped, pursed his lips to blow out his breath disgustedly. Things had indeed changed. How could he contrive to change them back?

# IV

First, the fear. Then hot blood had flowed to her extremities while the red rage had welled up inside. She had been ready for a fight. Then the awe and exhilaration as she had watched the stranger—what was his name, now? Bal-something or other—put on that magnificent show.

All of these Tuya had felt in succession. Now she felt only shame, for having been a thoughtless little fool who blundered into places where she did not belong, where she caused trouble and exposed innocent people to great danger. Her handsome savior could have been badly hurt—even killed!

She shuddered and increased her pace, heading homeward through the back alleys. If only it were dark, so no one could see her straggling home in borrowed—no, stolen! —clothes. But in the dark she would be back in trouble again. However well she had been able to get by in the streets of the delta cities she had grown up in, the night world was tougher here, more dangerous. She would never be safe after dark in the poorer quarters in Lisht.

She stopped at a corner, peered around, stole out from behind the sheltering wall, and made her way furtively down the passageway, her hand tightly gripping the knife she had hidden under the outer robe the two men had given her. Only when she was back into a street of now-deserted warehouses did she relax. And suddenly she realized she was

more afraid of being seen by someone she knew than she was
of running into danger once again.

*Fool! Petty, selfish fool!* What right had she had to draw
other people into danger on one of her idiotic whims? She
owed the man an apology!

At the thought she stopped dead in the street. For the
first time, her feelings began to make themselves clear. *Why,
you want to see him again! You'd pretend that it's only to
apologize, but what you really want is to see him, to speak
with him once more.*

Horrified, she put one hand over her mouth. No! She
could not be wanting to do that! She was a married woman,
with a husband whom she loved very much and—

But then a small, clear voice in her mind told her terrible things she did not want to hear, took the side she did not
want to acknowledge.

*You're lonely.*

*Your husband is away, and you need him.*

*You need someone to comfort you. And a woman won't
do.*

Oh, yes, she knew what the women she knew would tell
her, reminding her of her wifely duties. But the other kind of
woman was no good, either. The other kind of woman would
say, "Look, Tuya, he's away, and he's been neglecting you
anyway. Why deny yourself? Go out and find some pleasure.
Don't sit home like a fool and die of loneliness! You'll be old
and gray all too quickly as it is. Find your pleasure while you
can, while you're still attractive to men."

In the hope of driving these thoughts from her mind, she
set off again down the dusty street, her steps quick and
nervous.

But the voice in her mind would not let her alone. *You
need someone to talk to,* it said. *Someone who'll understand.
You need a man.*

As though the words had been spoken aloud, she put her
hands over her ears. *Change the subject,* she thought. *Try
thinking of something else.*

Seeing the long, narrow street deserted before her, she
squeezed her eyes shut for a moment and leaned against the
wall of a warehouse, taking deep breaths to calm herself. But
when she closed her eyes, all she could see was the stranger,
Bal-whatever. He was tall, powerfully built, with shoulders
even broader than Ben-Hadad's, as wide as Shobai's, in fact.

She saw his curly hair, his strong jaw, and slightly crooked soldier's nose. She saw his ready smile. . . . No. She saw *both* smiles: the one, amused, mocking, that he had given to the soldiers he was about to fight, and the kind, gentle one he had given her when the fight was over.

She opened her eyes, blinked, swallowed hard.

What an attractive man he was! Big, lean, hard, and yet with a streak of tenderness. Powerful and quick and brave, without a trace of foolish recklessness. Who else would have had the guts to tackle three men unarmed? To mock them as he fought them, make jokes, clown a bit?

She came to the end of the alley and once again stopped to look ahead. As she did, the servant of one of Ben-Hadad's court friends came down the street; Tuya ducked into a doorway and hid until he had passed. Why, if he had seen her here in the poor quarters . . .

She peered out and this time saw a clear path just ahead. She hurried down the street, heading for the little market square that fronted on her own street.

What *was* his name? Bal . . . Bali . . . How strange that she could not remember, when she had no problem remembering the name of his companion, Mekim, the one who had stolen the clothing for her. Balin . . .

Clothing! Why, she had been naked before him! He had seen her as only her own dear husband had a right to see her! At the very thought, a thrill ran through her, like a sudden chill. She felt the gooseflesh up and down her arms, bared as they were by the short sleeves of the robe Mekim had stolen.

And the thought was not repugnant to her. Or embarrassing, or indeed anything unpleasant at all. Instead, it was rather exciting! She closed her eyes for no more than an instant and saw his face again. His eyes had run up and down her body rapidly and had missed nothing; he would be the kind who would notice everything he saw, everything. But his eyes returned to her face and looked her in the eye. Not boldly. That was not the word. It was more as if he knew her—had known her well for years, the way family knows you, the way a dear friend or a lover knows you . . .

A friend or a lover . . .

Her eyes snapped open. *Tuya! What are you thinking? Has one act of foolishness turned you foolish altogether?* What would Ben-Hadad think if he knew his wife was thinking such thoughts about another man?

She bit her lip and tried to restore the relative peace of mind she had known before the attempted rape. But the more she tried, the more indelibly the whole memory of it seemed to be etched on her brain. *Naked and helpless before him . . . he rescued me. . . . He treated me like a lady, like a person of consequence. . . .*

She sighed. How long had it been since she had felt like a person of consequence, in this hateful court society where she did not belong, among women who despised her for the guttersnipe she was?

Tuya continued on, into the market square, and her thoughts centered on getting through the thinning crowd without being recognized. Too late she realized that the outer robe Mekim had stolen for her had a hood; she turned it up to cover her wigless hair just as Heket, Shobai's servant, came out from behind a greengrocer's stall and looked up, startled, right into her eyes. "Why, Tuya!" Heket said. "How nice to see you!"

But the servant's eyes went up and down her body and took immediate note of Tuya's ill-fitting clothing, clothing of the civil-servant caste. Tuya fidgeted and wished she could get away altogether. She forced a smile onto her face and said, "Good afternoon, Heket." She looked around. "I don't see the twins."

"I didn't bring them. A neighbor is watching them. Ketan has a bit of a cold. I thought it better not to bring the two of them out." Her eyes once again wandered over Tuya's unfamiliar apparel, but she did not comment. "Have you heard from Shobai and Ben-Hadad?"

Tuya flushed. "No. I don't expect to for some days now. It'll be sometime before the first couriers come back. Ben-Hadad isn't much of a correspondent anyway. He hasn't written his mother since I've known him." It didn't sound loyal to say so, somehow; a little lamely, she added, "It doesn't mean he hasn't thought about her."

"Of course not," Heket said, looking at Tuya's hood. She seemed to be having a hard time making sense of what she was seeing. Her hand went out to straighten Tuya's disordered hair, almost involuntarily: a servant's gesture. "Well, it was good seeing you. Come by and see the children sometime. They ask about you often, you know."

"Give them a hug for me," Tuya said, and, smiling a little uncomfortably, moved away through the crowd. As she did, panic flooded into her. *She knows I did something foolish! She can tell something's wrong! The way she looked at me, at these clothes . . .*

There was little reason to wear the hood up now. It did not cover her face anyhow; it did not even hide her messy hair—a real rats' nest. She frowned and threw the hood down onto her shoulders. But the act was mere bravado; she did not feel defiant or brave or even able to cope. She felt frightened by her awakening passions, excited by them, yet ashamed also. She felt—

"Tuya? Is that you, Tuya?" The voice was deep, friendly, and familiar. She wheeled around and looked into the calm brown eyes of Baka, general in charge of all the armies of Dedmose's command.

"B-Baka!" she said, grinning broadly and feeling greatly relieved but not knowing why. "I haven't—"

"You haven't seen me in quite some time," he said, taking both her hands and finishing her thought. "The fault's mine. I've let myself get so busy with soldiering and such that I haven't had time for my old friends and fellow insurgents. Well, the more fool I!" He smiled and pressed her hands warmly. "How's— But I forgot. Ben-Hadad's off in Nubia with Shobai, on that mission of the king's, isn't he? Let me look at you. . . ."

"Oh, don't!" she said with a bit more feeling than she really wanted to put into her voice. "I'm a mess. I . . . I took a spill. Messed up my hair. . . ."

"No matter. You look splendid," the soldier said with real affection. "I ask myself, 'Is this the same skinny little urchin who used to fight with my irregulars back in the delta, when I was called Benu, the Phoenix?' And I can't quite believe it. You're lovely, Tuya. Ben-Hadad's a fortunate man."

Tuya turned away, shame on her face. "Not so fortunate," she said. "I have yet to give him a child. I've been a disappointment to him, I'm afraid."

"Oh, no," Baka said. "You're still very young. There's plenty of time yet."

"He feels it, Baka. I can see it in his eyes." She started to speak again, but stopped herself. *What are you doing, telling him everything like this? You fool!*

But Baka had been like a father to all of them, back in the days when he had been the leader of the anti-Shepherd rebel forces in the delta after his imprisonment. She apparently still had the habit of confiding in him, just as she had done in the old days.

And it would appear that he still had the habit of treating his friends like his children. "Tuya," he said reprovingly, "I can't believe he holds that against you. If he were here, I'd have a little talk with him. When he returns I'll take him aside and—"

"No, please! Baka, it was good seeing you, but I really have to run."

"Well, if you must. Actually, I've work to do myself. Imagine: I'm faced with putting down a conspiracy against Madir and Dedmose. And I haven't much to go on. We caught one of the rebels recently, but he didn't know anything, really. If *you* hear anything suspicious, would you get word to me? The little information we do have suggests that the cabal—it may be a large one, for all we know—is quite dangerous."

"Me?" she asked. "I'm totally out of touch here, Baka. Nobody ever tells me anything. But if I do hear something suspicious . . ."

"Fine," he said. "I'll let you go. Don't be such a stranger. Let's see each other again soon and talk about old times."

"Yes," she said, turning away. "Yes, let's." But she hurried away as if he had been more of an enemy than a friend.

At the date merchant's stall, Dede stood holding his parcel, a puzzled look on his face. That girl, the one in the white robe, where had he seen her before? And—more to the point—what was she doing talking to a man like Baka, commander in chief of all the Egyptian armed forces and a man close to Dedmose and Madir? And she, only a woman of the civil-servant caste? From her clothing that seemed to be the case, but how could she then know such a highly placed man so well that he greeted her like family?

He shook his head. Best forget it. The meeting he and Hefget had had this afternoon with Mereb had produced work for him, and it was time he went home and got ready. There was packing to do; he had to make it out of town before the city gates were closed, to meet the guides who would take him to the Fayum tonight. He had to hurry; Mereb had said there was no time to lose. He was told not to disclose the nature of his mission to anyone, not even to his woman. *What* can I tell her this time? he wondered. *Perhaps that a relative is dying, and I have to pay my respects*.

Satisfied, he hefted his parcel of dried dates and set out through the back streets toward his home. He found that he was eagerly looking forward to the trip. At last they had given him something important, if Mereb's tone was to be believed. There would be no more of this business of people treating him as if he were some sort of great overgrown booby who could not be trusted with secrets or vital responsibilities. Perhaps even Hefget would start treating him with a bit of respect.

But at the back of his mind was still the question: *The girl! Who is the girl?*

# V

After the next three days, Mekim became exasperated with Baliniri. The big man would not go roistering with him in the taverns, and if they shared a jug of wine after dinner, Baliniri would nurse a single cup, staring thoughtfully at the wall, nodding when spoken to, but quite certainly not listening. As for visits to the Street of Lupanars, he was not at all interested. One night Mekim talked him into a midnight stroll down the street, where the merry young whores sat in their windows and called out to the men passing by. Baliniri hardly noticed them—even the beautiful Cretan twins who stood in full view of their audience, one clothed and the other naked, caressing each other to excite the passersby. In the end Baliniri went back to bed alone, and Mekim, despite his own best intentions, found the exploration of the bawdy houses little sport without his friend. Giving the twins a last, lingering look, he reluctantly made his way back to the room they shared.

To his surprise Baliniri was still awake, sitting up and looking out the window at the nearly full moon. A forgotten cup of wine stood on the bedside table beside him. "Oh, it's you," he said, looking up, no particular expression on his face.

"Of course it's me," Mekim said. Disgustedly he picked up the cup of wine and drained it in one gulp. "Who did you expect? The great Hammurabi?" He wiped his mouth. "Really, Baliniri, you're not much fun these days. You're either moping around or hanging out in the marketplace, looking for that girl."

"She'll be back," Baliniri said. "She said she would. I just expected I'd have seen her by now. Maybe she's frightened. Embarrassed. Yes, most likely that's it."

"Look," Mekim said, taking down a wineskin from a hook above his head. "It isn't as if there were only one girl in Lisht. I could have talked those twins into a decent price tonight if you'd been at all cooperative. And they'd have put on a show for us before we—"

"Whores," Baliniri said with distaste, reaching for the wine. "It just isn't the same." He drank, but without enjoyment. "I keep thinking about old Kirakos and that new slave of his, and of the look on his face. A few years ago, if I'd watched the old man look longingly at her, I'd have found the sight funny. I'd have laughed at him. Then, later, I'd have pitied him." He drank again, handed the skin to Mekim, then wiped his mouth with the back of his hand, a little wearily. "Now . . . now I think I understand him."

"Huh?" Mekim said. "Understand what?"

"Kirakos bought a slave, and whether he's admitted it to himself or not, he's in love with her. As her master, he could bed her whenever he wanted. But if he cares for her, just taking her as if she were a whore wouldn't satisfy him. She has to be free to say no, or saying yes won't mean anything. And he knows if he frees her, she'll say no. He's old, she's young. Why should she tie herself to an old man like him, even if he is rich and powerful?"

"I don't understand a word of what you're saying. What has Kirakos got to do with—"

Baliniri ignored him. "Worst of all, one of the slaves told me that the woman has a husband and children somewhere, and she thinks of no one else. This puts her in a place Kirakos can't ever touch. She'll always have her heart elsewhere. And it's killing him. He's lonely, terribly lonely. He misses his wife. Perhaps the girl reminds him of her somehow—of what she was like when she was young."

"Baliniri, you need this worse than I do." Mekim offered

the wineskin, but Baliniri did not reach for it. Mekim looked at him disgustedly, then drank again.

"If it were just lust . . . well, I'm sure that Kirakos has some of that left in him, despite his age. But I don't think that's what he needs right now. What he needs is companionship, of a kind that only a woman who's very dear to him can give. And when he wants it and needs it and knows whom he wants it from, nothing else and no one else will do. It's like seeing a man who's dying of thirst and telling him you can't give him water, but he can have bread or cheese. It doesn't work. Nothing will satisfy but precisely what he needs." He looked at Mekim now, and his eyes had a distant, thoughtful look. He looked away, up at the gibbous moon; a stray cloud drifted across its face, wispy, translucent. "And the funny thing is, Kirakos himself doesn't have anything to do with it. He can't change it. He can't control it. His life suddenly changes, and he can't change it back."

Mekim, realizing that his friend was not talking just about Kirakos, frowned, drank, then tried to change the subject. "Baliniri, don't you think it's time we looked up Madir and tried to sell the information about Salitis you picked up in Lower Egypt? We're running short of money, and if we're going to mope around here looking for a girl instead of heading off up to Nubia where we can at least make an honest living—"

"Look up who?" Baliniri said, coming back to himself for a moment. "Oh. The vizier. Yes, of course. It's just that . . . well, I was hoping for . . ."

"I know what you were hoping for. Look, Baliniri, would you mind if I stepped in and made inquiries? Maybe I can find out who the proper intermediary is and get the process started. I know this is the sort of thing you usually do, but you're so preoccupied just now. Maybe it's time for me to take some action, eh?"

Baliniri's mind was again far away. But he had been listening, if with no more than one ear. "Uh, yes, yes. Do whatever needs to be done. Madir, his name is. Talk to someone; see if we can get in to see Madir. I'm sure he'll be interested in what we learned about this Joseph fellow, predictions and all."

"All right," Mekim said. "Tomorrow. But if I do make an appointment with somebody at court, you'll show up, won't you? You won't go off haunting that little marketplace looking for—" He would have continued, but the look on Baliniri's face stopped him. "All right, all right. I won't say any more. But I have to know you won't let me down. Promise me you won't."

"I promise," Baliniri said. But there was little conviction, little involvement, in his words. His eyes were on the great moon, and his mind was far, far away.

In the street, in front of the place of rendezvous, in a pool of moonlight, Mereb extracted promises from Hefget. "Now, remember," he said, "you must speak only when spoken to. And don't embarrass me. Several of the people here tonight will be masked. Don't gape at them like some innocent."

"I won't," Hefget said. "But masked? Among friends?"

"There's a reason for everything," Mereb said in a low but piercing whisper. "The other day, as you know, one of our members was captured and tortured. We have just such security measures as these to thank for the fact that when he finally broke, he couldn't reveal any names or describe faces."

"I see," Hefget said. "I'll mind my manners. Don't worry. Well, now I understand why you sent Dede away."

Mereb took Hefget's arm and steered him to the door. "Dede is a useful man, I suppose, in his place, but he can't be trusted with secrets like the ones you'll hear tonight." He lowered his voice and looked around as he spoke. "Just between us, they're going to discuss where and when." In the moonlight Hefget could see Mereb's serious expression.

Hefget's own face showed his surprise. "Then it's soon?"

"Quiet, you fool! Yes. I was shocked myself when they told me." He approached the door and knocked: three times, pause, two times, pause, and three times again.

Instead of the expected voice from within, the door opened a crack. "Come in—quickly," a voice said from inside the darkened room. "The meeting's already under way."

In darkness they made their way to the back room, entered blinking from the sudden light, and sat down on a bench to one side. Hefget, despite his promise, gaped at the sight of the central speaker at the long table: His face was totally veiled in a mask representing the crocodile-god Sobek. But Mereb angrily punched him in the ribs, and he settled back sober-faced. Several others at the table wore god masks: hawks, lions, jackals. The choice of god masks obeyed no religious hierarchy; the Sobek-faced man seemed to be in charge, in defiance of the usual relative positions of the gods.

He was speaking now: ". . . Dedmose was born in the delta, near Buto, north of Sais. Because the Shepherd invasion makes him an exile from his native earth, certain of the year's festivals hold a higher place in his heart than others. He takes great pains to observe these festivals personally and requires that all members of his court participate, also. *All* members, mind you—including Madir." He paused and looked around the room as a murmur of understanding followed close on his words.

The festival in question, he continued, the one about which the present meeting had been called, was the feast of the erection of the pillar Ded, the symbol of Osiris, at the close of the great festival of Ptah-Sokaris-Osiris, in the month of Choiakh. It celebrated a great mythological fight, which, in remotest antiquity, had engaged the inhabitants of Buto, in the days when it had been called Dep.

It was a festival of the death and revival of Osiris, the god of the dead and of resurrection. In the opening ceremony, the king would salute a dead Osiris with a sacrifice. The god, mummified, would be lying on a slab, with a small amulet, a replica of the pillar Ded, on his forehead. The pillar represented the back bone of the god, and the festival celebrated the joyous moment when the god's backbone became straight. After the sacrifice, a second, larger, replica of the pillar would be raised by Dedmose and a priest, aided by royal relatives. When the pillar was brought erect, the restored god would arise.

The moments before the resurrection would be celebrated with music and joyful dancing. But once the god was again alive, the ritual would change, with the reenactment of the mythological battle. First the priests of Osiris, then a chorus of fifteen persons beat and pummeled one another for reasons lost in dimmest history. Chaotic crowding and a great deal of noise traditionally accompanied this part of the ritual; the joyful restoration of the revived god called for the abandonment of the celebrants' usual orderly behavior.

"Now," the Sobek-figure went on in his precise, emotionless voice, "you may begin to see where a certain advantage might accrue to people wishing to eliminate two, perhaps more, great enemies of the people." He paused significantly. "Dedmose will be a part of the ceremony. So will Madir."

"I begin to understand," said a man in the front row. "They and the priests will battle with bamboo swords and reed spears. What is to keep one or two of the spears—"

"From being real? Nothing except the predictable inspections by the guards in charge." The Sobek-figure rose and stood behind his chair. "Until now the whole procedure has been in the hands of the priesthood, and we have been unable to penetrate their inner circle. But last year, the young armorer Ben-Hadad was commissioned by the priests to create reed spears that looked exactly like the originals. If Ben-Hadad were here, he would have been commissioned again. But he's been sent away along with his uncle to Nubia. This plays perfectly into our hands. The person selected to replace him in this year's festival is one of ours."

Now the murmur of understanding became one of approval as well. Hefget looked around him, seeing the bizarre masks nodding enthusiastically.

A thrill ran through him. His heart was beating faster, faster. For the first time he could begin to really believe in this conspiracy. For the first time he could take the whole thing seriously. They were really going to assassinate Dedmose and Madir at one stroke—and perhaps others as well! Soon! This was no little cabal of petty malcontents, wasting their time with wishful thinking and blathering talk of high deeds; this was a group bent on a real revolution!

And he, Hefget, would have a part in it!

Suddenly he felt a wave of panic. If they failed—

*But no! Think instead of what'll happen if we're successful!* They would be able to put their own men at the top of the government, men who would run things the way *they* wanted, for a change. Riches! Power! What would he do with them?

# VI

The dawn of the fourth day found Tuya sitting up in bed, tense, restless, again unable to sleep. Sleep had come hard ever since her little adventure. There was an all-pervading disquiet in her soul now, one that no amount of housewifely busywork could exorcise. Perhaps if Ben-Hadad had been here, she thought, she never would have gone through with her ridiculous charade, dressing up in rags and going into the streets as if she were still the homeless ragamuffin of her youth. She never would have blundered into trouble and risked not only her own life but also that of her savior. But what was the use of pursuing this line of reasoning?

A shudder ran through her, and she closed her eyes against the thin dawn light streaming through the window, hoping to blot out the thoughts. But closing her eyes only brought back, in exact detail, the great, powerful, graceful figure of Baliniri, standing there unarmed, taunting her three attackers—each armed to the teeth—daring them to kill him, his white teeth flashing, the low, good-humored laughter rumbling in his throat, the merry twinkle in his brown eyes. . . .

Oh, curse it all, why did he have to be so very attractive? Why could he not have a badly broken nose or a potbelly? But as it was, even the scars on his rugged face and big masculine body only served to make him more handsome. His smile! That roguish, tolerant smile! And those courtly manners, the way he had treated her at the end. Then there was the look in his eye when she had taken her leave of him—

*Tuya, stop it!* she told herself. *You're a married woman. You love your husband. Ben-Hadad is everything you ever hoped for in a man. How can you think of doing anything that would endanger your life with him? How can you think of another man that way?*

She turned, pushed the coverlet back, and put both feet on the floor. Her body was warm from the bed, and the morning air had a delicious chill in it. She stood up and, naked, walked to the window to look out onto her own rooftop, with its chest-high wall piled with potted plants. The chill of the air on her body was exquisite; on an impulse she opened the door and stepped out onto the rooftop, nude in the morning air.

Ecstasy! The light wind stirred; it caressed her with a feather-light touch; she felt it on every surface of her naked skin. She threw back her head, closed her eyes, and slowly ran her own hands over her body, over breasts and belly and thighs. She moaned softly, shivering more with sensual delight than from the morning chill.

But then a cock crowed just outside the city wall, and in the next street a child cried out. As the daytime sounds of the city forced themselves into her consciousness, Tuya opened her eyes and found herself standing naked on the rooftop. She felt stupid and ashamed. She stepped back inside the house and put on her robe.

*What a silly goose you are!* she thought. *Doing a thing like that. . . .*

But all the time one corner of her wayward mind replied: *Ah, but for a moment your troubles were far away. You weren't love-starved and lonely. You weren't a drab housewife with a humdrum life and a husband who's more in love with his work than with you. For a moment you were a beautiful, sensual young woman with love to give—a woman with needs. . . .*

How long, after all, had it been since she had had a thought for herself, for her own pleasure, her own good? She had lived for Ben-Hadad almost from the first day she had met him. Everything she had done had been for him. She had followed him around, brought him food and drink, warned away enemies, waited on his every whim—only to see him taken out of the bazaars by a rich man who had wanted to sponsor him to play at court. And the rich man had had a daughter who—

She scowled, remembering. Well, thank the gods *that* had not worked out as planned. She had learned of Baka's planned raid on the rich man's house and had saved Ben-Hadad, pressing him into service in Baka's little band of rebels. Even then Ben-Hadad had hardly noticed her, even when she had gone to work as his helper at the forge, helping him make weapons for Baka's campaigns; he had hardly even taken note of her when she had worked naked beside him.

A flash of anger coursed through her. He had been such a dunce! Why had he not seen her? Why had he not paid attention?

But then she remembered the night he had finally taken her, there in the moonlight on the island where they were hiding after the raid. She had thought him badly wounded, but he had come out of sleep fully aroused, full of passion and tenderness for her. She had been in heaven itself, feeling for the first time a man's caresses, hearing his words of love, finally coming to know, at his hands, the full extent of her own feelings, her own senses, her own passion.

Ah! How sweet it had been! How exquisitely sweet and warm and loving and—

But where had it gone? Why did it have to fade? Had he ceased loving her altogether? Was that why he no longer came to her as he used to? Had he—

An idea forced itself into her mind. She felt it coming; she tried to avoid it, but it worked its way into her thoughts and would not be denied.

Did Ben-Hadad have another woman somewhere?

She sat down suddenly, all the air going out of her. She gasped, stared in horror. *Another woman?*

Surely it was not possible.

But . . . what other reason could he have for neglecting her so? It wasn't as if he had lost interest in the physical pleasures, that was sure. He had been just as lusty, just as potent, that last, rare, time with her, just before he had left for Nubia, as he had ever been. He certainly would not have been that way if he had been taking his love to another woman all that time . . . or would he?

Another woman! Who could she be? How could he have found time for an affair with another woman? He spent his days at the forge. He would come home at a regular time every evening—

But no, that was not true. Sometimes he had stayed late. And then he had come home tired, distracted, distant, just as if he had come to her table from the bed of another woman.

Tuya shook her head. Ben-Hadad? Unfaithful? It was not like him. He was constant and true. But by nature he was also warm and loving, and he had not been either of those for quite some time. All the more reason to believe that he had ceased to love her and had come to love someone else.

*Ben-Hadad! How could you?* she thought. And suddenly she was filled with rage at the injustice of it all. Why, she had not so much as looked at another man in all the time she had known him. She had been honest and faithful and true. Her affection, her attention, had not strayed for so much as a moment.

Once again the wind went out of her, and her shoulders slumped. Closing her eyes, she saw his face—not her husband's, but the face of the big foreigner who had saved her from the would-be rapists. She saw his easy, athletic stance, his air of absolute assurance, his fearless and upright manner. She saw his open and friendly smile, and the good-humored look in his eye.

She forced herself to open her eyes, to drive the vision of him out of her mind. Now she could hear his voice in her mind, as clearly as if he were speaking, and the sound was like music.

*Oh, Ben-Hadad! Why did you have to leave me? Why did you neglect me and make me prey to these thoughts? I don't want to think about this man! I don't! I don't!*

But when she closed her eyes again, all she could see was Baliniri's face: his broad forehead, his wayward curly hair, his wide mouth, curving in a merry smile, his brown eyes, warm and wise and understanding.

The waiting list for Madir's morning divan was very long. Mekim, taking a look at the long line of applicants, shook his head in disgust and started to turn away. But an official saw him and, coming up from behind, took him by the arm. "Pardon me, sir," he said. "Whom are you looking for?"

Mekim, startled, turned and looked the official up and down. He was not sure he liked what he saw. *One of your effete types.* Governments were full of them, here as in Hammurabi's realm. A boy-lover, from the look of him. "Uh, well," he said, "I had hoped to see the lord Madir. My partner and I came here from the army of Hammurabi, lord of the Lands of the Two Rivers. We were looking for employment—"

"I'm sure you'd benefit from talking to Baka, the general of our armies, but—"

Mekim was not about to be put off that easily. He looked the official in the eye, recoiling just slightly from the faunlike languor he saw there. "Not only employment," he said. "We've just been at the court of Salitis. Some interesting things have been happening there, developments that may not have been reported here yet. The lord Madir may well want to hear of these."

The official stepped back and looked *him* over now, eyelashes fluttering. "Oh? Well, now. I'm Sitra, secretary to the lord Madir. Anything you can tell him, you can tell *me*. Let's go over there by the palms and discuss it. That way I'll have a better idea just what priority to assign to—"

"I, uh, beg your pardon. We were hoping to *sell* the information. If we just give it to you—"

"Sell it?" The man made a little moue. "Well, that's all very well. But I'm here, you understand, to screen applicants for private access to Madir. *No* one reaches him without going through me." Mekim shot a sharp glance at him; was he making some sort of obscene joke? But no, the remark seemed straightforward. "You'll have to tell me, whether you like it or not, and take your chances."

Mekim snorted. "All right. I guess I have no choice." He let himself be led by the arm over to the inner court, where tall palms shielded an empty area from the sunlight streaming in. Once there, he shook off Sitra's grasp and faced him. "Well, it's a long story," he said. "But you know Salitis? His reputation?"

Sitra nodded. "He's said to be rather unstable."

"He's worse than that. He's crazy. And very recently he's gotten a great deal worse. He's on the verge of shaking up his government from top to bottom. He freed a slave the other day—a young foreigner with a reputation as a sooth-sayer or something—and elevated him, right there on the spot, from slave to second in command of the entire Shep-herd establishment. Above all the Shepherds themselves."

Sitra frowned, looked hard at him. "Above Kirakos?" he said. All too obviously he didn't believe a word of it.

"Yes, I know," Mekim said. "I didn't believe it either. Neither did Kirakos. But the old man had his spies look into the matter, and when they came back that night and visited him at his house, where we were staying—"

"Wait. *You* were staying with Kirakos?"

"Yes. He said that he checked it out, and it was the straight truth. It seemed crazy, but Kirakos told my partner it was another example of Salitis's insanity. He said—"

"Your partner is intimate with Kirakos?" The faun's eyes were wide with amazement.

"Yes. He tried to hire us, but Baliniri said no. If—"

"Baliniri. Where have I heard that name?"

"Baliniri of the siege of Mari," Mekim said. "The young-est general in Hammurabi's army."

"*That* Baliniri!" Sitra's tone had changed. "That's another matter altogether. I'm sure the lord Madir will want to talk to him. And Baka will, as well. Your comrade's reputation pre-cedes him. Not too long ago we had visitors from the north-ern countries, and they told of the siege of Mari, and—"

Now it was Mekim's turn to be impatient. "All the more reason to expedite our getting through to see your master," he said. "Now if you could make us an appointment—"

*     *     *

After Mekim had left, Sitra lingered on, thinking, in the cool shade of the tall palms. It had been something of a temptation to hear all the information himself, even before Madir got it. But it had been all too obvious that this Mekim chap was no more than a flunky for his companion Baliniri. He would likely have the information all garbled anyhow. Better to let the two of them through to spill their guts to Madir, and to be there to overhear. He would get a better précis from a man like Baliniri, who had a reputation for brains as well as soldiering.

And then, of course, he could pass everything on to the cabal, and they could use the information for their own purposes. It did not matter much if Madir got the information first. *His* days were numbered. Sitra smiled. *Quite literally numbered,* he thought. Absently he began counting days until the festival, when Madir and Dedmose would die.

# VII

The naked, sun-browned children frolicked and gamboled before the shallow pool, their shrill voices filling the air with laughter. Only the older girls were clothed, in simple white shifts. They played with a little ball made of hard-packed barley husks covered with stitched leather. The boys, lean, nude, spun and leaped, leaped and spun, in the thousand-year-old game called going around four times.

Seated on the long stone bench beside Heket, Tuya watched them play. At her feet Teti and Ketan sat, playing with the clay before them. Her eyes focused on them idly. Ketan, refined and artistic even at his young age, shaped a sphinx, long and delicate and graceful, while Teti modeled a very realistic-looking fortress with high walls and battlements. *How curious!* Tuya thought. *Each obeys the voice inside, and becomes the person he or she must.*

She looked up now and, desperate for talk, said the first thing that came into her mind. "I saw Baka the other day. He looked fit and well." Heket did not answer; Tuya went on.

"He seemed to think there was some sort of dangerous movement afoot in the city. Aimed at rebellion."

Heket's calm eyes looked at her. "I shouldn't be surprised," she answered. "I've heard things in the marketplace. I didn't pay much attention at the time, but—" She shrugged.

"What kind of things?" Tuya asked, interested now.

"Oh, I don't know. It wasn't much." A strange look appeared on her face. "Wait. There *was* something. A rumor. Something somebody was going to do soon. Some sort of demonstration or other. It had something to do with one of the festivals." She was about to dismiss it again, but another thought struck her. "If I remember correctly, the woman I was talking to had just broken up with her boyfriend. He was some sort of, oh, you know, political type. The kind that is never happy with whoever's running things. She was quite bitter about him."

"That's a good time to learn about someone's bad side," Tuya said. "A disaffected lover will spill things she'd keep mum at other times. What else did she say? Baka asked me to keep an ear to the ground."

"That was about it, really. I didn't get which festival. There was going to be some sort of protest or action."

Tuya put a hand on Heket's knee. "Where was this? How long ago?"

Heket pursed her lips in thought. "Oh, no more than a day or two. Was it the Bazaar of the Twin Palms? Or the Well of the Four Winds?" She shook her head. "It was one of those. I haven't been shopping anywhere else in quite some time. I can't leave the babies with the neighbors for too long."

Tuya pondered the information, watching the twins. There was a third child with them now; the little boy stepped up to Ketan's sphinx and, in a moment of childish malice, kicked it to rubble. Ketan, stunned, sat looking at him for a moment before bursting into tears. Teti, in a rage, attacked the stranger with fists and feet. "You leave him alone! You go away! I'll hurt you!"

*Always the little warrioress*, Tuya thought, smiling. Well, if the men would not do the fighting, sometimes the women had to step in. . . .

"It was the Market of the Four Winds," Heket said. "I'm sure of it. The woman's name was Taheret. . . ."

\*       \*       \*

*Well,* Baka thought, *he certainly looks like a soldier.* He stopped six paces away and looked the big man over as he sat on the platform at the top of the stairs and looked down, burly arms crossed over his chest, expression neutral, taking everything in. Below, the traffic in the square was at its height; people were shoving and pushing one another, trying to get past.

Baka stepped forward, took the stairs two at a time. He stopped a little more than arm's length away from the big man. "Pardon me, sir," he said. "You'd be Baliniri, perhaps?"

The big man looked down at him, eyes not unfriendly. "Yes," he said. "And from the look of you, you're a soldier."

"I'm Baka, general of the armies of Egypt," he said, extending a hand, which was instantly swallowed up in Baliniri's much larger palm. "One of my men said I might find you here. You'll pardon my keeping tabs on you. We're technically still at war, and anyone entering from the delta lands . . ."

"I understand," Baliniri said with a grin. "Come, let's share a bottle of wine at the tavern upstairs and talk."

Half a jug of wine later, they were, if not fast friends, at least on good terms. They had talked of Mari and the rise of Hammurabi, of the situation in the North, where, Baka was astonished to hear, the Shepherd lines back to Hayastan had been cut by Hittite attacks near the headwaters of the Euphrates. They had talked of Baka's years fighting the Shepherds, first with regulars, then with untrained civilian terrorists. They had taken each other's measure: Baliniri, the poor boy who had come up through the ranks on sheer ability alone, under pressure of war; Baka, the young scribe who had taken to war only because no better leader had emerged in the desperate fight against the invader. They had compared the scars of war, both mental and physical. They had come, provisionally, to like each other.

"By the way," Baliniri said, passing the earthenware jug, "my comrade Mekim says he was intercepted on the way to Madir by some little puff of wind named Sitra. He says he doesn't trust the man a bit. He wanted to know how to bypass him."

"Tell Mekim he's right," Baka said. "But I don't think anyone can bypass him. As the vizier's secretary, he'll be there when you talk to Madir, whether you see him or not. He has almost as many ears as Madir. Look, keep your appointment, but don't tell Madir much of anything—certainly not what you've told me about Joseph and Salitis's plans." His voice lowered as he said this, and he looked around the all-but-deserted tavern. "Then I'll arrange another meeting, just the three of us, and you can spill your guts. And don't worry about being vague at the first meeting with Madir; he'll understand what you're saying. And he'll be appreciative."

"But will he do anything about it?"

Baka grinned. "Not anything you can immediately see. He moves quietly and covertly, and this leads people to think he's ineffectual, that he's losing his grasp. Don't be fooled. That's just what he wants people to think. It's obvious that your information will prove extremely valuable—the more so if we can keep it confidential—you, me, Mekim, and Madir. You may have saved Upper Egypt's neck. Without this tip, we'd be at Salitis's mercy a few years from now. We'll have time to arrange for our own supply of food. Salitis won't be able to starve us out."

"I'm glad to be of help," Baliniri said, accepting the jug from him again and drinking. "Between your cause and theirs, I'd choose yours, in spite of my liking for old Kirakos. I have this feeling about the underdog."

"Then join us!" Baka said, leaning forward, speaking up for the first time. "If your information's correct, the war will be postponed while both of us arrange for grain storage against the famine. When Salitis has the rest of the world begging for food, accepting it on whatever terms he dictates, we'll be growing stronger while everyone else grows weak. Then we can strike a blow that—"

"I'll be an old man by then. So will you. No, I'll move on to Nubia. From what I hear, I should be able to make myself useful there. If I thought your people were going to fight, really fight, well, that'd be different. But"—he looked Baka in the eye now, hard—"you're not, are you? You're not going to initiate any major offensive."

Baka shrugged. "Frankly, my friend, we're not up to it. The battle that preceded our move to Lisht took more out of us than the Shepherds apparently know." Baka shook his head and sighed. "Losing Memphis the way we did was demoralizing. In order to save the army—and the rest of Upper Egypt with it—we had to abandon the city while there were civilians still in it. My soldiers had friends and family in the city when it fell and were close enough to hear the screams of the dying as the victorious Shepherds hacked their way into the city." He took the wine from Baliniri, but sat looking at it for a moment without drinking. "The only way an army can recover from something like that is to come up with a great victory. But we're weak, dispirited. If the Shepherds knew—" He looked Baliniri in the eye: a piercing, distrustful look. "Of course, you wouldn't—"

"No," Baliniri said quickly. "Not even if I were going that way. But don't worry. You're in no danger of immediate attack. They'll be having an internal revolution on their hands now, and their army will have its hands full putting it down. The borders will be the last thing on their minds." He yawned. "As for me, I'll be heading up to Nubia. I gather you know this Akhilleus?"

"Oh, yes." Baka grinned. "A great character. He's about half the height of the great Sphinx, and more than half as big around. When you first meet him, he'll sound like he's all bluster and bragging. But then you'll find he can do anything he says he can do." Baka's face turned thoughtful now. "And since Akhilleus returned to Nubia from the high country in the South, rumors have it that he's taken on a new dignity and solidity. I was told he turned down a great kingdom there. Why, I didn't hear. Perhaps he has ambitions in Nubia. For better or worse, he does seem to have not only unified the Nehsiu, the black Nubians, under his command, but drawn some support from the Medjai, their traditional enemies. This is the first time in history that Medjai and Nehsiu have fought on the same side." He smiled. "Experienced soldier though you may be, you may have something to learn from Akhilleus. He has depths none of us has plumbed yet." He changed the subject now, sitting up straight. "Do I take it you're leaving immediately, after you've talked with Madir?"

He again took note of Baliniri's roving eye. From time to time through the conversation, Baliniri had turned his eyes from the table, past the railing beside them, to look down from their second-floor position at the passing crowd in the marketplace below. Now he seemed to have spotted something; his eyes lit up, and he sat up straight, looking intently down, but then the light left his eye and he slumped back, almost dejectedly. "I beg your pardon?" he said. "Oh. Oh, no. I . . . I'll leave in a week or so. I have some . . . unfinished business here." With a rueful smile he watched his finger trace circles on the tabletop. "Even if I'm not quite sure what that business is. . . ."

\*   \*   \*

"She's the one," the baker said. "The one with the scarf."

"Thanks," Tuya said. Because of her tiny stature, her dark head hardly showed at all as it moved through the clot of people. In a moment she was at the woman's side. "Pardon me," she ventured. "You're Taheret?"

The woman stepped back to look her up and down and quite clearly wasn't impressed with what she saw: Tuya in her torn clothing, barefoot. "Who wants to know?"

"I'm nobody special," Tuya said, quickly moving through the lines she had carefully practiced that morning. "I heard you had been shopping for a new robe and weren't happy with what you were shown at the clothing merchants'. I have a line into some very good material, just in from Punt. Ridiculously inexpensive. No questions answered, if you get my meaning."

The woman was about to turn away, but Tuya reached inside her tunic and came out with a sample of cloth. The dye was a brilliant, vivid blue; the cloth, the highest quality, a hard-finish weave. It had cost Ben-Hadad quite a sum when he had bought it for her. "Take a look at this before you dismiss me," Tuya said. "There's plenty more where this came from."

Taheret frowned, took the cloth, inspected it. "Hmm. This is very nice. And you have—"

"Plenty more," Tuya interrupted. "Look, I admit I watched you at the merchant's stall. I was drumming up business and saw how close you came to buying the blue scarf."

"It *was* a nice pattern," Taheret admitted, still holding the sample. "If I could find a matching robe in the same pattern or something very like it, and if the price were right . . ."

Tuya grinned. "I'm sure we can work out something," she said, taking the material from Taheret's hand with one hand and her arm with the other, and steered her gently through the crowd toward the side street where she had cached her samples.

As they left the marketplace via the eastern exit of the square, Baliniri entered it from the western side. There was a vague, unsettling disquiet in his soul, and his eyes eagerly, desperately, searched the crowd for a sight of her, wherever she might be. If only . . . if only . . .

But after half an hour's searching he could find no sign of her. Then it had been wishful thinking after all, and it had not been she he had seen from the café window. He had not expected to have this much trouble finding her.

After a time he sat down, weary from all the wine he had drunk and his disappointment, on the step before the well and let his eyes scan the passing parade. What was the use of kidding himself? She would not show up here. Probably she was embarrassed about what had happened. What girl would want to show her face again after a terrible, frightening, humiliating experience like the rape attempt?

*You don't even know her name,* he told himself. *You don't know where she comes from. You don't know a blessed thing about her. She could be a thief or a prostitute. So stop this ridiculous obsession, this foundless infatuation.*

A pretty face passed: a young woman in a dark red headrail, with lovely, dark, almond-shaped eyes and full lips and a long, deliciously curved nose that set off the sweet line of her high-boned cheeks. Any other day he would have eagerly followed her with his eyes all through the square. He might even have got up to go after her, to get a second look. Now, morose, dispirited, he let her pass, and his eyes did not follow her as she strolled, hips swaying voluptuously, past the well.

*The girl . . . the little one . . .*

He could not get the little urchin out of his mind: her tiny upturned nose, the look in her eyes—at once fearless and vulnerable.

*Well, you've talked a good game about heading upriver, but you know good and well you can't leave until you've seen her again, until you've found out—*

Found out what? What precisely did he want? He was not sure. He just knew that he had to see her again, to talk to her. There was something surpassingly strange about it all. It was as though the finger of some nameless god had reached inside him and written on his soul, written a message he could not understand. But one thing he knew for certain: If he went away without seeing her, something inside him would dry up and die, and he would never be the same again. He would be less of a human being than he had been before. And less of a man.

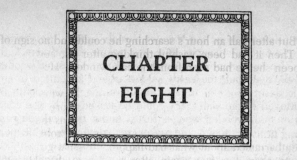

# CHAPTER EIGHT

## Avaris

### I

Flanked by two towering Hai bodyguards, Kirakos emerged from the imposing side entrance of the palace of the Golden Pharaoh and paused for a moment at the top of the low staircase to look down at the workers building the palatial new home of Joseph, newly named vizier to Salitis.

Just below where Kirakos stood, construction was in progress on the wall that would seal off Joseph's dwelling and its spacious grounds from the eyes of the poor. It was typical of the entire venture that the wall would be completed before the great house itself was started. This was done in part to contain the widespread resentment felt against the extraordinary measures Salitis had taken recently at the behest of the young seer. An entire city block of middle-class dwellings abutting the royal property had been razed in order to make room for the new vizier's home, which, the king had ordered, must be as close to his own as possible. Settlement for the demolished homes had been made at a fraction of their real worth, and there was great bitterness over this.

Once the wall had been raised, the work would proceed more safely. Already there had been rock-throwing incidents, and several workmen had been injured as they cut and dressed the wall's great limestone blocks. Now soldiers—the ubiquitous soldiers—lined the streets. Heavily armed, their orders were to take into custody anyone attacking the workers.

The huge stone blocks were lined up on massive wooden rockers that could be easily swung around and tilted to any angle desired. When time came for raising the blocks to be positioned in the wall, they could be jacked up by the addition of stout wooden wedges thrust under their curved runners. For now, though, the rockers rested on wooden sleepers to keep them from sinking into the clay underfoot.

One of the blocks was further along to completion than the others; a burly naked workman stood atop it, shaping it roughly with a maul made of harder stone. Next to this, an almost completed block was being tested for high spots by three men with honing rods; when a high spot was located, it was quickly chiseled away by an expert workman with a bronze chisel and wooden mallet.

Kirakos scowled and looked across the open space, where another detachment of soldiers was headed for the marketplace. Where people gathered, there tended to be trouble these days: speeches by dissidents (who were quickly battered down and hauled away to jail), near riots, even attacks on the fearsomely armed soldiery.

"Come along," Kirakos said harshly to the bodyguards. He set off down the staircase and crossed the open space, nodding curtly at the man in charge of the soldiers who guarded the workers. As he moved into the broad street beyond, the two bodyguards stepped into place, flanking him. "Strange as it may seem," Kirakos said in a voice made sour by irony, "I can actually remember when I could walk these streets without needing a pair of musclemen to guard me from harm."

"Yes, sir," said the guard on the left, the one who answered when spoken to. Kirakos had never heard the other guard's voice. "Changing times require changing responses."

"Spare me the platitudes," Kirakos said. "I can also remember the days when one could walk from the palace to my villa without tripping over fifty soldiers along the way or having to show credentials every time he turned around. Bunch of damned nonsense."

"We're just here to protect you, sir."

"I know. And to this end the soldiers have been yanked away from our borders, from Sile and Memphis. They've been called in from the lands across the Sinai, where we once had an unbroken line of impregnable forts stretching all the way across the headwaters country of the Euphrates, through Padan-aram down to Canaan. I could send a message all the way to Hayastan and have it delivered without my messenger having to cross any land we did not govern. But now the Hittites have cut that line through, and there have been attacks on the refortified walls of Ebla by the rabble we drove out of the city when we conquered it and rebuilt it for our own uses. And all because we've had to call in troops to protect us here in the delta, from people we conquered nearly a generation ago."

"They were called in before this last, uh, edict of the Lord of Two Lands, sir." The guard was being bold and knew it.

"I know. I fought it the whole time. I couldn't see any sense in it then, and I can't see any sense in it now. I suppose Salitis's insistence upon it back then meant that he was planning something like this the whole time, and young Joseph's auguries only furnished him with the excuse and the occasion to carry it out." Kirakos looked down the street, where a squad of soldiers blocked the path. "You there," he said as they approached the squad. "You, in charge. I'm Kirakos. Please stand aside—"

"Sorry, sir," the captain said. "It's for your own protection. There's been an incident. Someone threw rocks down from a rooftop, and several infantrymen were hurt. We're here to escort you home by a safer route." Behind him, from the rabbit warren of narrow streets where the lower-class quarter began, Kirakos could hear angry shouts, the sound of running feet and fighting. "If you'd be so kind as to come with us, sir . . ."

Kirakos, scowling all the more blackly, assented in sullen silence. He let himself be led through a dogleg path the soldiery had already cleared for him. Looking up, he saw soldiers standing on the rooftops looking down, their eyes hard, their posture upright and alert. And it occurred to him in a sudden epiphany: *We're the prisoners. We, the conquerors, are the prisoners now. And all because of this madman on the throne of Egypt. Him—and this strange young foreigner he's elevated above our heads and given a free rein over our destinies. . . .*

Sun-browned, naked except for a spotless white loincloth, his neck, wrists, and fingers glittering with golden ornaments, Salitis stood looking down at a beautifully carved cedar game board inlaid with panels of blue faience outlined in gold. The senet problem he had laid out for himself was a knotty one, with his hypothetical opponent's men blocking virtually his every move. Impatiently he juggled the four flat wands in his hand and impulsively let them fall to the table. They landed in a random pattern and indicated the number of moves he could take in his next turn. He thought about the consequences of first one move, then another. Each was more disastrous than the last. His opponent would surely win. . . .

A slave appeared at the door. "Joseph has come, my lord."

"Ah!" Salitis said. "Show him in. Maybe he can solve this for me." The Golden Pharaoh stood, hands on hips, watching his young vizier enter, conservatively dressed for his high rank, his face set in the usual expressionless mold. "Ah! Joseph! Look at this senet problem! I can't figure out what to do with it. I think he's beaten me."

Joseph looked first at the problem, then at the cast wands. "Pick them up and cast again, sire. I know it's against the rules, but you're the king, sire."

Salitis grinned his mad grin. "That's what I like about you. You cut right through all the stupid obstacles in my path and leave me free to do whatever needs to be done."

"It's the only way to look at it, sire," Joseph demurred. "We both know what needs to be done. We're privy to information the objectors don't have, information from the God of my people. We must act on it. A wise king does what is needed for the continued welfare of his people, whether or not they think the action wise."

"Right. Right!" Salitis clapped his hands, and a slave appeared at the door. "We'll eat on the patio," he ordered. The slave bowed and disappeared. "Actually," Salitis said, turning back to Joseph, "it's something much like that that I wanted to talk to you about. I've decided that the army alone isn't a strong enough ally for us. To force this program through, to convince the people to accept the state's control of food production, we also need the priesthood on our side. And they've been against me from the start. But I have an idea."

"I bow to your superior insight, sire," Joseph said, no trace of detectable irony in his voice. "What are you going to do?"

"I'm going to get the priesthood on our side. More specifically, I'm going to get them on *your* side."

Joseph, startled, looked sharply at Salitis. "I don't understand, sire. They regard me as a foreigner, an infidel. I'm a large part of the reason you've had trouble with them since you elevated me to my present position."

"I know. But I have an idea, my young friend. It *will* require your cooperation, but I'm sure you won't withhold it. Come with me." He led the way to the rooftop patio where he and Joseph could look over the wall to an outdoor garden below on the ground level: a charming little patch of green flanking a clear pool of brilliant blue. Beside the pool a young woman gathered blooms from one of the flowering shrubs.

"She's very beautiful," Joseph said.

Salitis smiled. "One of my counselors is a man named Ersu. I think you know him."

"Yes, sir. He lent the money to Ameni to purchase me."

"The very man," Salitis said. There was the odd glint in his eye, the strange edge on his voice. Joseph had learned by now not to oppose a decision of Salitis's—or even to question it—when the madness showed itself. To do so brought on fierce rages, fits of uncontrollable anger. "Ersu's brother-in-law is the high priest of On and is highly placed in the priestly hierarchy. He is a master politician, and most of the others of his calling either owe him something or are vulnerable to him by other means. I think he knows where some very big bones are buried."

"I understand, sire. But what does—"

"The girl's his daughter. You, my young friend, are unmarried, and so is she. I think it's time for you to make a good marriage, one that will ally you not only with the political power of the priesthood, but with—I add this advisedly—the money Ersu represents. After myself, he is the richest man in all the lands I control. He's the only one who had the good sense to sell his agricultural properties and invest his entire fortune in urban lands. All the people he sold to were wiped out when we took over the lands under cultivation. He now owns most of the inner city." His words had a wildly nervous quality about them, and his hands moved jerkily as he spoke. "We need this alliance. We have to have it. We can't do the things we have to do without it." He turned on Joseph now, his eyes glittering. "You'll do it. You'll marry the girl. Won't you? Won't you?"

Joseph's mind raced frantically. Thus far, in all he had done, there had been no direct conflict with the dictates of the God who had guided him to this high position, to whom he owed everything. But this? The girl was not of his race, his people. It was a terrible sin to marry out of his faith!

And worse, the girl was the daughter of a high priest of a false god! Could this be the woman he married? Who would bear his children? How could he justify this? He could just imagine his father hearing about it. It would kill him!

"I don't hear any answer," Salitis said sternly. "Look at her: She's a vision of loveliness. Strong, lithe, she'll bear you fine sons. It's the sort of alliance any man in his right mind would dream of."

Joseph looked down at the girl again. She *was* uncommonly pretty, with a charming oval face, raven-black hair. There was a natural grace about her as she moved easily from flowering shrub to shrub. "I . . . I beg your pardon, sire," he said. "It's just that—well, I wasn't expecting it. It came as a surprise to me. I'm still getting used to the—"

"Well, you'd better get used to it quickly," Salitis said, real anger in his voice. "I've told Petephres that the deal's arranged, and now I'm telling you. All that remains is for the contract to be drawn up." He shot a look of warning at Joseph. "Foil me in this, and you do so at great peril to yourself."

Joseph's mind was in turmoil. How could he not comply? Salitis was a madman and would order Joseph's death on a moment's notice if he thought he had been betrayed. In the days since he had lived at the palace, Joseph had come to learn that the wrong word could cost a man his head.

And yet, how could he go through with it? Such an alliance was a betrayal of his God, of the faith of Jacob and Abraham and of his people. And if he violated that faith, would his God not cast him down again? Who, then, would protect Egypt, Canaan, and the lands beyond from the terrible days of famine and want that lay ahead? It was only he, Joseph, who stood between his father's people and the slavery that Salitis could impose upon them once the great famine struck; he had no doubts that without his moderating influence, the people of Israel were lost.

"You haven't answered me!" Salitis said, his voice rising to a scream.

Joseph's stomach ached. Cold sweat had broken out on

his forehead, and he wiped his face with one hand. "The girl," he said. "What's her name?"

"Asenath," the king said. "Her name is Asenath."

# II

Under Kirakos's arbors the naked slaves reached high over their heads and pulled down the dark grapes to load them in wicker baskets. Only the taller men were used for this chore; the smaller or younger slaves, who could not reach the grapes, carried the baskets to the nearby winepress. Half-grown boys, also naked, their legs stained up to the thighs by the purple juice, trod on the grapes while holding onto ropes suspended from a framework overhead to keep from falling into the slippery juice and mash.

The juice would escape through a trough at the side of the winepress and would be stored in resin-lined pottery jugs capped with mud stoppers that had been pierced to prevent the fermenting juice from blowing its container open. The stoppers bore stamps identifying the wine as coming from Kirakos's estate. In time a scribe would write the vintage on the side of the jug; now, however, stout slaves bore the jugs to Kirakos's storage cellars, suspending their burden, in woven slings, from long bamboo poles.

Mereet watched the process with a somber eye. The soldiers had left only moments before, and she wondered now how she could convey their message to Kirakos without alarming him. That was probably impossible, because virtually everything that happened these days seemed to alarm him. His whole world was being cut out from under him; he had far less influence at court than he had had when he had purchased her only a short time before, and he, like all the rest, had lost richly lucrative lands when the king's troops had seized all privately owned agricultural areas. Kirakos had, at the time, professed to understand; there could be no exceptions to the Golden Pharaoh's orders, or bloody revolution would be upon them before the season was done.

But when the confiscation had begun, it was only of

grain-growing lands. Now the soldiers had come to inform her, as nominal mistress of the house, that the crown intended to seize all vineyards. This would be a heavy blow to Kirakos, who had taken great pride in producing the finest wines in Salitis's lands, using vine cuttings from lands the Shepherds had conquered, as distant as Padan-aram. These particular vines had sprung from a vineyard in Carchemish.

The thought tore at her heart suddenly. Carchemish! Her husband, Shobai, had worked in Carchemish before the Shepherds had come. He had armed the city against them, working for King Hagirum, the wise and valiant warrior-king who had been the first to rise against the invaders. Carchemish! Perhaps the grapes from the vineyard that these cuttings were taken from had been made into wine that Shobai had bought in those half-forgotten towns of the remote north so many years ago.

She stifled a sob and steeled herself. This was no time to let the past tug at her heart. She would have her hands full, finding a way to tell Kirakos. She had begun to worry about him these days; he had the look of a man whose heart could give out. A great shock was all it would take.

She turned and headed back along the long, curving path through the fields to the manor house atop the little rise up ahead. How strange it was, she thought, to find herself, a slave, worrying about her master. But the only way to live through the terrible changes and not go mad was to try to take all things in stride.

For a piercing, heartbreaking moment, her resolve failed her. *My babies! My darlings! Where are they now?* She balled her hands into fists and blinked away the hot tears. *No! You mustn't think that way. Better to think about Kirakos.* It was better to see things as they were.

Ah, Kirakos. There were worse masters, to be sure. How strange it was to think of becoming fond of a Shepherd overlord, after all these years of hating them categorically! Yet the old man had, over decades, won his way through his bloody and barbaric youth to a certain wisdom, to mature and sane behavior, to a certain kindness, particularly to the few people in the world who were still close to him.

She turned from the main road to the path that led up to the entrance of the great house. *Close to him* . . . she mused. *I suppose I'm as close to him now as anyone is. He confides in me. And sometimes, in the cool twilight hour, there'll be even a sort of gentleness in him toward me   We'll stop sparring. Our conversation will take on a certain easy humor, a certain quiet intimacy. . . .*

She stopped dead, eyes wide, understanding.

*The old man is in love with me!*

Of course! When you once introduced that one fact, everything made sense; without it, nothing did, not really. He had lost his wife, and he had been devastatingly lonely. There was no one to lean on, no one to consult, no one to talk things over with at the evening hour when all was quiet and peaceful.

At last she understood the looks he had given her now and then. She could understand why his voice changed in tone, why things were easy between them, as if they were family.

Thinking about it, there was a flash of quick resentment and anger in her heart. How dare he! How dare he think that she—

But then reason once again took over. She knew, as surely as if the answer lay in her heart and not his, that if there were any intention in his mind of taking advantage of his position, he would have done that by now. From the first, behind the banter, there had always been enormous respect for her, evident in everything he had ever said and done around her. Respect—yes, and affection.

No doubt about it. He was in love with her.

And the strange thing about it was that the fact pleased her, flattered and reassured her immensely. For it meant that, in this strange land, among enemies, she had a friend.

That was what he was, was it not? He was an old man. The compelling urges of youth had given way to other considerations. Instead of wanting to—to exploit her, *to use* her the way a younger man would have done, it was enough for him to have her friendship and companionship, to have around him a woman still young and comely, a woman he did not have to share with anyone except, perhaps, the memory of her own lost love. There was, in this, comfort enough for him. He did not need more than devotion and friendship.

And look what good they had done him! To be sure, his physical condition was deteriorating a little at a time, aging, getting ready for death. But his mental condition had gotten better. His eyes, dull and guarded when she had arrived, twinkled now. He took pleasure in life, in the observation of people and their follies. He enjoyed good food and wine. . . .

The thought was a stab at her heart. Wine! And here they were seizing his vineyards! Cruel! Thoughtless!

On impulse she went around to the side door and down the narrow stairs to the wine cellar. Once there, she looked around her, where the tall jars were stacked side by side in long, even rows. She counted the jars, estimated their contents. *He won't live long enough to use all of this.*

The thought should have been reassuring to her; instead it tore at her heart, and she felt powerfully like weeping inconsolably.

Life was short and fleeting. You were a child for the blink of an eye; a young mother for a heartbeat; an old woman for a moment, no more. Life had gone, and you had missed it all.

*Oh, my children, my dear, blind husband . . .*

To her amazement, she found her thoughts also going to the old man who, under the law, owned her body and soul. Her heart went out to him, too, in his own need, his need of her, and she realized how deeply she needed to *be* needed just now, to be someone whose presence could bring comfort and solace—who could bring color, warmth, life back into another person's heart, even if he was an overlord from a strange and unwelcome culture, even if he owned her like an animal. How very strange: Despite the great aching hole in her heart, there seemed to be enough love left over for a dying old man.

She turned to go, but paused on the stair. A thought had suddenly burned itself into her brain: What if there were some sort of destiny that governed human life? What if it were her own destiny to be here, in the strange foreign country her homeland had become, among strangers? What if it were her fate to be at the side of this slowly dying old man, to bring comfort to his last days?

If she could accept this in her heart, could not the thought help bring some comfort to her, too, while it lasted? While he yet lived?

While *she* yet lived?

And now, for the first time in a long, long time, she remembered Djedi. The first man, other than her father, that she had ever loved. The first man, other than her father, that she had ever lost. . . .

She had been only a child when civil war had struck the lands where she was born, not far from here in the delta. Her breasts had just begun to bud. Her father, the magistrate Indi, had been driven from his lands by bands of roving bandits and cutthroats. In defiance of his superiors, his friend the soldier Djedi had brought his little unit to help evacuate them, and in the battle that had followed, her father had been killed and Djedi had been seriously wounded. She had brought Djedi down the great river to safety, only to lose him to his wounds. In the brief time they had had together, Djedi had left an imprint that had lasted her whole life. Ever after, she had always known what it would be that she would admire and love in a man: It was an odd, uneasy—and yet, when you found it, strangely natural—mixture of valor and gentleness. Djedi had had the brave heart to lay his life on the line to save her. He had also had the greatness of soul to take note of a child's foolish talk and listen carefully, as if she were speaking words of wisdom. He had treated her as if she were an empress, a goddess, a person of great moment, and not a frightened, dowerless, featherheaded little orphan.

She had found something of this quality in Baka.

When she thought Baka dead, she had found the same quality in Shobai, ennobled by his suffering, a strong and violent man made gentle by what he had been through.

And now there was a grain of it in the old man the fates had sent her to nurse in his latter days.

She dried her tear-filled eyes on her robe and started up the stairs. Her thoughts were now tranquil, accepting. There was the beginning of peace in her heart. And she thought: *I could die in a moment—any moment. Under the circumstances, the only thing to do is . . . why, just what I'm doing.* Death could take her as it had taken Djedi: one moment here, the next moment gone. It could take her as it would soon take Kirakos. Death, then, would take her doing her duty, and part of that duty included kindness and caring and the honoring of this sick, hurt, strangely honorable, strangely decent old man in his last days.

She smiled, a strange, secret smile. And, her back straight, head held high, she headed up into the light. There were the evening chores to supervise. There was supper to attend to and the many duties attendant upon the winding down of the day and the coming of night.

## III

All day long people had milled around in the Market of the Date Palm, waiting for the government vendors to arrive to distribute the produce the soldiers had seized from the former owners. The few shops and stalls that were open—those selling clothing, sandals, and other nonedibles—had had little business all day; the usual customers of the small bazaar had arrived, looked around at the devastation caused by the crown's seizure of the means of food production, and left in search of a better provisioned market. Some of those who had left had returned—some of them more than once—hoping the produce had been delivered in the meantime. One or two of these shoppers were still in the square commiserating with the vendors when word came that three government wagons were finally coming, bearing produce.

The little market began to fill quickly with people as the word spread up and down the streets, and shoppers began to return in force. Fifteen minutes later the market was full of people, some of whom had come from all the way across Avaris. Virtually all of them had been waiting in one or another of the marketplaces all day. The vendors of dry goods welcomed the sudden influx of shoppers with eager anticipation; but now they learned that these shoppers were interested only in food. The exceptions were the thieves who had slipped into the square with the crowds and who now pilfered from the open stalls almost with impunity.

The masses were impatient for the arrival of the government wagons, and they complained to each other about the shortages and inconvenience. At last there came a call from the far fringe of the crowd: "They're coming! The wagons are coming down the street!"

The crowd surged forward in the little square; a clothing stall was knocked over; a fistfight broke out between two men, one of whom claimed the other had shoved him.

"Make way there! Make way in the name of the crown!" a loud voice boomed out. From the rear, bystanders could look over the heads of the massed people and see tall soldiers in Shepherd helmets, spears high above their heads. "Make way! We can't get the food to the stalls if you don't make way!"

Then the crowd parted, grumbling and cursing, and the sweating soldiers pushed through to an open space in one end of the square. As they did, a small wagon drawn by a donkey moved out of the side street and into the clearing. The crowd craned their necks; they could see crates of olives, dates, but the wagon was not piled high. Into the clearing came a second wagon, sparsely loaded with provender. The wagon was followed by a second contingent of soldiers. These deployed around the two wagons. "All right," the leader of the soldiers said. "If you'll just get in a single-file line now . . ."

"You mean that's all?" a woman in the front row said shrilly. "Those puny wagons are all there is?"

"There's more," the soldier said brusquely. "The rest has been delayed. Tomorrow or the next day—"

"Tomorrow?" the woman said in a strained voice. "The next day? What do you mean? Delivery was supposed to be this morning! There wasn't enough to eat yesterday as it was. My family went to bed hungry—"

"That's enough from you," the soldier said. "I'm going to have to ask you to get in line now."

His words were lost as a man climbed atop the platform surrounding the well in the middle of the square, saw the two wagons, and called out, "There's not enough! There's barely enough for the first few dozen people!"

The soldier looked up, annoyed. "You'll have to be patient," he said. "The first weeks of any changeover are always full of problems. We have soldiers harvesting the produce, people who aren't used to this kind of work—"

"You could try giving the land back," one man spat bitterly. "You could give the work of harvesting back to those who do it well, whose families have been doing it well for centuries. We never had this kind of trouble before, not even in days of famine."

"There now. Move along, you. And you back there! You by the well! Get down there! Or I'll have to—"

"Give us food!" a woman cried. "My children are home waiting!"

"Food?" the man on the well platform said, laughing ruefully. "All the food's probably gone to feed the soldiers they've brought in from the field to guard the food. These foreigners don't give a hang about us. They're not going to give us anything!"

"You!" the soldier commanded angrily. "I told you to get down. Now I'm telling you to shut up."

The man on the platform made an obscene gesture. Then he gesticulated dramatically and bellowed out to the crowd in an angry voice, "You might as well go home. There's not enough for six large families to live on for a day or so. They're not going to—"

The Shepherd bowman was poised, waiting for the order, his arrow drawn, the bowstring taut. The soldier in front nodded curtly. The bow sang. The arrow sped swift and true. It caught the speaker in the middle of the chest, between two ribs. His mouth went wide open; his eyes stared. He was dead almost before he had fallen to the ground.

"They killed him!" someone shrieked, her voice angry and indignant. "Did you see that? They killed him, just for—"

"All right!" the soldier said. "Get that woman! Bring her to me!" Two burly Shepherd swordsmen plowed into the crowd, making their way with elbows and shoulders.

But the crowd was not going to take this passively. As the soldiers surged forward, the mob pressed in and bore them to the ground. From the rear a rock flew over the heads of the shoppers and struck the commander of the guards on the forehead, knocking his helmet askew. Blood ran down his face in a thin line. He drew his sword, but this only further angered the crowd. They charged him. He hacked one of them down, but others grabbed his sword arm and wrested the weapon from his hand. The bowman nocked another arrow and let it fly, but someone jarred his arm, spoiling his aim. The bolt flew wide. The crowd was upon him and pulled him down. The soldier who had led the first wagon started to run for help, but one of the shoppers tackled him and brought him down hard on the packed earth just as another man came up, bearing the stolen sword, and stabbed down, hard and true. The fallen soldier let out a choked cry and died.

A dispute broke out over the pitifully inadequate contents of the two wagons. The fight spread. Screams pierced the air, and more soldiers came, but these were not so easily disposed of. A half hour later the little marketplace was awash with fresh blood, and a dozen men lay dead. Many were carried off to prison, some with wounds so fearful that they would probably not survive the transport to jail. Order, such as it was, had been restored, but at a terrible price. And almost all the shoppers went home empty-handed—if they went home at all.

In the morning the streets were full of soldiers, soldiers on virtually every street corner, soldiers in the inns and taverns and markets. It had suddenly become a punishable offense for more than six people to congregate at a time, except at officially designated places where the indigent queued up for food or jobs. There was little food. There were no jobs.

And in the city, there was an appalling shortage of places to live. Many slaves of the former growers had been pressed into government service, and the crown fed them and housed them. But there was no work or housing provided for the freemen. As the great farms and orchards were taken over one after the other outside the city wall, the freemen—former small farmers whose fields had failed in bad seasons and had been taken over by the big landholders, former slaves whose masters had freed them but not taught them new trades—streamed into the city, hoping to make a living. Those who had relatives came to live with them, but these newcomers soon found they had placed their kin in desperate want—most had barely enough food for existing family members, and times were daily getting worse for everyone. Some of them were asked to leave; others were literally thrown out, with no place to go.

The dispossessed drifted out of the city, to live as they might, sleeping under the stars, finding food by stealing from the orchards the government had taken over. Any of them caught in the act were executed without trial.

The ones the soldiers could not catch, the quick, the able, the lucky, moved covertly to the banks of the great river. There, at least, one could fish for his dinner. Convenient hideouts could be found on the river islands. As the days passed, numbers of the dispossessed began to band together for mutual aid and protection. As their numbers grew, the complexity of their living arrangements, added to the natural competitiveness of the hungry and dispossessed, led to the selection—sometimes by violent means—of a leader for each roving band, often a rough plebiscite.

One day the caravan bringing produce from the rich

tenth, eleventh, and eighteenth nomes into Avaris was attacked, all its goods seized. The sole survivors of the raid told of being attacked by armed bandits, fifty or sixty strong. The next day patrols scoured the area, but found nothing. The number of guards on the next caravan was tripled, and the bulk of produce shipments coming from On were shifted over to boat traffic.

This was not the solution some had thought it. The bandits took to the water, using stolen boats. The shipment from On fell to the robbers after a brief fight. For a week or so, many leagues of the great Nile itself were in the hands of the bandits until heavily guarded Shepherd galleys could make their way upriver from Avaris to clear the lanes, their oars manned now by slaves seized from the great plantations.

Petephres, high priest of On, called on his kinsman Ersu one afternoon. Petephres was surrounded by burly guards brought from his own region far upriver; it was no longer safe to walk the streets without bodyguards, and Petephres had refused to use government guards, preferring to trust his own men.

Ersu's servants let Petephres in. The principal house slave bowed low and said, "My master is in the garden. I'll summon him if you—"

"That's all right," the high priest said brusquely. "I'll go out there myself. Feed my men, will you?" Tall and dignified, he let his cloak be taken away and strode through the open door to the rear. Ersu and Ameni were talking at poolside. As Petephres entered, Ameni jumped nervously to his feet, like a common soldier whose superior officer had just entered his area. "There now," Petephres said, the smallest trace of contempt in his tone. "Stand easy." He turned to Ersu, ignoring Ameni altogether. "I gather you've talked with Salitis. How did it go?"

Ersu motioned to him to sit down beside them, but the priest remained standing, towering high over both of them. "He's brought the matter up to Joseph," Ersu said. "There seems to be some minor problem about Joseph's family traditions. He's not supposed to marry outside his faith."

"Faith?" Petephres snorted. "He was a slave only weeks ago. Who respects a slave's gods, his reli—"

"Wait," Ersu said, holding up one hand. "Sit down. You don't know what we're dealing with here. Joseph may have been a slave, but at the moment he's number two in all of the lands controlled by our friends the Hai. As such, he must be humored . . . or, at worst, accommodated."

"Accommodated? Nonsense."

"Nonsense yourself," Ersu said. "You've been living a charmed life upriver, insulated from reality. You haven't had to deal with our gracious lord Salitis. You don't know what he's like." They were in Ersu's own garden, and the servants and slaves were his own—loyal, trusted; nevertheless, he looked around cautiously before he spoke and lowered his voice to say, "He's quite mad, you know. He's dangerous, raving, given over to violent rages. If he says Joseph must be accommodated, then that's the way it must be."

"You've got to be exaggerating," Petephres said. "The letter I got from Salitis was very reasonable, rational, in fact. He seemed—"

"Forget the letter, Petephres. It was drafted by a rational man, a paid scribe. Salitis had nothing more to do with it than affixing the royal seal. And he was probably flat on his back, with his eyes rolled back in his head. He has the falling sickness, you know, among other things."

"Ah," Petephres said. His tone was thoughtful now. "Explain everything to me. I'm ready to listen."

"All right," Ersu said. He shot Ameni a secret look of triumph; it was not every day you could get the haughty high priest to sit back and listen, kinsman or no. "The story is this: Before he became a slave, Joseph was the son of an uncrowned king of sorts, up in Canaan."

"Uncrowned?" Petephres snorted again. "Nonsense. He's either a king, or he's not. Go on."

Again Ersu smiled behind his back at Ameni. "All right. As son of his father, he's also a priest of his God. As a priest of this barbarian religion, he can't marry a woman not of his faith. And here we're asking him to marry the daughter of a high priest of the true religion."

"Ah. Well, now, are we talking about a real belief on his part? Dogmatic? Or is it the sort of thing one professes to please his family, his father?"

"Apparently it's a real matter of conscience."

"Then there's no problem," Petephres said, brightening. "We can work something out. The marriage doesn't have to be a public one."

"Not public?" Ameni blurted out suddenly. "The second most highly placed person in the land? But—"

Petephres gave him one withering glance, but when he spoke, it was to Ersu. "We can have a private ceremony by his rules, whatever they may be, in which my Asenath becomes a member of his religion." He waved the whole thing away as unimportant. "Nobody need know about it. Then we can hold another, more public, observance and do it our way. It will look like a normal Egyptian upper-class wedding. Nobody will be the wiser, except you and me and a few others."

Ersu smiled. "I'm surprised you're so reasonable about this."

"Oh, come now," Petephres said. "We're practical men, after all. And we're arranging a politically expedient marriage that every last one of us will benefit from. I see no reason to niggle over minor details. Tell the young man that I'll give him his marriage on his own terms if he'll give me in return a nice empty ceremony on mine. Just for show, you know." His tone changed again. "Has he seen Asenath yet?" His smile was cynical and superior.

"From a distance. They haven't met."

"Have them introduced. She's a lovely, intelligent girl, even if I do say so myself. He can't help but be pleased with the match."

Ersu pursed his lips in thought for a moment, brow knit. "I hadn't asked," he said. "What does she think about all this?"

Now the full measure of Petephres's cynicism spilled over into expression and tone alike. "Think?" he said. "Asenath is a girl, and a young and inexperienced one at that. She's been raised to be obedient and respectful, so she'll marry the man I've chosen for her and be a dutiful wife. Joseph is said to be personable enough, and he's rich and powerful. I don't foresee any difficulties." His smile was knowing. "Tend to your own end of the bargain. Leave the girl to me."

# CHAPTER NINE

## The Nubian Desert

### I

The caravan had stopped dead before a great rock that towered over the surrounding countryside. Growing impatient, Ben-Hadad put one hand on Shobai's shoulder and said, "My curiosity is getting the best of me. I'm going up there to see what's going on. Anup just rode up to the top with a couple of his lieutenants."

"We've reached the Nile," Shobai said tranquilly. "I can feel it." He smiled. "You said 'top.' Top of what?"

"There's a ridge up ahead. It juts out of the rock irregularly, with a sharp projection at the top of it."

Shobai wiped his sweaty face with one huge hand. "It sounds like the rock of Abusir. If I'm right, then we're in Nubian territory, and have been for quite a little while—a league or so."

Ben-Hadad chuckled. "You're supposed to be the blind one, yet you miss so much less than I do. Wait here. I'll go up and see what's going on."

He pulled his pony out of the path and trotted up the long, sandy slope, feeling the solid rock under the drifted sand. As the path grew steeper he could feel the pony laboring under his weight. After a moment he stopped and dismounted to lead the animal to the top.

When he reached the apex of the path he saw that

Shobai's intuition had once again been correct. Below, the strange unearthly landscape of the second cataract of the great Nile lay spread out before his eyes. Anup and six of his men stood by their mounts, looking down at the countless black-rock islands in the dark water, stretching out as far as the eye could see. Anup turned and beckoned him nearer. "Well, there you are," he said, smiling. "That's what we've come all this way to see. Upriver it's all Nubia."

"Shobai says it's been Nubia for a league or so downriver, as well," Ben-Hadad said. "Perhaps more than that."

"Perhaps," Anup agreed. "It's an area we've never contested during my own brief career in the military. Down there"—he pointed to the right—"is where the forts begin. Just who happens to occupy them at the present moment is a matter for speculation."

Ben-Hadad scratched his head. "You know, of course, we've been spied on for days. Sentries standing atop a hill, looking down at us as we passed. They're probably from the forts. Either they didn't know we could see them or they didn't care whether we could or not."

Anup squinted down at the river below. "More likely," he said, "they wanted to be seen. I've seen them myself now and then. We all have. But which faction it is, I still can't say. If—" He stopped dead, looking back up toward the towering heights to either side of the path. "Well," he said. "What do you know? We have company."

Ben-Hadad looked first one way, then the other. To both sides of the path, tall warriors stood, bows bent, their long arrows pointed—so it seemed—directly at him. One of Anup's soldiers reached instinctively for his sword, but Ben-Hadad held his arm down. "Don't," he said. "They mean business." He held up his hands to show their emptiness; Anup did the same, then the soldiers followed suit.

He could see them now. They were black, tall, very thin, totally naked except for the odd ornament on a wrist or ankle and the quivers that hung from their necks. Black! "The Nehsiu," he said in disbelief. "They're this far north?"

In the thin air his voice carried, and as his words hung in the air, another figure, much unlike these, stepped from behind a rock projection. He was a head shorter, white-skinned, a little portly, with a half-bald head whose remaining hair was totally gray. Like his companions, he was naked, except for a sword belt; his lined old skin was sunburnt to the color of cured leather. "We certainly are," he said in accented Egyptian. Then, with a smile, he repeated the same in the language of the fierce Moabite riders of Ben-Hadad's youth in Canaan. "Welcome to our domain," he went on. "And where is my friend Shobai?"

"Musuri!" Ben-Hadad said. "Musuri of Moab!"

The reunion was a joyous one. They made camp in the shade of the great rock, by the river's edge. Musuri and Shobai, who had met at the siege of Ebla when Shobai was newly blinded and Musuri still had all his hair and a flat belly, embraced like brothers, while Anup and his men deployed beside the dark water. "Musuri!" Shobai said, genuinely pleased. "It's good to hear your voice! Where is Akhilleus?"

"Farther upriver," Musuri answered. "He and Ebana are mustering troops for an all-out attack on Kerma. If we can take it, I think the Black Wind has the whole of Kush. It'll just be a matter of mopping up pockets of resistance after that."

"The Black Wind? But—" Shobai stopped, nodded. "Oh, I understand. That's the name of your organization. But I heard that some of the white Nubians have joined you."

"They have," Musuri said, grinning. "A good thing, too. I was getting a bit lonely, being the shortest man here and the only light-skinned person. Now there are whole units who have come over to us."

"Marvelous!" Ben-Hadad exclaimed. "I won't ask how Akhilleus has managed this feat. I presume it's some sort of magic."

"Yes," Musuri said. "The same magic he worked in his homeland, unifying the headwaters country under one rule. If I hadn't seen that, I wouldn't have believed this. He's come into his own. I thought I knew the old man before this. But, Shobai, something happened up there in his home country. He shucked off all his old mountebank's ways and became a king once and for all, in spite of giving away the kingdom the moment it was offered to him."

Shobai's voice was thoughtful as he responded. "Perhaps that's the surest test of power. The more you give it away, the more it remains yours."

Musuri looked thoughtfully at the soldiers bringing the boats up. "That may well be," he allowed. "But if this present enterprise gives him a kingdom—and I think it will—I don't think he'll give it up." His voice lowered, became almost inaudible as another thought occurred to him. "Unless . . . unless there's a better or bigger kingdom to give it up for. . . ."

The boats were of very shallow draft and were poled by several of Musuri's towering black warriors, one standing at the bow and the other astern. Ben-Hadad at first feared for their safety; the water was full of terrible, frightening snags just below the waterline. But the soldiers evidently knew the channel well, and they slowly made their way upstream in the sluggish current, far from the main channels.

During their short trip Ben-Hadad had grown quiet and thoughtful, watching the tall, black soldiers of Musuri's command as they negotiated the twisting current. He took note of their relationship to old Musuri and watched as they responded with respect and efficiency to his smallest command. *They'd die for him*, he thought. *It's as if he were their father. . . .*

After a time they passed between the twin forts of Semna and Kumma, towering on the two banks of the river. Atop the walls he could see more of the tall, black warriors, standing storklike, their tall spears pointing to the heavens. "Musuri," he said, "surely *these* aren't Nubians. I'd no idea you'd brought so many of Akhilleus's young compatriots downriver with you when you came back from the headwaters."

"Oh, we didn't bring many of them back at all. Not at first. But a while back Kimala, the young king Akhilleus left in his place in his home country, sent a detachment of his more adventurous young men north, and they joined us. Those are the ones you see. Once Kimala had pacified the various tribes of his own land, it made sense to get some of his more restless young fellows out of the country for a while, before they got into mischief." He grinned and clapped one of the tall warriors on the back, muttering a few words in a language Ben-Hadad did not understand. The warrior smiled and answered in a tone of rough masculine affection. "We're using them for the most part as border guards. It was important to Akhilleus that the bulk of the real fighting should devolve on Nubians: Nehsiu loyal to us, plus those of the Medjai who came over to us."

"That makes sense."

"Yes. But there are exceptions. Wait until you see the women's detachment Ebana has developed and trained!"

"Women?" Ben-Hadad said, incredulous.

Musuri chuckled. "The women of Akhilleus's people are nearly as big as these chaps, and they're born fighters. That fort we passed a while back, the small one—"

"Dorginarti?"

"Yes. The women took that one by themselves. Scaled the wall at night like a bunch of lizards, surefooted and agile. By the time the defenders saw them, the women had taken the fort. Marvelous. I wish I'd had them back in my youth, at the siege of . . . Ah, there I go, talking old-soldier stuff again. I must be getting old."

Old? Ben-Hadad looked at him, trying to add up the years. *He has to be . . . what? Fifty or so? Yet look at him. He looks a good ten years younger than that, maybe more.* The casual nudity practiced by Akhilleus's troops was perhaps less kind to Musuri's aging body than the formal court dress of an Egyptian captain might have been—but he suffered by comparison only with such rock-hard, lean specimens of manhood as the soldiers he led.

"I wasn't going to mention it," Ben-Hadad said. "But I see you've adopted a different dress code up here."

Musuri smiled. "So will you," he said. "The farther south you get, the more sense it makes. You work naked at your forge, after all. Clothing is always catching on something, and it gets sweaty and filthy and smells bad, and you have to carry spare outfits with you. You'll notice we've abandoned sandals as well. Makes better sense, in the long run, to toughen your soles. Nothing to repair, nothing to lose. This way you travel light: nothing but yourself and your weapon and a little water. I had a hard time getting used to it at first, but Akhilleus convinced me it was better this way." He scratched his bald spot. "I've learned a lot from him in the past couple of years. I, who thought I'd learned it all about fifty campaigns ago."

An hour or so upriver Ben-Hadad, who had listened to all this with skepticism, began to learn the truth of Musuri's observations. White water announced they were approaching the Dal rapids, a huge cataract broken by dozens of rock islands fringed with scrub grass. All of them, Nilotic soldier and downriver visitor alike, had to step into hip-deep water and help shoulder the light boats. Ben-Hadad's clothing was soaked. Later, drenched with his sweat, it would stick to him for the rest of the afternoon; the Nilotics, however, got only their skin wet, and this would dry quickly in the sun, cooling their bodies as the water evaporated. And as they moved the boats up the bank to portage past the rapids, Ben-Hadad's sandal slid underfoot, and he almost fell; the soldiers remained as surefooted as mountain goats. He scowled; they smiled at him, easygoing, tolerant.

From the path above he could see why the portage had become necessary. The current whipped through the rocks, and with the rock outcroppings on either side, it would have been dangerous to try to negotiate the rapids. Even the few animals they saw only came to the backwaters to drink, where drinking water had been trapped in an eddy. And this was desolate country: The animals were few and far between. A gazelle here, a jackal or jerboa there.

As the trail wound upstream, high above the raging water, Ben-Hadad could see parallel and horizontal lines, evidently made by the hand of man, on the rock wall opposite. "Musuri," he said. "What are those?"

"The marks give you the various heights of the Nile at a given time of the year," the old man said. "If the sky were blotted out above and you couldn't tell the seasons by the usual means, you could probably tell them accurately by the height of the river measured against those marks. The top one is the Nile in full flood, swollen with the melted snow carried by a dozen rivers many days' march from here."

But now their progress slowed as they climbed, seeking footing on a steep path. Nearly at the top, the Nilotic soldier in the lead stopped suddenly and held up a hand to call them all to a halt. He said something in that exotic tongue that Ben-Hadad could not understand. Musuri nodded and translated. "Trouble of some kind. Hold it up there! I'll check it out." Then, as light as a man thirty years younger, he jogged up the curving track. When he returned a moment later, there was a serious look on his face.

"What's the matter?" Ben-Hadad asked.

"From the top you can see smoke," Musuri said grimly. "One of our forts—it's on fire."

# II

As Ben-Hadad looked down, one of Musuri's guardsmen brought Shobai up to speak with him. "Ben-Hadad," the blind man said, "tell me what you see."

While Musuri conferred with six of his more experienced warriors, Ben-Hadad answered his uncle. "The enemy doesn't seem to have taken the fort yet, but they're a much superior force. There aren't many soldiers inside the walls at all—maybe just a token force, all Nubians, instead of the tall soldiers here with Musuri. I'd say that under normal conditions, if they had a sizable defense force inside the fort, they could hold out a long time. With all the towers manned by regulars, it'd be very difficult to scale the walls. Those projecting towers, manned by bowmen, command a view of the walls between them." He described, tersely but specifically, the physical features of the fort in an expert's technical terms.

"Yes, yes," Shobai said. "Your description of the angle of the turrets' walls reminds me of the ones I helped design for the cities fortified by the Shepherds so many years ago. It's a good principle all in all. Where are they attacking now?"

Ben-Hadad looked down at the scene below again. "On several fronts," he answered. "The attackers are scaling the wall in two places. There's another detachment that, under cover of bow-and-arrow fire, is bringing in a battering ram."

"Not good," Shobai said, just as Musuri dismissed his lieutenants and came toward them. "They're spreading the defenders very thin, then? There's a good chance of their getting the ram up to the gate?"

"I think so," Musuri replied, clapping the blind man on the shoulder. "Unless we can get down there very quickly and drive them off."

"No," Shobai said. "There probably isn't time for a pitched battle. You've got to get your own bowmen up above the gate to protect the archers already inside the fort. Your bowmen—if they're not under constant fire from the archers on the ground—could pour boiling oil or water down or fire at the men with the battering ram. You have to take their bowmen out, and quickly. Scatter them. Make them take cover. Make it impossible for the ram to breach the gate."

"Good idea!" Musuri turned, barked orders to his subordinates in the guttural tongue he had learned in the lands upriver. Instantly the black bowmen scurried down the path. They took positions directly parallel to the part of the fortress wall that fronted the main gate, then took aim on the besiegers below. Musuri, grinning, turned back to Shobai. "If I ever tell this to anyone," he said, "half the people won't believe that I got advice from a blind man, and the other half won't believe that I took it or that it worked. Now, old friend, what would you have me do?"

"How many warriors do you have left?" Shobai asked. Musuri thought a second, then named a figure. "All right." The blind man mused. "That's enough, if my figures are right. Come up behind and cut them off from the river. Attack from behind."

"Right you are!" Musuri said. "Ben-Hadad, you stay here with your uncle. I'll leave two runners with you. If he's got any advice as the battle progresses, based on your descriptions, send a runner down to me immediately. These boys can run like gazelles, and they'll have the message in my ear before you can blink twice. I'll leave two boys who understand your language. All right?"

Ben-Hadad snorted. "If the runners can speak my tongue well enough to understand a complex order sent down by Shobai, I don't need to stay up here. Did you think you could keep me out of the fighting that easily?" He touched Shobai's arm penitently. "Sorry, Shobai. But I have to join in the fun."

Shobai frowned. "It's not an armorer's job to get involved in the fighting," he said. But whether Ben-Hadad chose to ignore his uncle or didn't hear him, Shobai could only guess as the young man followed Musuri down the sloping path.

Shabako, captain of the attacking force, screamed at his men as they brought the great ram forward. "Get a move on, there! Are you going to take all day? Are you—"

He never finished the sentence. The man in front of him suddenly staggered, bent double, fell on his side. A long arrow had passed through his chest. Almost before his body had touched the ground, a second soldier took an arrow through the thigh and toppled to the ground, his weapon abandoned at his feet.

Shabako looked up, astonished. On the hillside above, a dozen black warriors stood naked, their skins gleaming in the sunlight, and aimed a second rain of arrows at his troops. Their slender shafts poised in the air above, then fell among his men. Another three soldiers were hit. One of the shafts narrowly missed Shabako himself.

"Bowmen!" he called out, pointing. "Over there!" The second volley of bolts was aimed at his own archers; two of them fell as he looked on. "Fall back!" he shouted. "Fall—"

But from above, on the fortress walls, came yet another attack, this time of boiling water. There were screams of agony from the soldiers closest to the wall. And a third hail of arrows fell among them; one of them caught a man as he ran away from the wall, his body scalded, his hands clawing at his burnt eyes. He fell backward, heavily, the long arrow buried deeply in his throat.

"Archers!" Shabako yelled. "Get them! Kill them!" His hand pointed up the hill at them—and then was battered back. A spent arrow had caught him in the middle of the palm. He cursed, yanked it free. There was a gout of fresh blood. "Fall back!" he bellowed, as much in pain as in anger. "Retreat!"

As he looked back along the high path to the river, he could see the black warriors coming, spears at the ready—black men, fierce Nehsiu from the high mountains of the far south, led by a sun-browned Medjai much like himself—but old, bald, and as naked as the blacks he led!

"Deploy!" Shabako called out, panic creeping into his voice as he looked again at his ruined hand. "Fan out! Regroup!"

But now another rain of arrows felled two more bowmen. "Back from the walls!" he screamed, and a group of men who had been trying to scale the nearest tower obediently pulled back from the high walls, just in time to avoid an avalanche of rocks dropped over the edge on their heads by the defenders. "Bowmen!" Shabako cried. "Take cover!"

Now the fierce Nehsiu foot troops were upon them. His men met them bravely enough, but were battered back; the blacks' spears were longer than any used by either Taharqa's or Kashta's armies, and their points, razor sharp, stabbed through the Medjai bucklers and found their mark. Ten of

Shabako's men toppled heavily to the ground; the rest gave way. As they did, the rear echelon, coming up from the walls of the fortress, ran into another attack from the archers on the slopes above.

Shabako gripped his sword tightly and plunged into the line. He parried a thrust from one of the blacks' spears, hacked lustily at the ebony arm that held it. The black giant fell back. Shabako, elated at his own success, slashed right and left and wounded another of the black behemoths.

His quick eye landed on another stranger—a young, pale-skinned, and broad-shouldered warrior, well below average height, and much, much shorter than the blacks he accompanied—hacking away with a bronze sword. With a cry of rage Shabako made for him. "Traitor!" he bellowed. "You shall die! Die!"

The young man, occupied as he was with another opponent, did not see Shabako coming. Shabako's blow would have landed full strength on the young man's neck if another blade had not suddenly fended off his swing. The parry brought Shabako's sword arm down; he turned to face his attacker.

It was the old man, with the bald pate! Shabako's eye took in the potbelly—but also the still-powerful biceps and upper legs and the fearless look in the brown eyes. "All right!" he said through clenched teeth. "If you want to die first, so be it!"

He feinted high, lunged low. The supposed dotard parried with practiced ease and cut mightily at Shabako's neck with the backswing. The cut was itself a feint, though, and stopped halfway to its target. Instead of a wild hacking blow, which, if it had missed, would have left the old soldier open for attack; now Shabako had to contend with a blade pointed with deadly accuracy at his own unprotected middle.

He struggled to bring his guard up, but it was too late. The old man's point came forward, but inexplicably stopped short of gutting him. Instead the tip of that bronze sword touched him on the belly, drew a soft line across it. No more than the finest, most delicate line of blood traced across his stomach when he looked down. The old soldier stepped back, saluted sardonically. "I was going to draw the pyramid of Khufu on your skin," he said above the din, in a surprisingly strong voice, the voice of a tough old soldier. "That's the line for the base."

"Why, you—" Shabako croaked in a strangled voice. He lunged again, hard. The move was one he had taught hundreds of recruits over the years; it had won him the fencing championship in his own class some years before, and a commendation from the late Nubian king. But this old man parried the attack with ease, and the dancing blade once again drew its point in a featherlight sweep across his belly. He looked down, astonished. One side of the equilateral triangle rose from the horizontal line, a bit wavery.

"Confound it!" the old soldier said with a frown. One of the defenders lunged at him from one side; he stepped aside nimbly and, as the soldier flew past him, slammed him on the back of the neck with the pommel of his sword. The soldier skidded forward on his face and took a spear in the back from one of the black warriors. The old man turned back to Shabako. "My apologies, dear fellow," the old fighter said in an ironic voice. "I was interrupted. Now, where were we?"

Shabako's eyes clouded over with red rage. *The old soldier—he's toying with me! Me, Shabako!* "I'll show you where!" he said. And, feinting at the old man's face, he lunged instead at his throat.

The blow never landed. The old soldier came in under the lunge, quickly, deftly, with a skill perfected over forty years of soldiering, and put his entire weight into the thrust. Shabako felt a terrible blow in his midsection. He staggered back. As he did, the blade that had gone deep inside him came out again, red with blood. *His* blood! He looked down, saw the fearful wound, and dropped his weapon. His knees felt weak, and his vision seemed suddenly indistinct. There was a sick, giddy feeling inside him. He was falling, falling. . . .

"Good blow, Musuri!" bellowed Ben-Hadad, pausing to look back. He had just hacked an attacker to his knees and then half-brained him with the flat of his sword. "But—*look out!*"

Musuri turned. An attacker made at him with a battle-ax; the blow might have fallen if one of the black bowmen's long arrows had not caught the axman in the shoulder. He dropped the weapon and clutched his arm. As he did, one of Musuri's tall swordsmen dispatched him with a single mighty sweep of his crooked blade.

Musuri looked around. The offensive against the Black Wind's fort had failed! Musuri's warriors had killed all but a handful of the attackers, and several of the survivors were surrounded, about to be killed. The old commander grinned. "No!" he called to three Black Wind archers who surrounded a Medjai soldier. "Spare that man!" he said in the language of the Upper Nile. "Disarm him and bring him to me!"

The battle once ended, they inspected the fallen. The cadre of defenders had put out the fires the attackers' flaming arrows had started some time before, and now they came out into the field to confer with Musuri.

Ben-Hadad lingered in the field, walking among the fallen bodies of the Medjai attackers. Musuri called out to him. "What are you looking for? Come inside."

Ben-Hadad waved him away. "No, wait," he said. "I thought I saw something while we were fighting. A Medjai I tangled with back there struck my blade such a blow, it left a dent in it. Perhaps if I could find him . . ."

"Well, come in when you're done." Musuri barked an order to one of the blacks, who went over to Ben-Hadad and stood beside him, as if on guard. The runners were coming down the hill with Shobai now, and Musuri greeted them in their own tongue. The blacks grinned and chuckled, evidently pleased at what the old man had said.

Ben-Hadad, bent over, eyes intent on the ground, went back to his search. He was thinking: *What a marvelous old fellow Musuri is! He's as strong and cunning as a boy, but with an old man's wisdom, experience, and understanding to guide him. Why, he handled that Medjai soldier like . . .*

The thought died. *There it is!* And, his heart pounding with anticipation and excitement, he trotted to the spot where the fallen attacker lay. Only a handspan from the man's inert fingers the weapon lay. It had a curious handle, with a heavy hand guard. But it was not the handle that had attracted his eye.

It was the blade. Its shape was the traditional one of the Nubian Medjai. The material it was made of was a dark gray, oxidized here and there where water had contacted it and the rust had not been cleaned away. Ben-Hadad, his hand trembling, picked it up. It was half again as heavy as his own sword was.

Well might it be. It was made of iron.

Iron! Smelted and worked iron, here in Nubia!

# CHAPTER
# TEN

## Lisht

### I

The villa of Madir, vizier to the Lord of Two Lands and highest ranking official in all the territory governed by Dedmose, was not of an opulence befitting his rank. His own great town house in Memphis had been lost with the fall of the city to the Shepherd invaders, and upon the move to Lisht, the present house had been commandeered for his use. It had formerly belonged to a well-placed, but not particularly wealthy, priest of Ra. Thus, when Baka, at the head of a small force of guards, took Baliniri to visit the real ruler of Upper Egypt, the home they entered was of modest size and unpretentious appointments.

The front of the house was shielded from the sun by a great canopy borne by six blue wooden pillars, forming a sort of porch where the inhabitants could spend the evening hours. There they enjoyed the sweet breath of the north wind and the flowers and trees of the garden that lay between the house and the high, heavily guarded walls that set the estate off from the rest of the city.

Baka dismissed his troops at the gate, and both men surrendered their personal weapons to Madir's household guards. He turned to Baliniri and waved a hand at the garden and the house's facade. "It's not large, particularly for a man of Madir's rank," he said. "But it's comfort of a sort."

187

Baliniri nodded. "After that ridiculous display at Salitis's court, a house where things are kept in proportion is more than welcome. I gather Madir isn't much for show."

Baka steered him toward the house. "No. He's a practical man. I'm sure you already got that impression of him from our formal meeting in the palace."

Baliniri smiled. "I got whatever impression he wanted me to have. He'd not be an easy man to read unless he wanted you to read him. There was a chap a lot like him at Hammurabi's court. In my experience, the power behind the throne usually turns out to be much the same sort of man; he wants the power and knows that ostentation usually gets in the way of power."

Baka looked at him with new respect. "You've a sharp eye about you, my friend," he said. "It's too bad I don't seem to be able to talk you into staying around. I think you'd do well here."

"Staying around?" Baliniri said. His voice changed in tone, took on a much more thoughtful note. "Well, no. Not permanently. But . . . something is keeping me from moving on as quickly as I'd intended. A bit of unfinished business."

Baka took note of the odd expression on his face, but did not comment. *It is the second time he's mentioned this. Perhaps he'll be more specific about it as time goes by,* he thought. *Best not to push him.* "Here," Baka said. "One of the servants just spotted us. Madir will join us in a moment or two. One generally doesn't enter the house proper. Ah, here he comes."

Madir came forward out of the central room, dressed simply in a light white robe. "Greetings." Madir extended his hand and grasped the wrist of each man in turn. "I'm glad you arranged this meeting," he said to Baka. "It was wise of you to restrict our conversation in the palace to trivia. Here we can talk as openly as we like."

"Ah," Baka said. "You know about Sitra, then?"

"Of course. He's been passing information on to the conspirators. I've been feeding him a mixture of sound information—always trivial—and false for some time now." His smile was informal and warm, with a touch of mischievous satisfaction. "It keeps the lot of them off their guard, you know."

"You *know* about this little sand fly?" Baliniri asked, incredulous. "You know about the conspiracy—and yet you let them live?"

With uncharacteristic delicacy Madir bent to sniff a flower. "Oh, yes," he replied. "You see, I don't know who *all* of them are. Not yet. Or what *all* of their plans are. I know that there's a serious assassination plot in the works, but I don't know precisely when and where they plan to attack. You see, young man, there's no sense in casting my net and pulling it up before all my fish are in it."

Baliniri leaned back against a railing and looked at Madir with wonderment. "Can't you just dig it out of Sitra under torture?"

Now it was Baka's turn to explain. "This lot of conspirators is more clever than most. They are organized in such a way that the right hand literally does not know what the left is doing. Nobody knows the whole picture except the inner council—"

"Nobody knows," Madir corrected, "except the man who wears the Sobek mask. And I'd give a king's ransom just now to know who *he* is."

Now it was Baka who turned incredulous. "You *know* about the man in the Sobek mask? Pardon me. I should have known you would be ahead of me. But—"

"I know quite a bit," Madir said, enjoying himself immensely. "What I don't know is who is leading it and who is funding it." The vizier became serious. "Creating a revolution costs money, and someone is spending freely to back this cabal. I want to know who that someone is. And I won't pull in my net until I have that man in it. You'll be interested to know that Aduna is on the job in this."

"Ah," Baka said with a smile. "Aduna," he explained to Baliniri, "is another of the 'thousand ears' of Madir. A very good man."

"One of the best," Madir said, clapping his hands for the servants. Instantly two women appeared at the doorway, bearing dates, bread, wine. "I asked him about *you*, Baliniri, after your little skirmish with three of our soldiers." The women came forth, and the men took wine in plain gold goblets.

Baliniri flushed. "I had hoped that had escaped your notice. In some jurisdictions I'd have wound up in the dock for that."

"Nonsense," Madir said, raising his goblet to the young Mesopotamian. "A little gallantry is desirable in a soldier. Aduna had a report on the incident in my office before nightfall. And by the next day he had a complete dossier on you. I can tell you the name of your superior at the battle of Mari, the one you replaced when he was killed. I can even tell you where your scars are." Madir's smile changed character; the heavy-lidded eyes opened just a trifle, and Baliniri could see the twinkle in them as he added, "I can tell you most, not all, of a certain anecdote involving you and a certain Greek woman, in a tavern in Arvad a year and a half ago. . . ."

"Ouch!" Baliniri said. "Mekim! He's been letting his tongue get loose in the taverns again. If—"

"Not in the taverns," Madir said. "The 'thousand ears' of Madir include not a few in the brothels of the city. It would appear that your compatriot is less fastidious than yourself." He chuckled. "But let's get down to business. Tell me what you know of this affair in the delta, in as great detail as possible."

Coming across the market square, Hefget routinely patted the front of his garment where his purse was customarily carried and found nothing there. Nothing! All the money he had for the week— He patted the whole front of his robe frantically, up and down, with both hands, panic sweeping through him. Gone!

"Sir?" a quiet voice said at his elbow. "Is this yours?"

He wheeled, looked down into the dark eyes of the little urchin he had seen several times before in the bazaars. Her hair was bound in the back to keep it out of her eyes, and she wore a ragged tunic. His practiced eye could make out the long line of a knife under her dress. She held up his purse in one tiny hand. "Pardon me, sir. But a thief took this from you back at the greengrocer's stall, when you were looking at cabbages. I . . . well, I stole it back from him."

Speechless, Hefget took the purse from her, opened it. The money was still there! "You stole it back from him?" he said. "From a professional thief?"

She grinned, a cynical street-gamin's grin, merry-eyed. "It was either that or call the guardsman. And there's something about them that I find distasteful. I'm not too fond of the guards, you understand."

He took her elbow and steered her to a quieter spot by the side of the fountain. "Yes, yes. I don't like them much either. Look, I'd like to express my gratitude." He opened the purse.

"No, no," she said, shaking off his hand and carefully moving away, wary of unwanted advances. "That's not necessary. I have a confession to make: I was keeping an eye on you. I'm a friend of Taheret's. She was Dede's woman, you'll remember. . . ."

"Ah! Well, give her my best when you see her." Something in the girl's tone struck him as being odd. "Have you two known each other long?" he asked.

"No," the girl said. She looked around, lowered her voice. "I . . . I sold her some contraband a few days back. In the course of things she let me in on a thing or two. She judged me as someone who could be trusted."

Hefget frowned, looked her hard in the eye. "What sort of 'thing or two'?" he asked, instantly on guard.

"Look," she said. "I'm no friend of this regime. I lost friends and family when Memphis fell. Somebody's going to pay dearly for that sometime. The rich, the people of the court, *they* managed to escape down here to Lisht. But they left hundreds to die when the army pulled out." Bitterness entered her voice. "There was a young man. He and I were going to marry. Instead—" She turned and spat angrily into the street.

"I understand," he said, steering her this time to a blind alley behind them, where they would not be overheard. "Why are you telling me this?"

"Taheret's no fool," she whispered. "She knows her man Dede's just about smart enough to come inside when it's raining. She says you people sent Dede away to the Fayum to get him out of your hair before he spoiled something."

Hefget started. "A lot of people know that Dede's stupid. So what? You say 'you people.' What do you mean by that, young lady?"

"I'm not a lady," she said defiantly. Then, seeing the look in his eye, she added, "And I'm no tart, either, if that's what you're thinking. You try laying a hand on me, and you'll draw back bloody stumps for fingers. Let's say I'm just someone who wants revenge. I had a man who would have married me, me with no marriage portion. We had things planned. We were going to—" Her voice broke; she mastered herself and continued in a bitter voice, "Let's just say that if I were to run into a bunch of people who thought as I did about this bunch of butchers who sold Memphis to the Shepherds and gave up the city and everybody in it without a real fight—"

"Yes?" Hefget said. "You'd do what?"

She shot him an angry glare. "I can be very useful to people I choose to befriend. I have a quick hand and a quicker eye. And I can keep a secret, which apparently is more than your friend Dede can."

"How do I know you're telling the truth about stealing my purse?" he challenged. "You could have picked it off the ground where I'd dropped it. How do I know you've got a quick hand?"

"Pat your pocket," she challenged. "Go ahead, try it." He did. The purse was gone again! He went over his whole body, patting. "Don't bother," she said. She held the purse up, handed it over. "Here it is. I took it when you brought me over to the fountain. Now you've seen what I can do. I'm small, too. I can get in and over and under places that most people can't squeeze into. I can run fast. I can do a lot of things. And there's little I wouldn't do to get back at the people responsible for the death of my lover."

He looked at her, hefting the purse in one hand and putting it back into his tunic. "Suppose there were such a group of people. How far could they trust you?"

"Right up to the point where they betrayed me," she said. "How far can anybody trust anybody, ever? But I'll tell you one thing: Money means nothing to me. I could make an easy living any time I want to, just by picking purses. But I'm not the desperate kind. *They're* the sort that would betray you—the kind who gets behind on the rent or on the payments to the usurers, and has to do something quick, to raise the money."

"I understand," he said. "What *does* matter to you? Revenge?"

"Yes. But I'm practical, too. If such a group won, they'd be grateful. They might remember someone who did them a favor, back before it was fashionable to do so, when you could get impaled for getting caught at it."

"I'd say that was reasonable," Hefget said thoughtfully. "Look, let me think about it. I have to ask a few questions here and there. You'll be in the neighborhood if I need you? I've seen you around here before."

For a split second her eyes went wary. But then she relaxed, grinned. "Sure, I will."

Tuya watched him go, her hands on hips, a triumphant

smile on her face. Well! *That* was interesting. He *was* one of
them. She was sure of it. And she was working her way into
his confidence.

The shadows were long now; the food stalls were beginning to close. She could hear the guard high atop the city
wall call out the last warning for entering and leaving the
city, before the gates were shut for the night. She turned and
went to the well, pulled up the bucket, drank. It was time to
get back home before night came on and the city grew
dangerous. She wiped her mouth and turned away . . .

. . . And saw him standing there, looking at her. Baliniri!
He was even bigger and broader than she remembered, and
every bit as fetching as memory had painted him. But he was
not smiling. Instead there was an expression on his face very
like . . . anguish? Pain? But in her pounding heart she knew
the answer, knew it as surely as if she could look into his
mind.

## II

Her first impulse was to dissolve in embarrassment: her
hair! Her clothes! How could she meet him looking like this?
But his eyes were on her eyes, and she knew he could not
have cared less what she was wearing, or what her hair
looked like. He looked so vulnerable.

"I'm Tuya," she said, dry-throated, a little hoarse.

"Baliniri." He smiled warmly. "I've hoped to find you.
You said you were often in the market. And from that first
day I've haunted the place, but you weren't here."

"I'm sorry," she whispered. "I don't know what to say."
And indeed, she did not know. What should she tell him? *I
have a husband. I can't see you anymore.* She should,
but she could not. "I . . . I've been busy." It all sounded
so lame!

Now his eyes went around her face, up and down her
body. There was in them a great hunger, a great tenderness—
more, she was willing to wager, than he wanted her to see
there. "Well," he said, getting his voice under control and

smiling, "at least I've found you now. And this time I won't let you go without talking to you."

"It's getting late," she said nervously. "I can't be out like this."

"I'll walk you home."

"No, no. I mean—"

"I insist. Look what happened last time you tried to go home by yourself." He looked her in the eye. "Afterward, if it's just a matter of not wanting my company . . . well, I'll understand. But—"

"No, no." She reached out impulsively and touched his hand. "It's not that."

As her hand rested on his, a shiver ran through her. She tried to draw her hand away, but he quickly closed his huge hand around it. She looked in his eyes again, and what she saw there made her heart go out to him. *He's so good,* she thought suddenly. *He has a good heart.*

His thumb softly stroked the back of her hand.

"Tuya," he said, "I won't take no for an answer. Not on the matter of seeing you safely through the streets." He looked at the western sky. "Sundown is minutes away. It won't be safe for you to be out alone."

The pressure of his fingers increased slightly. It was as if a great warmth were flowing between them. "When I let you go before," he said in a low and husky voice, "I cursed myself six ways for a fool. The only thing I knew was that you were sometimes in this market. I thought: Idiot! How could you let her go like that!" He shook his head ruefully. "As the days went by, I thought that I'd lost you altogether, that all I'd have left was a memory."

She tried in her own turn to smile. "You're a soldier," she said. "Soldiers come and go. You must have many such memories stored away. Unless you've forgotten them by now."

Hurt came into his eyes. "That's unfair," he said.

Instantly she was ashamed, and drew away. "You're right. I'm sorry. After all you've done for me, I had no right—I . . . I was just flustered and didn't know what to say. I didn't mean to—"

He smiled. "Never mind. But I'm not letting you out of my sight unless you drive me away." He stood in deep shadow now, up to his face. She looked at the good mouth, the deep brown eyes. Those eyes . . . "Some women don't like soldiers, Tuya. We have a bad reputation. I have to admit, a lot of us deserve the bad name we have."

"No, no, that's not it," she said. "I'm afraid I can't explain just now why I can't let you take me home. I want us to talk, too, really I do. I know! The top of that building there . . . if we went up there right now, we'd see the sunset. Come."

Together they walked to the stairway on the side of the warehouse. As they went up the stairs their bodies touched once, twice. There was the same shivering, the same thrill each time. Atop the building, on the flat, wall-enclosed roof, they stood looking out over the city to where the sun poised for its dive into the western haze.

A light breeze stirred the palm fronds above the little square. The sun, now a dull, elongated ball, painted the sky with bright strokes of purple and red. Darkness hovered over that last stripe of light in the western horizon. Tuya moved closer to Baliniri, took his arm. Their hips touched; their thighs. A shiver ran through her again. It would have been so easy to run into his arms and let him hold her tight.

"Isn't it lovely?" she said. "I'm so glad we came up here. And it means so much more, sharing it."

Their fingers intertwined. She felt the great strength in his broad, callused hand. "At first I had the best of intentions," he said with a slow sigh. "I was going to leave town the moment we'd paid our respects at court. . . ."

He let his words hang in the air. She looked up, saw his rugged face in profile.

"There's no work for a soldier here?" she asked. Her bare foot touched, for a second, his sandaled one beside it. She pulled it back.

"Not for one who doesn't like training troops," he said. "Just between the two of us, my dear Tuya, the days of war are largely over around here." He shook his head, eyes on the fading sun. "There *is* a war going on in Nubia now. That's where Mekim wants us to go."

"And you?" she asked. She turned her face up toward his, towering above her. "You don't want to go to Nubia?"

He turned and took both her hands in his. "In a way I must. I'm a soldier. I became one as a child, pressed into service. I've known virtually no other life. And I'm even rather famous back in Mesopotamia. I don't know how to do much of anything else. If I were to stay here, with no war in sight, I'd become a guardsman or I'd train Baka's troops for him. He asked me, only today. But I don't know if that would make me happy."

*Ye gods,* she thought. *He knows Baka! If he knows Baka, I couldn't . . .*

"But I couldn't leave," he admitted helplessly. "Not until I'd seen you again. I felt something when we first met, and when I look at you now, I feel the same way. I'm not new to women, Tuya, but I've never had such a strong reaction. That little face of yours has haunted me day and night."

Suddenly she was in his arms, hugged close to his heart. He lifted her to sit on the roof's wall and held her close, close. She felt his heart beating through her tunic, his warm breath in her hair. His lips brushed her eyes, her ear. When her arms closed around his neck, his lips found hers. *Oh, gods above,* she thought. *How can this be happening to me?* "Baliniri," she whispered, gently pulling away. His heart was pounding, pounding! Or—was that hers?

The muscles of his great arms went rock-hard. And now he was covering her face with kisses. "Oh, my dear. My very dear one . . ."

Tuya pushed gently against his chest. "Please," she pleaded weakly.

Then, as suddenly as he had embraced her, he lifted her, put her down again, let her go, stepped back. "I am sorry," he said. "I let myself get carried away. I want nothing from you that is not freely given."

Now it was her turn to embrace him, although she only reached halfway up his chest. She held him, felt the strong muscles of his back. Her arms did not reach all the way around, even with his great arms free. She patted his back. "No, no," she said. "*I've* offended *you*. And it's the last thing in the world that I want to do." She hugged him close. "You're such a sweet man. Baliniri, you deserve more than I can give you. If I could . . . If I were . . ."

An evening wind had struck up with the dying of the sun in the long valley, and her last words were blown away. His great gentle hands fell on her arms and peeled them away from his big body. In the moonlight she could see his slow, sad smile. "Well," he said. "Time to get you home, then, before the streets get really dangerous." He kissed her palm, then squeezed her hand—a friendly squeeze.

For a time, walking through the quiet streets in the

moonlight, they did not speak. Now and then their hands touched, swinging alongside each other. Finally Tuya could take it no more. She grabbed his hand and tugged him to a halt. "Baliniri," she said, "we've got to talk. I don't want to hurt you."

"Don't worry, Tuya," he said. "An old man I served under once told me that we men were a bunch of fools, thinking we'd chosen a woman when, in fact, it was they who did the choosing. I should have paid more attention. When I couldn't find you in the marketplace, I should have known."

She thought: *I wish I could surrender to my own impulses. I wish I didn't have to deal with my conscience.* "Baliniri, please. I *do* want to see you again. But it's so difficult. I have things that monopolize my mind just now." She held his huge hand to her breast. "If I had a little more time to sort out my thoughts . . . do you understand?"

He turned back to the road, releasing her hand. "I understand," he said, not understanding at all, and the tone of his voice tore at her heart.

"Baliniri, you've got to listen. I do care for you. More than you think. It's just that I'm not in a position where I can choose. If I were free—"

"Free?" he asked. "Are you a slave? I'll buy you." He stopped, looked down at her. "No? I've misread you again? Well, it doesn't seem to be my evening." He grinned self-mockingly, unpleasantly, a grin that did not reach his eyes. "Come on. I've got to get you home before—"

"I can't let you take me home." There. She had blurted it out. "Please, Baliniri, trust me. It doesn't mean I don't want you with me. You must let me go on alone. And not follow me. Please, my dear. No questions." She sighed bitterly. "Oh, if I could only tell you everything!"

He stood back, looked her in the eye. She could see his pained and distant expression quite clearly by the moonlight. "I'll be leaving in a couple of days. But I'll be back here again tomorrow, at sundown, in the square. I'll look here just once. If you come, I'll know how you feel. If you don't, I'll understand the way it is."

He bent and kissed her hand and was gone. With a sob she looked after him, her hand still burning where he had kissed it.

# III

Ahead, however, was the dark street: a whole block and a half of it, with only the dim light reflected off the building at the end of the passage to guide her steps. She squinted through the gloom. *I should have let Baliniri get me safely back into my home neighborhood.*

But of course that was the one thing she could not have done, not if she wanted to keep the secret of her strange double life. And what if a neighbor saw them together? If Ben-Hadad were to find out . . .

Walking cautiously, feeling each step, she moved slowly down the long, narrow street. She stopped dead. What was that sound behind her? She froze against the wall, hardly daring to breathe, waiting for the sound again. The memory of her recent attack was horribly vivid in her mind. *Please,* she prayed, *don't let it be—*

But just then a hairy, hard little shape pressed against her bare thigh, and a rough tongue licked her calf. Her heart skipped a beat. "Lion!" she said joyfully. "Where have you been, old fellow?"

The dog moved out into the middle of the path, then stood, only partly visible, waiting for her. His stubby tail wagged furiously.

"All right," she said in the same low voice. "I could have a lot worse company on the way home. I wouldn't be surprised if Ben-Hadad had told you to look out for me while he was gone." She set out after him, a little more confidently now.

But—Ben-Hadad! The thought struck like a white-hot knife in her heart. In truth, she had already betrayed him. Her heart had gone strongly out to the Mesopotamian soldier, and she wondered for a heart-stopping moment what it would be like to lie in his arms and feel his kisses all over her body, feel him entering her. . . .

*Stop that!* she told herself angrily, shamefaced.

Lion led her past the corner, where an overhead torch lit

the intersection of two important avenues, and into a new street she hadn't been in before.

"Ssssst!" The voice came from the shadows. She let out a stifled shriek of fear and alarm. Lion stopped, turned, growled. Tuya's hand went inside her garment to the long, razor-sharp knife hidden there. "W-who's there? Don't come any closer. . . ."

But the man now moved closer to the pool of light. "It's Hefget. You talked to me earlier today."

Her fingers remained on the hilt of the knife, but relaxed a bit. She peered at him. "What do you want?" she asked warily.

"Don't be afraid," he said. "I talked to my superior. I explained your motives for wanting to help out with—well, with what we were talking about." His eyes looked cool and shifty in the half-light, but his voice had a not unfriendly ring to it. "There might be a thing you could do for us, something that requires a sharp eye and an ability to see without being seen."

For some reason she was suddenly wary again. "What do you want me to do?"

"Come over here," he said. Lion growled and crouched, ready to leap. "Call the dog off."

"Down, Lion!" The dog moved back, but stood watching the two of them. "I'm as close as I want to come. Tell me whatever it is from there."

"I just don't want my words to carry." He looked both ways and lowered his voice. "There's a stranger in the neighborhood. He could be a spy. We do know he met with a high official of the government earlier today. He may be reporting on what he's learned in the bazaars. If he is, we need to know about it. Just follow him around. Keep your eyes and ears open, and report to me every day. On the quay, beside the dock where they unload the boats coming down from On. Just after dawn. You won't have time to get anything on him by tomorrow, so meet me the morning of the day after. And—keep your own counsel."

"All right. But this fellow I'm supposed to spy on. Who is he?"

"You won't have any trouble recognizing him. He's a foreigner, very large, a head or so taller than most men. A mercenary soldier from Mesopotamia named Baliniri."

* * *

There was a party at the inn where Baliniri and Mekim were staying. Extra lamps and candles had been put out; there were decorations up on the walls and hanging from the ceiling. The servant let Baliniri in, recognizing him; but it was obvious from his manner that no one else would be allowed inside. In the big room thirty or more men, all habitués of taverns and acquaintances of Mekim's, were drinking from leather bottles, roaring out the off-color verses of the lusty drinking song the players of flutes, shawms, and kitharas were playing. In the middle of the room a dark-skinned woman danced, her costume no more than a veil or two left around her waist. As Baliniri entered she cast him a look of desire and removed yet another veil. Her brown belly gyrated voluptuously. He could see the thin film of sweat on her dark-nippled breasts.

His partner, Mekim, was sitting behind a table, a half-naked tavern slut on his knee, his hand clutching her thigh. "Mekim!" he bellowed. "What's going on here?"

"Ah!" he said. "Baliniri! Come on over here!" He held up his empty leather bottle and called loudly for more wine.

Baliniri stood, hands on hips, looking down at him. The girl on Mekim's lap was as intoxicated as the little mercenary was; her dress had fallen away from one shoulder, and one brown breast peeked out at him.

"A little bonus from Mad—from a friend of yours, whom you did some sort of f-favor today." Mekim hiccuped; the girl fell off his lap to the ground. "He sent a fat purse over by a messenger. I thought it was enough to allow us a good-bye party."

"Good-bye party?" Baliniri let out a disgusted snort. "How much has this cost?"

"Half the purse," Mekim said, looking around for the girl, but she had been picked up by another man, and this one had worked the other strap of her garment down and was fondling her enthusiastically. "Don't worry. There's still plenty of money left to outfit us for our trip to Nubia. Have yourself some fun! Grab a girl and sit down. Or lie down, or whatever."

Baliniri looked around him. Two of the partygoers were indeed locked in amorous embrace over in the corner, on the floor. Under the lights in the center of the room the dancer now removed her last veil, and her dance entered an even more frantic phase. A look of ecstasy came over her face. Candlelight gleamed on the film of sweat that ran down her back into the cleft between her full buttocks. As he watched, she began to shake again, her rear end twitching seductively.

He blinked, exhaled, as she turned to face him. Totally alienated, Baliniri found himself looking at the revelry as if he were a displaced spirit from the netherworld, unused to humanity and its strange ways.

It all looked so stupid. Vulgar. He felt sickened, and yet this was the sort of evening he would have enjoyed immensely only a little while before. Only a few weeks ago, he would have grabbed the naked little dancer, made off with her to the corner, and, with enough drinks in him, taken her right there in the middle of the floor, with everyone watching. He would have laughed and sung as loudly as anyone, gotten as drunk as Mekim, and futtered six women before the night was over.

What was the matter with him? He looked at the dull faces of the drinkers. He saw them as poor devils, lonely, benighted. And the women: pitiable creatures eking out a harsh living in a difficult time, showing their bodies to drunken fools, giving themselves to whoever wanted them during the course of the evening, pretending to like it. He wondered if they went out into the street afterward, to wash away the unwanted drunken kisses with well water, to wash away the odors of lovemaking, to wash away, if they could, the memories of the night.

He shuddered. *Am I growing old?* he wondered. He remembered, suddenly, having stood at the window in Avaris and watched old Kirakos look down with such longing at the young matron he had bought at the slave market. Now, instead of thinking Kirakos a fool, a senile dolt, he understood why the old man, moved by memories too profound to express, had looked on the woman's graceful body and wept.

Somehow, in the last few days, he had been given a gift of empathy that he had only suspected in himself before this—a gift or a curse; he could not say which. Whatever it was, he was helpless before it. He was not the same man he had been. And it had been caused by falling in love.

There was one thing about love: It grabbed you when you least expected it, when you were least well defended against it. And look at him now. What a fool he had made of himself, forcing himself on Tuya that afternoon in such a stupid and clumsy way! He was no better than any of them, the drunks or the whores, no less pitiable, no less contemptible.

*Tuya*, he thought, *if only* . . .

Suddenly, with savage motion, he grabbed the bottle out of Mekim's hands and drank deeply. The wine spilled down the side of his mouth and stained his robe. He wiped his mouth with the back of his hand and, gritting his teeth, threw one arm around the naked little dancer, pulling her roughly to him. "Musicians!" he bellowed in a voice full of smothered rage. "Can't you play any louder? Can't you play any faster?"

## IV

Madir's customary morning divan had been canceled. In its place he had scheduled an emergency meeting of his highest ranking advisers—men from the great houses of the nobility, the powerful landowners, the hereditary rulers of the southern nomes, the priesthood. The army was represented by Baka, and the others attending were of comparable rank in the hierarchy of the Red Lands.

Sitra scurried around arranging chairs as the advisers arrived one by one. It was of surpassing importance that each man be seated in exact accordance to his rank, and Sitra had been planning the matter ever since Madir had announced the meeting the afternoon before. Even so, he checked and rechecked the seating plans, making quite sure no guest received less than his proper due.

Now, as he stepped back to survey his handiwork, they were coming into the great reception hall, each attended by his servant: Pentu, who owned the greater part of the land and buildings in the middle-class quarter where most of the government workers of rank lived; Sokar, chief priest of Osiris, the most powerful man in the state religion; Montu, owner of the state's finest vineyards; Akhethotep, a great landowner from the Fayum, with his neighbors and fellow agricultural tycoons Dagi, Pabasa, and Idu.

Sitra frowned; still missing were Madir and Baka. It bothered him, not knowing where they were, because they were talking somewhere in the palace, far from his listening ears. He sniffed and pouted.

Unable to vent his displeasure on the real offenders, he approached the servants of the Fayum landowners and said in his high, piping voice, "Sorry. No servants here. No slaves."

Dagi reacted quickly, bristling. "Indeed? By whose orders?"

"The lord Madir's, your grace. He specifically ordered this. Sorry, but no exceptions." He bowed, not a little insolently.

"The very idea," Pabasa said, dismissing his slave. "Well, this had better be important, calling us out on such short notice."

"It's very important, I'm sure," Sitra said. "The subject . . . I'm not at liberty to discuss it." This was true enough; for a change, he had no idea at all of the intended subject matter. Perhaps it had something to do with that foreigner Madir had interviewed a couple of days before—although the interview had seemed harmless enough. "It may just be that all four of you lords of the Fayum were in the city at the same time. That happens all too seldom. Perhaps the lord Madir wanted to take advantage of the occasion."

"Well, that makes some sense," Idu said. "But I do hope he gets on with it. I'm a very busy man."

Sitra did not answer. Instead he looked around him at the patrician faces. *Which one is it?* he wondered, for perhaps the fiftieth time. Pentu, elderly and soft-spoken; Sokar, still strongly built in his sixties, cold-faced, basilisk-eyed; Akhethotep, his hawk features set in a perpetual sneer. The conspiracy had a second man—at least a second man, perhaps more—in this council besides himself. But it was an unbroken rule that no one was to know who it was. *Does he know that I'm in the conspiracy?* Sitra wondered.

From a curtained window that gave out on the gallery, Baka looked down, unseen. "They're all here," he said. "I wonder which one it is."

"I don't know," Madir answered. "I doubt if Sitra himself knows. That's the way they're running things. An uncommonly intelligent adversary, all in all. It's cost me a fortune in bribes, assassinations, kidnappings, and interrogations to find out what little I do know. Now my sources have run into a granite wall. I know that the one who's here, other than Sitra—if indeed there's not more than one—may very well be their leader, who wears the Sobek mask in their meeting."

Baka's eyes widened. "Then what's to stop us from simply casting our net right now, if we know he's here?"

Madir smiled thinly; as usual, his heavy-lidded eyes were unreadable. "We could. And we could have the same sort of revolution on our hands that Salitis has in the delta. And remember: He has that huge army to put down a revolt with. We have . . ." He held up his hands in a dismissive gesture.

Baka nodded ruefully. "I see your point. Half the army would bolt and go over to the other side. They're still bitter toward us, those who had family or friends in Memphis when it fell. Understandable, of course."

"Yes," Madir said. "As it is, keep an eye on all of them. Watch their reactions to our announcement. Watch their eyes."

"Yes, sir," Baka said.

Madir held up one finger in a cautionary gesture. "Only one of them—the conspirator—will know in advance that I intend to announce total government control over the whole means of food production. I hope his reaction won't be quite the same as the others'."

"I see," Baka said. "But only the four are from the Fayum. Why—"

"Montu has silent holdings there through his wife's family. Pentu is the chief member of a group that banded together to purchase water rights for half the arable lands. Sokar—" He hesitated for a moment. "Sokar is the spokesman for the priesthood. The state religion lost all its delta lands when we retreated upriver. But they now control not only lands in the Fayum but levies on the lands of others."

"Ah, yes. This is more than just a threat to them."

"Watch Sokar even more closely than the others. Let me tell you, I'd be relieved to hear that he reacted in honest astonishment," Madir said, a look of apprehension clouding his face.

Baliniri sat up and looked around the tavern with horror and disgust. His head hurt. He had a foul taste in his mouth. Beside him, the little dancer snored loudly, her mouth wide open, her hair a rats' nest. By the morning light, imperfections that had seemed charming the night before now struck him as loathsome. He shuddered. A raving beauty would look bad just now, because of his present vile state of mind. No one but Tuya would satisfy him.

He shuddered again, hating himself.

He looked around. Mekim slept happily on the floor, his head resting on the bare rump of the flute player. Around the room men and women, all nude, slept, sprawled out in awkward and unflattering positions. The floor was covered with spilled food, discarded clothing, puddles of wine.

He got up unsteadily, staggered over to the door that led up to the rooftop. He squinted at the sudden glare as he opened the door, but forced himself to walk out onto the roof, naked as he was. Across the street, on another rooftop, a young matron saw him and giggled. He looked around. There had been a little rain in the morning hours, and a basin on the roof had enough water to cover the bottom. He picked this up and upended it over his head, letting the water splash down over his dirty, befouled body. The young matron's laughter grew louder. He cursed and went back inside. On the floor, his dancer yawned cavernously, scratched her pubis, rolled over, and went back to sleep.

*What am I doing here?* Baliniri asked himself. He looked around, found his loincloth, put it on. His sandals were a little harder to find, but he located them. He reached for his tunic, but someone had vomited all over it. Perhaps himself, for all he knew. He grimaced and felt like vomiting here and now. He tossed the tunic aside, scowled, then remembered that the big fellow over in the corner was about his size. What had *he* been wearing last night? Oh, yes, there it was: the robe trimmed in blue. He walked slowly toward the corner. Every sudden movement made his head ache worse. Baliniri put the robe on, then looked around the room once more before heading for the door.

It wasn't just this scene before him. *Everything* looked stale and repellent and worthless these days. *Everyone* looked ugly and disagreeable. He, who had taken such pleasure in the bodies of women for so long . . .

*Ah! Tuya! Tuya!*

He closed his eyes for a moment and suddenly saw her: tiny and clear-eyed and honest and fearless. He opened his eyes, tried to bring back her image. Was she pretty? Was she graceful? He could not say. He only knew that he was in love with the total person, not a collection of attributes. She had the power to affect him in a way no other woman had ever affected him. He wondered if he could live without her. He was not sure. He had not been sure ever since their first meeting. If she rejected him . . . if she did not come to the marketplace tonight . . .

The meeting broke up in sullen, hostile silence. Pentu's icy glare swept across Madir and Baka; he nodded curtly to them and went out. Sokar nodded to Montu; the two went out together. The four men from the Fayum straggled out, Pabasa with Akhethotep, Dagi with Idu. Baka's eye caught Madir's; the moment he knew Sitra was out of sight, he shrugged as if to say *Sorry: I couldn't tell.* The advisers' reactions had all been much the same: incredulity, outrage, bewilderment, all stirred together into an unaccepting stew. He bowed to Madir and went out.

In the vestibule he met Tuya, dressed in a spotless white robe, bewigged, bejeweled—a wealthy young matron. "Tuya!" he exclaimed. "What brings you here?"

She looked to right and left worriedly, beckoned him into a corner. "The conspiracy. You told me to keep my eyes open."

"Here," he said, and steered her to a far corner he knew to be an acoustic dead spot. As he did, he saw Sitra's eyes on the two of them, and he positioned Tuya away from Sitra's line of vision. Had the secretary seen Tuya well enough to recognize her? "Now," Baka said. "What did you say?"

"This conspiracy," she said agitatedly. "I think I may have a line into something."

"What do you mean?" He looked over her shoulder; Sitra was still watching.

"I may be able to get inside it. If I—"

"Tuya! No! This thing is very dangerous. Stay out of it, please. I only wanted to know if you'd heard anything."

"I haven't. One of them has asked me to shadow someone. If I do it, I'll probably be in their good graces. They'll trust me. But the person they've asked me to shadow—"

"Tuya! Stay away. I mean it!" He put his hands on her shoulders and looked her hard in the eye. "It's too much. It's too serious. Big things are going on here."

"I know," she said miserably. "It's precisely because I do know how serious all this is that I feel I have to do something."

"No! Absolutely not!"

\* \* \*

The afternoon came and went. Tuya had sat unmoving in the same chair in the middle of her bedroom for over an hour, thinking how much easier it would all be if she could just obey Baka's suggestion! She could just drop it all; go back to being the lonely little housewife.

Above all, she could try to forget Baliniri. She would never have to see him again, never have to struggle with her conscience, never be tempted to betray Ben-Hadad again—whether in her heart or in the flesh.

*Yes, and then what?* her mind said. *Go back to being a neglected wife whose husband doesn't love her anymore? Go back to loneliness and unhappiness and despair? And turn aside real love when it's offered to you? Cast away a man whose love for you is evident in every word he says, every look he gives you?*

She sighed, stood up, and reached for the old-clothes box on the shelf beside her bed. She held up the ragged tunic, hesitated, threw it on the bed. She was about to turn away, but then, with a great sigh, she unfastened the brooch that held her robe. It fell to the floor at her feet, leaving her naked, staring down at the torn garment on the bed. A great shudder of some emotion she could not name ran through her. She picked up the rags and put them on.

## V

The sun was high when Hefget finally made his way to the door of the abandoned warehouse near the city wall where the meeting was to take place. He had made sure no one had followed him; the meeting—evidently an emergency—had been called in the daytime for the first time. This made him, and the others invited to it, more vulnerable than usual.

He knocked: three times, pause, two times, pause, three more. The guard let him in quickly. "Go in right away," he said. "They're all there, and already in session."

As Hefget entered the back room, the Sobek figure was speaking: ". . . intends to do pretty much what Salitis has done in the delta, if with a bit more finesse. It's the finesse that we have to worry about. Salitis's blundering has caused him trouble already, for all our spies tell us. Madir will take the same measures, and people will hardly notice they're being done. The results will lead to disaster, make no mistake about that."

The man in the mask of Khnemu, the ram-god of the Nile, leaned forward. "We have no choice but to submit?" he asked.

"No," the Sobek mask said. "I was at the meeting with Madir. Later in the day I approached one of the Fayum landowners, after he'd had time to talk it over with his friends. All four of them were understandably upset. The one I talked to may join us, once it's all had time to sink in."

The Horus mask nodded. "And what are the chances then of him talking to his friends? Of their support? After all, they have more to lose than anyone else."

"A very good chance, I think. But on the other hand, there's our coup to think of. If things go according to plan, seeking their support may be no more than asking them to approve of actions already taken. The time for the festival of Ptah-Sokaris-Osiris approaches apace." He looked around at all the masked faces, then at the row of lesser, unmasked members like Hefget and Mereb. "Which brings up an interesting question . . ."

"Which is?" the Khnemu figure said.

"There is reason to believe that this Joseph, the seer Salitis has chosen as his vizier, may be a genuine prophet. What if Salitis and Madir were doing the wise thing by seizing the means of production and warehousing grain against a very real famine? Would it then be wise for us to interrupt and cancel Madir's plans?" He paused to let his words sink in, then went on. "If there *were* no rain for seven years, what then?"

There was no answer; they were all thinking it over. He went on: "Salitis would control us if we had not done as he did. He could demand our surrender in exchange for food."

"What are you suggesting?" the Horus figure asked.

"That we allow the takeover to take place," the Sobek figure said softly, "and that when it has been accomplished, then we seize power." There was a sudden shocked sigh around the room. He continued: "Everything remains the same. Except that instead of Madir saving the Red Lands, *we* will have saved the Red Lands—we, who will then control all means of production."

\* \* \*

As the meeting broke up, Mereb drew Hefget aside. "I heard from Sitra. He mentioned that Baka has had several clandestine meetings lately that for one reason or other he was unable to eavesdrop on. Madir. Some court woman, who drew him aside for furtive conversation. The big Mesopotamian—"

"That's what I wanted to talk to you about. I've got someone shadowing the Mesopotamian. Now don't get angry, but it's someone new. A tough little street urchin who lost her boyfriend in the fall of Memphis. She's very bitter against the government. She wants revenge."

"You discussed things with a *woman*?"

"It'll work all right. Trust me. She's a thief—the best I've ever seen. She could steal your shadow out from under you, and you'd never miss it until an hour before sundown."

"But if she knows—"

"She'll know only what I tell her, and that won't be much. So far I've only told her we need someone to follow the Mesopotamian fellow around and report on him to us. She only knows me. There's no risk involved."

"Except for you. And whomever you happen to know. Including me, remember."

"You don't trust me? Me?"

"Well . . ."

"Lion!" Tuya said. "Go away! I can't have you following me around just now. Go home!"

The little dog backed away, but stood his ground, tongue lolling, his tail wagging good-naturedly. Tuya stamped her bare foot in the dust, angrily. Sometimes he could be so difficult! She poised to grab him, but he backed away just in time.

"Lion! I'm going to tie you up. So help me I am." She thought a moment, then she jumped in the air and yelled loudly. The dog leapt back, but came to rest no more than another body length away. There he stood, his short tail still wagging furiously.

"Oh, I give up. Do what you wish." Hands on hips, she scowled at the animal.

What an annoyance! Here she was, about to start out ingratiating herself with Hefget and his band of conspirators, and she couldn't shake a little dog—one that could, if she were unlucky, allow her to be traced back to her home neighborhood, could ruin her disguise. How could she do as Hefget had asked her to, if—

The thought came unbidden: *Come now, Tuya. You're not just doing your duty toward Hefget. You're not just spying on the conspirators. You are really serving yourself, because you know that's what you really want. You want—*

She shut her eyes tight, gritted her teeth. No! No! That was not it at all! She was doing what she had to. She was—

*Fool! Liar! Pretender! Admit what you're doing! Admit it!*

Through clenched teeth she denied it once more. "No! No! That's not it at all!"

When she opened her eyes, the dog was gone.

*Now. Now's your chance. Down the street, now, before he comes back.*


"Oh, go on," Baliniri said to his companion. "Take the rest of the money. Go have yourself another night of it. I don't care. Spend it all. There'll always be more."

"Not if you won't get back to soldiering," Mekim said. "Look, Baliniri, roistering is part of soldiering. If you don't enjoy the one, you're not going to be able to put up with the other."

"You say that because you sleep it off easily. For some reason when I've had too much to drink, I'm really punished for it the next day. Headaches, a bad stomach. Worst of all, though, is the way I feel inside. Dirty. Soiled. Diseased."

"Oh, come now. You're turning into a real goody-goody."

"I can't help the way things are."

"Aw, Baliniri. Why can't things just go on as they were?"

Baliniri scowled. Mekim would never change. But that was the trouble, was it not? He, Baliniri, he *had* changed. The whole rhythm and texture of his life, his needs, his tastes, and wants had changed. And there was nothing he seemed to be able to do to reverse it. It was as much beyond his control as was the fact that Mekim was still his old self and showed no intention or inclination to alter himself.

*I'm getting old*, he thought.

Perhaps that was it. Old, for a professional soldier, was anything much over twenty-five. After the newness began to wear off, proper caution, self-preservation, and confidence began to seep in. Then came a strange world-weariness, an inability to enjoy the old sensual pleasures.

"Well," Mekim said lamely, "I guess I'll go on then. I won't be back tonight. I'll go up to the House of the Golden Lantern, I suppose. It sure would be nice if—"

But he left it there. And, with a sheepish grin, a little

reluctantly, he turned and walked slowly away. Baliniri watched him go, and there was sadness in his own heart. Mekim had been a good comrade, a good soldier. It would be a pity to break up so fine a partnership. He would never be able to find a better man to stand beside him in a fight, whether in the field or in a back alley. He was loyal, valiant, resourceful.

Well, what was the use thinking about all that? It was what he himself was not that mattered now. Perhaps he, Baliniri, was no good for the whole life of a mercenary soldier itself.

Well, what *was* he good for? He would never make a courtier, he was sure. Just a glimpse of Madir's court—and more than a glimpse of Salitis's, over in the delta—reminded him how much he had hated life at Hammurabi's court, back in the Land of the Two Rivers.

He scowled and kicked a rock in front of his sandal. His thoughts a heavy burden, he began walking slowly toward the Market of the Four Winds. While they had argued, the shadows had grown longer. In a while the fat moon would rise over the river.

If she came tonight . . .

If she *did not* come tonight . . .

He stopped dead, his eyes staring at nothing. What if she did not come tonight? What could he do? How would he handle it? But she could not decide not to! She *couldn't*.

But of course she could. After all, who was he? A big oaf who could plan a campaign and lead men in battle. He had never given the smallest sign of being any good at anything but killing and fighting. Could he make a living once he had left the army? Could he build a house, settle down, raise children? He had never had a relationship with a woman that had lasted more than a few days, not even in the days back at Hammurabi's court, when he had tried his best to become the kind of show officer the great king had wanted him to become.

He spat into the street angrily and set out again through the curving avenues. As he did, he happened to look down and spot the little Canaanite dog again—the one he had seen the night before, hanging around Tuya! Perhaps she was here, then?

He hurried forward, following the little animal as it half walked, half trotted, through the streets. The shadows grew longer every moment. He stepped up the pace.

And then he looked up at the top of the same staircase they had ascended the night before.

Tuya was there, standing waiting for him. Barefoot, wigless, very plain. But there was her natural grace, her quiet dignity. Looking at her, he knew it was enough and was sure he would not have wanted her any other way. There was a sweet half smile on her face as she stood waiting for him. "You've come," he said in a hoarse voice.

Her lip trembled. She looked as though she were going to cry. "Yes," she said. "Oh, yes."

# VI

There was another one of those sunsets. This time he could not have paid attention if his life depended on it. All he could see was what the fading rays of the sun, coming at that low angle over the top of the city wall, did for her tanned skin, for those dark eyes, bright now with fearful anticipation, with something else he could not name.

"You came," he said again, taking her tiny hands in his. "I'm so glad."

"I wasn't sure I would," she admitted. "I'm afraid. I don't know what to think." She looked up at him, her eyes flickering over his face. "You said you wanted me. I don't know why anyone would want me. I'm nobody, nothing."

"Nobody?" he asked. He let go of one of her hands to run one hand gently over her hair, coming to rest on her cheek. "It's funny—I was just thinking that about myself. I mean, look at me, all beat up like this, all covered with scars. I've never owned anything but the clothes on my back, and toys to kill people with. The one time I had a bit of money, a bit of security, I threw it away as fast as I could because I was afraid of it."

"No, Baliniri, you're beautiful." Her voice trembled, and she squeezed his hand.

"Let's get away from here," he suggested. "Where we can be alone."

"Yes, somewhere we can talk," she said. "I don't care where. I just want to be with you again."

He thought a moment. "My partner won't be back tonight. We have rooms at an inn. I could have the owners send up dinner."

She mastered the fear and doubts that assaulted her. "Yes," she whispered. "Anything. Anywhere." Suddenly she pressed herself close to him. "But hold me, please, just for a moment. Now. I'm so afraid."

His arms went around her. "I know. This has never happened to me before, and I'm not sure I know quite how to handle it, either. I do know that we can't ignore it, though. It won't go away. It will be all right. Come. Come, now. We have a lot of talking to do." He stopped, stepped back, looked at her, an incredulous grin on his face. "Come. We can watch the moon rise over the river from the rooftop, back at my inn. Nobody will bother us."

"Good," she said. "I want to know you. I want to know all about you."

And as he embraced her again, her heart was beating fast, and her mind was racing even faster. *You little fool!* she told herself. *What are you letting yourself in for? What about your husband?*

But she choked the thought off angrily, and tried, desperately, to lie to herself about her reasons for coming.

The innkeeper sent up wine, dates, olives, bread. Baliniri and Tuya stood on the rooftop, their sides touching all the way down his leg and hers, his great right arm enfolding her, her right hand intertwined with his left. On the river the great moon shimmered. Below in the street the sounds of the city winding down its day had grown softer. Down the way someone plucked a kithara and sang softly in a lilting contralto:

> Disturb me not, O swallow!
> I have found my love in his bed;
> My heart leapt up when he spoke to me:
> "I shall not go away from thee.
> My hand is in thy hand.
> We shall walk together,
> I shall be with thee forever."

Tuya listened, shivered. She moved closer, turned her face up to his. She saw his smile in the moonlight. He picked her up, as easily as if she had been a baby, and set her down on the top of the roof wall. And now, still holding her so that she could not fall, he leaned forward and kissed her.

The kiss was soft, gentle. Their lips barely met. Then his lips went to her cheek, her eyes, her ear. The kisses grew slowly more insistent; more impassioned. They roved over her face, her neck, the hollow of her throat. She leaned forward, thrust her breasts against his face, held him close there.

"Oh," she said. "Oh, Baliniri, if I—"

Suddenly she found herself trembling uncontrollably. Her skin was on fire. "*Oh, gods,*" she said. The wind blew softly against her sensitized skin. He unpinned her garment and slowly pulled it away from her body. He caught her up in one arm and drew her tunic down, past her legs, tickling her as it fluttered to the ground. She could feel the breeze on her bare back, her sides, her shoulders, her bosom.

She was naked with him, and his hands—hard and yet so soft—were on her. His mouth found her breasts, kissing, teasing, first one, then the other. She pressed herself against him, threw her arms around his neck.

"Now. Please," she said in a voice she could barely recognize as her own.

His kiss took her breath away. She gave herself wholly up to it. Her body was afire with desire. He again picked her up, softly, as if she were a tired child being taken to bed, and carried her into the open room behind her, to the cushions on the floor where, lit only by flickering candles, he set her gently down and threw his own garment aside. His body was massive, barrel-chested, broad-shouldered, like some great bronze statue of a god, towering over her.

He lowered himself onto the cushions beside her. She pressed herself to him, and he took her in his powerful hands and held her high above him as he rolled onto his back. He sat her down atop him, impaled her.

"Now," he said in a deep gentle voice. "Now, my dear." Filled, she rocked above him. His hands caressed arms and shoulders and breasts, and she could not have said which sensation was the more exquisite. Sensations she had never experienced before, had never dreamed about, began. She entered a different world, one unlike all her previous experience. Eyes closed, she rocked, reeled above him, beside herself, moaning softly.

"Now," he said. "Now. *Now.*"

Afterward, she curled atop him in a fetal ball, held firmly

and securely in his enormous arms, while he rocked her gently to and fro, humming a tiny wordless song.

When she was able to rouse herself, she craned her neck to kiss him on the chin. "Oh, Baliniri," she said. "I don't know what I could possibly ever do to deserve feeling the way I do just now."

He held her all the more tightly and hummed the song into the top of her head. "I was thinking," he said at last in a voice full of dreams, full of moonlight. "In a way I don't know you at all. I don't even know where you come from. But it's all right, because in an entirely different way I know you completely. I think I've always known you, that I always will know you. And when I die, and when I go to the next world, whatever it is, I think there'll be a place where I'll find you there. . . ."

Suddenly her duality was too much for her to bear, a red-hot knife in her heart. "Baliniri, I have to tell you. I—I'm not what I seem." She sat up suddenly, her voice tight and constricted as she spoke. "If you—"

"It's all right. I know there's something between us. But it's enough for me that you're here."

She shut her eyes, but this was not enough to keep the bitter tears back. "Oh, I feel so terrible. I can't . . . I can't—"

"It's all right," he said, hearing only what he desperately wanted to hear. "Here, lie back. I'll pour some wine, and we can eat some olives. After we have a bit to eat, we'll talk a while, and then . . ."

She stared wide-eyed. His hand was on her: gentle, proprietary. She smiled, picked up his other hand, and kissed it. "No," she said. "You stay here. I'll bring the food and the wine." And as she stood and stretched sensuously in the pool of cool light from the moon, she could feel the soft wind on her naked skin. The nearby candle flames danced on the bare body she was taking such pleasure in showing him.

"You're lovely," he whispered. "Beautiful." His words caressed her. "It's strange: If someone had asked me what you looked like beforehand, all I could have said was that you were small. I couldn't remember isolated details. All I could remember was you. And now, it's as if I were seeing you for the first time. And you're beautiful, Tuya. Beautiful . . ."

After a time he took her again, this time mounting her like a god come down from the skies, and with what little rational thought remained to her now she once again marveled at his harnessed strength, the extraordinary gentleness. This time was as sweet as it had been the first time, if less of a surprise. He had awakened in her soul potentialities of passion she had never known before. Ben-Hadad, the only man she had lain with, had hardly been more than a boy when they had come together. Baliniri was a *man*, a widely experienced man, one who could show her depths of feeling that even she had never suspected within herself. Despite the range of his experience, he was indisputably in love with her. To him she was something special, a goddess come down to earth in human form.

This haunted her, tore at her heart. She knew she did not deserve this. She was betraying her husband by committing adultery with another man, and she was betraying Baliniri by not telling him about Ben-Hadad; by loving him— yes, she did love him in a way—but not enough, not the way he deserved to be loved.

The thought caused her to pull away when he would have taken her a third time. "N-no, please," she said. "I can't. . . ."

He pulled back. "Did I hurt you?"

"No. Oh, no. No, my dear. If you could be patient with me . . ."

"It's all right." He took both her hands in his, smiled. "We'll just lie here and talk. Or would you like to sleep for a little while?"

"No, no." She pulled that great hand of his up to her lips and kissed it warmly, almost desperately. "No, my darling. But let me lie beside you. And hold me. Hold me tight. That's what I need right now. There'll be time for talking later."

She nestled against him, feeling the strong welcome weight of his arm atop her, feeling his hard thighs against her rump, his broad chest against her back, glorying in the welcome warmth and strength of him. Time for talking later? How ridiculous. There would be no time for anything. She would have to give him up—not because she had betrayed Ben-Hadad, although that alone was bad enough. It was much more serious than that. If she were not mistaking the symptoms, it was the one thing she had wanted most only months ago, but that now she would not even know how to handle.

She felt against her body a new hardness: strong, male. She shivered, unable to resist the powerful feeling that seized her. Almost desperately, she turned around to embrace him, to receive him. "Yes," she said in a voice heavy with despair. "Yes. Now. Please."

## VII

Morning light came too soon. With the first rays of the dawn Tuya was suddenly awake. There was no slow acclimation to consciousness; instantly the horror of her present predicament was upon her. She clenched her hands, bit her lip, closed her eyes again—trying to shut it all out, trying not to scream. The tension sent a violent tremor through her body. Still asleep, Baliniri stirred beside her.

She pulled out from under his great protective arm, thrown over her during the night, and moved off the cushions to sit up and look at him for a moment. His great square face was peaceful in the soft light, disarmed by sleep. She could see the childlike gentleness of him, which was usually subjugated by the strong male spirit within him. His breathing was deep; the lips that had kissed her hungry body all over lay open, and she could see one crooked tooth. It was not a flaw; it humanized his strong soldier's face as did the artlessness of sleep. Tousled hair hung down on his forehead.

*Oh, Baliniri,* she thought. *What am I going to do about you?*

But of course she knew. She would have to give him up.

*If you couldn't have come along back before Ben-Hadad, when I was free, why couldn't you just have stayed out of my life altogether?*

She reached out gently to stir that wayward hair on his forehead. It was their destiny. It would not have done for him to come along before she had met Ben-Hadad, because she had had no sense of herself back then. She might not even have thought well enough of herself to aspire to a man like him, and because of that, she would not have attracted him—men were attracted to women who thought well of themselves.

Ben-Hadad's love had taught her to value herself, to find something in herself that a good man might love. Destiny. She had become someone—and she had drawn his attention —at just the wrong time. It was hopeless. The only thing to do was to leave him and try to forget everything. . . .

But she would never forget. Never. This night, the hours spent in his arms, the quiet small talk about the life he had led, ignoring his hurt when she would not speak to him with the same openness. . . .

Ah! How it hurt! The more precious the memory, the more it would hurt to recall it.

She rose, looked down at him again, and reached for her garment. Holding it, she stood, relishing for one more moment the thought of being naked with him and feeling reluctant to clothe herself, wishing against all her better judgment that his eyes were open, looking at her with love and desire . . . and then with a sigh she shrugged on the simple ragged tunic.

"Good-bye, Baliniri," she said in a whisper he would hardly have been able to hear even if he were awake. She tiptoed through the door to the roof and slipped down the stairs to the street.

She had gone no more than three steps before a harsh whisper beckoned her from an alleyway. "Ssssst!"

She wheeled around. "H-Hefget," she said, astonished. "You startled me."

He pulled her into the alley, spoke with enthusiasm into her ear. "On the first night?" he said. "Already you're sleeping with him? Gods! You're a fast worker, girl." He patted her on the arm. "What did you learn?"

She forced herself to stare him down. "I didn't have time. It was the first night. It was largely taken up with . . . other things." Her flesh crawled to speak of it with him; but there was no other choice. "You, uh, know how it is."

His leer made her feel like throwing up. "Yes, yes. Now listen, little one. This soldier's been to court. We want to know why. What'd he tell Madir. I assume you pleased him. He'll be seeing you again?"

"He was pleased. Yes." She wanted to go, but as she tried to pull away he held her. "Please," she said, "you're hurting my arm."

He held on, and his eyes bore into hers. "You're not losing your nerve, are you? We can't have anyone who isn't totally given over to our plan. If I thought for one moment that you were wavering—"

"No, no," she said hastily. "It was a long night. I'm tired. I didn't get much sleep." She pulled away now, rubbing her arm. "I'll, uh, get in touch with you the moment I've learned anything. In the meantime, go a little easy, eh? It's a measure of my devotion to the cause that I haven't stuck a knife in you for grabbing my arm like that. I'd have put my mark on anyone else."

He pursed his lips in thought for a moment or so before speaking. "Go about it as you will. But my people will want to hear about your progress at regular intervals, or they'll get suspicious. They don't know you, so they're wary. I don't know you, either, come to think of it. Your name. I don't know your name."

Tuya brightened a little. "That can be settled easily enough," she said, improvising quickly. "Call me Ti. And next time you have a meeting, take me along. Your people can all look me over and judge for themselves."

Hefget frowned. "Take you along?" he said. "I'll have to ask my superior about it. Perhaps after you've actually performed some real service for us—"

She bristled, tired as she was. "Service? I call last night service, my friend."

"Now, don't get angry. I appreciate what you're doing for us, but my friends are understandably cautious." He looked past the alley's edge, where the street was beginning to fill with people going to the well for water or to their jobs. "We can't talk here much longer. I'll expect you to check in with me daily, as we arranged, at dawn."

"All right. But remember what I said about the next meeting. I want them to get rid of this suspicion you say they have about me once and for all."

"I will," he said, and saluted her. They emerged from the alley into the street and went separate ways.

He started to leave the matter right there, and then hesitated. *What if she is a spy? I don't even know where she lives.* It was better to be safe than sorry, he decided. Imagine what harm an infiltrator could do to their organization. Imagine the trouble he would get into, for bringing her in as a member. They would kill him with the same weapon they had assassinated her with!

That settled it. He would have her followed day and

night until his suspicions were allayed or confirmed. The next time she came out of the soldier's apartment at dawn he, Hefget, would have a man shadow her.

Better safe than sorry.

But after two steps he stopped and looked after her, catching a last glimpse of her tiny form as she scurried down the lane. He tried to dismiss his suspicions. *Look, she's done what you asked her to do, and very quickly and efficiently, too, from the look of things. Take what you can get from her and stop worrying about it.*

Hurrying furtively through the streets, Tuya felt worse than ever. *Now look what you've done!* she thought. *You've ruined everything!*

Backed against the wall by Hefget, she had committed herself to seeing Baliniri again. But how could she go back to him? If Ben-Hadad had taken advantage of his prerogative as the husband of a barren wife and had had their marriage annulled, she would have been free to do whatever she liked about Baliniri's coming into her life.

But now it was different. She had new responsibilities. Even her husband's relationship to her had changed, whether he knew it or not.

She balled her hands into fists, turning a corner, and almost bowled over an old man walking heavily on a stick. "Sorry!" she said, but she did not stop and look to his welfare— there was no time, no time at all. Instead of returning at dawn, when she might get to her neighborhood without being seen, she was now returning a good many minutes later, when people were up and about. All she could hope was that no one would recognize her.

She *could not* leave Ben-Hadad for Baliniri now. She had missed her flux twice. To be sure, she had had false pregnancies before. But always there had been the doubt.

Now she knew, knew in her heart of hearts, that she was carrying Ben-Hadad's child. That meant that she had to return to him. It was her sacred duty.

*Gods!* she thought. *Please, please, get me out of this!* But the thought echoed hollowly in her mind, and there was no answer.

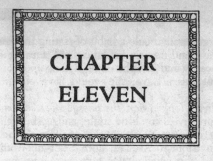

# CHAPTER ELEVEN

## Avaris

### I

Restless, nervous, frowning, Petephres, high priest of On, stood behind a screen in his town house in Avaris, watching the maids prepare his daughter for the wedding that would unite her, in less than an hour, with the second most powerful man in Lower Egypt.

*Well*, he thought, *she's pretty enough, especially by the standards of some benighted tribe up in Canaan. If this Joseph fellow finds fault with her, at least it won't be on that account.*

Now, as Asenath's personal maid, old Baket-amon, supervised the dressing of the girl in the traditional simple pleated white gown, her father's eyes wandered from the image of her virginal innocence to the naked bodies of the two slaves who assisted Baket-amon in her duties. The girls were not well matched; the elder of the two, Idut, was graceful, ripe in the buttocks, and long-legged, while the other—he had never learned her name—had an undistinguished body that, even naked, awakened no carnal thoughts. He would have to get rid of that one, or perhaps banish her to less prominent duties. The other . . . well, whether Idut knew it or not, she had a little tussle in bed with him in her future, one he was distinctly looking forward to. She turned now, artlessly displaying firm, high breasts; he licked his lips.

221

Petephres generally made a habit of tasting the flesh of every woman, slave and free, in his household, but somehow these two, the beauty and the plain one, had escaped his attentions so far. Idut was a slave; she would have no choice but to submit.

*Ah, there, look at her, the hussy. She's seen me watching her.* The girl gave a coy little smile, and as she walked around her young mistress to straighten her dress, she was for a moment invisible to Asenath and Baket-amon alike; in this split second she wiggled her bottom at him provocatively. Finishing her chore, she stood back—and shot him another glance, checking her effect on him. *The little slut! Won't I give her something to remember me by. . . .*

He shook his head, pursed his lips, and drove the thought from his mind for now. *Time enough for that later, once Asenath is safely delivered to her rich husband.* He watched the slaves fasten gold bracelets to his daughter's wrists and ankles and slip slender rings on her fingers and toes. Idly he wondered if anyone had given her any preparation for marriage—told her what her young husband might expect of her in the way of wifely duties. He suspected not. *Well, let her learn from her husband. My wife learned from me and was none the worse for it. Better for the boy to break her in for himself, the way he wants her.*

Tiring of watching, he wandered out into the great hall of the house. His brother-in-law Ersu was waiting for him; a slave had brought a jug of wine and two gold cups, and Ersu motioned to Petephres to share the wine with him.

He took the proffered cup, drank deeply, and looked around him. The town house had never pleased him; he preferred a bigger place like his villa at On, but there was little room for palaces within the city walls of Avaris. Well, let it be. With this advantageous marriage made, he would be able to do as Salitis had done for Joseph: have a block or so of middle-class houses razed to make room for a bigger house for him to entertain in. He took another gulp of the wine and turned to Ersu. "I'll be glad when it's all over," he confessed.

"She's almost ready?" Ersu asked.

"Ready as she'll get. I was just wondering what she knew of the ways of men and women. Slaves will talk, but that makes little difference. Talking about it isn't doing it. I'll wager she'll have a surprise or two in store for her when His Lofty Eminence gets her legs in the air for her."

Ersu winced at the manner in which Petephres spoke of his own daughter, but said nothing. "Does she even know what he looks like?" he asked, looking down at his cup and sloshing the wine idly back and forth.

"She's had a peek at him. Thinks he's beautiful. Well, he isn't a bad-looking chap, for a foreigner."

At the door a slave appeared, bowed. "My lord, the bearers and their escort have arrived."

"Good. Go tell Baket-amon to bring Asenath as soon as she's ready, will you?" He strolled to the window and looked down. "Ah, good. They've sent a couple of squads of troops to accompany her. Shepherd devils, burly and mean. I was apprehensive because of the recent attacks on, ah, people of our class in the streets."

"I know. Some bum threw a rock at me yesterday. Me! When they caught him, I had him flayed, of course. Only way to handle rebellion."

"We'll have more of his ilk to deal with in the months to come," Petephres said testily. "Unless we can talk Salitis into decisive action. There was another riot at one of the markets yesterday."

"The system has to be improved somewhat, you know. Terrible food shortages. The soldiers aren't getting enough food into the markets these days. That's a fact."

"That doesn't excuse rebellion, insubordination, and outright violence against the state. Come now, dear fellow. The unwashed must be kept in their place. Surely we all agree on that."

Ersu wasn't so sure. "Of course, you're, uh, right. But even a pack animal has to be fed regularly if you're going to get any work out of him."

"Yes, but there's no use feeding him when he's trying to kick your brains in or bite off a finger or two. Discipline must be established, whether we're talking about four-legged animals or two." Petephres helped himself to more wine. "It's getting late. What's keeping that daughter of mine, anyhow?"

Baket-amon made up Asenath's face, dipping unguents and dyes out of priceless boxes made of alabaster and obsidian. "Oh!" Asenath said, watching the process in a gold mirror. "I wish my nose weren't so long. He'll take one look at me and laugh."

"Your nose is perfect," the servant said. "Good heavens,

girl. You're a prize fit for royalty. Now, stop fidgeting and let me make up your eyes." Dipping a slender ebony stick into a gold-mounted jar, Baket-amon delicately spread the black cosmetic on the girl's smooth skin, outlining her large, meltingly beautiful brown eyes to call attention to their haunting quality. "There, now," she said. "Turn your head this way. Now that way. All right. Now for the necklace."

The slave girls brought out necklaces of amethyst, carnelian, lapis lazuli, and gold. "Which of these will my lady—" Idut began.

"No, no. The gold and turquoise one." The servant took the indicated necklace from a box of jewels, and the girl let her put the necklace around her neck. "I look like a painted doll," she said. "Do men really like women who look like this?"

Baket-amon stepped back to survey her handiwork. "He'll adore you. Don't worry. One would think you had no experience of men at all."

"But I haven't. You know that this is my first trip to the city. Father always kept me on the estate, and the only men I ever saw were priests. Most of them paid little attention to me. What the girls here tell me of men . . . why, it makes them sound like a bunch of horrible, barbaric animals."

Baket-amon turned on the two slaves, her eyes blazing. "Who's been talking to her about such things? You, Idut? I'll have the skin off your back for this! Do you have any idea how Petephres would react if he caught you filling her mind with your filthy drivel?"

"But I didn't—"

"Silence! I can tell from the guilty look on your face. Get out of here, both of you!"

"But—" Idut began petulantly, until she saw the look on the elder servant's face, and scurried away.

Asenath looked after them, noting Idut's slender legs, her pertly rounded bottom. Since the earliest days of puberty, Asenath, like others of her caste, had not been allowed to run around the house without clothing. *Am I that pretty with my clothes off?* she wondered. *Oh, if only I could see myself as others might see me . . .*

Baket-amon had been Asenath's personal maid long enough to guess what the girl was thinking. "You don't have to worry," the servant said. "You're smaller in the bottom than Idut, but you've a nice figure, very nice indeed, and a lovely, long neck. You could be mistaken for a queen—except that my lord Petephres tells me that queens seldom look quite as beautiful as the court painters would have you believe they do." She fussed with Asenath's wig, straightening it. "Now hold still."

Suddenly a wave of wild, unreasoning fear swept through the girl, and she closed her eyes and crossed her wrists protectively over her chest. "Oh, Baket-amon! I'm afraid! Going to live with a stranger! I don't want to go! I don't!"

"There, now, darling, it'll be all right. . . ."

"No! No! Why can't I just stay here? Why can't things just go on as they have? I don't want to grow up! Not if it means everything changing! Can't I go back to On? I was so happy there."

Baket-amon shook her head and wearily sat down opposite Asenath, taking the girl's hands in hers. "Look at you!" she said in a gentle voice. "You've spoiled your face with all those tears. I'll have to make your eyes up again." Asenath pulled her hands away and rubbed her streaming eyes.

"Look, darling," Baket-amon said. "Every girl is afraid just before her marriage. It's normal. But leaving home to become a wife is part of life. I didn't want to go to the husband my first master had chosen for me. My master had my bottom beaten with a switch until I could hardly sit down. I went willingly then, I must say. And my husband turned out to be a good and caring person, and we had a long and happy life together. Twenty-five years of it. If he hadn't taken the fever, during that spell of—" She sighed, stopped, started over again. "Darling, don't you want children? Little babies of your own? They're ever so much nicer than dolls." She stopped, thought for a moment, and added, "And worse. But mainly better."

"I don't know what I want, except to be left alone!" She covered her face with her hands and cried. The black kohl rolled down her cheeks in grotesque patterns.

"There, there, sweetheart. Don't fret. Everything will go so much better than you think it will. I've seen the young man. He's tall, slender as a reed, beautifully built. Very handsome, if in a way some local girls might find unfamiliar. There's red in his hair. Those people from up north can be very handsome people. The two of you will make beautiful children."

Asenath mastered herself now and saw herself in the

mirror for the first time. The sight provoked instant laughter that drove away the tears. "Oh! Look at me! Quick, the face cream! If my father sees me looking like this . . ."

Baket-amon's palm came out of the unguent box covered with cleansing cream. She slapped this gently on the girl's smeared face and began to work it in. "Here, now. Let me get under your eye."

"I'm sorry," Asenath said in a changed voice. "I won't do that again, really I won't. I'll do what's expected of me, and I'll just hope for the best. But I'll be glad when it's over with, really I will."

Baket-amon wiped her face clean with a fresh towel. "I'm sure you will, dear. In the meantime we've our womanly duty to consider, haven't we? And that includes bringing babies into the world. You can be thankful you'll have a nice husband when that baby comes along, a husband with money and power and a big house. It could be a lot worse, let me tell you, a lot worse." She stopped what she was doing, and a faraway look came into her eyes. "You could be a slave, for instance, with nothing of your own, or a serv—"

But she shut her eyes and shook her head violently, as if to exorcise the thought. "No," she said in a low voice. "Pay no attention to what I said. Pay no attention at all." And she sat up suddenly, back straight, head held high. "Now. Let's do those eyes once more, shall we?"

## II

Ayla turned away from the window, her face animated, her eyes bright. "My lady," she said. "Quick! Come quick! They're coming down the street! Now, before you miss them!"

Mereet carefully put down her papyrus scrolls containing Kirakos's house accounts and walked to the window to stand behind the girl, looking down on the scene in the street outside. The narrow street was lined with townspeople, and heavily armed Shepherd guardsmen were everywhere, eyes more on the crowd than on the procession that was making its way slowly down the street. More Shepherd troops advanced, guarding the front and rear of the processional, spears at the ready. The sharp blades gleamed, deadly, in the sunlight.

Ayla climbed nimbly up onto the high step before the window, craning her neck. "I can see her!" she said enthusiastically. "Oh, my lady, come up here! You'll get ever so much better a view! Why, she's simply lovely!"

Mereet debated for a moment the dignity, or lack of it, of the act; then, smiling, she took Ayla's hand and let the girl pull her up. The marble of the step was cool against her soles. A light breeze stirred through the latticed window. She looked down. In the open litter, the girl who was to wed Joseph of Canaan sat rigidly against the back of the seat, her long legs crossed daintily at the ankles, feet peeking out from under her gleaming white gown. Her little feet were bare and gleamed with toe rings and golden anklets; her hands were delicately splayed against the white gown. It was as Ayla had said: The girl was exquisite, with skin as smooth as a baby's. Her eyes were large and beautiful, as she looked up at the open sky; outlined in dark makeup, they fairly gleamed. A thought came to Mereet: *The poor thing, she's been crying. She's frightened! She daren't look down at the crowd; they scare her to death.*

"Oh, to look like that," Ayla said. "It makes me feel so ugly and awkward."

"She's quite a prize. I hope Joseph is good to her."

"Has Joseph much experience with women?"

The thought took Mereet by surprise. "Why, no, he hasn't had much opportunity for that. He spent much of his time in Upper Egypt in prison, you know. Before that he was a slave, closely watched. So unless he . . . but no. No, he wasn't very demonstrative or affectionate. I very strongly feel that when I knew him he was quite innocent. And Cherheb led me to believe that Joseph was busy day and night with Salitis, working out the details on the new regime in Avaris. It would be consistent with what one knows about the king for him to be obsessive, to demand all of Joseph's time."

"Well, he'll have to share him now," a voice said from behind them. Mereet turned, startled. Kirakos had wandered into the room, bent over a bit—the broken rib sustained in the street fight still pained him, and he tended to favor it. "This is quite a sight. The mistress of my household, standing in the window to peer down at a procession in the street. Women! Curious to a fault." He almost smiled through the gray-flecked beard. "Even the most dignified and haughty of them."

Mereet forced herself to climb down slowly; she wasn't about to let him spoil her composure. "If it is a natural characteristic of ours," she replied coolly, "then I assume I need not apologize for a fault so universal among my sex. I knew Joseph once, my lord. I was anxious to know what sort of woman the king has picked out for him. I wonder if Joseph even knows what she looks like." She turned to help Ayla down.

Kirakos's back straightened; the quick motion brought a wince of pain. "I was going to advise you to ask for yourself," he said. "You're already getting almost as much information out of my spies in the royal household as I am these days, enough to make me wonder if you oughtn't to have to help pay their salaries."

"You were going to, my lord? What made you hold your tongue?"

Kirakos's smile was little more than a mask for the humorless resignation that informed his tone. "Cherheb will no longer be spying for me," he said. "His head is sitting atop a pike in front of the palace gate." He let the thought sink in. Mereet stood, wide-mouthed, eyes wide open. "Our Golden Pharaoh took exception to the notion of my having a window on his household."

"Then the pharaoh knows—"

"I'm told by, uh, informants who were at the scene when he was put to the torture that our friend Cherheb went to the knife without openly revealing the name of his employer. But I have no illusions about this. He'd been seen coming and going from here."

"But—my lord, that means—"

"I don't know what it means—except that I'm quite out of the inner circle at the court of Salitis, of course." He turned away, and the quick motion again occasioned a grimace of pain. He cursed under his breath at his own weakness. "I intend to dissociate myself, as publicly as I can, from whatever's happening at the court. I'm reconciled to the death that will come upon me one of these days, but I wish to die in my own bed, quietly and peacefully, and not in some gutter, victim of an assassin's knife." He snorted derisively. "What a thought! Dying in my bed, like an old fool! See what the warlike Hai have come to! Kirakos, conqueror of Melid, hoping to die abed!"

"My lord is eloquent today," Mereet said.

"When people don't like what you're saying," Kirakos said, "they become critics of oratory. Remember that, Ayla. You never know when you may be able to make use of these stray bits of wisdom." The girl stared. He had never addressed her by name before or even taken particular notice of her. "What are you standing there for, girl? Haven't you any duties?" She gulped and beat a hasty retreat.

Kirakos sat down heavily, wincing. When he came to rest, his shoulders were slumped, and his face was gray. "My lord!" Mereet cried, rushing to his side. "Are you all right?"

He pushed her away. "I'm not having an attack, if that's what you mean. Save your concern for times of real distress."

"You can't drive me away," she said. "Any more than you can drive away that death you keep talking about. You should lie down. You look terrible."

"You sound like Arpena again. I never got any proper respect from her, either."

"And I'll bet you drove her to distraction, just as you try to do with me. But I won't let you, any more than she let you get by with your nonsense."

Now, as he looked up at her, his grin was a real one. "You're a tonic. Your sharp tongue will keep me from sitting around here like an old fool feeling sorry for myself for my loss of status. With you badgering me, I won't have time to indulge in the self-pity of an unemployed courtier."

"My lord, if you'd only—"

"I'll lie down when I feel like it," he said. "And you listen to me, for once: I can't help you get through to Joseph; I'm largely cut off from those circles, and he's pretty much insulated from the outside world." His tone was less sharp, more thoughtful, when he continued. "Perhaps you should give up trying. He may not be the same Joseph you knew anyway, my dear. People have a way of changing, as their lives change. He may have decided not to remember where he came from. Having been a slave isn't the most pleasant memory to carry around. He might wish to lay down such a burden, and—"

He saw her stricken face, though, and now he tried to get up, to go to her. The effort brought a stabbing pain. He sat back, his face drawn. "I'm sorry. I didn't mean to remind you—"

"It's all right," she said in a distant voice. "I'm used to it.

As for Joseph, my lord, I'll go back to trying to smuggle a message through to him by my own means. He may not be quite as small a man as you think him."

"Wait," he said. "I didn't mean—"

But when he looked after her, all he saw was the flourish of a trailing skirt, the flash of a bronze anklet, the warm skin tone of a bare heel retreating around the corner. And he wished, not for the first time in recent days, that he could call his words back.

After the first nods at ritual ostentation—the trumpet flourishes, the processions through the streets, the formal welcome to the court, with the assembled nobles gathered to greet the betrothed couple—the wedding ceremony itself was surprisingly brief. Joseph and Asenath were sworn to fidelity, mutual respect, and obedience, and pledged to the service of the state. There was no reference to the official state religion or to any of the great pantheon of Egyptian gods. Then the reason struck Asenath: *It must be Joseph's wish they're obeying. He must have asked for this sort of civil ceremony*. After all, there was that strange monotheistic religion he practiced, the one she had been "purified" to appease.

She stole a glance at Joseph while the priest of the city continued in his singsong voice. Her new husband was handsome as a god! Tall and slender and fit and fair of face, with red hair. It was strangely attractive, although an oddity among her uniformly dark-haired people.

Someone nudged her. "Take his hand," a voice said in a loud whisper. She did. And the touch of him—the first time she had had physical contact with him in any way—was really a most pleasant feeling, for all that his hand remained cool in hers, fraternal, neutral. She let her hand close on his, gently; she was astonished to feel him pull away a bit, until their hands were barely touching.

Her first reaction was hurt, then she stole another glance at him, at his stiff bearing, his nervous expression. *He's frightened! He's as afraid of this new life as I was an hour ago*. Look at him, she thought, young, new at court. Worse; he was from a foreign country, with no roots, no relations, no real home. The poor thing, he was petrified.

The thought was very comforting, to realize, as she did now, that of the two of them she was the less fearful. This would help her make friends with her new husband—she would comfort him, make him feel at home when they were finally alone. She would be gentle and sweet and caring. She would win him over, make him love her and appreciate her for the sweet girl she was. And as they became friends, perhaps the physical thing between men and women, the thing the slaves had prattled about so, would be a sweet, loving coming together, which she would remember the rest of her life. . . .

The ceremony completed, the young couple—still strangers with never a word passed between them except the ritualized ones necessary for formal agreement to marriage—were led out to the great hall of the palace, where Salitis himself, majestic, overbearing, with wildly intense eyes, a man who looked to be on the edge of madness, gave them his blessing. He told the priests attached to the royal household to usher the pair to Joseph's new dwelling. Thus it was among strangers that the two of them were escorted to the palatial new house the Golden Pharaoh had built at fabulous expense. On the steps of the new house, the priests conducted a second, brief, ceremony for the benefit of the public.

Emboldened by her new understanding of her husband's situation, Asenath reached out one small hand and grasped Joseph's fingers. He started to draw back his hand, but forced himself to retain her hand in his. She felt his hand: cold, covered with cold sweat. *Still frightened?* she thought maternally, protectively. *Poor darling.* She pressed his hand softly, but felt no answering response.

Then they were entering their new home! She looked around. Other than the palace itself, she had never been in such a spacious place. They entered court and vestibule, marched through a tall colonnade to the great central hall, with its high ceiling. There were enough tables to seat a hundred people. High on the walls, brightly colored murals told the proud story of the coming of the Shepherds, and the coronation of Salitis. Prominent in the picture was her husband, Joseph, standing straight as a reed and quite recognizable despite the obligatory formal beard the court painter had added to his youthful features. "Oh, look!" she whispered. "There you are! See?"

He looked at her for almost the first time, and the stiff formality of his face relaxed at last, if for no more than the blink of an eye. "You don't have to whisper," he said. "It's your new home." And he almost smiled! She wanted to hug him, but the priests were still there. *Time enough for that,* she told herself. *Just wait until we're alone.*

The doors of the master bedroom had been closed for several hours behind the newly wedded couple when dusk approached, and servants came to light the lamps for their master and mistress. After the slaves had knocked three times, Asenath came to the door, a light wrap thrown hastily over her shoulders. "What do you want?" she asked in a tight voice.

"We're here to light the lamps, my lady. Would you like food? Wine?"

"No. Please go away. I'll light the lamps myself."

"Yes, my lady. But does my lord—"

"Just go away. I'll call you when we want anything."

She heard their retreating footfalls through the half-open door, shut it tightly behind them, drawing the bolt. Now she turned back to her husband, standing naked by the latticed window, hugging his arms. "You're cold," she said. "I'll get you—"

"No. No, please." He reached down and found his robe and threw it over his thin body. She sighed. He looked at her, his eyes mirroring the desolation in his heart. "I'm sorry. It's not you. If I—"

"Oh, Joseph," she said, forcing the tenderness into her voice to hide, if she could, all sign of her own unhappiness. "It's all right. You're just nervous. It's been an exhausting day for both of us." She walked over to him, all soft submission, and tried to put her arms around him.

But he pulled away. "Please!" he croaked, his voice constricted. "I can't help it. I've never been able to stand being touched. Just be patient with me. Please . . ."

# CHAPTER
# TWELVE

## Nubia

### I

South of the second cataract the ascent of the great river by land became impractical, so that Musuri's party, with Shobai and Ben-Hadad, had slipped back into the desert west of the Nile and picked up the ancient track that connected the string of oases. This track, and all the trade routes, were now controlled by the Black Wind, Akhilleus's revolutionary organization, and from time to time their party would meet with Black Wind patrols policing the desert trails. This far south the patrols were mixed, with both light and dark Nubians marching side by side with the gigantic black mercenaries Akhilleus had brought north with him from his journey to the source of the White Nile.

The patrols greeted Musuri with affectionate respect, saluting the old soldier and inquiring after his health. He would curse them for a lot of unfledged, newly hatched offspring of diseased crocodiles, and send them on their way. This routine had continued almost from the first time the Egyptian party had joined up with Musuri's welcoming contingent. But now, as the desert route wound southward, they found more closely clustered oases, each capable of sustaining a considerable force of fighting men for a relatively long time. Token Black Wind forces occupied the first two of these; the third was quite another matter. The caravan passed two heavily guarded outposts before arriving at the largest oasis, and the approach to the most heavily settled section of the watering place led them past rows upon rows of tents, each tent capable of sheltering a dozen or more men. In open spaces between the tents, the troops, Nubian and Nilotic alike, were taking weapons drill under the tutelage of towering African warriors. On the other side of the path bowmen practiced archery on targets that looked like silhouettes of men.

Ben-Hadad gave the leading of his mount over to a Nubian ostler and jogged to the head of the line to march beside Musuri and Shobai. The blind giant walked easily, one hand resting on the back of Musuri's weathered hand. "I'm amazed, Musuri," Ben-Hadad said. "Just how big is this encampment of yours, anyway? I've been expecting to come to the end of it for some time now, but there seems to be plenty left to come."

"We're almost to the command area," Musuri replied. "Hah! You think *this* is large! You should see Akhilleus's camp across the river! It's twice the size of this!"

"Then Akhilleus isn't in charge here?" Shobai asked, breaking his long silence. "I'd hoped to meet with him."

"You will," Musuri said. "We're totally among friends now, so I can talk. In a day or so—we're awaiting the word from Akhilleus now—the final push against Kerma will begin. We've been amassing troops for it for a month, and now that we have all the northern river forts secured and control virtually everything north of the Dal Cataract, we think it's time to make an end of it once and for all. Of course, the enemy has got wind of this, more or less. And believe it or not, Kashta and Taharqa have made peace to join forces against us. They still hate each other, but they hate us even worse."

Ben-Hadad touched Shobai's arm. "Shobai, there seems to be a delegation of women approaching—women warriors!"

The blind man's face broke into a broad smile. "Musuri, you old devil. You wanted to surprise me! Is Ebana—"

He never got a chance to finish. Ben-Hadad looked on with astonishment as the bloc of warriors parted and a tall black figure came forward, arms outstretched, to embrace Shobai. "It *is* you!" the blind man said. "Ebana!" His arms went around her and hugged her close. But then he released her, stepped back. His hand went to her body, touched her swollen belly. "What wonderful news! You and Akhilleus—"

Her response was a great belly laugh and another hug. "—are going to have a baby. Can you imagine there being any other reason why I'd be here, commanding this desert garrison, and not across the river in the main camp with Akhilleus?" She grinned at Ben-Hadad, standing openmouthed, and Musuri. "Imagine me, at my age, pregnant! But there you are. Akhilleus won't let me within a league of the battle anymore. He says, 'If anything should happen to my son . . .' How he knows whether it's going to be a boy or girl, I don't know."

Ebana stepped back and took in the sight of her old friends and new. She grinned broadly. "This is indeed a time for feasting. Welcome, friends all! Welcome back, Musuri. And—you'd be Ben-Hadad, wouldn't you? Yes, I can see the family resemblance." She embraced both of them in turn, just as Anup brought up the Egyptian complement. "Welcome, captain! Welcome in the name of Akhilleus!"

The feast brought together the whole contingent, assembled before the campfires to celebrate the coming of Ebana's friends and the rest of the Egyptian delegation. There was from the southerners dancing of a kind Ben-Hadad had never seen before, with great leaps the height of a man's head, much fierce waving of spears, all to the boldly rhythmic music, great soaring songs from a thousand throats, accompanied by the powerfully virile sounds of a dozen different sizes of drum.

Ben-Hadad, thoughtful and sullen, had sat silent through the better part of the evening. Twice he called for more wine and drank deeply when the goatskin was passed. Afterward, he would sit staring at Shobai, but he did not speak, although it appeared that he wanted to. Musuri watched, shrugged; the lad had problems, it appeared, but he would not interfere. It was up to Ben-Hadad to solve them for himself.

Now, however, Musuri saw Shobai lean toward his nephew and speak in a low voice. In other circumstances Musuri might have indulged his curiosity and strained forward to overhear the conversation between the two; but instead, deciding to keep his own counsel, he sat back, face neutral, eyes mere slits, and watched unobtrusively, picking up what of their words he could hear without concerted eavesdropping.

Shobai was speaking: ". . . been very quiet of late. What's bothering you, my friend?"

The wine had at last loosened the young man's tongue. "Quiet? Me, quiet? Twenty times or more on this trip I've tried to draw you out, to talk to you. But you always change the subject and turn me away. Me, your kinsman. Your apprentice—"

"Not my apprentice anymore," Shobai said mildly. "You're a certified tradesman now, as of—"

"Don't change the subject again!" Ben-Hadad said angrily. "And that's not true anyway. You've taught me all I need to know to work bronze, and I'm grateful. But there's more than that. You may be the only man in the world south of the Hittite lands who knows the secret of smelting iron. And you won't teach it to me."

"Please," Shobai said. "You'll alarm the others. Besides, it's hardly a pressing question. There's no ore here, and—"

"That's not being honest with me! We were sent here to find ore. You know there's ore here. We were supposed to find out why Akhilleus reneged on his promise to—" Ben-Hadad realized what he was saying and lowered his voice. "Shobai, what happens when we do find ore? What happens when all of your excuses are exhausted? Even without iron, you could have been discussing the matter with me, talking about working methods."

Shobai sighed, slumped in resignation, then straightened up once again, sitting even taller than he had been before. His jaw firmed; a frown appeared on his usually expressionless face. "I didn't want to discuss this before all these—"

"Don't mind them," his nephew said angrily. He looked around him, took note of his neighbors' scattered attention, and misread Musuri's apparent inattention. "Their minds are a hundred leagues away. Tell me, Shobai! What have I done, that you should treat me this way? You're keeping this from me as if I were an enemy or a stranger."

Shobai pursed his lips in thought. "Enemy?" he repeated softly. "I sometimes think the iron itself is the enemy. Look what the pursuit of its secret did to my father. It brought him unhappiness. And his leaving to find the secret left our family alone—left my mother to go mad, left your father to grub for a living in the street. Left me, fool that I was, to follow my own misguided instincts, go my own selfish ways, and do incalculable damage. Don't you see? One foolish decision of Father's affected so many lives, and hurt so many people."

"Yes, but—"

"Think, now! You're asking me to let loose a veritable revolution in weaponry on an unstable world. You're asking me for a secret that can be worked for good *or* ill. Into whose hands will the secret fall? Tell me that, eh? Would you trust a man like Dedmose with it?" He shook his head. "The Shepherds could overrun Upper Egypt tomorrow. I don't understand why they haven't, because Baka tells me that our own army couldn't hold out for a week if the Shepherds came across the frontier at us."

"Well, we've been counting on Akhilleus to bring us men. Instead, he decided to stay in Nubia and fight this war."

Shobai waved away Ben-Hadad's objections. "And what would happen if Salitis were to attack, and triumph, and find in the camp of the defeated a captive like yourself who knew how to make iron weapons that would make Salitis invincible?" He pressed forward, his words growing in intensity. "Even the Hittites could not stand against the Shepherds if they were armed with iron. Imagine so terrible a secret falling into the hands of that mad son of Manouk's! Imagine—"

"I wouldn't give it to them! They couldn't drag it out of me!"

Shobai's smile was sad, knowing. "Ah, a while back I might have believed you, when you first came to me. You were a fine apprentice, hardworking, dedicated. The blood of the line of the Lion is in you, there's no doubt about it, although, like me, you will always fall short of the complete mastery of Belsunu or the artistry of your father." Ben-Hadad started to protest, but Shobai cut him off. "Come, now, let's be honest with ourselves. You and I are fine armorers. But the true genius of our line does not come in every generation. You and I were passed over."

"But—"

"A real artist knows who he is. He has no vanity or false modesty about it. All of us, I think," he said sadly, "wish to be other than we are—ethically, morally, spiritually. Me most of all."

Ben-Hadad tried again. "Shobai, if I—"

"Hear me out," the blind man said, and rather than raising his voice, he lowered it. "I now know that it was a good thing Father didn't master so terrible a secret as smelting iron until wisdom had come upon him, and did not pass it on to me until I was blind and couldn't use it for my own purposes."

"Shobai! I can be your hands, your eyes! If only—"

Now the blind man did raise his voice, just a trifle, and Ben-Hadad listened, stunned, mouth hanging open. "Before I lost my sight I was a self-centered, heedless, thoughtless fool, who never gave a moment's consideration to others— least of all to those who loved me. My mother could go mad with loss and loneliness; my brother—your father—could grub for a living in the gutter while I lived like a king. Not once did I think to help them."

"Shobai, what has this to do with—"

But now the blind man's huge hand reached out and fastened on Ben-Hadad's arm. "You are as great a fool as I was."

Ben-Hadad was frantic. "I don't understand. What have I done to—"

"Done? What *haven't* you done? You've a mother who loves you, who raised you with love. When was the last time you gave her a moment's thought? When did you send a message to let her know that you're still alive?"

There was no answer. In the shocked silence, Shobai went on. "You came to Egypt to find your friend Joseph. When was the last time you gave *him* a moment's thought? Joseph, the only childhood friend you ever had?"

There was no answer. He went on. "That wonderful little wife of yours, who adores the ground you walk on, who fought for you and saved your life? Gods, man! Do you think that a blind man can't tell? I can hear it in her voice, feel it in the very air around her! She's desperately unhappy. You've left her alone in an environment that's cold and distant to a person like her, but you never pay her any mind. You stay long hours at the forge and go home and fall into bed. When you go to bed, do you reach for her? Comfort her? Tell her you love her?"

He paused for a reply, but there was none. Instead, only the same shocked surprise.

Shobai let go of his nephew's arm. His grip had been so tight, Ben-Hadad could see red welts where those great fingers had been. "My words have struck home?" Shobai asked. "You see the truth in my remarks? Very well. It now remains to be seen whether you allow the seed of understanding to grow—or dig it up and root it out. Blind and useless though I am, I hold in my hand a secret so terrible it could change the world—and shall I pass that secret into the hands of a fool, like the one I was myself? Or shall I resolve to take this terrible secret to the grave with me?"

"S-Shobai, if you'd only—"

But the blind man waved away his words. "Unless I find a man wise enough to trust it to," he said in a voice so soft his words could hardly be heard. "And . . . forgive me, kinsman. But you are not that man."

# II

After a discreet interval Musuri, having watched Ben-Hadad's precipitate departure, edged over toward Shobai. "Your kinsman is angry," he said. "Is there anything I can do?"

Shobai's brow knitted, then he let out a deep breath and smiled. "You can get me some wine. And don't worry about him. Either he'll pay attention to what I've told him about myself or he won't. All I could do was acquaint him with his choices and their consequences. He has to make the hard decisions himself."

Musuri pressed a full goatskin of wine into the blind man's hands. "He just needs to grow up a bit," he said. "What a pity we can't go through being young without also going through being stupid." He sighed, old and world-weary. "Heaven knows I didn't. Damned heedless young ass that I was. Luckily, there weren't very many people my stupidity could hurt."

Shobai paused, the bottle poised before his lips. "How I wish I could say that of myself." He drank deeply, once, twice, then wiped his lips before handing the bottle back. "There's good in the lad. But youth is quick and rash and reckless. He wants me to teach him the secret my father passed on to me. He wants it now."

"Ah." Musuri looked into the fire, a knowing look on his face. "And you turned him down flat."

"I left the door open. If he becomes responsible, maybe. But—"

"But?"

Shobai shrugged. "I wish Father had died without learning the process. I even wish the Hittites themselves didn't have the secret. So far, they've spent their time fighting each other, when a more rapacious people would have conquered the world with so awesome a weapon."

Musuri drew his own weatherworn weapon, held it up, and watched the firelight play on its bright surface. "Shobai, would iron weapons really make that much difference?"

"They will cut through the weapon you hold in your hand, my friend, as if it were wood. Such a thing could change the world. I must see that it does not change for the worse. If I thought there were the slightest doubt in my mind about the people I was passing the secret on to, I would take poison rather than reveal it. Not to friend, blood kin, anyone."

Musuri chose his words very carefully as he spoke. "You know that when Akhilleus wins out here, he will be a king in Nubia, a king over white and black alike."

"When?" Shobai said, quick to catch nuance. "You say *when* and not *if?*"

"You have been only on the very fringe of our operations here, my friend. Kashta's forces lay farther south, and you've seen none of these. Now that Kashta and Taharqa have declared a truce, their armies are encamped before Kerma. They number perhaps sixty thousand, the greatest single force ever assembled in Nubia at one time, and they're all crack troops, tested and blooded—mainly in battle against each other."

"So?"

"So far we've only harassed them, pecked away at their rear guard, and subverted their own soldiers, who have come over to us by the thousands. But they've never met us in a head-on fight."

"And you think that when the big battle finally takes place—"

"—We will have a new king over Nubia. A king who will rule over all. Shobai, you haven't seen Akhilleus in his true form yet."

"I've never seen him at all," Shobai said softly.

"Sorry. I keep forgetting how one ought to put things. You and I traveled with him for years. He was a big clown, a mountebank of amazing gifts, perhaps, but a mountebank nonetheless."

"There was always substance to him, despite his clown-ish ways," Shobai said. "Imagine a slave becoming the owner of the greatest merchant fleet in the Great Sea like that. This isn't the stuff of which charlatans are made."

"No, you're right, of course. Remember, I went with him to his homeland. It was the greatest journey I'll ever make, a trip to a world as different from this one as Lisht is from Arvad. We climbed into the very clouds and saw sights I'd never even imagined before. Great cataracts, higher than fifty men's heads. Mountains of fire, so high that you can't see the top even after days and days of climbing. As we climbed, the years fell off Akhilleus. There came a time when he cast off the clothing people wear in the North, and naked against the elements, he was in his own world. He seemed to grow a handspan in height, right before my eyes. The world we entered was strange and savage. But the farther we went into that strange land, the more fearless Akhilleus became. He belonged there, in that land of mystery and majesty, was born to it."

"Go on."

"Shobai, the people were like black gods! The boys who came north to fight with us—they're marvelous, but they weren't the best of the lot. The finest of their warriors were, man for man, the best fighters I've ever seen. Shobai, Akhilleus defeated the best of them in a fair fight. And when the chieftains of the tribes offered him the kingdom that was his by blood-right and by virtue of victory at arms, he turned it down. Turned it down!"

"There's a nobility in him, all right. There always was."

"Ah, yes! And among his people, he has the virtual status of a demigod. I've known him for years and years, but he's not the same man."

Shobai leaned forward now, his face animated. "The real question is—why did he turn down a kingdom he'd won in the land of his birth?"

Musuri looked to right and left. Ebana had gone to bed sometime before. He kept an eye out for any of her towering sword-maidens and found none within earshot. "Ebana and I are good friends," he said, "and she shares most everything with me. She's puzzled, too. She honestly doesn't know what his final plans are. All we have is idle conjecture. He remains an enigma to both of us. And about his prediction regarding the sex of Ebana's child-to-be: It means a lot to him to have a son. A son to pass it all down to: the kingdom he's planning, his seed, the line of kings."

"And?" Shobai said.

"And I don't *know* what else. But I do know that tomorrow, when the battle begins, it won't just stop with the inevitable victory. It'll be more like a beginning than an ending—the beginning of something I can't begin to fathom. And then Akhilleus will control the greatest single source of iron ore in the entire region. *Iron*, Shobai."

"Ah," the blind man said, and sat back, slumped over a bit. He was thinking. "Then there will come a time when I will have a choice to make. That's what you're trying to tell me, isn't it?"

"Yes. A very important choice. One on which a great many things will depend. A choice that I'm very glad *I* won't have to make. And how will you choose when the time comes, Shobai? What then?"

Although Musuri waited patiently for many minutes, Shobai did not answer.

# III

The sound of drums woke Ben-Hadad at dawn. Drums! Hundreds of them, near and far; drums of all sizes and shapes, of all pitches, high and low; drums that sang to one another in intricate counterpoint, that whispered and bellowed and boomed and chattered. Drums!

He sat bolt upright, rubbing his eyes. He had had a bad night, sitting up late and staring at the stars and cursing the unfairness of it all. At the first glimmerings of light in the eastern horizon, he had finally slipped off, too tired to stay awake any longer, the anger and resentment from Shobai's reprimand boiling in his brain. Now, with the constant and insistent sound of the drums, he could sleep no longer, exhausted though he was. With a muttered curse he struggled to stand and searched for his outer robe and sandals.

To his surprise the entire camp was awake around him! The tall black soldiers of the Black Wind scurried to and fro, carrying weapons, guidons, and bucklers. To one side, in the clearing behind where they had feasted the night before, a mustering of an elite unit was taking place; they were hand-picked troops, standing stiffly at attention as a naked, sun-browned figure before them barked orders. Musuri! Rubbing his eyes again, Ben-Hadad stumbled forward toward the old man's lean, still-powerful figure.

Musuri saw him coming. He spoke gruffly to a subordinate and turned sharply to face the young man approaching. "Ah!" he said with a flinty-eyed smile. "You're up! Good! Just in time for the fun. The runner came in half an hour ago with word from Ahkilleus's encampment: We attack immediately. Some of those drums you hear—the faraway ones—are all the way from the other side of the Nile. They're saying much the same thing the messenger said, but in the language of the drums."

"In time for the fun?" Ben-Hadad said. "You mean I'm going with you?"

"Yes, if you like." Musuri took immediate note of the young man's enthusiasm. "Ah, I knew you'd like hearing that. Poor Shobai and Ebana have to stay here, by Akhilleus's orders. But you and I can get in on the thick of it. The attack has already begun over there, but we can get in on the second wave—that is, if you've a mind for fighting."

Ben-Hadad thought of something. "The people who attacked the fort a while back, back on the river near the cataract—they'd have come from one of the units we'll be fighting today?"

"Yes. They were a unit of the Fifth Mobile Infantry. We've faced them before. A good, strong outfit, but we've always licked them. Why?"

"Oh, nothing. But, yes. I want to be in on it. You couldn't keep me away!"

"Good. I'll be taking this unit over in just a few minutes. You'll have the honor of accompanying the finest unit that came downriver to fight with us. They're a particular favorite of Akhilleus's, and thus far they've been stationed here keeping Ebana safe. You can imagine how they've been champing at the bit. If you could see them on a forced march! They're tireless. They can keep up the pace for a day and a night and still be fresh enough to fight when they get there." He looked back at them now, squinting in the morning sun, a happy smile on his wrinkled old face. "I never in my wildest dreams imagined I'd get to command the likes of them."

"Then we'll be marching with them?"

"March? Bless you, boy, heavens, no. They don't march; they dogtrot, and at my age I couldn't keep pace with these two-legged gazelles. You and I will ride. Ebana told me to saddle her own horse for you. Come along, now. We'll draw rations and water, and then we'll be ready to go. It's a great day, son! Wonderful things are going to happen! And when they've happened, we may well have a new king in the Nubian lands!"

In the great encampment before the walls of Kerma, King Kashta of Nubia impatiently awaited the runner from the camp of his cousin Taharqa, on his left flank. Already present beside him in camp was Akhratan, his best general, who commanded the right flank, nearest the river. "Any sign of the runner?" Kashta said, pacing back and forth.

"No, sire. I don't know what's keeping him." Akhratan looked out across the open field beyond their front lines at the distant tents of the enemy: strange shapes, the tents of an alien race. Akhratan had never hidden his hatred of the black Nubians—the Nehsiu—and would have none in his units, regardless of their loyalties. Kashta had been forced to put Taharqa's legions, with their Nehsiu contingents, on the far side of his own central unit to avoid open conflict within the ranks.

"Damn those drums!" Kashta said. "If the black bastards are going to play them, you'd think they'd at least learn to keep time."

Akhratan looked amused. "They keep time well enough, sire," he said. "One of our captives taught me the drum language, so I understand the message. They're saying that I am a boy-lover with pomaded hair and that you—forgive me, sire—are a spindle-shanked eunuch with a piping voice. They say that by nightfall they will kill us."

The king cleared his throat. *If he weren't such a good soldier,* he thought, *he'd be sitting down on a sharpened stake by now, with ravens pecking out his eyes.* Suddenly he conceived an acute dislike for Akhratan, with his acid, rasping voice and ingrained prejudices . . . but he remained glad to have his services all the same. The man *could* fight and lead.

There was no doubt about that. "Confound it!" he said. "What's keeping that idiot runner?"

Akhratan peered out over the ranks of the massed troops to his left. "Ah! Look, sire. Taharqa hasn't sent a runner. He's coming himself. That'll bring the three of us together. Good. I wanted to coordinate the attack—"

"I'll coordinate it myself. I'll be commanding today."

"You, sire?" There was the bare ghost of a hint of icy contempt in the general's tone. "Surely we can't spare the person of our great king in such a perilous undertaking. I thought you were going to give over the command of the middle unit to your subordinate, Aspelta."

"I can't delegate this," Kashta said. "Too much depends upon the success or failure of today's battle. If we lose . . ."

"Lose?" Akhratan's laugh was raucous, mocking. "Lose, to this dusky rabble? To that great blustering oaf of a black braggart who calls himself Akhilleus? Sire, if it were anyone but the great king of Kerma himself speaking"—here there was deep irony in his voice, stopping just short of inso-lence—"I'd think you had been out in the sun too long and had baked your brains." He drew his sword lightly, slashed the air, and returned it to its hanger. "Sire, I'll kill the snaggle-toothed bastard myself if he's fool enough to wander over to the riverward flank of his own line."

Kashta had grown tired of this bragging and was glad to see Taharqa approaching at last. "Cousin!" he said, all for-giveness and reconciliation. "It's good to see you. Is your unit in readiness?"

"It is," Taharqa affirmed. Tall, hook-nosed, he towered over the shorter, stouter Kashta. He barely exchanged nods with Akhratan; there was little love lost between the two in the best of times. "The Black Wind will die on our spears like moths skewered on a needle. We will crush them today once and for all. My scouts say there are no reserves for Akhilleus to bring up, and his numbers are, all told, no more than half of ours."

"Make that two-thirds," Akhratan said. "You forget that garrison that defected to his side, my friend." There was cold hostility in his voice as he added, "My spies say it was one of yours, of course. Nehsiu. Can't trust them, not a one of them. Wave some bribe in front of them, some bauble or worthless gewgaw, and—"

"That's enough of that," Kashta said. "There have been

defections from all our camps. That's not the point. We need to make certain there are no new defections. The best way to do that is to obliterate the enemy. Now," he went on, squatting down on the clean sand and drawing lines with his finger, "here's the plan of attack for the day. Here's the Nile, and here's Kerma. I'm here, before the city wall. You're on my left flank, cousin. You, Akhratan, are on my right, by the river. Across the field . . ."

Across the field the three massed units of Akhilleus's force stood at ease. The drums had stopped. There was silence across all the great host. Striding up from the rear, half a head taller even than the tallest of the Black Wind soldiers, came—Akhilleus!

He was older than the oldest of them. Older, even, than Musuri, who had just crossed the river with his elite guards and Ben-Hadad. Yet he stood tall and straight and commanding. The sword in its hanger by his side was the only ornament of any kind on his broad-chested, wide-shouldered frame; in his huge hand a spear was held lightly; it was taller even than he himself and was renowned among his lean and powerful young soldiers—it had been brought all the way from his ancestral homeland and had once belonged to Ramogi, heir apparent to the throne Akhilleus had won and then declined. Ramogi had been his people's mightiest fighter until he had been bested in single combat by Akhilleus, a man more than twice his age.

Akhilleus held the spear high and peered out over the great throng before him. Despite the awe and enthusiasm glowing from the young faces, there was not a sound.

That great, deep voice boomed out, strong and commanding, carrying to every man, even to Ben-Hadad, far in the rear.

"Soldiers!" Akhilleus called out. "We have come far, you and I. Indeed, it seems that I have traveled across more years than leagues. All the years of my life have brought me to this one place and have had no other purpose than to bring me here. If I am to live and prosper, I shall live and prosper here. If I am to be buried and forgotten, here is the place, and today is the day, when people shall begin the task of forgetting me. *If, on the other hand, we win this battle and I live to reign—*"

There began a great rolling sound over all the enormous

throng, and no one could have said from which throats it came. It began softly; it grew; it developed power and body; it became a great full-throated hum, from all of the many thousands of soldiers. Ben-Hadad, listening wide-eyed, thought it would surely bury the giant's next words; but Akhilleus's voice carried still, over the hum, over the wordless song all those throats were singing.

"If I live to reign, we shall be remembered always!" He lifted his arms to acknowledge the soldiers' cheers. "Too long," Akhilleus said almost softly, in the pensive tone of a man just beginning to enunciate such thoughts, "too long has tyranny reigned here. Too long the policies of Kashta have kept black and white at one another's throats, have pitted brother against brother, neighbor against neighbor. You of Nubia have suffered too long from these policies. We, your brothers from the headwaters of the Nile, have come to stand beside you in a last battle to drive away all tyranny and bring peace and brotherhood to all men of goodwill in the Red Lands."

*Red Lands!* Ben-Hadad thought. *But that means Egypt!*

"Now," Akhilleus said, his voice rising in pitch, "the massed armies of our common enemy stand before us. Their numbers dwarf ours. But their hearts do not. Their hearts are small." He held up the great spear and waved it before them. "Does this hand wield this spear? No. This heart"—here his free hand pounded that great chest of his—"this heart wields this spear. If the heart weakens, the spear will fall, and I shall fall with it."

The humming grew; the voice rose above it. "Yet the heart will *not* weaken." The humming rose. "The spear will *not* fall." Again the humming swelled; the tune soared; the sound from thousands of throats called out their loyalty, their trust, their willingness to follow this great man to the ends of the earth, if need be.

"And *I* shall not fall!" Akhilleus said. "We shall prevail! Tyranny will disappear forever from the banks of the Upper Nile and from all the regions of this ancient land! Forever!"

Now the drums began again, each struck in perfect unison. The beat began slowly, then accelerated. Ben-Hadad's heart pounded with the drums; his eyes glittered with a mad light. His own sword was in his hand; he was bursting with the same wordless oath of allegiance as the troops. And for some reason he could not fathom, he was weeping with joy!

The great spear waved once more in the air, and then flashed downward!

The battle had begun!

The massed thousands moved forward across the great plain, the drums beating behind them! The song had words—words Ben-Hadad could not understand—and it burst forth, loud and strong, from the myriad throats! The drumming increased in tempo, and the soldiers trotted, then ran, to meet the enemy, and he, Ben-Hadad, was running with them!

## IV

As Akhilleus's legions charged the center of Kashta's line, the bowmen of Taharqa and Akhratan, on the two flanks, unloosed a mighty rain of arrows. Many were deflected by the stout bucklers of the black warriors; others found their marks, and a number of the tall soldiers fell behind. The rest, grinning and singing all the way, hit the enemy line with a controlled savagery before which Kashta's men gave way, fell back to prepared positions, then finally stood and fought back in vain. A huge hole opened in Kashta's salient line, and Akhilleus's warriors surged mightily into this, cutting, hacking, slaying. And still wave after wave of black warriors came on.

On a hill above the battle, Kashta watched, his right arm raised high to hold above the battle his baton of office. At his side his subordinate Aspelta, a death's-head of a man with hardly any flesh on his bones, hovered anxiously. "Now, my lord?" he said in a constricted voice. "Now?"

"Just a moment," Kashta said. "Let them get deeper into the apparent break in our line. A little more now . . . a little more . . ." He smiled, an unpleasant smile, dripping with malice. "Good, good, keep letting them in."

"Now, my lord? I can see Akhratan waiting for the signal. He's fuming. He's bouncing around like an angry child."

"Let him fume. He'll be all the angrier for the battle, when it comes his way. A little more . . . *Now!*"

His arm flashed down! And, below, on the field of battle, the commanders reacted. From both sides the full force of the flanking armies besieged the two sides of Akhilleus's troops. Seen from a distance it looked like the pincers of a gigantic crab, closing on some dainty morsel. The armies came together, and Akhilleus's force was split in half by the flanking attack! The first wave was surrounded! Cut off!

The second wave of the attacking force fell back, regrouped, divided into two sections to meet the flanking attacks. Kashta's own forces struck back, slashing into the surrounded first-wave units!

"Ah!" Kashta said, his eyes gleaming. "We have them! We have them! If only Taharqa can press hard enough—"

But on the field the encircled blacks counterattacked with an awesome ferocity. The circle around them widened, wavered, broke. The fighting was terrible, intense, the men jammed together, sword to sword, spear to spear. Kashta's men labored mightily to reclose the circle around their towering foes, but to no avail. Instead, Kashta's men seemed on the verge of utter disorganization. "Close it up!" bellowed Kashta from his height. "Close it up, you cowards! Stand and fight! Stand!"

Kashta's left flank, under Taharqa's command, seemed to lose heart and fall back. They lost ground, stood firm again, were beaten back. Only Akhratan's men, by the shores of the great river, held their ground and even advanced a trifle. "Good man! Hang on there!" Kashta bellowed down at him. "Ah, if only the rest of those cowards would hold firm! Look at them, Aspelta! They're breaking!"

As if in response to his chiding, the left flank turned and fought its way back to its original position, and the eastern frontier of the battle looked to favor Kashta's victory. Then almost miraculously, Kashta's own band succeeded in closing the circle around the embattled black vanguard of Akhilleus's legions. Kashta looked right and left. "Where's Akhilleus?" he said agitatedly. "I want him killed!"

Ben-Hadad, in the left flank of Akhilleus's force, in the second wave of the attackers, found himself facing the superbly trained troops of Akhratan, standing firm with their backs to the cliffs overlooking the Nile. Akhratan had asked for this position, knowing his troops would fight more fiercely if they had no land behind them available for a retreat.

Although Ben-Hadad had no way of knowing that, the first flush of contact with the enemy convinced him that he and his colleagues were up against what had to be the toughest part of the enemy force.

Untrained in the use of arms, Ben-Hadad had hoped to get by on sheer enthusiasm, on his native quickness of eye and of hand, and the considerable strength his years as an armorer had given him. But his first Nubian opponent had had all of these qualities, plus training.

Ben-Hadad's first thrust, then, had been parried easily, and on the backswing the Nubian had hit him a glancing blow on the shoulder—not a deep cut, but enough to bring a fresh flow of red down his arm. Ben-Hadad, stunned by the hit, had fallen back a step, but had then counterattacked and landed a lucky thrust below the man's ribs that had felled him. It had been no more than an accident, and when he had bent and given the fallen Nubian the coup de grace with a thrust to the throat, it had been with a bad conscience and with a realization of his own undeserved good fortune.

There had not been much time to reflect on the matter, though; unlike the other defenders, the ones facing his unit had stood firm and given Akhilleus's soldiers a lusty battle of it. Now, standing just behind a towering black warrior, he looked around and tried to get his bearings.

Where was Akhilleus? He had thought he would be able to locate the black giant by now, but there seemed to be no sign of the big man. Perhaps he had gone in with the first wave, which was buried inside a wall of encircling defenders. If he—

Suddenly, in the line before him, a fierce surge! Kashta's defenders attacked. The black stalwart in front of him staggered and fell, a Nubian spear in his guts! Ben-Hadad raised his sword, caught the next thrust of the spear, and shoved it aside only barely in the nick of time! Both weapons tied up, sword and spear pressing hard against each other, he found himself face to face with his attacker!

He blinked, saw the hawk's face, hook-nosed and hateful, and looked into eyes filled with hatred. "You!" his attacker said, his voice showing the strain. "What's a white man doing fighting alongside these filthy black bastards?"

Ben-Hadad blinked again, looked at the insignia of rank on his opponent's chest, and gaped in astonishment. A Nubian general!

"I am Akhratan, general of the army," the other man said, struggling to get his spear free. It was pinned now to Ben-Hadad's side by the young man's arm, which held it firmly. "Yes, boy! You ought to know the name of the man who kills you!"

Ben-Hadad's arm was the stronger, though, and he was able to keep Akhratan's spear under his arm while he brought up his free hand to smash his opponent in the face. The spear fell to the ground, but the general staggered back, clawing for his sword in the hanger by his side.

Ben-Hadad recovered his balance. Out of the corner of his eye he could see the men on his flank had driven the defenders back. He and Akhratan, with the widening gap around them, had room now for single combat. Ben-Hadad gripped his sword and wished that he had held on to the buckler he had been given before the battle. It had been knocked out of his hands during the first advance, and he had not had time since to find another.

Now the enemy general, a contemptuous sneer on his face, advanced on him, his weapon held tauntingly before him. With a sinking feeling of horror, Ben-Hadad looked down at the weapon that was pointed at his belly as the man moved toward him.

The metal was black! Touched here and there with rust! Rust! It was an iron weapon!

Ben-Hadad stepped back cautiously. "That sword," he said in a voice that broke like an adolescent's. "Where did you get that sword?"

Akhratan shot a glance at it, and his smile grew the more unpleasant, a vulture's hideous grin. "Ah, you recognize the black metal, do you! It strikes fear into your heart, does it? And well it might. It's got your death written across it, boy. It will cut through that paltry bronze sword in your hand as if it were flesh." He swung the blade; the air seemed to hiss around it.

"*Iron,*" Ben-Hadad whispered. "Smelted iron." His gaze stayed fixed on the weapon's dull blade as it circled now, pointed at his own vitals. "What Nubian knows how to smelt iron? That's no Hittite design. How did you come by—"

But he did not get an answer or a chance to finish his question, for the Nubian bellowed in rage and attacked with terrible ferocity. Ben-Hadad stepped back, dodged, and tripped, stepping back again over some obstruction on the ground behind him. Instantly Akhratan was upon him, towering over him, a look of triumph on his hateful hawk's face. Ben-Hadad held up his sword defensively, but Akhratan swung his awesome black sword with fearful force, and the power behind his blow nearly tore the sword from Ben-Hadad's hand. He looked in astonishment at the weapon in his hand; its blade was chopped clean in half, and he held only a stub. Akhratan's smile was all the more deadly as he pressed in for the kill; he drew back for one last hacking death stroke at the fallen man's neck—

"Akhratan!"

The voice was huge, echoing, commanding. The voice of a god in human guise—or of a king! Towering high over the two of them was Akhilleus, fierce and frightening, his eyes flinty, his great chest heaving with excitement, his huge hand holding a sword twice the size of an ordinary man's!

"You!" the Nubian said in a strangled voice. He stepped back, and Ben-Hadad scrambled to his feet and out from between the two of them. Then Akhratan, hatred and contempt in his throat, spat out: "Ah! The black savage at last! The headhunter! The blood-drinker! A fine meeting indeed! Now I can give the rabble a lesson in the fine art of dissection, having so excellent a jackal to practice on!"

For an eye's blink Akhilleus did not speak; then, solemnly, he stepped back and saluted his smaller foe, with an air of religious seriousness. "Die, then," he said softly, almost tenderly.

Ben-Hadad stared as they circled each other slowly, unaware of the battle that raged around them. "Akhilleus!" he cried. "Look out! His sword—it's of iron! Don't parry! Don't—"

"It's all right," the black giant said in the same chillingly gentle voice. "To cut my blade in half, he has to touch it. He will not touch it."

Something in his tone awakened Akhratan's old hatred of all blacks. "I'll show you, you dusky devil! I'll—"

But when he lunged, Akhilleus was not there. Ben-Hadad could not believe a man so large, so old, could have moved so quickly. Akhratan cursed and attacked, lunge after lunge, wild swing after wild swing, at the dancing giant. None of the thrusts struck home; none of the cuts landed. Akhilleus smiled, the tolerant and gentle smile of a man playing with a child. Sweat poured from Akhratan's forehead;

his breathing was labored, but Akhilleus was not even winded. "Curse you!" Akhratan said through clenched teeth. "Stand still and fight, you filthy black coward!"

But the very moment Akhratan stepped back to catch his breath, the tide of the great battle turned. Until this moment neither side had gained an advantage, despite the superior numbers of the Nubian force. Akhilleus's warriors and their rebel-Nubian allies had evened the numbers in their first drive against Kashta's army. The fighting had been stalemated for many minutes, but now a great cry came up from the ranks of the Black Wind, and both Akhilleus and Akhratan looked up to see fresh troops pouring down the field to relieve and augment Akhilleus's forces. The new troops were tall, lean, black, naked—and female!

As Akhratan watched, horrified, the women charged into the flank of his force, hacking and stabbing with deadly effect. The Nubians, boxed between the male and female troops of the Black Wind, gave ground, demoralized. The women, grinning fiercely, cut them to pieces.

"Akhratan!" Akhilleus said in hardly more than a whisper. "Your invincible force crumbles. At the hands of the Black Wind!" He saluted again, mockingly.

"You filthy black scum!" Akhratan spat, and attacked with the fearless desperation of a man with everything to lose.

Akhilleus let a great swing go past, then watched the backswing cut the air audibly past his chest. He reached out, on the attack for the first time. His bronze point flicked out, like the tongue of some great cat, and cut Akhratan's throat across, as easily as if it had been slicing a ripe fruit.

Akhratan tried to speak; he dropped the iron sword and clutched his throat, then crumbled slowly to his knees.

Ben-Hadad scrambled forward to grasp at the fallen sword. In a last desperate move Akhratan's hand flashed out and grabbed Ben-Hadad's ankle. Ben-Hadad stumbled and fell. He saw the rock rushing up at him, and his hands went out before him, but too late. Then there was a sharp pain—and blackness.

Ben-Hadad awoke on a stretcher, being carried from the battlefield by two huge black soldiers. His head throbbed, and when he tried to sit up, an attack of dizziness and nausea forced him back down, weak and gasping. He looked around, blinking. Above, in the clear sky, vultures circled slowly, waiting to land. A detail of Akhilleus's troops was piling bodies high to one side; nearby, guards marched away the wretched Nubian prisoners, their wrists tied, their once proudly clad bodies now naked and filthy and bleeding from many cuts.

A familiar face swam into Ben-Hadad's field of vision. "Musuri!" he cried. "Did we win?"

"Yes!" Musuri answered, falling into step with the men carrying Ben-Hadad. "You missed the best part. The women swung the battle, Ebana at the head. Akhilleus is going to reprimand her for leading the charge herself, but she wouldn't have missed it for anything." He patted Ben-Hadad's arm. "Akhilleus entered Kerma in triumph and was acclaimed king. Kashta was killed in the fighting. I had the honor of assisting in his demise." There was a twinkle in the old man's eye. "Taharqa saw how the fight was going and ran on his sword. It was a complete rout." He smiled. "It's a great day!"

Ben-Hadad's recollection of the battle became clear. "I was reaching for something when I fell and hit my head. The sword! The iron sword!"

"This one?" Musuri asked, beginning to hand it over. Then he thought of something and delayed giving it to his young friend. "You've a special reason for wanting this, haven't you? Your uncle refused to teach you how to smelt iron, and now you think there's someone up here to learn it from. Am I right?"

Again Ben-Hadad tried to sit up and was prevented by a blinding flash of pain in his head. "Ahhh!" he cried, pressing his fingers to his temples. His hands came away bloody. "Please," he pleaded. "Give it to me. I have to find out who made it. I was going to ask Akhratan, but—"

"Too late for that," Musuri said. "He's dead." Walking beside the stretcher, he balanced the black-hued sword in his hand. "Most likely Akhratan knew who made the sword," he added. "It's not a sure thing that anyone else who knew is left alive. It may have come from another land—"

"*No! No!*" Ben-Hadad cried out. He tried to move again, with the same disastrous results. "The design's Nubian! Any fool can tell that! I have to find him, whoever he is, and—"

Musuri sighed and pressed the sword into the prostrate man's hand. "Here. Take it," he said. "For all the good it'll do you. But you're not going to spend the next few months up here looking for the armorer. You're going back to Lisht, with the new diplomatic delegation from Akhilleus's new government. You'll be leaving as soon as you're able to travel." He forced the young man back down on the pallet as he tried once more to rise. "No arguments," he said firmly. "Akhilleus's orders. And I'd think twice before disobeying him. He's a king now, and his word is law over everyone, friend or foe. If he says you'll return, that's what you'll do."

Ben-Hadad gripped the sword so hard, it cut into his hands. *That's it, then*, he thought. *Akhilleus and Shobai have me boxed in between them. I'll never learn! Never!*

High above, the vultures still circled slowly, slowly, but they seemed to be closer than they had been a moment or two before. Ben-Hadad turned on his side, painfully, away from Musuri. Everywhere there were signs of carnage. It was a great day, a day of victory, yet he had never felt so defeated in his life.

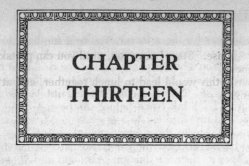

# CHAPTER THIRTEEN

## Canaan

I

There came a time at last when the feasting was over, when old times could be profitably talked over no more, when Imlah and Danataya could no longer delay returning home, and Jacob could find no new reasons for keeping them from their journey.

Nevertheless, when Imlah came to announce that his party would depart before noon, tradition demanded that the elaborate formalities of Canaanite ritual be respected. Both Imlah and Jacob enjoyed the formal observances of hospitality and protocol; both went through the prescribed steps of the ritual dance with the same great air of seriousness and the same twinkle in the eye.

Thus Imlah, bowing low, said to Jacob, "Your exceeding bounty has covered me far above my head; may the God of your people perpetuate your house and prolong the lives of your dear ones. May the gods of my own people enable me some day to reward you for your boundless generosity. And now I beg you to permit me to depart." He bowed again, deeply.

Jacob's own performance, following the rigid dictates of custom, was equally flawless. He confessed his utter unworthiness of such lofty praise and his surprise at the compliment, and in the next breath begged Imlah to take no thought of departing.

Imlah insisted then that he must go, and Jacob made the expected response. "Stay, I pray you, until you can partake of our noon meal."

Ordinarily this would lead to lunch together, and at the end of a lengthy meal and siesta, the host would declare that the day was already well spent, the journey long, and the road far too dangerous for night travel—and that there was nothing to be done but to stay the night and depart on the morrow—at which time the ritual of delaying departure would begin anew.

But at a certain point in the present proceeding, Jacob, catching Imlah's eye, saw his old friend wink and then bow. He threw up his hands and abandoned the formalities. "Ah, my friend," Jacob said, "as much as I have enjoyed your company, I tire easily now. I've been a poor host, running out of energy and going to bed early every night. And I know you have urgent business at home."

"I do. Otherwise I'd stay. You're very nearly the perfect host, my dear fellow, and you know what Danataya and I think of you. I'm grateful for all your generosity to her over the years; a kindness to Danataya is more to me than a kindness to me, and your fatherly concern for her is a debt I'll never be able to repay."

"I'm so glad she's found a man like you," Jacob said warmly. "I only wish she'd found you right after we came south to Canaan. Instead she had all those years of pain and horror with Hashum and that swine of a son of his. . . ."

"I meant to ask," Imlah said. "Is Shamir safely out of the country? Have your sons seen to the matter? If I find him bothering her again, I swear I'll have him taken down to the river some night and quietly drowned."

"Don't think about him anymore. With that brand on his face, he can't travel in these lands by day, and you're a day's ride from the Moabite wilderness where my sons turned him loose. He won't easily find friends in that country either; they've heard of his antics down that way, too. And the Ishmaelites will not take quickly to a man who carries my brand on his forehead; they're my distant kin, you know. I think we may well have seen the last of him."

"Good. Danataya took a little ride yesterday afternoon on the new horse you gave her. She says it's a magnificent animal, proud and gentle."

"I'm delighted she likes it. Its sire and dam were presents from the Ishmaelites, during a peace parley some years ago." He shook his head, thinking of the slain horse. "That such a one as Shamir stayed in the region, bringing shame on us all, while Joseph and Ben-Hadad . . ." There was a strange quality of reverie about his voice now, and Imlah looked at him sharply. The old man's face was full of mixed pleasure, pain, hope, and the heartache of hope deferred. "I had a dream last night," he said, quietly looking off into the distance. "It was about my son Joseph. I dreamed he was alive." He looked at Imlah now, puzzlement in his eyes. "One moment he was rich, famous, a great leader of men. The next moment, he seemed to be restricted, manipulated by others, a man in a difficult and dangerous place. He's lonely and unhappy, crying out for love and understanding but unable to tell anyone about it. Ah, Imlah, my son is alive, and he needs me, but there doesn't seem to be a thing in the world I can do about it. Where is he? In what foreign land? What language does he speak among the unbelievers?"

"I don't know," Imlah said gently, wishing he could say more to comfort his friend.

"When you think the time is right, tell Danataya of my dream, and that I think Joseph is alive. If he is, perhaps her son has found him and they're both safe." He turned and saw Danataya making her way up the hill to where they stood. "Let's change the subject; I don't want to bring this up when she's getting ready to go."

The two men embraced as warmly as if they had been brothers. And when Danataya came up to them, all trace of sadness was gone from Jacob's face, and his demeanor portrayed nothing more than his own undisguised love and affection for her.

The Edomite caravan stopped for the night on the fringes of Jotbathah, a dismal, painfully poor settlement comprised of tents and shabby mud huts gathered haphazardly around a well of brackish, bad-tasting water. Shamir gasped with relief when he realized they were going to stop. He couldn't have gone a step farther; he was sure of that. His tongue was black with thirst, and the alkali dust of the desolate Arabah coated his face and burned his eyes. His sandals had given out at last somewhere south of Tamar, and he had staggered along the rest of the way, in the straggling rear guard of the caravan, on bare feet that now bled from open sores made all the more painful by the hard alkaline soil underfoot.

Still he managed to stagger, whimpering at the pain, to the well and shove an old woman out of the way to get at the water bag. He drank, splashed hands and feet, drank again— and, suddenly nauseated, vomited violently beside the well. A herdsman traveling with the caravan saw Shamir, spat contemptuously at him, and kicked him to one side to help the old woman get back to her feet and fill her water jug.

Shamir shuddered and let the herdsman go, bearing the old woman's burden for her. He could think of nothing he would like more than to take off the head covering that shielded his face from the sun and splash the tepid water on face and head; but the head covering concealed the fresh brand on his forehead. He knew what would happen if a member of the caravan saw his forehead: Thieves were not tolerated in any caravan and were instantly thrown out to die when they were detected.

So when the rest of the party had drunk and washed their faces, the best he could do was to sneak back to the well, tear a piece of cloth from the tattered corner of his already ragged garment, and moisten it to wash the grime out from around his eyes, wincing and cursing at the pain. He drank again, more judiciously this time, and began to wonder where his evening meal was going to come from. Last night, on the fringe of the Moabite lands, he had had to fight four pariah dogs for discarded table scraps. He shuddered at the memory.

He remembered the scurvy little Canaanite dog that his old enemy Ben-Hadad had owned. The damned little animal had attacked him one time when he had given Ben-Hadad a cuff alongside the head. He wished he had killed the dog a long time ago, and Ben-Hadad with him. Perhaps if he had, his own luck would have been better. His own father, Hashum, would still have been alive now and figured out a way to help him. Hashum had always had a crafty scheme.

He wondered what Hashum would have done in his own present predicament. He would not go hungry, that was certain. Father and son, Hashum and Shamir had always found something to eat, even in the leanest of days, even if it meant that Danataya and Ben-Hadad went to bed without dinner.

How he missed Hashum at times like these! His father

had never for a moment allowed it to enter his mind that anything might be his own fault; it was always conveniently someone else's. It was hard for him, Shamir, to maintain that sort of flawless, seamless single-mindedness. Hashum would have cursed the things that stood in his way and gone about eliminating them with a terrifying economy of purpose. Well, he would have to learn to be more like Hashum if he were going to get ahead in a world full of fools and swine.

For now, he would find some dinner, even if it meant fighting the dogs or cutting some bastard's throat for it. After that, he would have a clear head to think about what to do next. One thing was certain: North of Ezion-Geber, he was a marked man. Only the luck of running into this grubby Edomite caravan had saved him so far, and they would be sure to catch on to him when the caravan reached Ezion-Geber, a border port full of people from everywhere.

Everywhere? There was a good idea. They would also be bound to everywhere. If a fumbling, stuttering oaf like Ben-Hadad could cadge a ride to strange and exotic places with an outbound caravan, so could he. New places, new opportunities, new victims.

Egypt, perhaps?

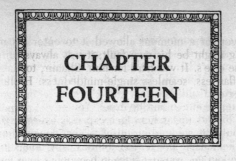

# CHAPTER FOURTEEN

# Lisht

## I

This time as she dressed to go, Baliniri awoke and looked around. He rubbed his eyes and sat up. "Tuya!" he said in a voice still husky with sleep. "You're not leaving now? Please . . ."

Tuya sighed deeply. Her shoulders slumped, and the comb dangled from her hand. Defeat was etched in every line of her little body. "Oh, I was so hoping I'd get away before you—"

"Please," he said again, standing up. The sight of him, brawny and naked and gentle and vulnerable, tore at her heart. "Please don't go like this, sneaking off before daylight."

"It's not before daylight," she said. "Look. There's light in the sky. If I don't get back before—"

"Before what?" he said, coming to her and trying to take her in his arms. She pushed him away; he took her hands instead. "My dear," he said. "What do you have to get back to? What is this other life of yours that you won't tell me about? Is it another man? Can't we be honest with each other?"

"No!" she pleaded, almost sobbing. "I can't! Please don't ask me! Don't you see how much it hurts to have to keep saying no to you?" Her shoulders shook while she fought mightily against tears. "Oh, this is no good. I have to go. And

261

Baliniri, I can't come *back*! I—" But now the tears came in a flood, and she pulled her hands away to cover her face. He tried to comfort her, but she turned angrily away. "Oh, I'm so miserable! Why did I ever start this? How could I have been so stupid and cruel?"

"Cruel? You couldn't be cruel. You—"

She looked up at him, her expression half-anger, half-pain. "You!" she shouted furiously. "What do you know about it? You don't have any responsibilities, any obligations! You just come and go, walking right into people's lives and doing whatever you like."

"How can you say that? You know how much you mean to me now. If I lost you—"

This brought a fresh burst of sobbing. "Oh, don't start *that* now! Don't you see how hard you're making it for me? Please, just let me go." She tried to push past him, but he blocked her way, his great arms trying to embrace her, his eyes hurt, imploring. "Please, Baliniri, please! I—I *have* to go! Now!" This time she did manage to push her way past him.

At the door she paused once and looked back at him, the morning sun shining full on him through the open doorway: big as a bear, gentle as a baby, his whole great body naked, his posture one of vulnerability, pain, loss, longing—and love. It came to her in a flash: This was the last she would see of him, ever. She tried to fix this one picture of him in her mind forever, and the very thought was heartbreaking. How sweet he was! What a prize for any woman! She took a deep breath. "Good-bye, Baliniri," she said, then ran down the stairs into the morning light.

Down the transverse alley came Hefget and Dede, the latter just back from his fact-finding trip to the Fayum. Hefget had decided to pump his dull-witted friend before taking him to the meeting of the conspirators; there was no telling what advantage he might gain to have the information ahead of the others. "Then you did get the letter I sent you?" he asked. "The one about Madir's plans for the Fayum?"

"Oh, yes," Dede said. "And you're right, the big land-owners are ready for revolt. If our people can get through to them right now, we'll recruit all of them at once, in one basket. I talked to key servants of two landowners, and they've had several meetings lately to discuss the takeover. If they were suddenly to learn of the existence of a really organized conspiracy, they'd join in a minute. Hefget, if I could get permission to talk to one or two of them—"

Hefget shuddered, but did not comment. "We need you here," he said. "We have an undercover man down there by now working on it. Don't give it any—"

Dede stopped, held Hefget back. His eyes narrowed. "Hefget," he said. "That short girl there, coming down the stairs . . . Who is she? I've seen her before, but I can't remember where."

"Oh, her." Hefget patted his arm reassuringly. "Her name is Ti. She's one of us. I have her spying on a soldier who's close to Baka. She's passed on some valuable information so far. A very useful person, really. You may have seen her at the Market of the Four Winds. A thief."

"A thief, you say?" Dede said, brow knit. "Why do I keep thinking I've seen her before? Why do I keep thinking she doesn't look right in rags! Huh. I wish I could remember. You say she's spying on General Baka? But—"

"She's seen us. Here, I'll call her over. Ti! Ti!" His call was hardly more than a loud whisper, but she heard it. Her reaction was delayed, halting. Finally she came over to the two of them. "Ti, this is Dede. He's been off on a mission for us. Dede, I want you to meet Ti, one of our best people in the city. She's been spying on Baliniri—"

"I wanted to talk to you about that," she said in an agitated voice, ignoring Dede. "Look, I can't—"

"Tell me about it later," Hefget said. "I'm glad I ran into you—I wanted to tell you that there's a meeting today, at noon, at the house on the Street of the Two Fountains. Be on time."

"But Hefget—"

"No buts. Be there. Afterward you can tell me what's on your mind. Now run along before we're seen together."

Her pained eyes lingered on his face, and it looked for a moment as if she were going to speak once more. But she did not. She turned to go without acknowledging Dede's presence at all.

"I wish I knew where it was that I'd seen her," Dede said. As he spoke, a small four-footed figure came out of the morning shadows and set off at a trot down the street after her. A scruffy little Canaanite dog, light-footed, its tail held high.

\* \* \*

At the palace of Dedmose, Madir's secretary, Sitra, dismissed the servants who had opened the windows and straightened up the offices of the royal scribes. Dedmose himself was due to visit the area in the late morning, and his passion for neatness and cleanliness was well known in court circles.

As Sitra passed from the scribes' workrooms into the great hall, a whispered "Sssst!" stopped him in his tracks. He looked around for the source.

"Sssst! Over here," the voice whispered. It seemed to be coming from behind a large woven wall hanging near the door that led to the royal apartments. "Just step near the wall. Don't make a fuss. Look as though you were doing something, or looking for something."

Sitra recognized the voice, even muffled. The man in the Sobek mask! Sitra did as told and took off his sandal, pretending to examine and repair a torn lace. "Yes?" he said softly. "What do you want?"

"Important meeting today. Noon. Street of the Two Fountains. Be there."

"I'll be there. What's up?"

There was no answer. Sitra moved back. The arras did not quite reach to the floor. He looked for the speaker's feet, but they were gone. He looked behind the hanging. No one was there. Puzzled, he stepped behind the arras himself, his back to the curtain, his fingers feeling their way along the wall. He came to a chink between the stones. Sitra probed and found that the chink extended the height of a man, continued up and across . . . a secret doorway! He marveled that the palace should still hold any secrets from him after all this time here. He felt here and there for handholds, but could find none. How did one go about opening the door? Well, no matter. He would consult the royal architect. Surely there would be some mention of it in the plans for the palace. He would get to the bottom of this soon enough.

In the street, stumbling along half weeping, half cursing the terrible destiny that had led her here, Tuya finally noticed the little form trotting along good-humoredly at her heels. "Go away, Lion!" she said bitterly. "Get away from me! Go home, now!" The dog danced around her feet, tongue lolling. She aimed a kick at its head, but the little animal pranced out of reach. She reached into the dirt at her feet for a rock and sailed it at the dog, but it flew wide of its target. Lion would not go away.

Tuya looked around. At the end of the street, the cul-de-sac ended in a high wall. She ran to this and scaled the wall, swinging down to the other side. There! The dog could hardly follow her over a wall. She looked around her; she was in a new street and was not certain how it connected with the rest of the quarter. She frowned, looked at the sun shining over the top of the building opposite. Plenty of time to get to the meeting.

She knew she had to go. What choice had she? The conspirators all knew her from the meeting Hefget had ordered her to attend, while she knew almost none of them. They had seen her face; they would recognize her anywhere, even in her court finery. So it was no good trying to drop out of the cabal now; she would have to brazen it out to the end, until Baka could step in and arrest them all.

Why had she been so stupid as to get into this thing in the first place? It had hurt her, it had hurt Baliniri, and—perhaps this was the worst part of it all—she now stood a good chance of getting caught at her spying game. And if she did, could she stand up under torture, refuse to talk? She doubted it. She would betray Baka, the whole thing. . . .

Well, there was no use thinking about all that now. She would concentrate on learning what she could today. If it were a really important meeting, perhaps they would let out some damning information, which she could take to Baka immediately after adjournment. During their last meeting, Hefget had revealed that the day of the coup was approaching, but he had not given her an exact date or occasion. She only knew that the day they were planning to kill the king and his vizier would have to be a festival day, when Dedmose would make a public appearance and therefore be vulnerable. But which festival day? The Egyptian calendar was studded thickly with festivals, and the king had the option of celebrating any or all of these privately.

If she could find out today where and when the plot was going to come to fruition and get the information back to Baka, perhaps it would all have been . . . well, "worth it" was the wrong phrase. There would always be the shame, the betrayal of herself and of both the men she loved, about this episode in her life, and she would have a hard time ever living it down. She would make it up to Ben-Hadad if she lived through all this—after all, she would have all the years of her life to do so.

But how could she atone for what she had done to Baliniri if she held to her resolve never to see him again? There was no answer; it was just one of those terrible things that people in their blind stupidity do to other people, blundering clumsily into each other's lives, causing hurt, and then going away without doing anything to salve the pain. She had always hated the sort of person who did this—and now she learned that she was one of them, whether or not she liked the truth.

She looked around at the row of shabby houses, at the fouled gutter thick with flies, at the filth in the open street. As she stood musing, a woman, back bent under a heavy burden of sticks for her fire, came trudging past. Her face was careworn and drawn, and there was in her weak and watery eyes a look of desperation. Tuya looked away quickly and almost started crying again. One was young for such a short time, and then one was old, then dead before she had even begun to learn to live. Could a girl be blamed for reaching out for happiness when it passed?

But she had reached out for happiness with Ben-Hadad, and then had seen it all go sour due to her barrenness, her inability to fit into the new life he had begun, here in Lisht. Then, giving up too quickly, she had reached out for the handsome soldier Baliniri, only to realize that she was finally with child by her husband and must abandon all hope of a future with Baliniri. She could neither go forward nor backward with any sort of grace. Any turn she took would be full of bitterness and peril.

There was only one thing to do, and that was to see the conspirators apprehended and the plot neutralized. She would have to go to the meeting. After that, she had a lot of hard thinking to do.

II

"Go away!" The angry voice, muffled, thick with sleep,

came from inside the bolted door. "We're not open until evening!"

Mekim, weaving unsteadily on his feet, pounded all the louder, drowning out whatever else the innkeeper may have had to say. "Open up!" he demanded in a raucous voice, blurred with alcohol. "I've got a fat purse to spend, me and my friend, and if you haven't got this door open by the time I've counted to ten, I'm going to find somewhere else to spend it." He pounded the door again for emphasis, then he turned to Baliniri and winked, his rough face set in an owlish grin. "There now," he said in a more normal voice. "If that doesn't bring him running—"

The door opened a crack. "Oh, it's you! Why didn't you say so? I'm always open for a good customer." The innkeeper swung the door wide. His hair stuck out on all sides, unkempt; his eyes were red-rimmed. "Even if I *was* open until dawn." He looked down with a critical eye at the purse in Mekim's hand, mentally gauging its contents. Then he looked up at Baliniri, towering high above his head. "Ah, Captain. We haven't had a visit from you in quite some time. A rare pleasure, sir."

Mekim pushed past the proprietor and marched, albeit in the crookedest of lines, to his customary table by the window, opened the shutter, sniffed in the fresh morning air, and sat down. "Now," he said, "my friend has some evil spirits to drive away, and I need some poison to neutralize last night's overindulgence. I think I was drinking palm wine. What's the antidote for that?"

"Well, sir, we have millet beer, brewed after the Nubian fashion, thick and strong. It's good for calming the stomach and"—he winked at an unsmiling Baliniri—"driving away the goblins." The innkeeper struggled into his working robe and combed his hair with his fingers.

"Good. Bring us *plenty* of that." Mekim dropped the purse on the table with an ostentatious thud. "Relax, Baliniri. You look awful. What did *you* have to drink last night?"

The big man sat down heavily. "Nothing much—a cup or two of wine. No more. No, it isn't that. I've lost her, Mekim. This time it's forever." He rubbed his eyes with the heels of his hands.

Mekim frowned. "The little one, eh? Picked up and went away, just like that?"

Baliniri buried his face in his hands. His words were

muffled, but there was no mistaking the despairing tone. "She's been trying to end it for some time. Always, after saying good-bye, she's come back. And then our time together would have a strange, desperate edge on it, as if she were trying to pack our whole lives into one night, as if she were going to die on the morrow. She'd hold onto me as if she'd slip off into an abyss the moment she were to let go."

The innkeeper came back and placed bowls in front of his customers, then poured a dark liquid to the rim. He placed the jug beside them and withdrew. Mekim took one bowl, sipped from it, and handed the other to his friend. "Here, try this. Not bad. Thicker and sweeter than we're used to, but not bad. Good for what ails you."

Baliniri took the bowl, but stared down into it rather than drinking from it. In a moment he set it down. "This morning I could tell that this time she'd not return." He sighed. "I'm glad I was able to find you, Mekim. I needed someone to talk to."

Mekim smiled, quite pleased with the turn of events. "Well, look," he said expansively, "I'll ask around about her in the marketplace. Surely somebody there will know where to find her."

"That's just it," Baliniri said. "Nobody knows anything about her. She just seems to have showed up one day at the Market of the Four Winds." He did pick up the bowl now, and he tried a little of the dark brew.

"No one knows where she lives? About her family? Friends? Nothing?"

"Nothing. Gods, Mekim, I've been preparing myself for this for days. But I had no idea her leaving was going to be so devastating."

Mekim took one look at the disconsolate slump of his friend's huge shoulders, frowned, took another stiff drink, then poured himself more. "Ah, me," he said. "How much simpler it was back in the Land of the Two Rivers, or along the coast of the Great Sea. One wanted a woman, he just took her, and that was all there was to it." He waved for the innkeeper again. "Here!" he said. "Could we have some bread? Maybe some cheese or salt fish? Suddenly I'm hungry as a bear." He looked down at his feet, where the innkeeper's pet hound lay, chin on paws. Absently Mekim reached down and patted the dozing animal on the head. "What a pity. Getting all sloppy over a woman. It would be a simpler life if we treated women like a pet dog or cat—if one of them runs away, you find another."

Baliniri raised his head and now had a look of intense concentration on his face. "Mekim," he said, slowly smiling. "Thank the gods for your tendency to prattle. You've given me an idea."

"Idea?" his companion said, draining the bowl again and reaching for the jug.

"Yes. The dog. Why didn't I think of it before? Always, when she came and went, there was a perky little dog with her, with his tail up in the air like a deer's, like a little flag. When we spent the night together, the dog would be sitting at the bottom of the stairs in the morning, waiting for her. He followed her wherever she went, even though she never seemed to pay much attention to him."

Mekim just stared. "I don't understand. If she's gone, so is her dog."

"Maybe not. Animals come and go. If I can find the dog, maybe he'll lead me to her, or at least take me to where she lives. From there I can start asking around. Perhaps somebody will recognize her description."

Mekim rolled his eyes heavenward. "Spare me, you gods. I thought perhaps this crazy notion of his had finally played itself out. Will we ever get back to soldiering? I'd hoped to be in Nubia by now. Instead—"

But Baliniri was on his feet. "Thank you, Mekim. Be a good chap and pay the innkeeper. I've got to go. If I can find that little dog of hers—"

"Wait!" Mekim cried, trying to stand. But the effects of a night and morning spent drinking and carousing were not so easily shaken off. He sat back down hard. By the time he could regain his equilibrium, Baliniri had gone out the door, a new sense of purpose in his steps, his posture. Mekim cursed him roundly, sighed deeply, and called for more beer.

On the way to the meeting Tuya's courage faltered, and she almost talked herself out of going through with it. But a few minutes' quiet sitting by the first of the two fountains from which the street got its name managed to calm her. She closed her eyes, listened to the sound of the bubbling water, and by and by she became more optimistic. *It'll be all right,* she kept telling herself. *Just concentrate on listening and remembering whatever you hear, so you can tell Baka afterward.* Once he had heard everything and could make mass arrests of the conspirators, surely she would be safe. Anyone who managed to escape Baka's nets would be in such a perilous position that he would be unable to—or unwilling to—pose a threat to her or her loved ones.

Her heart fluttering with anxiety, she started out once again down the wide street toward the warehouse at the end, past the second fountain. *Head up!* she told herself. *Act the part you've written for yourself: You're a tough street kid who isn't afraid of anybody, who walks down the streets as if she owned them, who feels at home anywhere.*

As she passed the second fountain, however, she saw someone at the end of the cul-de-sac approaching the door. The conspirators' first rule was simple and unbreakable: Let the other person enter, then wait a bit. Don't give any onlooker the impression that this is a popular address. She let the man enter, waited until she had counted to fifty, then made her way past the deserted fountain into the dead-end street.

*That must have been Mereb,* she thought, remembering the dark eye patch. Not a big man in the councils of the conspirators, but a key one: one who controlled the activities of several smaller cells at the same time. One who, most likely, knew the higher-ups and might possibly betray them under torture. Well, he would be easy to describe to Baka. She would try to memorize the masked conspirators' postures and their hands, especially if they had any peculiarities by which they could be identified when the time came.

*Hands!* Her own palms were sweating profusely as she stood before the door. She wiped them on her garment, then knocked. Three knocks, pause, two knocks, pause, then three knocks again.

The door opened a crack. "Ah. Go right in." The guard remained in deep shadow, his face concealed. The inner room was dark. Tuya blinked, trying to accustom her eyes to the gloom of the interior. The door was shut behind her, and she was locked in the camp of the enemy, once and for all.

Dede, watching from a shadowed doorway opposite the fountain, chewed on his upper lip nervously. The girl! Who was she? Where had he seen her before?

Wait. Yes. The little street-urchin he had seen in the Market of the Four Winds, stealing dates, the day Hefget had warned him against public recognition of Mereb. She had looked like a skinny child then—it had come as a surprise when she had turned and he had seen her breasts. Well, she was not so skinny now. Perhaps she had graduated from stealing dates in the market to something more lucrative.

How stupid of him! Of course she had, if she was spying on the Mesopotamian soldier for the cause. Doing well at it, too, from what Hefget had said. Well, Hefget was probably slipping her some money in exchange for her services, and the soldier fellow was no doubt feeding her these days. Anyhow, she looked downright healthy, for all the worry that had been on her face as she approached the door.

Still, why did he keep thinking that he had seen her elsewhere?

He looked at the sun, rising above the warehouse that fronted the little square below the fountain. Time to go. If he were late, Hefget would get mad at him, and that would not do when he had to present the information he had learned in the Fayum. He had to avoid getting upset if he wanted to remember, much less present, the information he had gathered. He squared his shoulders and crossed the street to knock with the signal he had been taught, rapping smartly on the thick door.

As he did, another furtive figure, robed, face veiled, detached itself from the deep shadows and moved quickly to the doorway where Dede had been standing, with the precise steps of a dancer. Only when the watcher had seen Dede safely inside did he turn to look right and left down the cul-de-sac to make sure no idle eyes observed him. Then he pulled the hood back and approached the door. His own pattern of raps was less assertive. "Who's there?" the guard demanded.

"Sitra," the man in the robe said. "Let me in quickly. I don't want to be seen." The guard let him in and closed the door behind him.

After a time Lion gave up sniffing and scratching at the base of the wall over which Tuya had disappeared, and trotted back out of the narrow street into the main thoroughfare, turned the corner, went back around the block of houses. Experimentally he sniffed his way into a side street and, finding no trace of Tuya's distinctive scent, tried another alley.

This time he stopped, tail wagging furiously, tongue lolling, and looked around him. There seemed to be some trace of the elusive scent, but it was masked under a host of conflicting smells. Had she come this way? The little dog stood his ground, confused; then, nose to the ground, he sniffed his way to the corner and into a short half block of dead-end street.

As he did, two men came around the corner and spotted the animal. One of them, tall, with a bald head, carried a net; the other, shorter, painfully thin, wore a coiled whip at his belt. "Look, Dali," the thin one said. "There's one. Quick, block off the street so he can't get away."

The tall one shook his net out with practiced ease. "You've a sharp eye, Kiki," he said. "The royal leopard will eat well tonight. I'd about given up on finding anything more today."

Kiki uncoiled his long whip and flexed it. "Given up?" he said. "With the number of strays in this quarter? Now, just stand there and keep alert, and we'll have him. I'll give him a touch of the quirt and drive him toward you."

"I'm ready," Dali said, holding the net spread wide, while crouching, poised for action. "Now stir him up a bit." He looked hard at the little dog, sniffing at the ground in front of the fence where the street ended, apparently unconcerned by their presence. "Come along here, doggie," he said in a wheedling voice. "There's a good boy!"

## III

Stretched out before the line of masked men was a long, narrow table, one with raised borders nailed to its corners. The table had then been covered with a shallow layer of fine sand. The viewers on the far side of the table could not quite see the surface of the table from a sitting position, but it had not seemed to matter thus far; after a quarter of an hour of talk, the masked men had yet to refer to it.

Up to now the discussion had not been of interest to Tuya: reports from this or that underling, on subjects outside her range of concern. The only exception from this pattern had been when Mereb, the man with the eye patch, had relayed to the council the precious little information—most of it fabricated, but having the sound of insider's authenticity— that Tuya had passed on to Hefget as having come from Baliniri. Mereb promised better revelations in the future. At no time did Mereb refer directly to Tuya; apparently his ego did not allow for the sharing of credit. Tuya silently breathed a sigh of relief at the fact and scrunched down even farther in her second-row seat while he spoke, as if by doing so she could avoid notice from the conspirators seated around her.

This was not altogether successful. A hulking, moon-faced fellow sitting next to Hefget, six seats away and one row back, seemed to have taken undue interest in her. She looked back once or twice, and both times found him staring at her. It was unsettling; she had taken great pains to look unattractive—her clothing was still a ragamuffin's, and her hair was a mess. So why was this man showing such interest in her?

Worse: Up on the stand where the masks veiled the leaders' faces, one could not even see the eyes of these chimerical creatures. Yet she could feel the eyes of one of them on her. No, she was sure it was not her nervousness that conjured up this feeling of being watched; someone up there was actually giving her something of the same kind of scrutiny the round-faced fellow had been giving her. But why?

The Sobek mask was speaking now: ". . . the takeover by the Shepherds of the means of food production in the delta is from all accounts now complete. The work has been done with Salitis's customary boorishness, with predictable results. There have been riots, stonings of guards, even one bungled attempt at assassination of a minor official. The reprisals have been quite brutal."

Tuya's concentration was interrupted by that strange feeling she had had earlier. She turned and looked back, but the moon-faced man was looking at the Sobek figure and not at her. Yet someone, one of the men behind the masks, was intent this very moment upon her face, searching her features. Who? Who?

"We had intended to delay the coup until later," the Sobek mask continued, "until the state takeover of the food-producing resources here in the Red Lands and in the Fayum was complete. But Madir has made amazing progress, and it now appears we can go back to our original date for the assassinations and our takeover of the government."

Tuya's eyes went wide, and she forgot her premonitions. Gods! This was it, then!

"It is Dedmose's custom," the Sobek mask said, "to attend the annual festival of Ptah-Sokaris-Osiris, which is sacred to all natives of his home city, Buto. Madir, Baka, and court members will also attend. This will place within our grasp, at one time, virtually every one of our enemies."

This brought a murmur of appreciation from the crowd, and set Tuya's heart beating even faster. The festival was only days away! What a stroke of luck that she had attended a meeting in time to learn of this! Armed with detailed knowledge, Baka could be prepared for their treachery.

"The ritual calls for Dedmose to stage a mock fight with several of the priests, who will be our allies. The 'weapons' should be made of reeds, harmless. Ordinarily these would be faked up by the armorer Ben-Hadad"—here Tuya's heart skipped a beat, but she forced a look of interest onto her face—"but, as our good fortune would have it, he's in Nubia just now and has been replaced in the present enterprise by—"

"Wait!" the Horus mask said. "I have new information. Ben-Hadad and Shobai have been sent back from Nubia. Apparently they're making their way back here quickly."

"When do you estimate they'll be back?" the Sobek mask asked. "Not before the festival, I hope?"

"Very near. They could arrive in time for the festivities."

The Sobek figure thought for a moment. Tuya's thoughts were mixed. Ben-Hadad home again, and soon! This was cause for joy—or should have been. Now she was not so sure. If there were physical danger in this, she hoped he would not arrive until after Baka had had time to arrest all of these people.

"We'll have to proceed according to plans," the Sobek figure said. "I'll have the returning party ambushed on the way back to Lisht."

"That'll take some doing," the Horus mask said. "There's a war party with them, led by Anup, a very able commander. And there's always the chance that Akhilleus will send some of his own people back with Shobai and Ben-Hadad. The blind man is an old friend of his and has tremendous military power at his disposal."

"Ah, yes." Another moment of thought. "Well, even that can be dealt with. There's bound to be confusion in Nubia, with the war ending so recently. Meanwhile, I'll explain the present plans. During the ceremony Dedmose and Madir will be quite vulnerable, and thanks to our subordination of several key people, some of the 'fake' spears will be real ones. King and vizier will fall in the first moments—"

"Wait!"

The voice, shrill and loud, came from the third row. Tuya's eyes went back to the source. To her horror, the moon-faced man was standing, pointing at her!

"There's a traitor here!" he cried. "The short woman there! Someone grab her, quick! I just recognized her! She's a friend of Baka's!"

The uproar was instantaneous. Rough hands grabbed Tuya's arms from both sides; she was dragged up to the table. The moon-faced man advanced on her, finger still pointing. "Yes!" he said. "I saw her talking to Baka! She must be the one who approached my woman a while back, when my woman and I were . . . having troubles! That little one's been asking about me! She's a spy! A spy for Baka!"

Tuya struggled, but the hands on her arms were too strong for her. "Let me go!" she cried. "I don't know what you're talking about!"

But this was the first time she had spoken, and in the end it was her voice that betrayed her. "Wait!" the voice of the Horus mask said. He stood, looked at her. She still could not see his eyes, but she did recognize his voice. *Sitra!* The secretary who controlled access to Madir. If only Madir knew—

"This man's right," he said. "I recognize her, too. She's no street urchin! She's Ben-Hadad's wife. She was at the ceremony when he was given the commission to go to Nubia! She was presented to Dedmose!" His voice was full of malice.

"Take her away!" the Sobek mask commanded in a harsh voice. "We'll find a way to deal permanently with her later."

"No!" Sitra shouted, his high-pitched voice distorted by the mask. "Don't put her to death! She's worth more alive than she could ever be dead!"

"Eh?" the Sobek mask asked, surprised. "What do you mean?" His hand motioned Tuya's captors to wait for a moment; they held her fast. "What do you propose? Ransom? What for? Once we've killed the king and Madir, her husband's life won't be worth anything, either."

"No!" the Horus mask said. "Get word to Shobai's caravan. Tell them to halt at the Bahariya oasis, or the girl dies.

All we need is to delay them for a day or two. Once the coup has taken place we'll control not only the court but the army as well, with Baka dead. When they arrive, we'll cut them down like cornstalks."

"No! No!" Tuya cried at last, despair in her heart. "Let me go! Baka knows all about you! He'll come and get you!"

The Sobek mask chuckled. "If you'd already tipped him off, this meeting would have been broken up moments after the last of us had entered. Half of us would be dead already. No, you're bluffing. And yes," he said, addressing Sitra, "your plan's a good one. We'll hold this little one. We'll need her." He turned to the guards. "Take her away!"

"Yes, sir," the guard on her left said, tightening the already painful grip he had on her arm. "Where shall we take her?"

The man in the Sobek mask paused. Then he looked at Sitra. "I think you should handle this," he said. "If we intend to follow your suggestions."

Sitra nodded, then looked at Tuya, and for the first time she could see his eyes: cold, dismissive. "Yes. Take her to my place. Until the coup. After that, we'll have no need for her. Perhaps I'll give her to the slaves."

"Good," the Sobek mask agreed. "Just get her out of here. We've had enough distraction. When you come back, we'll finish discussing our plans."

Going out the door, the grip of one of the guards relaxed on her arm, and Tuya yanked hard and pulled free. "Stop!" the guard cried.

She spun around, trying to pull free from her other captor, but his grip was like a vise. She pulled, twisted, and kicked viciously at his privates, but she missed, hitting him high on the thigh instead. Sitra pulled off his heavy wooden mask and smashed her in the face with it. For a moment there was a blinding flash of light before her eyes, and her knees buckled. She almost lost consciousness, but Sitra slapped her face, hard, with his open palm.

"You little slut!" he hissed, his face less than a handspan from hers. "Try to betray us, will you? You'll pay for that— not once, but many times!" He stepped back and let her two captors get a firmer grip on her. "Take her to the warehouse near the Market of the Four Winds, the one they boarded up last week. Bind and gag her and dump her in a basket. Cover her up with rags, old clothes, anything you can find, before you deliver her to my house. I don't want you dropping the basket for people to see what's inside. I'll tell my servants you're coming."

As he spoke, Tuya made one last attempt to pull loose from the guards. Their grip held. Worse, Sitra, his face contorted by hate, swung the mask at her once more. The blinding flash again, then darkness and oblivion.

## IV

"Come on, you fool!" Dali said, shaking out the net. "Can't you drive him over to me?"

Kiki sucked dolefully on one spidery hand, where the dog had bitten him. "The little devil nearly took my finger off!" he complained. "If you think you can do any better, you come try. I'll hold your confounded net for you." He eyed Lion warily, frowning, keeping the injured finger in his mouth. The dog, sharp-eyed, crouched, ready to spring again.

"Move over to one side," Dali directed scornfully. "Get him up against the far wall. Then give him a taste of the whip and drive him over to me." He advanced, shaking the net, blocking access to the street. "Just come over to me, now, you little bastard. . . ."

Kiki stepped to the extreme side of the narrow alleyway, whip in hand. As he did, Lion feinted, snarling, baring his sharp little teeth. Kiki, startled, almost dropped the whip. "Stay alert, damn you!" Dali shouted. "Don't let him get away!"

But as the two maneuvered into position, something happened in the street behind Dali that distracted Lion completely. Three men walked past, one of them carrying an unconscious woman over one shoulder. Lion caught the familiar scent immediately. His mistress! Where were they taking her? He forgot himself, rushed forward, and ran full tilt into Dali's net!

"Ah!" Dali said, throwing the net around the little animal. "Got him! No thanks to you, you wretched coward!" He watched as Lion, barking fiercely, struggled in the meshes. "I was beginning to wonder if we were going to catch him."

Kiki coiled his whip and stuck it in his belt, then went back to sucking on his injured hand. "You don't have to be so disagreeable," he said.

"Sorry," Dali said. "Don't take it to heart. We've got what we came for, anyhow. Now help me carry the little troublemaker. If we keep the net between us, he won't be able to reach us with those teeth of his."

Lion wriggled, trying desperately to get loose. Why were those men taking his mistress away? Why was she asleep? He chewed at the net, worrying the knots, his mind racing. What had that strange scent been, on the third of the men carrying her away? Could he remember it? If only he could get out of this strange thing they had him trapped in . . .

Now, however, they picked him up, still tangled in the mesh, and carried him down the long street, in the opposite direction from the one the three had taken Tuya. He struggled, bit angrily at the fiber. One by one the knots gave way; still he worried the net with his teeth, shaking his head from right to left. He would get loose; he would free himself from this thing, and get away from these men. Then he would find his mistress and learn what they had done with her, and why she looked that way.

"Wait," Baka said. "This is beginning to make a peculiar kind of sense. Let me see if I've understood you: This girl . . . she just seems to have showed up one day in the market? Nobody knew where she came from? Nobody knew where she lived?"

Baliniri nodded. "That's about it. I asked around, but all anyone could tell me was that she is light-fingered beyond belief—could steal a man's beard and be gone before he knew it was missing. And," he said after a moment's reflection, "that she is uncommonly quick with a sharp knife she always carries. Not that that saved her the time I first met her. Got in over her head, and I had to—well, I had to put a few of your least impressive irregulars out of commission."

Baka laughed. The two were walking by the canal that diverted Nile water into the king's quarter, looking down at the slow-moving, fouled water. "I had heard about that. I wasn't going to bring it up. Tell me more about the girl. She was short, then? Dark? With a thin face?"

"Yes. How did you know? I hadn't described her."

Baka sighed and pounded one fist into the other palm. "You've described her well enough," he said. "Damn! I know exactly what she was up to. I should have known! I should have figured it out beforehand and stopped her."

"How? How would you have known?" Baliniri said. "How do you know of her? They said she hadn't any friends. . . ."

Baka closed his eyes and seemed for a moment lost in thought, puzzling over thorny problems. Then, when he opened his eyes again, it was to look into Baliniri's, earnestly, intently. "Tuya isn't a street urchin at all. She's a very dear friend of mine, and she's been missing for a day. I have people out looking for her."

"So I was right about her— She never belonged in the rags she wore, really. She was so obviously so much more than a street-smart thief. But—you say she's missing?"

"You may have been the last to see her. Frankly, I'm afraid for her. Come, let's talk to the captain of the guard. I'll have him alert the city guards. I think Tuya has gotten herself into some real trouble. I have someone watching her house, and he's supposed to let me know immediately if she shows up. So far I haven't heard a word from him."

"Her house? She has a house? For the love of heaven, man, who is she?"

Baka took his arm and steered him away into the main thoroughfare. "We'll talk on the way. Hurry, now. If she's been up to what I think she has, she's in danger. I warned her, confound it, but she wouldn't listen. She's always had a stubborn streak."

" 'Always'? Baka, I'm not moving an inch till you tell me who she is."

"She's the wife of Ben-Hadad, the armorer from Canaan. You know the name. Shobai's nephew. I don't remember if you two met."

"No." Baliniri bit his lip, anguished. "But of course. That explains a lot," he said, more to himself than to Baka. "When she said good-bye, I knew there was something more to it. She was suffering, feeling guilty. She . . . she loves him, then?"

Baka shook his head, pondering, as the two started briskly down the long street. "If she's been suffering, she loves him," he said simply. "I wonder what made her stray? What made her transfer her love to you? Knowing Tuya, she wouldn't have done that lightly. We men can be damned insensitive at times. We neglect our women, mistreat them, break their bloody hearts." His face twisted in self-loathing. "I lost a wife that way. I neglected her for this damned war. Something like that was probably to blame here. Ben-Hadad has been spending most of his time at the forge in the past year and has left Tuya alone too much." He turned his head, still walking briskly, to face Baliniri. "You got involved with her, then? Really involved?" But, seeing the closed look on his friend's face, he turned back to the road. He stopped, seeing a uniformed guardsman approaching. He accepted and returned the man's salute and said, "The armorer's wife. Anything new to report?"

"No, sir. I was at her house only minutes ago. Someone came to see her when I was there, but—"

"Eh?" Baka said, perking up suddenly, all alertness and attention. "Who was it, man?"

"A friend of the family. Name was Heket—"

Baka turned to Baliniri. "Shobai's children's nurse. She's all right." He turned back to the guardsman. "Any other visitors?"

"No, sir. It looks like the girl didn't have any friends except this woman Heket."

"Good work. Continue the surveillance and keep in close touch."

"Yes, sir." The man saluted but did not turn to go. "Sir, the children's nurse . . . she may know something. There was something about her manner, maybe something she was on the verge of telling me, but was reluctant to—"

"Thank you. I'll talk to her myself. She may very well know something. She's intelligent, keeps her eyes open." He dismissed the soldier, then turned to Baliniri. "Come on. We'll talk to Heket. I'll fill you in as we go." He set out again at an even faster clip, but, rounding the corner, slammed into one of two men carrying a net between them. Baka was lean and hard for all his patrician appearance; he bowled over the smaller of the two men, who dropped his end of the bundle the two were carrying. The quarry in the net started struggling and barked ferociously.

Baka was about to apologize, but then he saw the face of the man he had knocked off his feet. "You!" he said. "Haven't I told you to stay out of this area? What have you got there? Don't you know the law against trapping animals inside the city limits?" The dog in the net, hopelessly stuck, barked all the louder. Baka's fingers tore at the netting, trying to untangle it.

The second man came forward. "Sir," he said. "We are from the royal household. We're to provide meat for—"

"Don't give me any trouble. You've broken the law. Trapping is permitted only beyond the city walls. Now report to the captain of the guard."

They did not wait for the rest, but abandoned the net and the dog inside it. Baka knelt and worked at the knotted ropes. "Here, help me with—" He stopped, aghast. "It's Lion! Ben-Hadad's dog!"

"It is?" Baliniri said. "Why, yes! This is the one I used to see her with!" He pulled his sword and cut through the remaining strands. "Come out here, fellow." He patted the little animal reassuringly. "Calm down, now. . . ."

"We may be in luck," Baka said. The little dog, recognizing him, licked his hand. "Lion used to follow her everywhere. Perhaps he knows where she is."

Sitra's house was one of the largest in town: much larger than the town house owned by the far more powerful Madir. Sitra's unique position as the man through whom access to Madir had to be arranged had made him the recipient of a thousand bribes, and he had accepted enough of these over the years to allow him to live in secure luxury. The high walls of his villa enclosed formal gardens, a pair of ornamental pools fed with waters diverted at great expense from the Nile, and a zoo second only to that of the crown. Under the flowering sycamore and figs, peacocks and other rare birds roamed freely; inside the great house, guests walked an uneasy path through a spacious vestibule in habited by half-tame leopards, cheetahs, and other exotic animals. On festive occasions, when large crowds were on hand, the carnivores were chained; at other times their presence in that area, which led to the villa's private quarters, was considered a security measure, and the animals were allowed to roam at will.

Thus, when Tuya, still unconscious, was delivered at Sitra's door and handed over to his servants, they carried her past curious animals that sniffed at her as she passed, memorizing her scent. And when she was finally deposited on a couch in Sitra's hall, and her eyes fluttered open, the first eyes she looked into were those of a great jungle cat: great, glowing, half-dilated eyes, regarding her with cool interest.

Tuya froze for a moment, and then screamed.

The leopard recoiled, roared, pawed the air with a powerful clawed forefoot. Tuya sat up, fell back onto the floor, the couch separating her from the animal, and sat paralyzed with fear. "*H-help!*" she said in a voice so constricted by her abject terror that it could barely be heard. "Please . . . somebody . . ."

One of the servants took note of her and walked up to the leopard, cuffing it on the ear. The animal snarled, but drew back, apparently used to such treatment. "Don't mind him," the servant said. He looked her over, noting her fear, and smiled unpleasantly. "These things are frightening to you? All the better. You'll think twice before trying to escape. You can only get out through that room"—he pointed— "and there are *more* cats in there. They're worse-tempered than this fellow is, by a long shot."

"W-where am I?" Tuya said. "Oh, I remember. Sitra's house." She shrank back against the wall, her eyes on the leopard. There was a throbbing pain on one side of her head. She reached up and felt a lump. Blood had dried on her skin.

"That's what he smells," the servant said, enjoying her obvious discomfort. "Blood. Don't let him get too close. He'll try to lick it off you. And if he gets used to the taste, you're in trouble." Tuya looked back at the leopard; its eyes were still on her. She closed her own eyes but could not blot out the sight of it. Her heart was pounding, pounding. How could they have known? The one thing in the world she feared . . .

## V

As Baka and Baliniri strode briskly through the city streets, Lion danced along ahead of them. From time to time the dog would stop at a street corner and sniff the wind or the stones underfoot or the high ground beside a puddle; but always he returned to the road.

Baka watched the dog. *He's on to something*, he thought.

He had heard again and again from Ben-Hadad about how the animal's loyalty had gotten him and Tuya out of trouble many times in the past. He shuddered. If he were right, if the thing he feared actually had happened, he would need all the help he could get finding her.

"I don't understand," Baliniri was saying. "What could have possessed her to do such a thing? If these people she was spying on are as dangerous as you say—"

"They are." He steered Baliniri around a corner now, always following the dog. "I tried to warn her after I realized that she was getting involved in the conspiracy. Damn! What a fool I was to tell her about it in the first place."

There was a wistful note in Baliniri's voice when he answered. "I don't know. If you hadn't told her, I might never have gotten to know her!" He looked at Baka. "You say she really was a street kid when Ben-Hadad met her?"

"Yes. Orphaned, living by her wits. She had a reputation in the Avaris markets for being absolutely fearless—and honest, in her own way. She would steal a melon, but only from a stall that had done good business that day and could spare it. She was a loyal friend, generous to a fault with whatever poor provender she had—and, until she met Ben-Hadad, she had never been touched by a man."

"I see. So when she took up with this armorer fellow—"

"He wasn't an armorer then. He'd just come in from Canaan and couldn't find work. Hardly spoke the language. He turned out to have a marvelous natural flair for senet, a game we play here. He was playing matches for money. Then the boy met his uncle, who took Ben-Hadad as his apprentice. The lad is good-hearted but thickheaded. He took the longest time to see that little Tuya worshiped the ground he walked on." He made a face. "He'll never be one of the great armorers, either. Bloodlines aren't everything. His father was an artistic genius. And a legendary hero—perhaps you've heard of Hadad of Haran?"

"Him?" Baliniri said, astonished. "I've been hearing about Hadad of Haran for most of my life. Somehow I had it in my mind that his confrontation with the Shepherds happened long ago. How old is his son?"

"Mid-twenties, but emotionally young for his age. And Tuya, poor dear, always seemed older and wiser. The only thing she wasn't wise about was her own worth. She had no idea what a prize she was. She—"

But he happened just then to look at Baliniri's face, and witnessing the other man's misery suddenly like this, his own sense of loss came back to him. *Mereet! Mereet! Where are you?*

Up ahead, Lion veered out of the path, heading for the market that bordered on Tuya's home street. The dog crossed the square, threading his way through the legs of a few shoppers, and came to a stop before a familiar figure: Heket, Shobai's pleasant-faced housekeeper. At her feet were Mereet and Shobai's boy and girl twins. The boy, Ketan, and girl, Teti, embraced the dog; Lion responded by licking Ketan's face until the child giggled and begged the animal to stop. Lion backed away, then scampered off, while Baka steered his friend to the group.

"Baka!" the servant said, smiling. But then her smile turned somber. "You haven't found her."

"No. Heket, this is Baliniri. He's a soldier from the Land of the Two Rivers, and a friend of mine and Tuya's."

A fresh crowd of shoppers surged into the square just then, and Heket bent to pick up Ketan. "Could one of you get Teti for me?" she asked. "They have a tendency to wander off in a crowd like this and get lost."

"I'll get her," Baliniri offered, and bent over to pick up the tiny, dark-eyed girl-child. "Hello!" he said. "My name is Baliniri. Who are you?"

"I'm Teti," the child said. "You're almost as big as Father. Are you an armorer too?"

"No, I'm a soldier. But I know your father's work."

"He's blind. He's going to teach me *and* Ketan how to make weapons, though." She was so intent, so serious, Baliniri's heart went out to her. A thought suddenly tore at his heart: He had been thinking just the previous night about the children he wanted to have with Tuya. Now they would never have the chance—

"I'm going to make swords, just like Father does. He said so."

"A girl? Making swords to kill people?" Baliniri asked, trying to hide his amusement. "Isn't that a little odd?"

"Father's going to show me how," the child boasted, ignoring his question. "I'm going to be a famous sword maker, just like Grandfather was, and Ahuni and Belsunu."

"Belsunu?" Baliniri asked. "I saw a sword of his once. It

was beautiful. I had my own armorer try to copy it, but it wasn't as good. Belsunu was of your kin, then?"

"He was Grandfather's grandfather," the child said, wriggling her tiny body around to show him her back. "Look, I'm a Child of the Lion, just like Ketan is." She pointed with her small, dimpled hand at the red mark on her back, like the paw print of a lion. "Only boys had it, until me. But I've got it, and Father says it means I'm special. He'll train me, just like he'll train Ketan." She curled up in his arms, happy and comfortable, as if she trusted him completely. "I'll make swords for everybody. I'll make one for you. You're nice." She smiled, and dimples appeared in her cheeks. Her dark eyes glowed with sudden affection.

"I'd like that," he said. "When you're old enough, I'll buy a sword from you. That's a bargain. Here's my hand on it." He extended his huge hand, and it engulfed her tiny one. "Would you like to see the sword I have now?" he asked. "It's not as nice as one of Belsunu's. It's not even the copy I had made."

"Yes! Yes! I want to see!" the child cried, craning her neck. He reached down and liberated the battered implement to hand it up to her. It was plainly too heavy for her child strength, but she tried to lift it unaided nevertheless. "It's very heavy!" she said solemnly. He kept a grip on it and let her feel the blade carefully. "You should sharpen it. Father says you ought always to take good care of your sword."

"He's right, of course," Baliniri agreed, smiling with genuine affection at the child. "Careful! You'll cut yourself."

"No I won't," she said. "I know how not to hurt myself. But this isn't a very good sword. I'll make one better than this. Just you watch. I'll make you a wonderful one, when I'm bigger."

"And I'll pay lots of money for it, too." Heket came over to them and held her arms out for Teti. "You two seem to be getting along well! I'll take her now."

"Oh, it's all right," Baliniri said, and Heket dropped her arms. "We're old friends. She's going to make a sword for me when she's bigger."

"Oh, heavens," Heket said, rolling her eyes. "Her father talks that nonsense, too. Pay no attention to it."

"I think she'll do whatever she says she'll do," Baliniri said. "She's quite a little girl. Aren't you, Teti?" He held her up, high over his head; she giggled and crawled into his arms when he lowered her to eye level. "But I have to go now. I think Baka is done here, and I have to go away with him. It's been nice meeting you, Teti. I hope we'll see each other again." He tried to put her down, but she insisted on hugging his neck warmly before he did.

"Good-bye, Baliniri!" the child called, standing beside Heket, looking up at him. "Come back soon!"

Baliniri waved, nodded to Heket, and fell into step beside Baka. "What does Heket know?" he said.

"Well, she spotted Tuya coming out of an inn in the early morning a while back. She's been suspecting something odd was going on. I told her that if Tuya gets out of this in one piece, Heket's not to say anything to Ben-Hadad. If Tuya wants to return to her husband, she should be able to do so. They'll have to work it out as best they can." He looked at Baliniri's face, and his own expression softened. "I know what you're going through," he said. "Be brave. We still have to find her." His sigh was deep and emotional. "I have this terrible feeling they've caught her spying on them. If they have—"

"Look!" Baliniri said. "The dog. He's back."

Baka looked down at his feet, where Lion was dancing again! He ran forward a bit, then stopped and waited, turned to run forward again, stopped and waited once more. "He's all we've got," Baka said. "It can't hurt to follow him. Maybe, just maybe . . ."

The two set out once again, a sliver of hope still in their hearts. But at the intersection of two major thoroughfares, Lion once again bogged down, confused by conflicting signals, by a welter of misleading scents. He walked disconsolately around in circles, nose to the ground; for a moment or so he seemed to favor a particular street, but after ten paces down it he returned to the intersection again and showed the same disappointing signs of confusion. The trail was cold!

*So he's the one*, Heket thought to herself. Somehow she had suspected that Tuya's unhappiness might eventually lead up to something like this. And she *had* looked so . . . guilty that morning. And now here he was, her lover, in broad daylight, trying to find her. And with Baka helping him!

Well, the husband usually had himself to blame in a case like this, and this was no exception. The poor little thing had not fit in from the first. Her whole life had revolved around Ben-Hadad, and what had he done? He had spent all of his days and nights working at that forge of his. *Or*, her mind suddenly suggested, *whatever else it was that he was doing!*

And just look at the fellow! He had turned a lot of women's heads before this, she would wager, and would turn more in the years to come. In her own youth she would have thought nothing of going after a specimen like him! Big, powerful-looking, with curly dark hair . . .

"Heket!" little Teti sang out, pulling on her nurse's hand. "I love Baliniri! Don't you? He's my new friend! I'm going to love him forever!"

"You do, do you?" Heket said, taking the two of them by the hand and leading them away from the market. "Don't you think he's a bit too old for you, Teti? Come, let's go home and—"

"No!" Teti said. "He's not too old! He's my friend! I love him! I'm going to see him again! I'm going to make him a sword when I get big!"

# VI

"It was a natural mistake," Hefget whined. "How was I to know that she was working for the other side? Please, Mereb."

The scarred man turned his one good eye toward him; the look in it was as cold as the southern snows. "I trusted you, Hefget. I authorized you to deal with important matters. And what did you do for me?"

"Please. You yourself thought her a good idea at first. Remember? You complimented me on what I was doing."

"Don't link me with this! It's no affair of mine! I've no intention of sharing your disgrace with you!" The man with the eye patch angrily shook Hefget's hand off his shoulder. "Keep your blundering hands off me! From now on you and I are strangers. Do you hear that? Strangers!"

He turned and set off down the alley, leaving Hefget shaking with desperation and fear. "Mereb!" he cried. "Wait for me! Please! I'll make it up to them!" He jogged down the uneven street after his former mentor, puffing a little. "Mereb, please!"

"Don't use my name in the street, you fool!" the scarred man said in a low, angry voice. "Get away from me!"

Mereb's face was like stone, and his acid words were flung from an angry, immobile mouth. "Don't you understand? The council tossed you out! I will not be seen with you—I'm under suspicion with the council for the first time, and all because of you!"

"You're d-deserting me? But you're my best friend—"

"Friend?" He chuckled bitterly. "I'd even turn down an invitation as a paid mourner." His words were malicious, biting, hurting. "Do you understand? I'm talking about an event in the very near future—that is, if you've anyone who cares enough to want to bury you." He snorted derisively. "More likely you'll end up on an ash heap for the crows to pick at." He turned away, then looked back just once. "Don't follow me. If you do, I may just save the council's assassin a bit of work." With that he turned smartly on one heel and was gone.

Hefget stared blindly after him, his eyes wide open and brimming with tears. "Assassin?" he said in a small and timid voice. "Assassin?" He swayed weakly on unsteady legs. "They're going to kill me! They're going to send someone after me to . . ."

The thought put new life in him. He gathered his failing strength and rushed down the alley. Dede's woman, Taheret, generally could be found at the Market of the Four Winds around this time of day. She would know where he could find Dede. Surely good old Dede would not forsake him! They had been such good friends!

Again Lion's trail had led to a dead end: a half-deserted square between the rich quarter and that of the servant caste. A passing cart had spilled a load of melons in the middle of the street, and the fresh scent had confused the dog; he wandered in small circles, unable to pick up the trail again.

Baka sighed. "It's no use. I think he's done about all he can do for us. Go home, my friend. I have some other ideas, but not all of them can be put to work as publicly as all this."

"Home? What will I do there? I won't be able to rest, or sleep, or think about anything else—"

Baka put a hand on Baliniri's shoulder. "Tell you what. Take the dog with you. He trusts you. I may be wrong about his being played out; he may yet pick up another lead. If he does, you'll be there. Meanwhile, there's somebody I haven't made use of yet." He whispered in Baliniri's ear: "Madir has a spy of great resource, who, in turn, has his own network of informants. They've infiltrated the lower level of this cabal. I'll see what his people know and get a message to you by nightfall."

"Let me come along."

"No. Madir's orders. Not that he doesn't hold you in high regard, but virtually no one except Madir and myself has access to this man."

"I remember a name. Aduna. One of Madir's 'thousand ears,' you called him."

"You're sharp. But it would be best for everyone if you forget that you ever heard that name." He clapped Baliniri on the arm. "I've got to go. Don't worry any more than you have to. I'll keep in touch." But as he turned to go, he saw the hopeless expression on Baliniri's face. *Poor man,* he thought. *However this turns out, it'll turn out badly for him. He knows he's lost her either way.*

"Dede! Please! Don't you turn me away too!"

Moon-faced Dede had acquired a new dignity since discovering the spy. He haughtily drew himself up on the tavern seat, all lofty condescension. "Go away!" he said. "Someone might see us together and draw incorrect conclusions. Haven't you any shame, Hefget? Don't you know what it could mean, having people think you and I—"

Hefget let out a long, despairing breath. "All right," he said bitterly. "Be that way. And after I got you in with these people in the first place . . ."

"I know, I know. And I'm grateful, really I am. But you can't go on trading on that gratitude forever. Not when it gets me in trouble."

Hefget turned away with a curse and left Dede there, sitting before a bowl of palm wine and a plate of olives, looking every bit the same ninny he had always been, despite his newly acquired self-importance. Where could he turn? If even a fool like this shunned him . . . if the council had put an assassin on his tail . . . Face drawn, eyes haunted, he staggered out of the dark inn into the blinding light of midafternoon.

* * *

Two pairs of eyes followed him to the door with interest. "Quick," said Teos, a dark-skinned, balding man. "Get to Aduna and tell him what we've seen. I've been following those two for weeks now. The round-faced fool shuns his former master. . . . Hmmm—something has happened. Hefget looks desperate. This might be a good time for me to see if I can contact him. If he's desperate enough, he might talk to me. You get to Aduna and tell him what I'm up to. Quickly, now!"

His companion, a burly, bearded rough named Penne, stood and nodded. "Be careful," he said. "Hefget looks to be at the end of his tether."

Teos nodded grimly and went out into the street after his quarry.

Sitra triumphant was a malevolent sight indeed. Gone were the birdlike gestures, the epicene mannerisms. In his complete victory over Tuya he was almost masculine, standing there with his puny arms crossed over his narrow chest, glowering at her. The servants, all male, stood by, waiting for his first reaction. Was she to be treated with courtesy or with contempt? They would follow Sitra's example in either case.

Tuya shrank back against the far wall, one eye on the still unchained leopard, which had sat down on the cold stone of the floor and was watching her. "Please," she begged. "Let me go. I won't tell anyone—"

"No, you won't," Sitra said, an unpleasant smile on his face. "I'll see to that—even if it means cutting your tongue out. After you write a letter to your oafish husband, I'll probably dispose of you to the field hands on my estates, those who insist on mating with the opposite sex."

"Why would you want to hurt me?" she asked earnestly. "I haven't done anything to you."

Sitra's expression turned savage. "You? You don't count at all—except as a way of getting back at Baka and his circle. That includes that ham-handed dolt of a husband of yours." He turned to the slave on his left, a slender, well-muscled man in his twenties. "Maya, keep her in the party room, the small one. She'll earn her keep serving wine at intimate dinners. Chain her to the wall. And take that disgusting rag off her. I can smell it from here."

Tuya tried to duck away, but she was too slow. Maya and

another slave grabbed her by the arms, and with one violent motion Maya ripped off the ragged tunic, which was all she wore. "The chain," he said. "How long?"

"Long enough to reach the couches," Sitra said. But now an idea struck him, and he smiled that nasty smile of his. "Wait. Give me that rag you took off her. I'll let the animals smell it. In case she should have thoughts of escaping, she won't get past the leopards after I've given them this to sniff." He took the dusty garment delicately between two fingers and walked over to the great cat in the room behind him. "Here, darling," he said to the leopard. "Dinner." He looked back at Tuya, cowering naked against the wall, her eyes fixed on the great cat. "Well!" he said. "She really *is* frightened. I can see I'm going to have some fun." He tossed the rag to one of the other slaves. "Here. Have each of the cats in the outer room get acquainted with this scent. Then toss the disgusting thing out." He shuddered. "Women!"

Silently, unobserved, the assassin stalked Hefget through the streets of the city. So far the doomed man had kept to the thickly populated areas and had remained relatively safe. But the assassin had experience killing in broad daylight and in thickly crowded areas; it was trickier that way but could be done. After all, his commission did not specify where or how. It just said "before nightfall." There were several hours left.

Someone brushed past him and took off at a brisk pace down the long street. As he watched, the man approached Hefget and took hold of his arm. Hefget stopped; the man spoke to him. The assassin paused, standing in shadow, looking out. He could not hear what they were saying. But Hefget, reluctant to talk at first, seemed now to relax his wariness around the man.

This complicated things. Before, he had had the rest of the afternoon to kill this man. Now perhaps only minutes. And what if Hefget had already told the stranger something the stranger should not know?

He reached inside his garment and loosened the sheath of his long, slender knife. And, silently, silently, he moved in shadow, from one shaded doorway to the next, toward the pair.

"It's all right," Aduna said, his face expressionless, his

heavy-lidded eyes masked. "You can talk in front of Baka."
Penne hesitated still. "It's all *right*, man. Get on with it."

"Yes, sir," the bearded man responded. "It's Teos. He
thinks he's on to something. He's been following a man
named Hefget—"

Both men were instantly alert. "Hefget?" Baka asked.
"Go on!"

"Yes, sir. Hefget has been friendly with a rather stupid
fellow named Dede." Aduna nodded. "A sort of hanger-on of
his. Today Hefget showed up at an inn, looking really frightened, desperate. He seems to have come to Dede for help,
and Dede, who all the time had been kissing Hefget's—"

"Yes, yes. We get the picture."

"Well, sir, Dede cuts him off, as if he's suddenly nobody. And Hefget is *begging* him, as if things had turned
around completely, and whoever had been on top was now
on bottom."

"Yes. So what did Teos do?"

"He went after Hefget. He'll report in. But he wanted
you to know."

"Good work. Now run along, will you? There's a good
fellow." Only when Penne was gone did Aduna speak again.
"I'm afraid this may turn out to be bad news, Baka. The girl
was brought into the conspiracy by Hefget. Something must
have happened today. She's gone, and Hefget is in disgrace."
His heavy brows went up. "I'm afraid your friend Tuya may
be in deep trouble . . . if indeed she's still alive."

Baka shook his head sadly, then was motionless for a
moment. Suddenly he pounded the table savagely with one
fist.

Hefget had pulled Teos back into a dark close between
two buildings. Teos stood with his back to the exit to the
street. "First you've got to promise me amnesty," Hefget
said. "If you do, I guarantee whoever you work for will pay
you well for what I have to tell you. This is big stuff! Very
big!"

But something happened just then. Teos's body jerked
suddenly forward toward him, and he collapsed into Hefget's
arms! Behind him a man advanced, a bloody knife in his
outstretched hand!

Hefget let the body fall and staggered back into a brick
wall. There was no opening. He was trapped! Trapped!

"Please," he said in a hollow, weak voice. "I'll pay you. Anything." But even before the words were out of his mouth, he knew what the unspoken and inexorable answer would be.

## VII

Early the next morning Dede joined Taheret at the Market of the Four Winds. He had rarely done that before, but something in her breakfast conversation had drawn his attention, and he wanted to see for himself. Now, standing unobtrusively beside the well, he looked across the square at where the big man, looking wan and disheveled, sat at the foot of the stairs, the nondescript dog at his feet. "That's the one, eh?" he said. "There sure is a lot of him. He and the girl must have been quite a sight, with her as small as she was."

"I wouldn't know," Taheret said. "I never saw the two of them together. I just wish he'd disappear. He's been asking around about her. All yesterday afternoon he was bothering people with questions."

"And of course you told him nothing," Dede said.

"Don't go bringing *that* up again. How was I to know when she first approached me that—"

"All right, all right." He sneaked another look at the big soldier. "He looks terrible—like he didn't get much sleep last night."

"Nor did I," Taheret said resentfully. "As you know. The faster this is all behind us, the better I'll like it."

"This may be our chance," Dede offered. "In this state he'll be more susceptible—"

Taheret put one restraining hand on Dede's arm. "Susceptible to what? You leave him alone. We came close enough to disaster as it was. It was my fault. I admit it. But we're out from under the cloud now. Don't go putting us back—"

Dede smiled. There was a new air of confidence about him since the day before, when he had denounced the girl to the council. "Don't worry. He looks quite beside himself with fatigue and worry. If I can plant the right suggestion—"

"Don't! Don't do it!"

"He's the last real problem we have here. You heard they found Hefget's body last night. There was someone with him, someone Mereb thinks was Baka's man. The assassin the council put on Hefget's tail could be put to use again. Would you like to redeem yourself in the eyes of my friends once and for all?"

"Why, yes, but . . ."

"Then get a message to Mereb for me, immediately. I'll give you his home address." And, his eyes still on Baliniri, he spoke rapidly into her ear in a low voice. As he did, her mouth went open, and her eyes went very wide.

Sitra's guest had long since departed, and the party room was a mess. Maya gathered up the fouled cushions and the dirty coverlets, and looked around him. The floor would have to be scrubbed, of course; there was spilled wine everywhere, and Sitra's little friend, unused to anything stronger than the sweet wines of the delta, had vomited up the powerful palm wine the girl had poured again and again into his cup at Sitra's bidding.

The girl! Ah, there she was, curled up in a tight ball on the cold stone floor, trying to keep warm. She seemed to be sleeping, but fitfully. Sitra had had her hair cut almost as short as a boy's, but the naked little body coiled up by the far wall, wide-hipped, was no boy's. Maya looked her over with slight distaste and sniffed disdainfully. As he did, she twitched—or was it a shiver? The chain on her ankle rattled. She probably was cold, particularly after working through the night in a room heated by a coal brazier in the center of the floor. She would feel the morning chill.

He put down the dirty cushions for a moment and went to the couch Sitra had left only an hour before. He shook out a spare coverlet and walked over to where the girl lay. For a moment he looked at her again, trying to imagine what men attracted to women might see in her strange body, with its lumps here and lapses there. He decided that by *their* standards, as strange as those might seem to him, she would be considered attractive. He shrugged and started to throw the coverlet over her.

But then a thought struck him, looking down on her soft and vulnerable nakedness. Necho! Of course!

Necho was Sitra's foreman in charge of his private kitchen garden: a tall, devastatingly handsome fellow whom he, Maya, had been trying unsuccessfully to seduce for the better part of a year. It was not as though Necho was not inclined at all in that direction, of course; he would submit gladly to Sitra's own advances. But Necho was as favorably inclined to women as to men, and none of Maya's many overtures had brought him any closer to enjoying Necho's manly embraces, not while there was such a plentiful supply of willing kitchen maids. The little sluts were always tripping out to the garden tempting him, waggling their bare behinds at him. . . .

But what if he, Maya, were to ask Sitra for the girl, to dispose of as he saw fit? And what if he were to use her to tempt Necho to his own bed? To trade her for Necho's affections? He chuckled. The idea had a delicious aptness about it. Why, the girl would be the slave of a slave, given to another slave! He closed his eyes and imagined, as he had so many times in the past, those brawny arms of Necho's, holding him tightly.

He shuddered blissfully. Yes! He would do it. He would be extra attentive to Sitra in the days to come. He would do special things for him—tell the cook to fix Sitra's favorite dishes, treat him to extra attention in his bath. . . . Then when the girl no longer had any value, surely Sitra would be generous when he asked him for her.

He smiled and laid the coverlet over her, almost tenderly. He would have to keep her healthy and out of trouble in the interim, of course. No colds, no beatings to bruise her smooth skin. He smirked benignly and retrieved the fouled cushions he had thrown down. Taking these to the outer room, he tossed them into the basket reserved for them. Used only once but soiled by love's secretions, they were now anathema to the fastidious Sitra. The cushions would be sold for next to nothing to secondhand dealers.

He was about to leave when he spotted a filthy rag on the floor beside a sleeping leopard. Maya recognized it as the tattered tunic the girl had been wearing when they had brought her in, which had been used to acquaint the beasts with her scent. Maya sighed and picked it up to throw it atop the pile. There! They could take it all away now.

"No, I'm not sure it was the same girl," Dede said affably. "After all, I wasn't there. But my friend, now, he was quite definite. 'That's the girl,' he said. 'The one the soldiers tried to have sport with, out behind the inn a week or two ago.' No, now that I think about it, it must have been more than a month." Casually, too casually, he glanced at Baliniri's red-rimmed eyes. "There was some big foreigner who saved her, my friend said—"

"That was me. Yes!" For the first time there was hope in the big man's tired face. "Your friend saw her being taken away? Loaded on a boat? To where?"

Dede looked around, then motioned Baliniri closer. "I'm not supposed to tell you this. I mean, if the authorities come to know about it, the boss gets in serious trouble. After all, nobody is supposed to be dealing with the Shepherds." He shot Baliniri a sharp look. "How do I know I can trust you?"

Baliniri wiped his face with the back of his hand. "Please. I'll pay you for the information. I'm trustworthy. All I care about is the girl. If she's in any danger—"

"Danger? Why, the man I'm talking about sells whores— slaves—to the Shepherd army. It must cost him a fortune in bribes to get the boats past the border guards. But the Shepherds pay well for women—and boys too, some of them."

"Gods!" Baliniri grabbed Dede's garment with one hand and fumbled in his own clothing for a worn purse, which he thrust into Dede's hands. "And this ship—it left when?"

"Last night. This is the sort of shipment that doesn't travel by day." Dede hefted the purse. "Not much chance of catching up to them now, I'm afraid." He waited a beat before adding, "Unless . . ."

"Unless what?" Baliniri asked, his voice hoarse. "If there's any chance of heading them off—"

"Well, I really shouldn't say."

"Don't be coy with me, damn you!" Baliniri shouted, angry for the first time. His huge hand went to Dede's neck and clamped down hard. "What do you know? How can I head them off?"

"L-let me go. P-please." The hand released its grip, but stayed round Dede's neck as a warning. "There might be a way. The boat with the slaves is slow and has to hide in the reeds while arrangements are made to pass the border. A fast two-man sailboat might make up the distance between you and them by, say, late afternoon. You might intercept them at the border."

"Where is the boat bound?"

"The Shepherd garrison at On."

"Where can I find such a boat and a man to sail it for

me?" When the answer was not forthcoming fast enough, Baliniri's hand once again clamped down on Dede's neck. "Quickly, damn you!" The red-rimmed eyes glistened with a single-minded madness, and the grip was that of an angry, desperate man. Dede wheezed, coughed, until the grip loosened enough to allow him to speak.

"D-dock seven," Dede croaked. "Slip five. Ask for Khunes."

Through the whole conversation Lion had stood quietly in the shadows, looking at the both of them. Now, as Dede moved nervously off across the square, rubbing his neck, the dog came up to rub against Baliniri's leg. "No, boy," the soldier said. "This is where we have to part ways. You can't come along. Better go home now. Baka will need you here." He looked down at the dog standing still before him. He backed away. The dog stood its ground. "There's a boy. Home! Go home!"

Lion watched Baliniri move away, then he turned and trotted, tongue lolling, back through the streets. It was obvious that wherever the big man was bound, dogs weren't wanted. Lion jogged easily down the long thoroughfare to the end of the avenue, then turned left. He passed a pair of graybeards, a child dragging her doll behind her in the dust, a pair of gossiping housewives, a cart full of old clothes, drawn by a slave. . . .

Lion stopped abruptly, sniffed the air, turned. The cart. There was something about the cart, with its burden of dirty cloth. A familiar smell. A smell of—

Suddenly he began barking loudly, excitedly. And, seeing a telltale scrap of cloth hanging over the edge of the cart, trotted up to the vehicle. He sniffed at the rag, let out a wild yip, reached up to grasp the overhanging cloth with his teeth. For a moment the cloth hung, and Lion hung suspended from it, holding on only by the grip of his jaws. Then the rag tore, and he fell to the ground with a scrap of it between his teeth. He rolled, landed on all four feet. Tuya! Tuya's scent! Clear as anything!

He stood in the middle of the street, confused. What to do? Chase the wagon? Or—

But now he had made up his mind once and for all. He set off down the street the way he had come, as fast as his short legs would take him. Try as he might, however, he could find no sign of Baliniri.

"All right!" Khunes said. "Steady as she goes! Tiller straight ahead!" He reached up and yanked hard on the line. The knot gave, and the sail, until now bunched tightly against the yard, shook down slowly. He made it fast, slack as it was. "Keep your eyes on the current there, will you? The place out in the middle of the river, where the water's going faster than it is here!"

"Very well," Baliniri said, turning his back to the boat's owner. "Just tell me what you want me to do."

"I will," Khunes said. He smiled secretly as he reached inside his garment for his sharp knife, the one that had dealt out death to the traitors less than a day before. *I could do it now*, he thought, *while he's watching the current*.

But no. Who knew just who was looking on right now, this close to the shore? There were still curious eyes on their boat. Wait until they were downstream a bit, set the big ox to fiddling with the yard, get both his hands tied up with something important, his attention totally diverted. Then, when he's not looking, strike. Hard! Decisively! Bury the knife in that broad back of his! Finish him off in one stroke!

# CHAPTER FIFTEEN

## Avaris

### I

Now over all the lands administered by the conquering Hai, the heavy hand of the Shepherd army lay like a crushing burden, pressing always down, down. Not only had the large farms been taken over completely by the crown, but the smaller, family farms were run, owned, supervised by the Shepherds. Production fell; some crops failed; freemen workers drifted away in the night from farms where they had worked happily for years, and did not return. Some of these workers found their way to the island hideouts of gangs of bandits that preyed on Shepherd caravans taking food to market in the cities.

The raids had provoked retaliation, and caravan and river shipments alike had armed Shepherd contingents to guard them. But the army was spread thin, and discipline and morale were in a bad state. In the great border encampments and in the cities and country, spot inspections by military higher-ups showed case after case of laxity, insubordination, and unpreparedness. There was even one case of a border sutler bargaining with the enemy—the Egyptians—for shipments of whores for the enlisted men. He was impaled amid much public outcry; but the laxity went on.

Kirakos, at one time commander in chief of the entire Shepherd military force, was excluded from the chain of command, but he had retained his rank and reputation for forceful leadership. This being the case, when he heard unsettling reports from various circles, he quietly organized a small task force of trusted officers and men and traveled to the key areas where malfeasance and apathy would do the worst damage. The conditions Kirakos and his task force found in the camps he inspected were even worse than anticipated, and his wrath had fallen on the commanders like a rain of boiling oil. The commanders and their subordinates trembled in fear as the old man berated them. But when he left—under heavy guard—he had not taken direct action.

The commander at On, where Kirakos's words had been particularly scathing, scratched his bald head and frowned. Why had the old man done nothing? Did he have intentions of firing the execrated leaders by bulletin from Avaris? Or—the thought was seductively reassuring—was the old fellow's bark worse than his bite? Rumor had it that Kirakos's voice was no longer heard in the places where power dwelt.

After the inspections at On and on the Libyan border, Kirakos's party had sailed beyond the delta, beyond the mouth of the Nile, and past the two arms of the mighty Nile and Lake Manzala, landing near the desert lands to make a surprise inspection of the garrison at Sile. By taking the water route, Kirakos's task force was able to approach the garrison from the same direction an attacking force would be coming in the event of war. Even at Sile they found laxity: They were able to march within shouting distance of the garrison before being seen, and when Kirakos was at last admitted through the Sile city gate, he found the garrison understaffed, racked with disease, poorly fed and housed, and lacking in the Shepherd discipline Kirakos had known in the great days when the Hai had swept victoriously across Mesopotamia on the way to Egypt.

His wrath was once again ferocious, but here, closer to the home base at Avaris, the commanders were aware that Kirakos was out of the chain of command and no longer a voice to be taken seriously. The camp's commander made ritual bows to Kirakos's authority, which basic protocol demanded, and showed no panic or fear. Kirakos caught the nuance, took note, and promptly returned overland to Avaris, encountering little military presence along the high road. At one point a bandit raid threatened the task force, but the handpicked troops drove away the robbers, who sustained heavy losses.

Tired and angry and depressed, Kirakos entered Avaris, disbanded his private force, and returned to his house.

It was an amazing thing, he mused. In one generation the greatest military force of its time had had all the guts bred right out of it. Even the older officers, who had been with the army when the Hai had conquered half the world, were over the hill, dead, or retired. They didn't care anymore.

His thought was interrupted by a sudden, squeezing pain—powerful, inexorable, centering behind the large flat bone in the middle of his chest and spreading to his left shoulder and down his left arm. He wanted to breathe deeply, but could not get his breath. He gasped and tried to cry out, but all that would come was a low, weak croak. "H-help me," he said in a constricted voice. He held on to the arras, leaning weakly on the hand that held it. "H-help . . ."

"My lord!" Mereet cried, coming into the room and dropping the armful of clean clothes she had been carrying. She went to his side, helped him into the next room, and eased him onto a cushioned couch.

Kirakos looked up at her from the couch and said weakly, "If I can just get my breath . . ." He massaged his left arm with his right hand, tried flexing his fingers. "I'll be all right. Don't worry about me. I've had these little attacks before."

Mereet had been about to go into the adjoining room and call for help when his words stopped her in her tracks. "You have, my lord? When?"

He shot her an angry glance: angry as much at himself for having let the words slip, perhaps, as at her for noticing. "Oh, on my trip. A day or two ago." He gasped, trying to get air. "At Sile. After I'd reprimanded the commandant."

Mereet stood looking down at him, horror in her eyes. "My lord! I'll have to restrict your activities! I'll give strict orders to the staff to—"

"You'll give no such order," he commanded, and tried to rise, but the pain forced him back down. He lay gasping. "I'd better not fight with you just now. It'll have to wait for a more propitious time."

"It'll have to wait forever," she said, taking a fresh coverlet from the pile she had dropped and covering him, tenderly and efficiently. "I'm not going to argue with you anymore, much as I'd like to, you going around having attacks and not telling me, refusing to take care of yourself. Imagine! Gadding about the whole of the delta making trouble for everyone as if—"

"As if the whole existence of the Hai kingdom depended on it," he stated, a touch of irony coloring his words. He paused to get breath, and went on weakly, "Which of course it does. The army's falling apart. The whole country's falling apart." The pain hit him again, and he gasped in agony.

Mereet knelt by his side. "My lord, it doesn't all depend on you. The world will go on whether or not you exert yourself this way." She put one soft hand on his forehead and wiped away the cold sweat. "Just lie still."

Her voice was soft and soothing. He shut his eyes, tried to catch his breath again, and felt the pain ebb ever so slightly. "Y-yes," he said in a thin, high-pitched voice. "There is something to what you say. If I remain silent, the result will probably be the same as if I speak my mind and expose to the king what I have learned." He looked up at the ceiling high above, with its rich frieze of Hai warriors marching victorious into fallen Carchemish. The sight was a bitter one.

"My lord," she said softly, taking his hand between hers and stroking it soothingly, "you've done all a man could do. If the king has his mind set on his present course, that's the way things will be."

Kirakos sighed. "You're right, of course. I ask myself why I even care. After all, I won't be around much longer. I won't have to live in this beastly world that Salitis is creating, and I've no kin to worry about. My wife, my sons, and their children are all dead. They've been spared all the trouble to come, as I will be."

But now, with the pain still showing on his face, he turned his eyes on Mereet's face, and something more sober, more thoughtful, appeared in his expression. "I have no one, really, to worry about but you. And I do worry about you. If this madness of Salitis's leads to chaos, to anarchy, to civil war . . ."

Mereet's tone grew more contemplative. "My whole childhood, my adolescence, were lived in civil war, my lord. I will survive, my lord. I thank you, however, for your concern. There is one thing, though, that you could do if you would think to please me."

"Eh? What's that?"

"My lord, under existing Hai law a free woman cannot be made property without a trial, but a slave could be seized after your death, or—"

"Or even before my death, if I were to grow too unpopu-

lar at court. Don't worry. I promise to take the steps necessary to protect you—upon my death you will be free. All in
good time I will instruct the scribe Pet-Osiris to draw up the
necessary documents. You have only to go to him after I'm
gone. He will give you your papers."

"My lord is kind," she said. Yet there was still sadness in
her voice. "I should have known you would think of this. . . ."
Her smile was sadder still. "But look at me. I think of myself,
when I should be thinking of you. And I importune you in
such a moment of distress."

Her hand once again took his, and pressed it, and she
was visibly shocked by the limpness of his grip; it registered
in her eyes. "Ah, Mereet," he said in an old man's voice,
"what am I going to do with you?" He turned his eyes
heavenward again and closed his eyes for a moment. When
he reopened them, they reflected brooding sorrow. "If I were
truly the wise man some younger folk thought me until my
recent fall from grace with our Golden Pharaoh, I would have
had the wisdom to free you some time ago. I know how you
must miss your loved ones, so far away. But in my folly and
weakness I think to myself, *I need her, I must have her by
my side or what will become of me?* As I weaken, I tell myself
that I will have you freed when I am no longer here to need
you. And thus I wrong you daily, you who have come to
mean so much to me."

Mereet took the aged hand that held hers and held it to
her cheek. "My lord, I wrong *you* by not telling you how far I
am from blaming you. My private sorrows have to do with
destiny. I am where the gods wish me to be for now. Perhaps
there is some reason why I am here—some duty that only I
can do. The gods have been kind to me. To all sides I see
worse masters, and I could have fallen to the lot of any of
them—"

But suddenly she realized he was no longer listening to
her. *Is he dead?* She felt the wrist she held, and the pulse
was there still. Her panic subsided. Tenderly she put his
hand down on his chest and watched his sleeping face; the
pain and anxiety left it slowly. Presently the deep breathing
came, as he entered a deeper level of sleep, and only then
did she feel free to relax, to sink from her knees to a sitting
position beside his bed. There she sat for many minutes,
thinking, her eyes never leaving his face.

## II

At the palace of the Golden Pharaoh, Salitis's spies had been at work. Even before Kirakos's inspection party had taken to the sea to surprise the garrison at Sile, army representatives had sent messages back to Avaris informing influential friends at court of the old man's meddling. These men had hastened to leak out a highly exaggerated version of Kirakos's activities to Nakht, head of Salitis's spy network, trusting his conspiratorial turn of mind to get the information to the king in a form calculated to further undermine Kirakos's position.

Nakht bided his time, waiting for exactly the right moment to introduce the information. This was no easy task; Salitis these days was much occupied with his young vizier, Joseph, transforming the Egyptian delta into the greatest granary in the world. And, as Nakht well knew, interrupting a session between the great king and his young protégé provoked a full-scale tantrum, with signs of homicidal madness. One improvident courtier who had dared to interrupt one of Salitis's sessions with Joseph had found himself hauled off to prison on the spot, and there he rested, despite all the efforts of his friends and relatives to have him freed. There were those who counted him fortunate still to be alive.

While Nakht waited for his audience with Salitis, he wondered if there truly was an "inner circle," from which Kirakos could be finally excluded. Or did the inner circle consist of the king and Joseph alone? Most likely that was the case, with people like himself merely having occasional access to the king. And even that status could change in one day. Salitis's rages were coming more and more frequently these days, and few of them were without their victim, be that person guilty or innocent.

Now Nakht sat on a stone bench in the anteroom to Salitis's audience room, looking at the murals high on the walls above: self-glorifications of the bearded Shepherd warriors putting Egyptian captives to the sword; Shepherds leading Canaanite or Eblaite captives, naked and bound, to captivity; Shepherds paying homage to their barbaric god Seth, a strange figure with the body of a greyhound, a long forked tail, a thin, curved muzzle, and pointed ears. And suddenly he knew what he must do to advance himself. *Forget Salitis!* the thought came, clear and unambiguous. *Concentrate on the vizier!*

Of course! The problem was to reach the young foreigner, to get past his habitual standoffishness. It was through Joseph, and through him alone, that Nakht could reach the pharaoh and exert influence, without prompting any of those kingly rages, which, so far at least, had never been directed at Joseph.

But how? Not only was the young man strange and solitary, he was reputed by some to be a sorcerer, a follower of a single strange foreign god, one whose name even he, a reputed priest, dare not speak.

Nakht frowned and, looking across the great room, saw emerging from the door to the king's reception room Mehu, a highly placed attendant to the Golden Pharaoh. He rose and went to meet Mehu, bowing courteously. "Greetings, my friend," he said in an unusually warm tone. "How is it today?"

Mehu looked around; the walls had ears. Motioning Nakht closer, he whispered, "Frankly, I think I'd wait a day if I were you. He's even screaming at Joseph. That's never happened before."

Nakht nodded gravely. "Since the news I bring is sure to set him off, even in the best of moods, I'll wait till tomorrow."

Mehu nodded solemnly. "There's no guarantee that will be a good time, either," he remarked, then paused. "You've news about Kirakos's voyage?"

"Ah," Nakht said, smiling appreciatively. "You haven't lost your touch, I see. That was supposed to be a well-kept secret. Well, I see I'm still dealing with a master of the courtly dance, who knows all the steps." The flattery was given lightly, but hit its mark. "Could I prevail upon your kindness for some advice, please? It's so seldom I have contact with a man who knows so much more than I do about the ins and outs of court life."

Mehu beamed. "How may I serve you?"

Nakht looked right and left before plunging in. "If a man wanted to get closer to the center of things, could he do better than to find a way to approach the young vizier?"

Mehu shook his head gravely. "That's perceptive, my

friend, but Joseph keeps to himself. If he has thoughts, fears, feelings, you'd never know it. He speaks little. He has no friends." He was about to shake his head and dismiss the whole matter, when a thought occurred to him. "But there might just be a way—"

"A golden purse for the man who finds it."

"Yes." He accepted the offer with a raised eyebrow. "The servants at Joseph's house . . ."

"Yes?"

"Well, there's a rumor. Young Joseph is newly married, to a daughter of the priest Petephres. Word has it that the marriage has yet to be, uh, consummated. At any rate, his young wife, Asenath, put out a discreet call for a soothsayer a day or so ago. Unfortunately, no one has answered her call. They know her father's opinions about their lot—he's had several of them impaled near the Egyptian border."

"I see. So if someone could find a magus who could cure the lady's distress . . ."

"It might be just the key. Domestic bliss restored. Wife prevails on newly amorous husband to do her a little favor. A friend of a friend craves a small boon. Audience with the new vizier. The rest is up to you."

"I see." Nakht pursed his lips in thought. "Would the doubling of such a golden purse, perhaps, produce the name and whereabouts of a soothsayer tailored to the lady's exacting requirements—someone guaranteed not to frighten a gently reared young woman of fine manners and sheltered ways?"

"It just might." Mehu smiled graciously. "It would require the greasing of perhaps half a dozen palms." He paused and said delicately, "In advance."

Nakht grinned. This was the kind of dealing he understood. He reached inside his robe and produced a small leather purse, hefting it in his hand. "This is earnest money—"

"—not to be applied against the total," Mehu said, completing the thought in a manner more calculated to please himself than Nakht. "I'll spread it around and see what it produces. I'll get back to you in a day. Will that be satisfactory?"

" 'Satisfactory' is a word we use when the entire transaction has been concluded in a manner acceptable to all. But I'll look for your messenger."

"Please. The fewer messengers the better. Show up here yourself tomorrow at this hour. I'll have word for you then."

\*　　\*　　\*

"Dissent! Obstructionism! I won't have it!" Salitis shouted, his voice beginning to show signs of hoarseness from an hour of almost uninterrupted screaming. "Who do they think they are? Defying me! Me, the emperor of the Black Lands! By heaven, I'll make an example of them! I'll line the high road from Athribis to Bast with bamboo poles, with a head decorating each and every one!" His face was red, and the veins on the sides of his forehead stuck out fearfully. Joseph was sure he was about to have another one of his falling fits.

"Please, sire," he said in a quiet and soothing voice. "Perhaps that won't be necessary. I'll have a man sent down to talk to them. Perhaps they just misunderstood the orders. You know these rustics. Communicating with them is a problem at best. In the present circumstances, it's all but impossible unless you send exactly the right man. I have the name of a—"

*"Don't argue with me!"* Salitis screamed. "Do you think me incompetent? Incapable of making a proper decision? Do you take me for a fool?"

"No, sire," Joseph said quietly, his face an impassive mask.

"Fools! Incompetents! I'm surrounded with idiots!" Salitis bellowed. "First the insubordination, the defiance, the deliberate contravening of my will. Now this! *This!*"

"Please, sire. The physicians told you—"

"Physicians? Charlatans! They're a lot of bawds!"

"But if you'd just try to calm down for a moment—"

This set off another round of oaths and imprecations. Joseph began to be seriously concerned. Twice in the past two weeks, Salitis's rages had led to falling fits. The second of these had been especially severe, and it had been some time before the physicians had been able to revive him. And when they had, he had had one of them whipped.

Joseph sighed, then went to the table for the jar of wine. "Perhaps," he said, his back to the king, his head turned so that he could look over his shoulder, "perhaps I could get you a cup of wine. . . ."

Salitis glared, but did not scream at him. Joseph took this as assent and started to pour the wine. Then he remembered what the doctors had told him after that last seizure: *"If he does this again, and you're afraid for his health or his life, give him this in his drink."* He fingered the hollow ring they had given him, thought for a moment, then, prying the ring open with a fingernail, he poured the liquid into the cup and filled it with wine.

He closed his eyes. He was shaking. *If Salitis tastes something odd . . .* he thought. *Oh, God of my fathers, help me. . . .*

After a moment he mastered himself and managed to proffer the golden cup to the king, holding it almost reverently in both hands. "Here, sire," he said in as natural a voice as he could muster. "Just try a little of this. You're hoarse. It will soothe your throat."

"Throat?" the king said, fixing him with that mad glare. But it turned out to have been just the right thing to say. "Yes, I am a bit hoarse. Give me that." His hand swept the cup out of Joseph's hands, spilling a little of the wine on the floor between them. He took it in both hands and drank, deeply. "Ah! You're right," he said. "That was quite good. Here, refill it for me, will you?" He passed the cup back to Joseph, wiping his mouth with the back of his hand. But now, very suddenly, he gave in to obvious fatigue and sat down on the couch beside him. "Here, I'm very tired. All this business has quite drained me. If these people would only have some care for my welfare, for my health."

Filling the cup again, Joseph for a moment wished there were more of the narcotic in the ring the physicians had given him, but that had been the last of it. He half filled the goblet and handed it over to Salitis, noting the already visible effects on the king's face: the relaxation of the facial muscles, contorted only a moment ago with rage. "Here, sire. A little wine is just the thing when one's feeling weary. Perhaps you'd like to lie down. Here, let me get you a headrest."

But Salitis had already begun to slump, and his hands would not hold the wine. Joseph caught the cup before its contents spilled, and gently eased Salitis's head down onto the couch. Then he lifted the king's legs up onto the cushions. After a moment he looked around for a coverlet, found one, and cautiously draped it over the pharaoh's unconscious form.

Afterward, Joseph stood, eyes shut, over the couch, and he began to shake uncontrollably. He gripped one hand savagely with the other and forced his palsied body under control. But when he had done so, he found himself suddenly nauseated. He rushed to the window and, dizzy from the strain, vomited up the little he had eaten that day into the ornamental bushes on the ground ten feet below.

*       *       *

"Why, yes," Baket-amon said. "My lady Asenath *has* been looking for someone, although I can't imagine how you found out about it."

Mehu looked at the servant and shrugged. "It's my business around here to do what I can to make things go smoothly for His Majesty's trusted and valued friends. If I'm to do a decent job of this, I have to anticipate trouble."

Baket-amon's mouth turned down. "Well, I'm afraid you're a trifle late for that," she said. "The trouble's already here, and it's been causing my mistress no end of pain and worry. Anything your friend can do to make things go easier between the two of them will be much appreciated, I'm sure."

"I'd be pleased to be of service. I want no recompense. Your young mistress's favor is all the payment I wish. And as for the magus's reckoning, I'll take care of it myself. After all, the bill would otherwise go to your lady's husband, and, if I understand the situation rightly, we don't want him to know anything about this."

"Oh, you understand. You can't imagine what a comfort that would be."

## III

The first two soothsayers consulted were obvious fakes and were summarily discarded. The third, a man named Neferhotep, lived in a richly appointed apartment near the palace. This in itself served to attract Mehu's interest from the start; surely a charlatan could ill afford to live in such a place. The soothsayer further impressed him by keeping him waiting for more than a quarter of an hour. It was a daring stunt, but it had its intended effect.

When at last Neferhotep appeared, tall, cadaverous, impressive-looking in costly robes, he made an entrance that Mehu could only applaud, looking imperiously around before advancing at a slow, measured pace. Stopping at last before Mehu, he bowed infinitesimally, maintaining his awesome dignity. "Neferhotep of Thebes at your service," he said in a silky voice. His sharp eye fixed Mehu with a piercing stare.

"You, sir, are in pain. You have an aching head. It is killing you."

"W-why, yes," Mehu said, taken aback a bit. "I do have a—"

"Isis prepared a poultice for Re's head when it ached," the soothsayer said. "Equal parts of the following: berry of coriander, berry of poppy plant, wormwood, berry of the *sames* plant, berry of the juniper plant, with honey for the vehicle. Mash the ingredients into a paste." He paused, and a tiny smile crept across his otherwise solemn face. "Let's be candid, though, my friend. A vendor of bogus spells will smear this paste on your forehead and say some mumbo jumbo, and it will all seem very impressive, but your head will continue to ache. The trick is to make the patient ingest a bit of the stuff before you smear the rest on his head. That's what the honey is for, to kill the bad taste." His smile was accommodating, conspiratorial. "I have heard of your mission already, my friend. You have come to the right place."

"Heard of it already? But—"

"I have my sources, just as you have yours. There is a certain couple, highly placed, who are having trouble with the first days of their union. You wish a love spell or potion. Am I correct?"

"You are. But—"

"Come, sir, have a cup of wine with me. Then I will give you a most impressive potion: a lock of hair from a man who died a violent death, seven grains of barley from the offering buried with a corpse; ten *oipe* of apple seeds . . ."

"I think it would be best for you to deliver the potion yourself. I think she'll be impressed with you, if you don't mind my saying so."

"Fine." Neferhotep continued ticking off the ingredients on one hand, one finger at a time: "Mix in the blood of a worm and the blood of a black dog. The petitioner will have to contribute a drop or two of blood from her own second finger and from the palm of her left hand. . . ."

"You're my man. I can see that. Save the spell for the meeting with the girl. First we'll have to meet with the chap who's putting up the money. A mere technicality, of course."

"I understand. He's well fixed, this man of yours?"

"I would say so. Of course, you understand that you and I will share the fee, including bonuses."

"Ah. Then the fee will be within a hair of excessive."

The smile this time was a shark's, but with a touch of humor in it.

"I think he can afford it. You'll have to bargain by instinct. Know when to push for more, when to seal the deal."

"I always do. Don't worry, I'll have him thanking us both for overcharging him. Come. Wine. I think this is the beginning of a beautiful working relationship. I've intended to find a liaison with the palace for some time now, but I had to keep a low profile during that terrible period when the king was executing soothsayers."

"A wise decision."

"All my decisions are wise ones, my friend. It comes with the trade. Know all, see all. Your health, sir." Now the smile was broad and warm, and the voice a purr like a contented cat's. "Drink up, there, my friend, then let me refill your glass."

He must have dozed off, sitting there in the chair next to the king's couch, because the next thing he knew, he awoke with a start, to look up into the mad eyes of Salitis, staring down at him. He jumped up, instantly awake, fear stabbing at his heart. "Sire!" he said. "I . . . I must have—"

"Yes, Joseph!" Salitis said. "You went to sleep." His words had a strange emphasis, and his face was unnaturally flushed. "No, sit back down. You probably haven't been getting enough rest lately. I've been working you too hard. There's so much to do to complete my great work here."

Joseph stifled a yawn and sat down, trying to look as alert as possible. His heart was still beating fast; he knew all too well by now how quickly Salitis's quiet, friendly spells could go over the edge into mad, howling rages again. "Sire, if you'll pardon my making a personal remark, I think you may be working *yourself* too hard. There are those of us around the palace complex who worry about your health. You drive yourself so."

Salitis's face assumed a quizzical expression. "I hadn't thought of it that way. Of course. That's how I came to fall asleep, isn't it?" Joseph, listening, trembled with relief. "Yes, it must have been," the king continued, "and you'd been sitting here watching over me. How loyal! I'll reward you. What would you like? A vineyard? No, that's all under the province of the crown now; if I go around giving away things like that, there'll be a lot of bother in the council. How about gold? Emeralds? I could have a statue made of you. I could—"

Joseph sighed. "Sire, the greatest gift you could give me would be to take a holiday and restore yourself. You've lost weight. You're not sleeping nights. If you could . . ."

Salitis stared, his eyes glittering. "Take time off? But of course you know I couldn't do that. There are still too many things to do, and they all have to be done now. Now! Right now! I'm behind schedule as it is!"

Then the mad face broke into a feverish smile. "Wait," he said. "*I* can't take off, but *you* can. Yes! That's a fine idea! Take a couple of days off! Go to the country! I've a villa some leagues out of the city, on one of the islands. It's safe enough; there's a detachment of troops there year round. Go there, you and that new wife of yours. Yes! I insist!"

Joseph groaned inwardly. The thought of what Salitis would do alone in the city, without his own moderating influence working on him, filled the young vizier with fear. "Sire, I appreciate your kindness and thoughtfulness more than I know how to say. But—"

"No! No! I absolutely insist! I command you, as your king! After all, I have to have you bright and healthy by my side if I'm to carry out my programs here! And if you're all tired out, falling asleep like that . . ."

Joseph closed his eyes for a moment, holding his hands over his face. When he opened his eyes again he wore an expression of chastened resignation. "Perhaps you're right, sire."

"Of course I'm right. I'm always right. Now go! Prepare for your holiday. Take three days. Take a week, if you like. Send me a daily report, telling me how well you're learning to relax again. Go! What are you waiting for?"

"Oh, no, sir," Baket-amon, Asenath's servant, said. "She was very impressed. This Neferhotep gentleman, after all, is a very striking fellow—and with that gift for speech . . ."

"Yes," Mehu said. "But will she use the remedies he recommended to her?"

"Oh, I'll see that she does, sir. She listens to me. I'll just have to be careful that her father doesn't find out. You know how he is about casting spells—I mean outside of the temple. If he were to find out that this gentleman were advising her . . . well, things would go very badly."

Mehu's eyebrow lifted. "But as old campaigners, you and I know that Asenath's father needn't hear of everything that happens around here." His hand hefted an imaginary purse, and his expression said more than words.

"Uh, yes, sir, I agree perfectly. Wise people keep their own counsels, sir."

"After all, the girl is no longer living under her father's roof. She's under the authority and responsibility of her husband now."

"Yes, sir. And whatever makes their marriage a better one has to be for the best in the long run. Even if it is, well, a thing previously outside my young mistress's experience."

"Everything is outside your young mistress's experience, my dear. That's what older and wiser heads like ourselves are for, to help the young and unfledged prepare for new experiences in life. You're doing her a favor; think of it that way, and it will take on an entirely different coloring in your eyes. You're doing her a valuable service."

"Oh, yes, sir. When you look at it that way, sir, it does look better. A service."

"It's good that we agree. Now go to work—and make sure she does as she has been advised."

"I'm afraid," Asenath said. "What if it doesn't work? What if Joseph finds out? I'd feel terrible. If he knew I was doing something like that to him . . ."

Baket-amon put down the clean robes she was packing for her mistress and looked Asenath in the eye. "If you'll pardon my forwardness, my lady, I'd say your first duty is to save your marriage, and how you go about doing that is your own business."

Asenath sat down and began combing out her hair. Her face bore much the same sad look it had worn ever since her wedding night. Her sigh was almost a sob. "It's just that . . . oh, I've tried so many things already. I've been warm and loving. I've even tried one or two of the things Idut suggested."

"Idut?" Baket-amon said, turning to her, eyes flashing. "Has that little slut been talking to you? Telling you a lot of her smut? I'll have her flayed! I'll—"

"No, no, please. She didn't mean any harm. Around my father's house, she and several of the younger slaves used to go about the house naked." She waved away Baket-amon's attempt to interrupt. "No, no. I know it was Father's idea. I know how his eye used to follow Idut around. I can understand that a man like Father enjoys looking at her."

"Hmmmph! Looking! As if that were—"

"I know, I know. Anyway, with that in mind, I listened to what Idut suggested, then I tried to arouse Joseph that way. Unfortunately, I don't feel comfortable going around naked, not even to please my husband." Her face was desolate as she added sadly, "Not that it had the intended effect anyhow. Joseph was more embarrassed than anything. He told me to put some clothes on."

"Well, don't pay any attention to Idut anymore. I've been meaning to send her back to your father." Her expression was cynical in the extreme. "She'll be more, uh, useful there, I suspect."

"No. No, leave her where she is. She means well. She's just one kind of girl, and I'm another. What would work for her wouldn't work for me. And," she said with a sigh even deeper and louder than before, "in Joseph we're dealing with someone very unlike Father."

"I know," Baket-amon said, coming over to embrace her. "Poor dear. If only he were an Egyptian . . ."

"No, no," Asenath said. "I wouldn't want him any different. He's really a very good person. He has a fine reputation in the palace for kindness. It's just that he seems to be hiding behind a high wall of bricks where I can't reach or touch him. As if he were a prisoner."

"Well, prisoner or no, you're going to have some time together with him, just the two of you. None of the servants will accompany you—the pharaoh's orders. There'll be food and drink and all the amenities, and but for the guards outside the walls, you'll be alone together. If I were you, mistress, I think I'd use the time trying anything and everything that could possibly have the desired effect. That includes casting away your inhibitions." She stepped back and held Asenath at arm's length to look into her eyes. "That includes taking the good advice Neferhotep gave you."

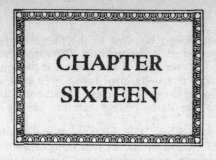

# CHAPTER SIXTEEN

## On the Nile

### I

From their hiding place in the reeds, Khunes and Baliniri watched the Shepherd war galley pass, making its wide turn as it approached the border waters. On the high deck, the sailors, who had furled the great sail only moments before, shipped the huge mast, while the rowers manned their long oars, looking bronze and fit in their single, apronlike garments. The hidden watchers could see the hulking helmsman, every muscle straining, leaning hard against the tiller and bracing one foot against the rudder post for better leverage. Slowly the tiller rotated the stock of the rudder oar and its blade far below him; slowly the ship turned downstream.

Baliniri waited until the boat was in the mainstream before speaking in a low whisper. "Look at that, will you?" he said in a disgusted voice. "Other than the ship's officers, there isn't a Shepherd on the whole boat! Haven't these people any shame at all, working for the people who invaded and conquered their homeland like that?"

Khunes smiled. "It is difficult sometimes to identify the enemy. You yourself, sir, are friends with leaders of the armies of both sides. You see no inconsistency in that?"

Baliniri's eyes focused on him directly. "As a mercenary, in theory it shouldn't matter whose coin I take. Remember, Khunes, I wasn't born here, and it isn't my land that has been invaded by strangers."

Khunes turned his eyes to the Shepherd boat as the oarsmen propelled it downstream. "Strangers, sir? I'd say Dedmose, our own king, is a stranger and the son of strangers. Dedmose is a delta man, ruling over men of the Red Lands. Some of the upriver people regard him with the same detestation the delta people reserve for the Shepherd overlords."

Baliniri nodded. "I understand. When I helped pacify the mountain kingdoms for my lord Hammurabi, some of the people welcomed us with open arms, thinking anyone a better overlord than their own kings. But from what I hear, Dedmose isn't a tyrant."

For a moment there was a tiny flaring-up of emotion in Khunes's eyes. "There are those who think otherwise, sir," he said flatly, then reached for the oars again. "We'll have to make up for time that we lost getting past the Egyptian lines. And now this Shepherd ship . . ."

"Right," Baliniri said, taking his oars and standing to make his way to the forward seat. "How far is it to the garrison?"

Khunes stood looking down at the seated soldier, plainly unhappy that Baliniri had not taken the stern seat. "Not far, sir. Could I change seats with you? That way I'll be ready to grab for the mast when it's time."

Baliniri smiled benignly up at him. "You mean that way I'll have my back to you. What need will you have of the mast? A sail would only betray our position to anyone who hasn't seen us already. The only sailing you intend to do is back upstream, after you've stuck that knife of yours in me. Right?" Now his smile became a mocking grin.

"I—I don't know what you're talking about."

"My partner and I haven't been in Egypt long enough to know everything about it, my friend, but the few friends we've made have been most informative. For example, I recognize the little tattoo that you of the assassins' guild wear under the bracelet on your arm." His voice had a silken quality to it now: slow, unhurried. "It was Dede, wasn't it, Khunes, who set me up? He sent a runner to tip you off."

Without warning Khunes swung the oar in his hand. Baliniri's hands went up to protect his face, but the oar caught him on the side of the head, knocking him sprawling. The boat rocked crazily, but Khunes was an experienced sailor and righted it by shifting his own weight. And, his hands moving with blinding speed, he dropped the oar and pulled out of his belt the long bronze dagger with which he had killed Hefget.

He lunged forward. As he did, Baliniri shook his head and dodged clumsily out of his way. His huge hand grasped the wrist that held the knife, then squeezed hard. Yelping with pain, Khunes dropped the knife, but Baliniri's wits had been addled by the blow, and Khunes managed to wriggle loose. As the soldier lurched after him, Khunes retrieved his oar again and used it as a battering ram. The heavy handle caught Baliniri over the eye, head-on. The giant fell forward on his face, stunned.

Khunes looked around frantically. A heavy ivory belaying pin lay on the deck by his feet. He reached down for it and, as Baliniri tried to rise, slammed him hard at the base of the skull. This time Baliniri's face hit the deck with a loud thud when he fell.

Khunes gasped for air. He looked for his knife, but it was under the big man's body. He bent over Baliniri's body and tugged at it. It seemed to be caught on something. Khunes pulled, cursing.

But once again the big man came groping back out of his stupor, and with a groan he pushed himself to his feet, while Khunes grabbed the knife, stepped back to avoid Baliniri's bearlike rush and encircling arms.

The boat had been untended too long and had begun to drift slowly out of the reeds and into the sluggish stream. Now, with the tiller no longer manned, it caught a crosscurrent and turned suddenly. Khunes lost his balance and toppled over. Baliniri's great hamlike hand fastened onto his ankle like a vise!

Khunes tried to pull away, but the huge hand held him, pulled him toward that angry, bleeding face, toward those terrible destroying hands! He cried out in terror and swung the blade in desperation. It opened a wound on Baliniri's arm. The giant released him for a second, then came after him again.

Khunes screamed, forgetting all caution as the boat turned round and round, out of control. He scrambled backward, but Baliniri, his eyes filled with cold rage, crept toward him, arms outstretched.

"No! No!" Khunes cried. Desperate, he lunged!

The blade, razor-sharp, caught Baliniri coming hard. It

buried itself in his chest. He cried out as much in anger as in pain. His hands wrapped themselves around Khunes's neck and squeezed . . . squeezed. . . .

After a moment Khunes was still. Only then did Baliniri release the limp form and sit back on his heels, swaying. With one final effort, he pulled the knife out of his chest. There was a quick gout of blood, but as he sank back, weakened by shock, his hand closed on the outer garment he had abandoned an hour before to row in his loincloth. He picked it up and pressed it to the wound.

The boat was drifting downstream, into Shepherd waters. He managed to drag himself aft to the tiller, and with one hand clapping the robe to the wound in his chest and the other, still bleeding, draped clumsily over the tiller, he lay in the bottom of the boat, growing weaker with every moment.

*Steer!* he thought, blinking the darkness back. *But where? Toward the main current? No, couldn't handle the tiller in a strong current. No. Toward shore.* On land there was a chance, if a slim one, that some villager would see him and help him. Gasping with the effort, he leaned on the tiller and turned the boat toward the far shore. He managed to hold it there all the way until he felt the current go slack under him; until the boat plowed into the reeds, and at last banged its prow on the bank. Only then, becalmed in the shallows and safe for now, did he allow the darkness to engulf him.

A Shepherd patrol found him there, unconscious in the bottom of the boat, the dead man at his feet. They decided to drop Khunes overboard to the crocodiles. The big foreigner was another matter. What was he doing in Shepherd-controlled waters? None of the usual paraphernalia that accompanied a smuggling operation could be found on the vessel, so the patrol's leader reluctantly abandoned his first theory, which had to do with a falling-out among thieves or blockade runners.

A second consideration came to mind: If the boat were turned over to the patrol's superiors, questions might be raised as to how such a boat had penetrated Shepherd territory when the commander at On had quite recently been given a blistering beratement by one of Avaris's most highly placed officials—Kirakos—for laxity and lack of preparedness.

The patrol commander looked down at his captive, frowning. He turned to his subordinate, Seranoush. "I'm of divided mind," he said. "We could just kill him right here and now. . . ."

"No, Baitsar, no!" his lieutenant said. "I recognize this fellow. I was up in Avaris on leave a while back. I know I saw him there. Just where and when I can't say. I think we'd better take him in for questioning."

Baitsar frowned pettishly. "It would be easier to order you to slit his throat, but something tells me you may be right." He stopped and looked hard at the wounded man, who was showing signs of life for the first time. The big foreigner opened his eyes; the lids fluttered, blinked. The eyes rolled back once, then focused on the commander. The foreigner's lips opened, and he tried to say something, but the words were so faint, the voice so hoarse and weak, that neither man could make it out.

Seranoush bent over, put his ear near the wounded man's mouth.

"Avaris," he whispered.

"What about Avaris?" Seranoush asked.

But the wounded man sank into unintelligible babbling. "Can't help her now . . . story about boat no good . . . set me up . . ." He tried to wipe his eyes with his hand, which was covered with dried blood from the knife wound on his arm. Then, blinking away the stupor in his mind, he croaked out, "Take me to Kirakos. In Avaris."

Seranoush, startled, looked up at his commander. "Sir?" he said. "Did you hear what he was saying? Kirakos? But—" Seranoush's face underwent a change. "Wait!" he said. "Yes, yes! *That's* where I've seen him before!"

Baitsar leaned forward. His mind was full of the terrible day when Kirakos's party had descended upon the post and inspected it without warning—and of the humiliations the entire officer corps had undergone at the old man's hands. "What's that?"

"This man is a personal friend of Kirakos's. He stayed at the old boy's house when he was in Avaris. Kirakos took him everywhere, including to court. Everybody was talking about it."

Baitsar looked down at the big captive, whose eyes were closed now. "Are you sure? What do you suppose he's doing here?"

"Oh, gods! Sir, what if he were on some kind of mission for Kirakos? What if he were testing our river defenses?"

Baitsar's eyes went wide. "Gods! And if he were, look what's happened. He managed to make it here in a boat obviously registered in Egyptian waters—right past our defenses, in midday, right under our noses! I can just hear what Kirakos is going to have to say about that!"

Seranoush's hand toyed with his dagger. "There is always, sir, the possibility that he could disappear now, without trace."

"No, no. This is much too ticklish for that! Imagine if he were expected somewhere and failed to show? We'd have inspectors down on our necks before the day was out. And while I can trust you and you can trust me, do you think we can trust the rest of those dolts in the patrol to keep quiet about this? After all, they've seen him, too." He shook his head emphatically. "No. We'd better patch him up." He sighed bitterly. "And, I suppose, do what he says—take him to Kirakos."

# CHAPTER SEVENTEEN

## Lisht

### I

"No!" said Sokar, the chief priest of Osiris, drawing himself up to his full height, his harsh features frigid and unyielding. "Absolutely not. I won't hear of it. It flies in the face of a thousand years of tradition. It's an offense against the gods, a sacrilege."

"Very well, then," Baka said, turning and pacing. He shot a glance at Madir, sitting impassively in his high seat in the big conference room. "We'll do without the festival this year."

"Do without?" Sokar said, raising his voice. "Madir, reason with him. We can't just *cancel* the ceremony. Besides the religious aspect of it—which, I thought it was understood, is my bailiwick, Baka, not yours—there's the social aspect. If the people hear we've canceled an important ritual, one intimately connected with the fertility of the soil and the growing cycle, there'll be riots, panic—"

"Better that than risk physical danger to the king!" Baka said, his eyes blazing. "Madir, doesn't he understand the problem? We have every reason to suspect—"

Sokar snorted. "Bah! Blather! The sort of drivel you soldiers use to befog the minds of the bureaucratic caste, to increase your influence with the crown. If the royal coffers haven't been opened to you the way you'd like, if one of your number gets snubbed at an official reception, all you have to do is scream about how the enemy's at the gates, or about how there's some conspiracy afoot out there, some dark plot to unseat the king or—"

"To *murder* the king!" Baka said. "To murder Madir, too. If we go ahead with the ceremony and don't have armed guards to prevent any—"

"Armed guards? In the temple? On the sacred grounds? Unthinkable."

"Now, look!" Baka said, exasperated. "We learned only this morning that the man who replaced Ben-Hadad in the preparations for the festival—the cabal had gotten to him. You know the harmless reed spears and swords usually used in the ceremony? Well, instead of those, we found lethal weapons. Inside the reeds were razor-sharp blades, long enough to stab a man through the heart. That's not all—there was poison on the tips."

The priest's eyes were wide with horror and surprise. "I . . . I had no idea," Sokar said. "Are you sure?"

"Quite," Baka affirmed. "We put the armorer to the torture. Before he died he told us about the plot. Not as much as we would have liked, of course, but enough to make it absolutely imperative that our plans be changed."

Now, for the first time in many minutes, Madir held up his hand and spoke mildly. "This fellow you tortured," he said, "he didn't by any chance reveal the identity of the man in the Sobek mask, did he? Because if he did . . ."

Sokar looked from one man to the other, his face under iron control. "What are you talking about?" he asked. "Mask? What mask?"

"Unfortunately, no," Baka said, ignoring Sokar. "The cabal network is organized so each man knows the name and face of only a few others—except at the top, where everyone knows everyone else. The armorer was an underling."

"I don't understand," Sokar blustered. "You claim to have precise information on this—this plot, and yet you do nothing? You know who these people are, and—"

"We know who most of them are," Baka said. "But not all. I learned a new name only this morning. For security reasons I can't divulge it, but he'll be under arrest this afternoon." Baka grinned a hard soldier's grin. "I rather know this one," he said. "He's not tough. He won't hold out as long as the armorer did. When the torturers start breaking his fingers and toes like sticks of bread . . ."

Sokar shuddered. "Of course, if there's a real threat to the person of the king . . . that makes everything different. Bring in all the guards you like. We'll disguise them as priests. For heaven's sake, Baka, why didn't you say all this before? Of course I'll cooperate." He looked up at Madir. "The thing's in your hands. Just let me know what you want me to do, and I'll rearrange the rehearsal. I'm at His Majesty's disposal."

"Dedmose will not be participating," Madir said softly. "That much had been decided even before we caught the armorer. His Highness's double will impersonate him." He rubbed his eyes and looked at the lowering sun streaming through the skylight. "It's getting late, my friends. I must go." He rose, slowly, deliberately, like an old man. "I'm glad you've worked it out between you. Now I'll take my leave." He turned to go, but an afterthought turned him around once more to face them. "Oh, Baka. Could I perhaps see you for a moment? There were some details I wanted to . . ." He let the words die out, waving them away with one hand. He nodded to Sokar. "My regards to your family, Your Eminence."

The two of them watched the chief priest of Osiris make his way through the door, increasing his pace with every step. Only when Sokar was safely out of sight did Madir wave Baka closer. "You saw?" Madir asked quietly. "You watched his face?"

"Yes," Baka said. "No doubt about it. He's one of them. Who would have suspected it? He has so much to lose."

"*One* of them?" Madir echoed. His lips smiled, but his eyes remained all but unreadable. "I've known that almost from the first. What I didn't know until today was that he was the one I sought. The principal one."

Baka stared, incredulous. "Principal? But—"

"The man in the Sobek mask," Madir said softly.

Baka tried to speak, but could not. He cleared his throat. "*Him?* And you're letting him go?"

"Of course."

"But surely he's being followed."

"No. What good would that do?"

"Good? Why, you could learn who the others are! You could find out—"

"My dear Baka," Madir explained, taking obvious delight in his commander's discomfiture, "I *know* all that. I know who *all* of them are."

"Well, then, why don't we just—" He began with his voice raised, resolution in his tone. But in midsentence the thought stopped, interrupted by a different and more sobering one. "Wait," he said. "You know, then. They have Tuya?"

"Yes. I even know where she is. We intercepted a messenger headed out into the desert. He was to have made contact with the returning party from Nubia and given them this note." He reached inside his robe and pulled out a papyrus. "She seems to have written it herself, at their dictation." He let Baka read the simple appeal. "Interesting custom, that. Teaching women to read and write."

"I taught my wife to read," Baka confessed. "I was nearly drummed out of the scribes' guild for it." He finished reading, rolled the papyrus, and handed it back. "Well. Sitra! I never liked the man, but I never gave him credit for having enough brains to—"

"Oh, he was the smartest of them all," Madir said mildly. "He's even found the secret passage we used to use to spy on him, although I have to admit Sokar found it first." He sighed. "I wish he *were* less brilliant. It'd make our subsequent decisions easier." He looked Baka squarely in the eye for the first time now, and his eyes opened wide to reveal a glare like a hawk's. "As it is . . ."

Baka stared back. "If we make a move, Tuya dies. And that place of his is a fortress."

"Exactly. The moment he knows we're on to him—"

Baka's mouth opened wide. "But won't Sokar tell him?"

"Sokar will go home. He will consider his options. He will think of himself first. He will consider making a run for it. He will be so upset he won't be able to eat. He will ask for wine and will have the hope of drowning his troubles in it." He pursed his lips and shrugged. "I know his habits better than he does."

"You have spies in his house!"

"The best. More of my 'thousand ears.' One of them will pour the wine. There will be a slight aftertaste. Perhaps he won't notice it at first. Perhaps he will. It won't matter. It doesn't take much. A touch, on the tongue . . ."

"Madir . . ."

"Come, Baka, don't look so shocked. We'll work together in this. I've kept you in the dark up to now, and there wasn't any good reason, really. I think I just wanted to see the expression on your face when I sprang something on you."

"What are you talking about, Madir?"

The vizier opened his eyes fully, as he seldom did, and looked into Baka's, even smiled a bit. "Come, my young friend. Don't you at all see what I'm getting at?" Baka's face remained blank, mystified. "Well, then I'll have to tell you. I'm getting old. I've talked it over with Dedmose. I told him I was going to start training my successor."

"Successor! But—"

"Oh, don't play coy with me, Baka. I'm losing my touch. In the old days this conspiracy thing wouldn't have gotten nearly as far as this before I caught and crushed it. I'd never have let a thing like little Tuya's imposture get past me. Now she's in very great danger."

Baka stared. "You can't blame yourself for that, sir! That was my oversight, not yours. If I'd taken her seriously—"

"A good sign! You take all the responsibility, the blame, on yourself. A true leader always does that, and always cleans up after himself."

Now Madir stood up and, to Baka's great surprise, reached out and put an arm around Baka's shoulder. "Baka, my son," he said. "You must know by now that I get my way, every time, as regular as the cycles of the sun and moon. If I decide you're to succeed me, that's all there is to it. You might just as well get used to the fact. You've experience on every level in the military, and you're a trained scribe, a man of learning. You've a bit of polish for court doings; the job doesn't require much— Eventually they'll all come to you, and it'll be to your advantage not to be too friendly with any of them."

He steered the two of them toward his private offices. "Come. It's time for you to meet some of my undercover people. You may recognize one or two of them, but you'll likely not have connected them with me. . . ."

The conversation would have continued, but a herald entered through the outer door, saluted, and said, "Sir, request permission to report."

Madir started to speak, but was delighted when Baka took the reins himself. "Report!"

"Sir, the scouts report that the Nubian party has been sighted. One of them appeared to be badly wounded or seriously ill. They may by now be on the outskirts of town."

Baka wheeled, stared at Madir. "But they're not due for another—"

Madir took over now. "Get someone out to them right

now," he said decisively. "Tell them to come here to report. Anup, Shobai, Musuri. And Ben-Hadad. Yes, especially Ben-Hadad." There was something in his voice that without words said "Dismissed!" The herald turned smartly on one heel after a sharp salute and went away.

The herald caught up with the returning party just as they entered the city by the western gate. So did a small, short-haired dog, which detached itself from the crowd at the little market. The dog dashed forward to dance excitedly around the sunburnt, stocky young man who led the procession.

"Lion!" said Ben-Hadad, bending down to welcome the small animal. "It's good to see you, boy!" He reached out to pet the dog, but the animal started barking frantically, jumping back out of reach of its master's hands. "What's the matter? What's the matter there?" He moved out of the way of the others, his eyes still on the dog, just as the procession followed him through the city gate. "You want me to follow you?"

But the herald broke in now, bowing curtly before him. "Sir, I have urgent orders from Madir. You're to report to him and General Baka immediately. You, Musuri, Anup, and Shobai."

Ben-Hadad took his eyes off the frantic capering of the dog for the first time. "We'll come," he said. "We can walk over with you, just as soon as I've attended to something—"

"Sir," the herald interrupted gently, "this is urgent."

"So is this," Ben-Hadad said, a somber look on his face. "Musuri, Anup, and I will accompany you back to the palace. But we have to make some arrangements—one of our party took ill on the way—so ill that we came back early to get some expert medical attention. Even with that I'm not sure he'll survive. Once I've seen to his safety and comfort . . ."

"Sir. Please. Let the others handle that."

"I can't. It's my uncle—Shobai."

## II

Dede stood open-mouthed before the unguarded door of Sokar's town house. It stood ajar. Unguarded? In these unsettled days? He reached out one timid hand and pushed the door; it swung wide. Still no guard came to stop or interrogate him. This, at the household of the chief priest of Osiris, a man with many and powerful enemies!

Dede stuck his head in, looked around. The courtyard before the main house was empty. Even Sokar's cats seemed to have gone. Dede summoned up all the courage he could muster and called out in a tremulous voice, "Hello? Hello! Anyone home?"

No answer. He began to wonder if the entire place was in fact deserted. Even as he thought this, a face appeared at a window. It was Sokar's personal servant. "You!" Dede said. "Is your master—"

But the servant's eyes were full of fear, and he disappeared from the window. Dede could hear the flapping of his sandals as he made off for the far end of the house. *Strange . . .* Dede thought as he crossed the court, pushed open the front door of the main dwelling, and looked in.

The front room was a shambles! Chairs, tables, and tall amphorae had been knocked over and broken, oil was spilled on the rug, and prominently displayed art objects he remembered from an earlier visit were now nowhere to be seen.

"S-Sokar?" Dede called softly, venturing forward cautiously. "Sokar, are you there?"

Then he saw the body, sprawled out on the floor in the middle of the big room. He rushed to Sokar's side and bent over, but there was no sign of life. "Sokar!" he said in a stunned whisper. And, seeing the spilled wine cup beside the fallen priest's hand, the liquid that stained the carpeting, he knew what had happened. When he arose again his eyes were wide with horror.

"Poisoned!" he said in a low voice. "But who could have—"

It came to him, in one blinding flash. Certainly not any member of his own circle.

*He knows!* Dede thought, sickened. *Madir knows!* Sokar had been poisoned by someone in the employ of Madir of the Thousand Ears.

His heart pounded. Fear, stark and cold, gripped his body. His hands trembled. A final, terrible realization nearly caused Dede's heart to stop. *Gods! I'm in terrible danger myself! If they know about Sokar, they also know about me!* Sokar, after all, had always worn the mask, and only in the last days, after he had exposed Tuya, had he himself been trusted with the identities of the men and women in the upper echelon. So if Madir knew about Sokar, he had probably known about him, Dede, for some time.

"Oh, gods! What will I do? Where can I—"

Mereb! He would go to Mereb! Perhaps Mereb would know what to do—that is, if Madir's assassins had not gotten to *him* yet!

Tros of Ilios, personal physician to Dedmose and one of Shobai's closest friends for more than twenty years, came out of the room where the blind man lay and looked at Heket and Ben-Hadad. "He's sleeping now," he said. "But he looks terrible. How long has he been like this? He's a shadow of the self he was when he left for Nubia."

"He started losing weight on the way," Ben-Hadad said, "but we all lost weight on the trip through the desert, so I thought nothing of it. And you know what kind of vitality Shobai invariably had. Even ill, he was always stronger than any three of us. I thought he'd bounce back. . . ."

Musuri came forward from the back of the room. "You and I have talked about Shobai and his family, Doctor," he said. "Is this what I think it is?"

"His lungs? Yes, I'm afraid so. There's a hereditary tendency to weakness." He looked at Ben-Hadad. "You'd do well to be aware of this yourself, young man. Your father didn't live long enough for the signs to develop, but your ancestor Belsunu died of lung disease. Just wasted away, Shobai told me. You all may have inherited his weak chest— for all your outward vitality—and it's made worse by your trade, breathing in all those noxious fumes from the forge."

Ben-Hadad looked like he was about to burst into tears. "B-but will he recover? He won't—"

"Who can say?" Tros said, folding his hands and looking down at them thoughtfully. "I don't think he has many days to live. A month at most, if he's lucky."

Now there was a disturbance outside, and the door burst open. Baka, breathing hard from recent exertion, stood in the open doorway, with three heavily armed attachés behind him. "I came as quickly as I could," he said. "How is . . ." But the somber expressions told the story eloquently. "Tros?" he said. "Tell me."

"Lungs," the doctor said. "Fairly advanced. Sometimes these big men go surprisingly quickly. I don't expect him to last too long."

Ben-Hadad looked pale and wilted. "He wouldn't talk to me. I thought he was punishing me, avoiding me. I went around resenting him for it. . . ."

Baka came forward and put his arm around Ben-Hadad's shoulders. "Ben-Hadad," he said gently, "come outside for a moment. I have something to tell you. . . ."

"Hey! What are you doing? Stop that right now!" Maya stood in the doorway, looking down with consternation at Tuya, who sat cross-legged on the floor, tugging at the manacle around her ankle. She had the manacle nearly off now, but the metal had rubbed her skin raw, and blood from her ankle stained the marble floor. Anger flared in her eyes as she looked up at him. "You little fool!" he said. "Don't you know what would happen if Sitra saw you trying to get loose?"

"What do I care?" she said defiantly. "I'd rather die than have to serve wine at another disgusting orgy. Where does he get those slimy little friends of his, anyway?"

Maya rolled his eyes heavenward. "It is not my place to question my lord's taste, dear. I've learned to look the other way, and you'd perhaps do best to do the same. Here, put that thing back on, now."

His eyes ran down her little body, and then opened wide. "You're—you're—" he said.

"Yes," she said, petulantly. "I'm pregnant. You won't be able to parade me around this way anymore. His lordship's little catamites wouldn't like it if I remind them that I can make babies and they can't. It's too much of a reminder of the emptiness of their sad lives." She saw the look on Maya's face, though, and softened a bit. "Here, I shouldn't have said that. I haven't any wish to offend you. You've been decent to me so far."

"It's all right. I'll get something for you to put on. You just wait here." He turned and went out.

" 'Wait'?" Tuya said. "What choice do I have?" She went back to the tugging and did manage to free her foot from the manacle. She threw the leg iron down on the floor and tried to stand up, but putting weight on her ankle made it all the more painful. She flexed it, biting her lip against the pain, and looked around. "Hmmm . . . no good to go out that door; he'll be back in a moment. And there are always those cats to worry about." She shuddered at the thought. She looked over at the high window opposite. If she could get up to that . . .

Limping to the far wall, she climbed painfully up the stones to the top of the wall where the high window afforded ventilation. She sat on the sill and looked into the street below. Her heart skipped a beat.

*Those men are soldiers!* she thought. Never mind the civilian dress. She recognized them; she had seen them in camp, back in the days when she had sometimes gone to visit her husband at the forge. What was the big one's name? Well, no matter; she knew him. But what was he doing here?

And look; down the street, at scattered intervals, there were more of them. They stood in doorways talking, two by two. They didn't seem to be showing any signs of moving on, either. They were . . .

"Gods!" she said incredulously. "The place is surrounded! It's—" But before she could call out to them, Maya returned.

"You get down from there!" he said, and his hand closed hard on her bloodied ankle. She yelped in pain. "Get down or I'll yank you down!"

She tried to pull away, but his grip was strong. "All right," she said. "Just let up a little. That hurts." And she jumped down, landing beside him on the cold marble. She got up and flexed her sore ankle. "You didn't have to hurt me."

"Here," he grunted, thrusting forward the simple tunic the girls in the kitchen wore. "Put this on. And you're going to have to put the manacle back on. If Sitra finds you this way—"

"If I find her what way?" Sitra said, his voice loud and acidulous. Both of them turned, shocked. "You fool! You've let her loose? You're giving her something to wear? Is this some sort of idiotic plan to help her escape? Because if it is—"

"No, no!" Tuya said, slipping the tunic over her head. "It's not his fault. Just look at my ankle. I got loose, and he caught me. As for this thing I'm wearing, surely it hasn't escaped your attention that I'm pregnant?"

"You're pre—" He let out a disgusted curse. "Your type is always breeding, like cows. Well, leave the thing on. There won't be much time for partying now." He turned to Maya. "Lock her in the cellar. There's been a change in plans. The Nubian party has been spotted in the city."

"Nubian party?" Maya said. "But—"

"Yes. It means either our message didn't get to them, or they got it and have decided to ignore it." He looked with hatred at Tuya. "Your husband," he said, "seems to be taking our threat to your safety rather lightly. Apparently he values your life very little. To save your life, he was supposed to camp outside the city until after the coup." He barked the next words at Maya. "What are you waiting for? Take her away! Kill her."

"Wait!" Tuya said. "Have you looked outside? Something's gone wrong, Sitra. The streets are full of soldiers. I saw them. Your house is surrounded." She took note of the skeptical look on his face. "Look for yourself!" she challenged. "Don't take my word for it."

The nearest eye-level window was in the next room. Sitra rushed to it and looked down. "She's right!" he said. "Something's gone wrong! Maya! Arm the servants! Bolt the doors!"

He looked back at Tuya and saw the unmistakable look of triumph on her face, and his eyes flashed with hatred. "Don't look so happy, little one," he said. "The first time one of them tries to set foot in this house, you're the cats' next meal. Do you hear? Torn to shreds by the cats!"

Tuya swallowed hard, trying to control her terror. She looked past Sitra, across the great room. Near the far door one of the leopards yawned. Its great yellow eyes seemed to look directly at her, and when it caught her eye, she could not force herself to look away. She stumbled backward until she could feel the wall against her shoulders. Her knees trembled. Sitra inspired little fear in her; she had dealt with his kind before. But the cats! The cats terrified her beyond description.

Breathless, bleary-eyed with fear and horror, Dede stumbled through the streets, elbowing his way through the clots of shoppers before the stalls on the avenue, caroming off the walls, shoving aside the unwary. Where could he go? What could he do? If the likes of Sokar wasn't safe, who was? Certainly not so powerless a man as himself! Wherever he went, they would hunt him down and find him!

Coming around a corner, he ran headlong into the one person he most wanted to see: Mereb. The two recovered, staring at each other, open-mouthed. Then the one-eyed man grabbed Dede's arm and dragged him forcefully into an alleyway. Looking around to see if anyone could hear, he said in a harsh whisper, "Good! I'm glad I found you! We've had a change of plans. We need every man we can get. Come with me!"

"Yes, yes, but they're on to us!" Dede, his words tripping over each other, managed to stammer out the truth about what he had found at Sokar's house. "I'm afraid to go home!"

The man with the eye patch scowled and waved aside his ravings. "Forget all that! We got a tip about Sokar and the return of the Nubian force. None of that matters now. The coup will still take place. But—" He saw an urchin standing at the mouth of the little alley, listening. "Get out of here, you whore's brat!" He stooped to pick up a rock and made as if to throw it. The boy took off, not bothering to look back. Mereb tossed the rock aside and turned back to his friend. "Just come with me. There's no time to waste."

"All right," Dede said in a high, whining voice. "B-but where are you going?" He let himself be pulled by the arm to the alley's edge and back out into the crowd.

"Never mind! Quickly! Every moment counts now!"


# III


Heket came out of the back room to find Musuri sitting placidly on a low bench, showing his sword to little Teti. "Now, *that* nick I got quite recently," he said. "It was my own fault. I'm getting old and careless and clumsy. But it's been a good sword. After all, your father made it."

Teti tried to lift the weapon one-handed, but found she could not. "I'm going to make swords like this," she vowed. "I'm going to make the best sword in the world, so I can give it to Baliniri." Musuri looked up at Heket, and one eyebrow went up sharply. The child went on: "Baliniri's my friend. I'm going to marry him when I grow up."

"Hush now!" Heket said, moving closer to gently pry the weapon out of the child's hands. "That's quite enough of that. Now go play with Ketan, darling. The captain has things to do." She patted the child on the bottom and shooed her off into the next room. "She's taken to you," she said to Musuri, taking note of the old soldier's crinkly-eyed, thoroughly ingratiating smile. "She has an affinity for soldiers. You, Baka, Baliniri . . ." She remembered her errand. "I wanted to tell you he's awake now."

"Good," Musuri said, getting up as nimbly as a much younger man. "I'll see him. Perhaps afterward you and I can talk a bit, eh?" His smile grew all the broader. It was the kind of smile that made one instantly feel at home with him, Heket thought. She took in the captain's bronzed, still hard upper body above his kilt and sword belt: the barrel chest, the powerful biceps. *He talks of growing old,* she thought, *but one doesn't perceive him in that way.* "I'll be out in a moment," the old soldier promised. "Don't go away, eh? Please?"

Looking down on Shobai in the bed now, Musuri was shocked at the deterioration of his friend. He had been aware for some time that Shobai had been losing weight, but while the blind man had still been ambulatory, Musuri had only been conscious of a slight diminution of vigor—such had been Shobai's basic vitality. Now Musuri took note of the hollow cheeks, the suddenly fallen biceps, the gaunt neck. Shobai looked *old.* Musuri cleared his throat softly. "Shobai?" he said. "It's me—Musuri. How are you?"

The blind man smiled. "Come, sit close by me, old friend. I heard my daughter's voice out there. Have the two of you been making friends?"

"Yes. Don't change the subject. How are you? You don't look well."

"I'm weak." His voice, once strong, masculine, was now an old man's. "How strange. I thought I'd keep my strength longer than this. But collapsing like that on the march home . . ."

Musuri sat down beside him on the bed and took his hand. It was huge, half again the size of Musuri's own, and there was still some strength in it, if immeasurably less than there had been once. "Happens to all of us sooner or later," he said.

"Yes, but Belsunu was supposed to have worked at the forge until a couple of days before he died, according to what Jacob told me. I'd be surprised if I ever lifted a hammer again." He sighed; it was like gasping for breath. "I felt this coming on. Perhaps I shouldn't have gone on the trip South. I had a dream that I was dying—"

"Well, you're home now. Rest. Take it easy. Maybe you'll get better for a time. That sometimes happens with the lung disease."

"I doubt it. It's as if all the strength had drained out of me, once and for all." He sighed again. "I wonder if I'll ever see her again. . . ." He shook his head. "Musuri. Promise me one thing."

"Done."

"Look after Mereet if she ever comes back. And don't let anything happen to Baka. Madir confided in me before we left; he's going to train Baka as the next vizier. Baka is a very important man here. Without him I don't know what will happen to the Egyptians and their dreams of getting rid of the Shepherds." The big hand weakly squeezed Musuri's. "Keep an eye on the twins, please."

"I'll do all of those things. Before we left Nubia I talked to Akhilleus. He doesn't need me anymore. I'm retiring from active service."

The hand squeezed again. "Good, good. You should settle down."

Musuri chuckled. "I've been thinking about that. Your servant Heket—tell me about her. To be honest, she interests me."

Shobai smiled broadly. "Yes! Yes! How often I've wished for her to find a man, but until now she'd never consider leaving my service. Talk to her, Musuri. I can't think of a better match for either of you." As sounds of loud voices drifted in from the other room, Shobai strained forward from the pillow to listen. "What's that?"

Musuri got up, patted the blind man's hand as he disengaged his own. "I think Baka and Ben-Hadad are back," he said. "You rest now. I'll be back to see you as soon as I can." He went out and closed the door behind him.

Baka turned to him, eyes flashing. "Musuri!" he called. "Come along. There's a problem. An assassination attempt on the king. And a riot near the temple."

"No!" Ben-Hadad cried. "*I* need him! What are you going to do about Tuya? If—"

Musuri looked from one face to the other. "Riot?" he asked. "Tuya? I don't understand."

Baka scowled. Then he threw up his hands. "All right,"

he growled. "Stay with Ben-Hadad. But neither of you should do anything rash. She's in great danger there. Sitra's house is like a fortress. Try a frontal assault and they'll kill her, as sure as anything."

"Kill who?" Musuri asked. But Baka had already hurried out into the street. "Ben-Hadad!" Musuri demanded. "What's happening?"

"Come with me," the young man said. Grim-faced, he drew his sword. Musuri's brow went up again; the sword was the iron weapon they had found in Nubia on the battlefield. "There's no time to lose! We've got to save Tuya!"

"Think about it," Sitra said nervously. "We aren't certain the soldiers are outside because of us. I admit it looks suspicious. But . . ."

Nebka, his bodyguard, peered out from the high window. "Those are members of the royal guard, sir. I can't allow it. It's too dangerous. I have your safety to think of, sir."

"Safety?" Sitra said in a waspish voice, high-pitched, nasal. "Do you mean to suggest that I'm safe where I am? Cooped up here like a caged lion? Waiting for them to swoop down and—"

"No, sir," Nebka said. "But you're safer than you'd be if you were already in their hands. Perhaps we—"

"Perhaps! Perhaps! A fine lot of good your 'perhaps' will do me when we run out of food and drink, eh? I think we ought to wait until nightfall and make a break for it." He elbowed Nebka aside and took his place at the window. "Nebka! Look! There's something going on down there! Look! Quick!"

The big bodyguard craned his neck and looked where his master pointed. In the street below, an elder officer had just come up and was speaking in an agitated voice to the man in command of the little ground force. Nebka tried to hear their conversation, but couldn't. From across the warren of streets, alleys, and boulevards, there was a distant sound of people in the temple quarter. As they listened there was a roar from the faraway source, as if from hundreds of throats. The commander of the guardsmen barked out an order; his men stepped into the street and fell into formation. They could make out a few of his words now: ". . . temple quarter . . . riot."

"Riot?" Sitra said, excited. "Did you hear that?"

Nebka looked for the bald elder officer, but could not find him. Now the junior officer barked out another order, and the soldiers wheeled and made off down the street, their spears held high. "Look, sir! They're leaving!"

Sitra nodded and looked up at the western sky. "Yes! And less than an hour to sundown. Under cover of dark we ought to be able to—"

"Dark? Sir, I think we should try now. We don't know when the soldiers are coming back. The riot could be quelled quickly. We could be just getting ready to leave, and there they'd be, back at their stations, surrounding the house."

Sitra scowled petulantly. "First you say stay; then you say go. I wish you'd make up your mind. But maybe you're right. How many do we have under arms now? Slaves and servants?"

"Sixteen, sir. Seventeen armed men, including yourself, sir."

"No more? No, it's too risky in broad daylight. We'll wait until nightfall."

"But sir—"

"No! My mind is made up! Not until the sun is down! Meanwhile we've got to send someone out to the gate, someone who can be trusted to handle a bribe. Maya! Maya, where are you?"

It had been one of Madir's few organizing failures. When the first orders had gone out to arrest—or, in the case of Sokar, to poison—the leaders of the conspiracy, the action had drawn away most of the available members of the city guard. Madir, thinking these sufficient to cover the work at hand, had not called for reinforcements from the garrison outside the city. As a result, his forces had been spread dangerously thin, scattered over a dozen locations around the city.

Unfortunately, at such a moment Dedmose had chosen to disregard Madir's warnings and make an unscheduled visit to the Temple of Osiris, accompanied only by his personal guard. These were a dozen hand-picked Shairetana warriors, superbly trained members of a hereditary caste of personal servants to the Egyptian crown and descendants of the great warriors who had served the mighty Twelfth Dynasty kings in the days of Sesostris and Amenemhet.

Under ordinary circumstances, such an escort would have proved more than sufficient. The king's party had only to cross a single, open square to reach the temple—a square usually empty of people in this sparsely populated sector of the capital. But today was a festival day, the first of the festival of Ptah-Sokaris-Osiris, and as a result, the street and square alike were thick with people from all quarters of the city. They were attracted by the bountifully stocked stalls providing free food: bread, sweet cakes, beer and wine, roasted oxen, and birds cooked on the spit. All this food had, according to the ritual, been offered to the god in solemn ceremonies and had presumably been accepted as valid sacrifice. But, the god once propitiated, the food was now, by order of the king, to be distributed to the people. Another festival might have been open only to members of the upper classes, but this one, being a special favorite of Dedmose's, had been arranged to include the lower orders as well.

Dedmose, appearing at the top of the palace steps, was surrounded by the tall, majestic Shairetana soldiers. At first he was cheered by masses in the square, in gratitude for his bounty. He graciously acknowledged their applause and began to move slowly down the staircase.

Then pandemonium broke loose! From the sidelines, someone lunged through the gap between two hulking guards. Afternoon sunlight glinted on a metal blade, and Dedmose, wounded, staggered back into the hands of his guards. Three of the Shairetana dived into the crowd lining the stairs. Knives, swords, spears flashed, and there were anguished screams. A woman fell face down onto the stairs, stabbed to the heart, and rolled slowly down two steps to die at Dedmose's feet. More screams, and a child's high-pitched wail.

First the crowd fell back in horror; but not all, even those in front, had seen the attack on the king, who had by now been rushed from the scene by two of the gigantic guards. All that the people at the bottom of the staircase could see was the dead body of the woman: the terrible gaping wound in her chest, the pool of her blood that stained the stairs. They could also see the soldiers fiercely hacking away at what appeared to be innocent civilians. One man, less timid than the rest, had approached one of the guards and put a hand on the soldier's arm. He had been cut down viciously, his throat slashed.

"Murderers!" someone cried from the rear. "Butchers!"

Several men up front charged forward at the Shairetana—some deliberately, others merely shoved forward by those behind them. Two of these were targets for the guards' spears; another pair, however, rushed through and pulled one of the guards down. He was clubbed to death with rocks picked off the street. Emboldened by success, the crowd surged forward again. Three men died this time, plus another guard. Now the men who had killed the guardsmen were armed with their victims' swords, spears, and long knives. With these they charged the remaining guardsmen—just as the first reinforcements arrived, called by the soldiers who had carried the wounded Dedmose to safety.

These young reinforcements were raw recruits still in training for work as gate guards for the palace; they had simply been the first men the retreating Shairetana had found en route to the palace's doors. Inept, clumsy, they were hacked down by the crowd in a matter of moments. Meanwhile, the remaining Shairetana slashed viciously at their unarmed opponents on the edge of the broad temple stairs. Drawn by the rising din of conflict, new onlookers swarmed in from the side streets to join the fray. The disturbance had become riot; the riot was in danger of becoming revolution.


# IV


"There," Tros said, fastening the compress down. "I've closed the wound and stopped the bleeding, sire. Now let me give you something for the pain."

But the king, white and drawn, eyes burning with excitement, tried to sit up and had to be forced back down by the doctor. "I can't just lie here!" Dedmose said. "There's a riot in the streets!"

Madir, who had been silent all this time watching Tros work, now moved forward. "No, sire. I'm afraid I must insist. You must rest. The doctor can't guarantee your swift recovery unless you do as he says. The body won't heal unless—"

Dedmose let his head fall back onto the bed and stared up at the ceiling. "How could this have happened?" he asked. "My own people!"

"The captain of the Shairetana has made a report," Madir said. "There were two attackers. One was killed on the spot. The other escaped, but the guards saw his face. He can be identified. Meanwhile the city is sealed. No one leaves, no one enters."

"But the riot! My own people, rising up against me!"

"Not against you, sire. I've been told that the crowd could only see the guardsmen lunging at the crowd, trying to get at the assassins. To the people it looked like an unprovoked attack by the Shairetana. The spectators could not see the initial attack on you."

Dedmose's face turned in his direction. "But who would believe that my personal guard would commit an unprovoked act like that?"

Madir started to answer, but Tros intervened, bringing a bronze cup and holding the king's head up gently so that he could drink. "Ugh!" he said. "That's bitter."

Tros moved back a step. "You'll feel better in a moment or two, sire," he said soothingly, then bowed with practiced ease and withdrew.

"Sire," Madir said, moving to the king's bedside and sitting down heavily on a low bench. "It's my fault. I shoulder the entire responsibility. I should have left specific orders that you were not to be in the streets without heavy guard."

Dedmose closed his eyes, struggled to open them again, then gave in to the nostrum's effect. "Whatever Tros gave me, it's making the pain go away. I'm dizzy."

"You'll be asleep in moments," Madir said. "Meanwhile, sire, I've come to a decision. I've given young Baka complete autonomy. He'll be able to quell the rebellion with minimum violence and bad effect."

The king remained alert enough to understand Madir's changed tone. "Ah," he said in a sleepy voice. "This is what we talked about, eh?"

"Yes, sire. In the old days such a thing never would have happened. I am getting old. Careless."

The king's eyes closed, and his face totally relaxed. Madir looked at the stained bandage on Dedmose's chest and at the gaunt face. He thought Dedmose asleep for a moment or two; but then the king half smiled and spoke even more slowly than before. "Well," he said. "We all grow old. Let's see how the young man does with the present crisis. Perhaps if he . . ."

He did not finish the sentence. His words slurred off into silence. He slept.

*    *    *

The fighting had spread all the way down the long avenue to the next square, which marked the border between
the quarter of the temple and that of the middle caste. New
recruits had stabilized matters near the original site, at the
temple steps; but other, battle-hardened, troops that were
called in to clear the streets and avenues separating the two
quarters were men who had had no experience handling
internal quarrels, in which the ordinary savagery of war could
not safely be brought into play. When the habitués of the
square began throwing rocks, the front-line soldiers, called in
from the garrison outside the city, waded into them, hacking
and stabbing, leaving dozens dead.

From above there was a rain of rocks from the rooftops.
A line-soldier captain barked an order, and bowmen were
brought in. They climbed the stairs of a house across the
street and, with the first volley, felled the rock throwers, one
of them a child of no more than ten. Then they turned their
bows with deadly accuracy on the crowd in the street, driving
back the civilian reserves who had begun to come in from the
quarters that housed the lower classes.

The civilians retreated, then regrouped in the smaller,
adjoining square. A citizen stood atop the raised rock wall
around the well and cried, "There are too many soldiers!
We've no chance against them at all! Our only hope is to
return to our own quarters and hope none of them has
recognized us!"

There was a shout of approval from the rear. The citizen
was about to continue when strong hands pulled him down to
the street, and hard fists battered him. The crowd roared; but
another man took his place atop the well's wall: a man with an
ugly, scarred face and a dark patch over one eye. "No!" he
cried. "They've cut down your friends! They've killed an
innocent child back there. Will you stand still for such butch-
ery? Has the blood of great Egypt been watered down so
completely that we will stand by and see the innocent murdered by armed troops too cowardly to drive the Shepherds
out of the lands of our fathers?"

Another shout of dissent sounded, but the speaker had
friends planted in the crowd, and two of these silenced the
dissenter with blows to the face. "There!" the man with the
eye patch said angrily. "That's the only way to deal with
cowards and traitors! My friends—would you fight the troops

more readily if you were armed? Eh? Armed with real weapons?"

"Yes! Yes!" shouted a man in front. "They cut down my nephew back there! Give me a sword, and I'll make two of them pay for his death!"

The man in the eye patch knew he had them now. "Look behind you! My friends are opening a warehouse of arms! Step up and draw your weapons!" They turned and saw the twin doors of a building closed these many months swinging wide. Inside, a roughly dressed man held up spears in each hand. "There you are!" the speaker bellowed. "One per man! But quickly, before the soldiers come!"

They formed lines and grabbed the arms; from there the conspirators herded them back down the street toward the marketplace. From the little square Mereb and Dede could hear the sounds of battle once again, as the newly armed townspeople engaged the soldiery. Metal clashed against metal; shrill screams hung in the air.

Dede, trembling, stood half supported by the warehouse wall, looking out with horror at the scene: citizens, peaceful only an hour ago, arming themselves against their own guardsmen. His face was a white mask of fear and foreboding.

Mereb spotted him there and scowled. "Dede!" he cried. "Take your weapon! There are plenty for everyone!"

Dede closed his eyes and shook his head weakly. His knees were like putty; it was all he could do to keep them from buckling. "No," he croaked in a broken voice. "You go on without me. I'll never touch a weapon again—unless it's to do away with myself."

Mereb stepped forward and slapped him backhand across the face. "Are you going to turn milksop on me now, after you've struck the greatest blow you'll ever strike?" he snarled.

Dede held up one hand to ward off any further blows, but his voice was a little steadier when he spoke. "Blow!" he echoed. "Do you realize what you got me to do, Mereb? You got me to strike at the king! At a god, Mereb! This hand of mine was raised against a prince of the blood!" He looked at his hand as if it were leprous.

"God?" Mereb ejaculated, grabbing him by the shoulders and shaking him. "You struck no god! Did you see the man bleed? He's no more a god than you or I! And if I have anything to say about the matter, my friend, by this time

tomorrow he'll be rotting meat in the boneyard, and we'll be
the rulers of Upper Egypt! Think, Dede! Think of where this
could lead!"

Dede wasn't listening. "I touched him! This hand held
the knife! And the guards can identify me!" He put both
hands over his face and sobbed. "I didn't mean it!" he cried.
"I never meant things to go this far! And now it's too late. . . ."

The man coming toward Ben-Hadad and Musuri, down
the street, was, from the way he walked, the set of his
shoulders, and his confident air, obviously a soldier, if one
out of uniform. His sword hung easily from his belt, and scars
showed here and there on the uncovered parts of his body.
He was short—shorter even than Ben-Hadad—but his shoulders were broad, and his muscular arms were a trifle too long
for his squat frame. His face was good-natured, open; he had
had more than a few drinks already, even this early in the
evening.

Catching sight of the two men, he slowed his pace and
hailed them, speaking with a slight accent Ben-Hadad could
not easily recognize. "Say, friend!" he said. "Someone told
me there was a disturbance somewhere around here. Do you
know anything about it?"

Ben-Hadad, nervous and drawn, was about to pass him
by without answering, but Musuri stopped him, one hand on
his arm. "Your ear will draw you to it," he replied, motioning
toward the sound of conflict behind them.

The stranger smiled, sizing up the speaker. "You're a
soldier, like myself from your speech, from somewhere up
near Canaan, but you've been a long time away."

"Thirty years and more," said the old man, grinning.
"You've a good ear. And you'd be from somewhere in the
Valley of the Two Rivers, and fairly recently." The stranger
acknowledged this with a smiling nod. "I don't think you'll
make any money out of joining either side just now," Musuri
continued. "It's a riot, and a serious one; but it'll be put
down. All you can do is get your self mistaken for one of the
rioters and have to fight your way out of the misunderstanding. You could end up bloody and in prison."

"Oh ho! And I thought there might be some fun."

Ben-Hadad tried to pull away. "Musuri, we have to be
going—"

"Wait," the old soldier said patiently. He turned back to

the stranger. "If you want a bit of sport, come with us instead. We have to rescue a lady. There'll be no pay—except the friendship and gratitude of Musuri of Moab." He thumped himself on the chest.

Ben-Hadad once again tried to pull away, but both men ignored him. "Musuri, eh?" the stranger said. "My compliments. I've heard the name before."

Musuri waved away any appreciation of his reputation. "There's a lady to get out of trouble. This gentleman's wife has been abducted and is being held in— Come along, and I'll explain on the way." He started off down the narrow street again. "By the way," he said. "I didn't get the name."

"Name?" the newcomer asked. "Why, Mekim—at your service."

The now-armed villagers charged the soldiers in the square, and the first wave was beaten back. But the soldiers sustained casualties, and as the civilians swarmed up the stairs, the bowmen on the roof had to turn their attention away from covering the action in the streets to defend themselves. Several archers fell, victims of spear thrusts; knocked to the ground under the mad rush and beaten to death by their attackers. Now the rioters were armed also with bows and arrows, and commanded the square from above. When fresh troops arrived on the far side of the little marketplace, they were met with a hail of ill-aimed arrows, a few of which found their mark.

The soldiers regrouped to charge, but suddenly a voice rang out, strong, loud, commanding: *"Wait! Wait, my friends!"*

For some reason the bows lowered, and the charge faltered. In this no-man's-land in the middle of the square, a well-known, instantly recognizable figure stood, hands on hips, feet well apart. The bright eyes scanned the crowd; rebel and loyalist alike held their fire, and the shouting trailed off rapidly to something not far from silence. The slim, fearless figure waited until the last sounds died, eyes calmly moving from face to face.

Then he spoke. "Yes," he said. "You know me. Baka. Plain, simple Baka, from the delta. Baka, who bears as many scars from the Shepherds' weapons as any man here. Baka, who has fought the enemy as long as any man in Egypt. If you want to kill someone, kill me. If you're angry at the soldiers, don't kill them. Kill me. If you've a quarrel with our king, take it out on me." His eyes went around the crowd again, and there were many who could not look him in the eye.

"Baka, the soldiers killed my—" someone began. But there was something in the slim commander's eyes that made the speaker hesitate. The crowd saw the pain on Baka's expressive face.

"The king lives!" Baka said. "One of the assassins is dead. The other we will have before dawn. We are satisfied that none of you had designs on the king's life."

"King? Assassin?" someone asked. "What do you mean?"

"That's how this all began," Baka said. "Someone tried to kill our king. The troops struck back, and in their haste, two innocents were killed. Most of you did not see what happened. All you saw were the deaths of your friends, and you retaliated thinking the soldiers wanton murderers." He paused, scanned the crowd again, taking in their shock and horror.

"Come," he continued, his voice solemn and compassionate. "We have had a misunderstanding. Let it end. Let the killing end with it. Our king lives, and he will mourn the fallen dead with us. I swear this. I will walk with the funeral procession of every man who fell today—the assassins only excepted. I will see the heirs of the innocents who died here today compensated for their loss. I will see their souls sung peacefully into the Netherworld. I, Baka, swear this. But we can only do these things when we are at peace with one another."

The silence was striking now. He looked around the square again, his eyes going from face to face. And in front a man slowly took the spear in his hands and laid it down gently at Baka's feet. Wordlessly, he stepped back into the crowd, a somber expression on his face. And one by one the others followed suit, in sorrowful silence. The riot was over. As the last rays of the setting sun lit the darkening skies, they heard the voice of the crier atop the city wall: "Sunset—and all's well. . . ."

# V

Sitra was coming apart, a little at a time. His thin face was covered with sweat, and a nervous tic had appeared on one cheek, contorting his face at irregular intervals. "Where is he?" he asked in a high, whining voice, wringing his hands. "Where can he have gone to?"

"Patience, sir," Nebka said. "These things take time. We aren't even sure who is manning the gate just now. It may be someone new, someone who doesn't know any of us. I'm sure Maya is doing his best, sir."

"His best? Damn his best! His best isn't good enough, that's obvious. If he were any good, he'd have had the whole thing wrapped up by now and been back here helping us. And I wouldn't be worrying like—"

"Please, sir." Nebka walked briskly into the next room to inspect the servants, who were lined up, weapons in hand, looking a little unsure of themselves. "Don't worry, now. Everything will be all right." But with his back to Sitra, he allowed himself a disapproving frown. The little pederast was beginning to show his true colors, he thought, and they weren't flattering.

He walked up and down the row of servants. "Look here," he said in a voice full of authority. "We're in a tight spot, and there's likely to be some fighting."

"Please, sir," said someone in the second row. "We're not fighting people, most of us. If we had some idea what we were up against . . ."

Nebka stopped, stared at him, then let his gaze go from face to face. "I'll give it to you straight," he replied in a harsh voice. "Our master has landed himself in desperate trouble, and the entire household is going to be blamed for it. When the government people come in, they're not going to accept any excuse. The soldiers and guardsmen are going to start killing, right and left, so you can forget any pretty illusions that you'll be able to throw down your weapons and say, 'Oh, please, my wicked master made me do it!' " He spoke the words in a mocking falsetto.

"But . . . can't we—"

"Forget it," Nebka said. "You're going to have to fight . . . unless you want to stand here and be cut down by the soldiers. You'll be fighting for *your* lives, not your master's." He let this sink in, then went on. "There's an outside chance that we'll be able to escape the city before the soldiers can catch us." He squinted through the gathering gloom and barked out an order. "You! Light a couple of lanterns." The man scrambled out of position to obey, as Sitra came into the room. "Now, if—"

But there was another interruption, a loud, frenzied knocking on the front door. "Quickly!" Sitra said. "That must be Maya! Get that, will you?"

When Maya finally staggered into the room, winded and panting, they could see by lantern light the look on his face. Sitra leaned back against the wall, his face an expressionless mask, watching Maya's trembling hands, his horror-struck face. "I couldn't get through," Maya gasped. "The gates are closed. All of them. Baka's orders. *Baka!* He's the new vizier. Word just came down. And—and, sir, the plan has failed! Our leaders are all either dead or captured! Baka stopped the uprising in the streets, all by himself! The rioters laid down their weapons in the square. There's a general amnesty. . . ."

Sitra's face lit up for a moment. His eyes widened. But Maya held up both hands. "No, sir. The amnesty doesn't include us. They have the names of everyone on the council who sat in on the decision-making."

Sitra croaked out, "They'll be here soon. It's only a matter of time."

Just then, Tuya poked her head out of the back room, and Sitra saw her. She had seen the look on Sitra's face, malevolent and vindictive. "Y-you!" he said in a tight voice. "You little slut! *You* betrayed us! You were informing on us! Reporting to Baka all the while! You'll pay! You'll be the first to die! I'll kill you myself!"

Nebka stepped forward and put a restraining hand on his arm as he was about to rush into the back room, sword in hand. "No, sir!" he ordered in a voice that carried the same sort of authority now that it had when he had spoken to the servants. "No, sir! I forbid it! I absolutely forbid it!"

Sitra stared, incredulous. "Forbid? You forbid *me?*"

"When we're as close to death as you and I are right now, sir!" Nebka said in a powerful voice. "My guess is that the soldiers will be here within the hour. And she's the only hostage we have, sir."

Sitra stood stock-still. Behind him a low rumble came from one of the great cats, wakened by all the commotion. For one terrible moment Sitra looked down into the horrible yellow eyes, looked at the yawning jaws and the huge clawed feet, as if realizing that he, too, was little more than meat to the great carnivores there beside him. And it was past feeding time.

\*        \*        \*

On the rooftop it was quite dark. The sun was well down, and the last reddish rays had disappeared over the western horizon. A damp, chill breeze had come up from the river, and Necho, guarding the roof alone, wished he had brought something to throw over his shoulders.

If only it were not so dark! And, worst of all, there was an unnatural silence hanging over the quarter now. Where were the people wending their way homeward after a long day's work? Where were the women with their straggling children, coming home from market, the topers lurching out of the taverns? Instead of the normal hubbub that would come at the end of a workday, there was this strange, unearthly silence, which, in the absence of moon or stars, his imagination peopled with soundless phantoms skulking in the dark streets below.

Once again he thought with regret of the girl. Now he would never have her. And what a lovely prize she would have been. He had peeked into the back room once or twice, three or four days ago, and had had a good look at her, naked and chained. He had felt powerful feelings of lust for her. Maya had promised him he would get her when the coup was complete, in exchange for that exhausting night of unnatural revelry up here on the roof, where no one could see . . . and now Maya would never deliver on his promise. He could not. It was obvious what was going to happen: Sitra was going to use her as a hostage, to get away. And when his own neck was safe, Sitra would kill her.

Suddenly it hit him. Why, *he* was in terrible danger! He, Necho! It was not just a matter of Sitra being in trouble; his whole household would be fair game for Baka's soldiers when they came, and they would not make distinctions between master and slave.

His hand tightened on the hilt of the sword at his side. He would have to fight! He, who had never raised his hand against another human being. He would have to kill or be killed!

With frightened eyes he looked out across the rooftops at the great bulk of the temple, whose upper windows were lit by torches and candles. On the other side of the temple were the prisons. In the cellars, the subterranean dungeons, the conspirators who had escaped the soldiers' swords would be awaiting the arrival of the torturers, who—

But no: It was too horrible to contemplate! He pictured

himself strapped to a table, watching the torturers approach, their horrid implements in hand. He shuddered. There had to be some way out of this. He could not let this happen. He would have to—

He never finished the thought. From behind, hard hands with a grip of iron pinned his arms to his sides. From the front, a third hand clapped over his mouth, and a razor-sharp blade suddenly pressed against his neck, hard enough to break the skin. The moon above peeked through the cloud cover, and he could suddenly see a pair of eyes staring malevolently into his own.

"There, now," the man in front of him, with dark curly hair, said in a silky whisper. "One word, one syllable, one move, and you're a dead man." As if to underscore the point, the knife pressed even harder into his flesh. The hand over his mouth relaxed just enough to let him breathe—but the arms pinning him from behind held him as hard as before. "Are you going to be quiet? Because if you try to call for help or alert the people in the house—"

"No!" Necho croaked hoarsely. "No! I'll be quiet!"

"Good," the man with the knife said. "Now tell me the floor layout inside." Necho's voice was barely audible as he stammered out an answer. "All right. Now how about the girl?"

"G-girl?"

"The one Sitra has been holding as a prisoner, damn you!" The knife, which had relaxed its pressure against his neck, pressed again. "The little one! Where are they keeping her?"

"The b-back room. The one where Sitra holds his parties. There's a stairway—"

"That's out," the man with the knife said. "They'll spot us right off. Have they harmed her?"

"N-no," Necho managed to squeak out. "No, she's all right. At least she was just before sundown, when they put me up here. They're c-counting on her to get them out of here. She's a hostage." The knife pressure at his throat relaxed; so did the rock-hard arms around him from the back. "You've got to find some other way. There's the cats."

"Cats?"

"Leopards. Cheetahs. They're not tame. Sitra fed a slave to them last year when he tried to run away."

"Where are they?"

"Right below us."

"Gods!" the man with the knife said. "Then Tuy—the girl will have to pass through that room on the way out! Is that right?" Necho nodded. The knife-wielder turned to his friends. "Tuya's scared to death of big cats. I remember how she was with Dedmose's lion. This is going to be tricky."

The man behind Necho stepped out into the light. The moon shone on his bald pate, and Necho's eyes widened. Was this old fellow the one who had held him so tightly? "There's only one way to do it. I have to make a fuss at the other end to distract them. Perhaps it wouldn't hurt if you, Mekim, were to join me. How many are down there?" he asked Necho.

"Uh . . . sixteen, including Sitra."

The oldster grinned, crinkly-eyed. "How do you like those odds, Mekim?"

The short man's smile was deadly. "Well, eighteen or twenty would have been better."

"All right. Is there another way"—this to Necho again—"down to the room the girl's in?"

"Y-yes. There's a high window, and if you get down to the ledge quietly enough, perhaps you can get in there."

The knife-wielder said, "I'll go down. You make enough noise to cover me. We'll hit them from two sides." He turned back to Necho. "You've been very helpful. You've earned your life, I think, although I can't let you go back to them."

"I wouldn't want to, sir. All I want is to get away."

"Go ahead. Good luck. But first give us a couple of minutes to get in. Then go down the wall and out into the street. If you can get into the Thieves Quarter, people there will take you in."

"Thank you, sir."

Necho watched them disappear over the wall. For one fleeting moment he was tempted to cry and betray them; but he stifled the impulse. He had been granted a miraculous chance at freedom and would be a fool to jeopardize it.

He took a deep breath, sent up a silent prayer of thanks to the gods of his people, and climbed rapidly down to the street.

# VI

"Oh, stop sniveling," Mereb said. "Face things like a man, you little coward." Dede did not respond, but stood in semishadow, the lamplight slanting across his frightened face. Angered, Mereb shook him by the arms, hard.

Footfalls down the path prevented a more severe beating. Hastily Mereb grabbed Dede and pulled him back into the shadows, just as a patrol of guardsmen marched by, the overhead torchlight glinting on the sharp points of the spears.

"That was a close one," he said when they were gone. "Now get hold of yourself. We're in a tight spot, but I've been in worse. We just have to think out our options."

For the first time Dede seemed to come alive. "What does it matter?" he said, his voice verging on hysteria. "Wherever we go, they'll find us. At the end of every road, there'll be a torture chamber, a sharpened stake. Why postpone it? Why—"

"You fool! You spineless, whining fool! If you hadn't botched the thing in the first place—"

"*Botched?* The only thing that I don't regret is that I failed in my attempt to kill the king. A living god, father of Egypt, without whose annual sacrifice the Nile's waters would—"

"Stupid superstition, fit only for idiots!"

"No!" Dede cried out. "The one thing the soothsayers agree upon, Mereb, is that if the people don't mend their ways, a great famine will come, and we'll all starve!" He began to whimper and fidget.

"Shut up and come along!" Mereb ordered, grabbing him by the arm. "I've got an idea. I know a place where we'll be safe until this has blown over. There may even be a little food there. The owner is in the Fayum, and it's unlikely he'll return until things are quieter."

Dede made no protest as Mereb half dragged him along the alleyways, following a tortuous route to avoid main thoroughfares. Twice they had to slip back into the shadows to avoid patrols that seemed to be everywhere in the city.

Finally they found their way to a modest house on the edge of the temple quarter. The door was locked, but Mereb went around back and found access through a window. He helped Dede up and said, "I'll go around front. You let me in, Dede! Did you hear me?"

"I hear you," came the reply from the complete darkness inside. The curious note of deadness was again in Dede's voice, but Mereb dismissed it with a snort. He retraced his steps and went back around to the front of the house, awaiting the call from inside.

How had it gone wrong? He frowned, puzzling things out. Everything had seemed so sure. The rabble had accepted the weapons to use against the guards. He had fired them up with his incandescent oratory. But then Baka had stepped in. When had Baka acquired such an ascendancy over them? What was he, anyhow, but a member of the privileged scribe caste who had turned soldier? Why would the poor, born to an infinitely rougher life, listen to such a man? Surely resentment should pit caste against caste here. Surely . . .

He tested the door. The lock still held. He looked right and left, then called out in a sharp whisper, "Dede! Open up! It's dangerous standing out here under the light like this!"

There was no answer. He decided against speaking out again; someone might hear him. He went back around the side to the open window and with difficulty managed to scramble up over the sill into the room.

There was a light in the adjoining room, visible under the door. He tiptoed forward. "Dede!" he said peevishly. "Don't you know better than to light a lamp before you—"

But as he opened the door, he could see why Dede did not answer. In the short time he had been inside, Dede had climbed atop a chair, buckled his empty sword belt around his neck, and fixed the other end around a heavy beam overhead. Then he had simply stepped off the chair.

"The fool!" Mereb said, gagging. But even as he spoke, the pounding on the door began. He froze against the wall, the horrid sight of the dead man before his eyes: the staring eyes, the protruding tongue. The body revolved slowly, slowly.

"Open up!" the voice outside ordered, loud, insistent. "We know you're there!"

Maya had sent one of the kitchen slaves up the staircase

to call Necho down. But as the slave rounded the corner, he was met by a mad-eyed old bald man, eyes wide, face contorted in a terrifying grin. *"Haaaaahh!"* the ancient bellowed, freezing the slave in his tracks just long enough for him to see the deadly sword in the old man's big-knuckled hands. Then the sword swung mightily. It was the last sight the slave ever saw.

The old man leaped into the room, still roaring at the top of his lungs. Two of the yard slaves attacked him immediately; one of them actually managed to engage the old man's blade in competent parry. But suddenly it was no longer there. Instead it was in the slave's belly up to the hilt. The slave fell, his partner faltered for a split second, and it was the end of him. The sword caught him in the neck.

At the same moment, as three other slaves moved forward to take on the old man, he was joined by a new face at the far window: a short, curly-haired, laughing figure, burly, long-armed. "You take those three, Musuri!" he said. "I'll see if I can keep the others busy." And, a grin fixed on his good-humored face, he set to, fencing vigorously with two men at once.

As he did, Sitra, panic-stricken, huddled behind one of the unchained creatures. One leopard, drawn by the scent of fresh blood, wandered into the room where the fighting was taking place. The old man, Musuri, chuckled and made mewing noises. "Come here, pussycat," he said, mockingly. "Here, kitty." The leopard, startled, stopped for a second, sizing him up. Musuri's blade lashed out like a striking cobra, slicing through the big cat's neck. The animal roared and pounced. But Musuri nimbly sidestepped its rush and buried his sword in the cat's side! The animal slipped in the fresh blood and slid forward, banging into the wall. The motion caused the sword to move inside the cat, and it let out a yowl of pain, pawing frantically at the sword buried deep inside its body. The old man laughed and picked up a weapon dropped by one of the fallen slaves. "Mekim!" he called to his friend. "Do you need any help?"

"No!" the short man said, lunging suddenly and skewering one of his opponents. "Go into the other room! See how the girl is!"

Sitra only had time to herd another leopard toward the doorway when he heard Mekim's words. As the great beast moved out into the room toward the fighting, Sitra righted himself and stood thunderstruck. Of course! If he could get to

Tuya before she got away, he could use her to make his escape. With a knife to the girl's throat, using her as a shield, they would have little choice but to let him go. With one final glance at the last remaining, restlessly pacing leopard he took off for the far room.

When he reached the room in which she had been held captive, he saw a burly dark-haired man bending over her, his mighty back muscles straining. As Sitra watched, frozen to the spot with shock, the broad back suddenly registered release, and Tuya staggered back. There was a *click*, and Sitra could see the young man toss the chain aside, having forced the manacle apart by sheer brute strength. "There!" the dark-haired man said. "Oh, your poor ankle! It's raw!"

With a malign bleat of rage, Sitra charged, his sword outstretched. "Ben-Hadad!" the girl screamed. "Look out!"

The young man turned as he rose from his kneeling position. The change in position threw Sitra's lunge a handspan off its mark, and the blade inflicted no more than a minor flesh wound. Sitra blundered into Ben-Hadad's big body and staggered back to recover.

Ben-Hadad looked at him curiously. He made no move to defend himself or to draw the strange-looking black sword at his belt. Instead, he motioned the girl to stand behind him and stood looking at Sitra, his hands held loosely in front of him. "So you're the one," he said. "Not only a traitor but an abuser of women."

For some reason his refusal to attack filled Sitra with an incoherent rage. "Get out of my way!" he shrieked in a shrill voice. He feinted with his sword, but even the feint did not provoke the young opponent to defend himself.

In a panic Sitra glanced over his shoulder into the main room. He could see the leopard hunched over the fallen body of one of his own slaves. The old man, Musuri, and the short fellow were fencing vigorously with his servants, and as he looked he could see Nebka—good old reliable Nebka—drive Musuri back with a volley of blows that the old man had apparent difficulty in parrying. There was hope yet! "Look," Sitra said. "Just go your way and give me the girl and I'll spare you. In case you don't know, I'm the fencing champion of the city these four years running."

"I know who you are," Ben-Hadad said relatively calmly. And now something familiar in his face came home to Sitra. Where had he seen that face before? "I saw you at court the day I got the assignment to go to Nubia. Forget about my giving her up. I gave her up when I accepted the Nubian commission, and it was a fool's errand. If I'd lost her forever by doing so, I'd richly deserve the pain it would cost me. But now I've found her, and I'll never give her up to anybody again, for any reason. So, master swordsman, the only way you'll ever touch her will be to kill me." Amazingly, he still had not drawn his odd sword. "Come, sir." The flesh wound on his chest was bleeding, and an irregular stripe of red ran down his front. An idea entered Sitra's mind. "Well, come on!" the young man challenged, a hint of impatience in his voice.

Sitra smiled and attacked.

To his amazement Ben-Hadad's draw was practiced, professional. His parry was clumsy but effective, and when he recovered into an on-guard position, he almost looked like a soldier. Sitra could see his own feint and thrust coming a full eye-blink beforehand, and had his parry prepared.

But to his surprise the parry shocked his hand so hard that he almost dropped his sword! He looked down, wide-eyed, at the weapon the young man held. "That's not bronze!" he cried in horror. "That's—"

"Yes," the young man responded. "Iron. And every time we touch forte to forte, your weapon will grow weaker. You see, it hardly matters what success you've had as a fencer. With this in my hand, I need be no more than mediocre. And if I choose to attack—"

With that word he *did* attack! The devilish sword hacked expertly at Sitra's head, and it was all Sitra could do to avoid the blow while simultaneously remembering not to try the usual sort of parry on such a wild swing. An ordinary parry would have left him with a sword hacked neatly in half by that demonic weapon. Sitra stifled the panic in his heart and remembered the insight he had had the moment before. He feinted; invited a counter lunge, and gave ground steadily, one handspan at a time.

Steadily, the young man pursued him back into the main room. Too late, Tuya saw what was happening and tried to warn her savior. "No! No, Ben-Hadad! The leopard! Watch for the leop—"

But Sitra had decoyed his opponent within reach of the chained cat, and the animal smelled the fresh blood on the young swordsman's chest. It stood, and one mighty paw lashed out! The blow knocked Ben-Hadad sprawling! The leopard pounced, crouched over his fallen body!

Sitra let out a shrill scream of triumph and backed into an almost matter-of-fact lunge by the old soldier, who, having dispatched the last of his enemies in the other room, now came up in time to stab Sitra in the kidney, hard. Sitra, eyes wide, staggered around, took one look, tried to form words with a mouth that could not find breath, and slowly pitched forward on his face.

Now the old man moved toward the great cat, his sword at the ready, but he was knocked aside by a flashing figure, who, wielding a dagger retrieved from one of the fallen fighters, leapt on the great animal's back and buried the slim blade in the animal's rib cage!

"Tuya!" Musuri said, adding his own blow to the great cat's raised neck. The girl fell off its back and rolled to one side, just as Ben-Hadad came up off his back and buried his great iron sword in the animal's unprotected middle. The leopard made one last powerful swipe at Musuri, then collapsed. With fearful efficiency Ben-Hadad, swinging the deadly black sword, hacked off its head. Then, standing, weaving, blood pouring from a dozen wounds, he looked down and offered his hand to the fallen Tuya as she tried to scramble to her feet. "Look at her, Musuri!" he said in a voice rich with pride and love. "Little Tuya, who said the only thing in the world she was afraid of was a big cat like this one!"

But now she was in his arms at last, her face pressed close to his bleeding chest and not caring what kind of mess it made as she hugged him again and again. "Oh, Ben-Hadad! I've got you back! That's all that matters! After that, what could I ever be afraid of again?"

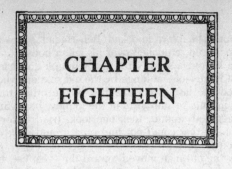

# CHAPTER EIGHTEEN

## The Delta

### I

Sunset was no more than moments away. The red ball of the sun hovered over the marshes, its roundness now compressed into a flat lozenge. The sky was a mad palette of reds and oranges. In the east, darkness already lay upon the land. Above, the water swallows swooped, dipping for the flying insects. A soft breeze stirred the waters and bent the papyrus reeds.

Asenath looked out on the terrace where her husband stood watching the scene, and then looked down at the cup in her hand, at the dark wine she had just soiled with the potion the necromancer had given her back in Avaris. *Will Joseph taste the difference?* she thought. *If he tastes it and spits it out, I'll have no one, slave or free, to blame it on. There are just the two of us here on the island. He'll know it was me.*

And what if the potion worked? Would she want the result—induced only by the potion and a spell?

Suddenly the thought occurred to her: *I'm not sure I want to do this.*

But she stiffened her back, and, taking a deep breath and closing her eyes, she mouthed the words, just as the sage had instructed: "Give me my wish, O blood of Osiris, which he gave to Isis to make her feel love in her heart for him night and day. Make Joseph, born of Jacob, drink of this cup and make him feel love for me in his heart."

Something disturbed her concentration, and she could not remember the words. She closed her eyes and tried all the harder. "Give me my wish, O blood of Osiris—"

The distraction, whatever it was, was still there. She opened her eyes and saw with a shock Joseph standing before her, his eyes grave and concerned. "Asenath?" he ventured. "What are you doing? What is in that cup?"

"J-Joseph," she whispered, "I . . ." She swallowed and could not go on. She tried to avoid his eyes. She was close to crying.

"Asenath," he said, looking hurt. "I saw you drop something in my cup. What did you do to it? Whose idea was this?"

"I . . . I didn't mean anything! Really!"

Gently he took the cup from her. "Is it poison? Did someone bribe you to do this? Did someone force you?"

She burst into tears and buried her face in her hands. She had never been so miserable in all her young life. "Oh, J-Joseph . . . I don't know what made me. . . . I was so desperate. . . . They told me nothing would happen. . . ."

But now the full import of his words registered at last, and she looked up, her face a mask of horror. "P-poison? Oh, no! No, Joseph, no! It was n-nothing like that!"

He sniffed at it again, his anger taking hold. "A sleeping nostrum, perhaps? Something to make me pass out, whereupon your confederates can slip in and—"

"Joseph! No! No! It's a—a love potion! It's to make you love me and care for me! There was a spell I was supposed to recite with it. It was supposed to make you desire me, as you have not done since we . . ." But now the weeping began again, and she could not finish her thought. "If I could get you to—"

"Love potions?" Joseph said. "Love spells?"

"Joseph," she said, looking up at him, one hand anxiously holding the other. "I'm so lonely. I've n-never been so lonely in my life. And I d-do everything I can to make you care for me, and still you stay apart. Somebody like me runs out of ideas very quickly. If I knew more about men, perhaps I'd know ways of attracting your attention. But I'm new to all this." The tears had stopped, and as he listened quietly, she gained confidence. "If I've offended you with this potion, I'm truly sorry. But I didn't know what else to do. If I could only make you see how much I care for you—" She stopped, sniffed, went on bravely—"You're a kind and good man. I can see that in all you do. And if you can't love me the way men care for women, I can learn to live with that. But I'm so alone here, in this strange place, among people I don't know and don't trust. I can do without a husband in the usual sense if I have to, but I need a friend—more than I've ever needed anything in the world."

She looked shyly into his eyes, and the suspicion was gone, replaced by a graver, gentler look. He put the cup down carefully on a table and drew her aside. "Here, sit beside me on the wall," he said quietly. The touch of his hands on hers as they sat down was soft, but commanding, protective, reassuring.

"I've wronged you," he said. "In my self-absorption, in my single-mindedness—"

"No, Joseph! No! I didn't mean—"

"Please." There was gentle pressure on her fingers. "I have to say this." She sat back and watched him with wide eyes, mouth open. "Asenath, I came here a slave. My life has been hard, and I was terribly bitter. I still am, sometimes, although I try to fight against it. You see, I've come to the conclusion that the God of my people wants me to be here, that He has work for me here, important work that may affect the future of the whole world."

His face now seemed lit by a strange light, transfigured by the last rays of the setting sun. Just as the sun set, she could see his eyes, large and warm and understanding . . . and terribly hurt. "Oh, Joseph, if I'd only—"

Again the pressure on her fingers. "Please. Let me finish." Now his eyes closed, and he spoke as if no one were there. "If the God of my people wants me here, then how can I be bitter and angry at my brothers, whose envy and jealousy prompted them to sell me as a slave? They may have just been doing His bidding, sending me here. Maybe the privations I suffered were necessary for the testing, the improving, of my character! If I'm right about His wanting me here to do His bidding, it's obviously necessary that I be strong and self-reliant."

He sighed, and she could dimly see his shoulders slump. "This is the most dangerous and frightening place of all," he said, "and the most fearful time of all the days I've been here in this strange land. From time to time I actually look back with longing on the days when I was a slave in prison.

Generally, after all, my masters were just and even kind men. But now . . ."

He fell silent for a long, long moment, and, emboldened by the gentleness and confidentiality of his tone, she gently squeezed his hand. There was an answering counterpressure, and she almost burst into tears again. "Please, Joseph," she whispered in a voice so soft as to be almost inaudible. "Tell me. Tell me all of it."

"For a long time now," he said, at last able to unburden himself, "I've known that the God of Abraham was speaking to me in prophetic dreams. He has told me in detail of the great famine that will fall upon all the world." His sigh was deep. "What He has not told me is what to do about it."

"But I thought—"

"The business of storing the grain? True, the dreams mentioned that. But without someone forcing the issue, who is going to give up the chance to make a quick profit selling his surplus? The farmers, large and small, all share a difficult trade. This year's good crop often has to pay for last year's poor one. How do we get them to reserve a large portion of this year's crop? Why should these people, not of my faith, believe me when I say that some God they've never heard of has told me in advance about all this?"

"But surely the king can—"

He patted her hand almost affectionately. "Now you're getting to the *real* problem," he said. "The king. If only his father had lived! My own father knew his father; did you know that? They were friends, of a sort. My father, not knowing who he was, did him a favor. In return, when the Shepherds attacked the city my parents and brothers were living in, they alone were warned in advance, and Jacob brought his family safely back to the Land of the Covenant. I have always thought that Manouk was doing the will of the God, whether he knew it or not at the time."

Asenath broke in now. "But Manouk's son—can't he be doing much the same sort of thing, Joseph?"

"There's a difference. Manouk's son is insane. And he's getting worse every day. And I haven't any idea how to handle him. He frightens me. If I could keep him at arm's length . . . but he insists on keeping me as close to him as possible. And he has turned on everyone who had ever been close to him. He's even turned on old Kirakos, the wisest of all Manouk's old counselors. Kirakos has been totally excluded from the government." His voice had an ominous ring to it when he added, "I'm the only one left. I've replaced all of them. And while that means Salitis has reposed all his confidence in me, it also means I'm the only one to listen to his rages, to hear his fits, to watch his rapid decay. Formerly, when he was angry, there was a whole list of courtiers to vent it on. Now there's only me!"

"Oh! Poor Joseph! Oh, my darling, I didn't know!"

Again the pressure of his hand. His face turned toward her in the dark, and his voice was low and serious. "There's more," he said. "While this man lives and rules and decays day by day—and grows more malevolent, more erratic, from moment to moment—no one is safe. No one is safe anywhere."

"I don't understand."

"When the famine comes, we may be the only place in our world with food. They'll all have to come to us, the Canaanites, the Babylonians, the Elamites, the Hurrians, the people of Tyre and Arvad and Ebla, and—" He swallowed. "—And the people of my father's land. If I can bring them here and shield them from Salitis's madness, perhaps I can save them. But will that also spell their eventual ruin?"

"But if they're here, Joseph, and you're vizier—"

"For how long? I could be killed by this mad king of ours. And with me no longer here to protect my people, what then?" He gripped her hands with a new urgency, a new warmth. For the first time the reserve between the two of them had melted away totally, and her heart beat all the faster for the fact. "Twice before, the leader of our people—first Abraham, then my father—has left the land promised to Abraham and his seed. Both times have resulted in disaster. Asenath, something inside me tells me that they should never leave the lands beside the Jordan—never! I foresee slavery, dispersal, hardship, and loss, every time my people leave the lands of Israel. And yet asking them to come here under my protection seems to be the only thing I *can* do. Worse, it seems to be the only thing that the God is telling me to do. How can He tell me to do the one thing that could ruin our people? Which voice that I hear inside me is His, Asenath? The one that says 'Bring your family to Egypt'? Or the one that says 'If you do, they'll wind up slaves to Salitis's successors'? Oh, Asenath, I don't know what to do, from one moment to the next. I have to steer as safe a course as I can, and at the same time keep this insane king from turning on me and ordering my death!"

"Joseph, if only I could do something to help!"

In the grip of the fear and self-doubt, it seemed that Joseph did not hear her. But the pressure on her fingers stayed firm and reassuring. "Asenath, everything I do to prepare against the coming famine increases the State's control over everyone in the region. I'm feeding power to a lunatic who can't be trusted with it. I'm going mad with worry. I can't sleep of nights."

"I'd noticed, my dear. But I'd thought it was—"

"It's more than I can handle by myself. And there's nobody to talk to about it, nobody I can trust. Salitis doesn't allow me any friends. Every day he increases the distance between me and the rest of the court and creates new enemies for me by the severity with which he executes the plans I've laid out for him. I've no one to turn to."

"Yes, you do! Joseph! You have me! I'll always be here, Joseph! Talk to me, if you can't talk to anyone else! I don't guarantee I'll have any answers, but—"

"I don't need answers. All I need is a friend. Oh, Asenath—"

He reached for her, and his hands on her body were like fire. His lips found hers, and there was nothing tentative or reserved about his kiss. His arms around her were like leather bands, binding her to him. He lifted her off her feet to carry her away. It was the moment she had been waiting for, consciously or not, not just all the days of their brief and, until now, loveless marriage; it was the moment she had been waiting for, all her life. And when, in their moonlit bedroom, he embraced her at last, she thought she would faint with joy. And the act of love, when it came, turned out to be nothing at all like what the slaves in her father's house had been talking about. It was so much more! So very much more!

## II

The learned doctors, long-faced, full of false dignity, trooped slowly and solemnly out of Kirakos's room. Mereet looked on and hated them all, but held her tongue. To all intents and purposes she was, after all, still a slave and had no right to speak her mind to such exalted creatures. Nevertheless she knew that they were fakes and that little of what they had to say would transcend the obvious. She wished that Tros of Ilios were here, with his effective medicine and plain words.

But this was the delta, and one had to put up with what one could find here. She saluted the chief physician and asked, "Has there been any improvement?"

The doctor struck a pose. "Kirakos has been struck down by the gods," he said. "It is the will of—"

Mereet could not hear any more. "Please," she said. "Will he recover?"

The doctor's brow lifted, and there was anger in his eye at her effrontery in interrupting him. But he chose to ignore it. "I'm afraid the paralysis will be with him to the end," he said flatly. "That whole side of his body is beyond his control. His vision and memory seem affected. He will have periods when he won't be able to say what's on his mind, because his lips will no longer obey him and because his mind will not focus adequately."

"I understand," she said. "I appreciate your being frank with me. There is a time when one simply must know the truth." She sighed. "How long has he got?"

The doctor shrugged, but there was concern for her in his tone. "Days. Hours. One never knows. It would be wise for him to make the appropriate sacrifices to—"

"Thank you," she said. "The lord Kirakos's feelings about religion are well known. Now let me have one of the girls fix food and drink for you and the other doctors."

"That won't be necessary—"

"Please. The lord Kirakos's truck gardens are exempt from the king's laws, and his melons in particular are famous in the court circles, as are his wines." She saw the light in his eye and motioned to Ayla, who approached and bowed. "Ayla, take the esteemed doctors to the terrace and bring food and drink—the best." The girl smiled and politely beckoned the doctors to follow her.

As she did, there was a loud knocking on the door. Mereet debated for a moment sending a servant to answer—Kirakos might need her own services—but after a brief hesitation went to open it herself. When she did, there was a captain of dragoons standing there. She could see others of his unit behind him, bearing a ceremonial litter. She could see the outstretched body of a man inside. "Yes?" she said.

"We have a man here who said he had to be taken to the lord Kirakos. We found him wounded near the border. He seems to be a personal friend of your lord—"

Mereet's eyes went wide. "Oh!" she said. "A foreigner? A Mesopotamian soldier, perhaps?"

"That's the one, ma'am. He's got himself all cut up somehow. We patched him up as well as we could, but he's got some sort of fever. Before he passed out he insisted on seeing your master."

"Bring him in," Mereet said. "We're in luck. The doctors from the court are here. Perhaps I can get one or another of them to look in on him." Turning, she spotted Ayla returning from the terrace. "Ayla! We have another sick man here. Have these men take him to a guest room, and bring the doctors." The soldiers carried him in. "Now, quickly. He's got a fever and needs treatment as soon as possible."

After the wounded man had been attended to, Mereet went back to Kirakos's room. She knew that two Mesopotamian soldiers had been staying in the villa as Kirakos's guests, but they had vanished one night shortly after her own arrival here. The men had never said good-bye or thank you. Kirakos had wondered what had happened to them, to whom he had extended his friendship. Now, perhaps, he would find out.

Going into Kirakos's room, Mereet saw, to her surprise, the old man's eyes open. "My lord!" she said. "I'd hoped you were asleep by now." She crossed and sat beside him on the bed, looking down with tender concern.

"I'll get all the rest I need from now on," he said weakly, only half his face moving. "Are the doctors gone?"

"They're still here. I have the girls feeding them. And the Mesopotamian is here. He's been wounded and asked to see you. Soldiers brought him from the border."

"Baliniri? Or Mekim? Interesting. And my name still carries enough weight that the soldiers obeyed his wishes? Amazing." His eyes were sharp, however little his face moved. "Well, bring him here."

"It's Baliniri. He's unconscious. He has a fever. I don't know how badly he's hurt. When he's fit to move, I'll have him brought in if you're well enough then. Unless his fever is catching."

"Catching? Don't speak nonsense, woman. What do I care if it's contagious? If my life is shortened by a day by something I catch . . ." But he softened his tone and said gently, "Don't mind me."

"I don't mind you, my lord."

"I'm used to people deferring to me."

"Your curse falls upon me like a caress, my lord. I know your mind as well as your habits. Don't worry. I'll have the man brought in as soon as it's practical." She rose as if to go, but his eyes signaled her to stop. "Yes, my lord?"

"Don't go. The advocate and the scribes were here yesterday, when you were in the city. Before my latest, uh, fall back to earth from the pinnacle of vanity and folly."

"And Ayla let them in to bother you? I'll have to speak to her. She knows better than to—"

"Hush. I ordered it. And a good thing, too. I did manage to get the proper documents witnessed and executed before the stroke. This way no one can say I was of unsound mind when I did."

"Documents, my lord?"

"You'll see anon," he said, his voice still weak. "It's a matter of insuring your protection, and that of the other members of the household when I die. I think I've adequately taken care of things. The document we settled upon will protect my property from seizure."

"By property, my lord, you mean myself and Ayla and—"

"Hush now, woman. Don't badger a dying man." He closed his eyes. "I'm tired. I think I'll sleep. Look in on me from time to time, will you?"

After a moment, Mereet, weeping softly beside him, could begin to hear his regular breathing as he slipped off into an untroubled sleep.

She left the room, wiped her eyes, and went into the great central hall, where the chief doctor awaited her. "He sleeps?"

"Yes. Have your people eaten?"

"Excellently. I looked in on this Mesopotamian fellow. He's taken a bad wound, but he's going to survive. He's a very strong type and, judging from the wounds on his body, has lived through a lot worse than this. The fever will pass within hours. They shouldn't have tried to move him so far, so fast. But he'll be all right."

"Good. When can I have him taken in to see Kirakos? My master wants to see him before—" Somehow she couldn't bring herself to say the words.

"Wait until morning, unless things take a turn for the worse for Kirakos."

"Thank you," she said, making the little bow required of a slave when speaking to a person of his rank.

"Why do you do that?" he said. "Force of habit? I'd think a freed woman would try to cure that particular habit as quickly as she could."

"Freed woman?" she said, staring.

"Why, yes. I was just talking to one of the scribes. Didn't you know? Your manumission is complete." Now it was his turn to stare. "Oh, of course. All the excitement . . . there wasn't time to tell you, and you've been so busy since."

Mereet stared, eyes wide, mouth open. *Freed woman?* she thought. *That means I'm free to go to Shobai. To my children.*

But then an equally shocking thought struck her. *Free? Not while that dear old man lives! Not while he needs someone to see him through his last hours, to comfort him as he prepares to go out into the great darkness.*

"Congratulations." The doctor had respect and friendliness in his voice.

Ayla had the blood-soiled rags taken off his body and was about to take them to the laundry, but somehow she could not bear to leave him. The sight of him lying there, all the fight and aggression gone out of him despite the visible masculine power of that great body, was so beautiful she wanted to cry. There was, in addition, a strange taste of stolen pleasure in the thought of watching him when he could not watch her back, a voyeuristic enjoyment that was at once sweetly asexual and excitingly carnal.

Men were so beautiful!

She sighed. Would she ever, ever find one of her own? And would he have even a trace of the beauty of this sleeping warrior?

She doubted it. Almost as if to taunt her own idle dreams, her mind raced back to Baliniri's earlier visit here, to the way he had been when he had first met Kirakos and come home with him, bringing that short friend of his. She remembered the soldier's rolling walk, and his ready and charming smile.

She remembered his hearty, full-bodied laugh, and the memory of it, even now, pleased her; a man with a good sense of humor was a fine catch.

*But listen to yourself! A slave—unless those rumors were true that the girls had told. But what would it matter if they were true: A freed woman with no marriage portion still had little chance of marrying a good man.*

But as her thoughts had run on like this, her eyes had traveled up his big body a little at a time, up the heavily muscled, but youthfully slim, legs, past the flat belly to the great chest, to—

She started! The eyes were open, looking at her!

"I know you," he said slowly, hoarsely, his voice betraying the drug the doctors had given him to ease the pain. "I must be at Kirakos's house. That's right, isn't it? And your name is Ayla. . . ."

# III

Toward evening Kirakos awoke, blinked, rolled his eyes. Force of habit made him try to get up, but then, when his limbs would not obey him, he remembered. *Ah, there. Those days are behind me now, aren't they?* he thought. *Well, so be it. Time enough for that when I was younger, more vigorous.*

Now it was time for contemplation, for letting his mind dwell on the past, for there was no future to think about. Nothing held any particular interest for him. He cared nothing for the future of the Hai. Try as he might, he could see no real future for them now that they had deserted the ways of their ancestors: the old ways of the tent and the cart, following the rain and the green grass wherever these might take them, leading the herds they had lived upon for generations immemorial. Sons of the wind, the Hai had lived the life that suited them for all those years and had prospered, even when the great famine had descended upon the lands around Lake Van and forced them to go on the march once more. Theirs, after all, had been the way of the sword. The hands that held the shepherd's crook could easily switch over to the sword and the ax and the spear.

Ah, yes, that was where they had gone wrong. Those hands had grown idle. When the calluses of the sword and the spear had begun to disappear, the spirit had gone out of the Hai—the spirit and the manhood. Look at their leadership now! What a fall from Manouk the crafty, the wise, to this unsound son of his!

He thought sadly: *Manouk! What have you done to us? We could have stayed in a harsher and less hospitable land and kept what we had, remained as we were. But you chose instead to bring us to this land of plenty, which sucked the strength from our arms, the vigor from our spirits. We needed the hard desert underfoot and the harsh and aggressive wind in our faces.*

Anger coursed through him and was as quickly gone, and an impotent curse died in his throat. What was the use? Better to work at calming himself, to see if his last hours could possibly be spent in peace.

For a moment his thoughts lingered on Mereet, and he closed his eyes. He envisioned her as he had seen her from the upper window, standing ankle deep in the cold water of the little pool, naked, her flawless body bathed softly in the light of the candles while the slaves washed her.

Who would have imagined that an old man could find as much pleasure and comfort in the mere company of a beautiful woman as he had ever had in the more carnal days of his youth? Who would ever have imagined the quiet joy her presence had brought him in his old age? He was pleased beyond description to have had it, and he had ensured her safety after his death; now it was a matter of letting go of this last friendship—last and, perhaps, best—in his life.

How easy it was to drift with the current now, not struggling against the inevitable. He let his mind wander as it might, and random scenes from his youth came to mind: his first command, when he challenged and bested an aging leader who had ordered him flogged for no offense at all; the day he won the title as the first horseman of all the tribes; the day he witnessed the legendary battle before the walls of Carchemish, when brave Oshiyahu of Haran won a place in the annals of all men by killing in single combat Karakin, the man they said could not be killed by mortal man; the storming of the city of Melid . . .

Now, however, a great sadness, a great regret, came over him, and he tried to slow the march of his thoughts, but found he could not. Melid, where he had tried to show compassion to the people, but where his men were bent on sating their blood-thirst on the hapless civilians after the city had fallen. Melid, where his men had committed atrocities beyond description, raping and killing women and children alike, using the sick and elderly with the utmost barbarity . . . and he had not been able to stop them. Melid, where the armorer Shobai had refused to make weapons for the Hai after seeing what they had done to the vanquished.

He blinked, tried to focus his mind on other things, tried to clear away the sudden gloom and guilt and shame; but they persisted and the hot tears came and there was no gentle woman's hand now to wipe them away.

"No, Captain! You shouldn't try to get up! It's too soon! You'll only hurt yourself!" Gently Ayla tried to force Baliniri back down onto the bed, but it was as if she had tried to restrain a bear. The pressure of her hand meant nothing to him, and she could feel the tense muscles in his chest, as hard and unyielding as the flank of a draft horse. He sat up, wincing, still a little groggy from the drug he had been given earlier. The soft breeze came through the open window and stirred the candle flame, throwing dancing lights all over his great naked chest. "Please, Captain!"

Baliniri smiled at her. "Here," he said, a gentle tone in his voice, "I don't mean to offend you by disobeying. I just have to get up. I'm the best judge of how fast this body of mine is healing." He took her slender, long-fingered hand in his very large one in an affectionate gesture. "But thank you for thinking of me."

Ayla blushed. "Please, Captain. If you will lie down again—" She sighed. "Mereet will be so angry with me if—"

Baliniri stared. "What name did you say?"

"Mereet. She's head of the household. I suppose she's actually the mistress now; she's been freed, so the story goes."

"Tell me about her. Her background?"

Ayla's face fell. So it was Mereet he was interested in. "She told me she was the wife of a blind armorer named Shobai. When she became a slave, she lost him and her twin children, Ketan and—"

"And Teti!" Baliniri said. "Yes! Yes! Was she ever the wife of Baka, the general of the Egyptian army?"

"Yes, but how did you know?"

"Never mind!" Baliniri said, his voice betraying his excitement. "Quick, send someone for her." He smiled and patted her hand. "I know the twins! I know her maid Heket! I'm a friend of Baka's!" He squeezed the hand he had patted. "How wonderful she's alive! How happy everyone will be to hear!"

Ayla smiled timidly. "You mean—" she said, not daring to hope.

Baliniri smiled at her and suddenly, impulsively, leaned over and kissed her. It began as a light, friendly sort of kiss, and ended quickly. Then he recovered and backed off, the better to look at her. After he had looked into her eyes he put his huge hands on her upper arms and drew her to him. This time his kiss was fervent, demanding.

"Ayla!" a stern voice said through the open window. "What are you doing? Captain, back in bed, please."

Baliniri released Ayla to look over her shoulder at Mereet, standing in the doorway, a candleholder in her slim hand, a look of grave disapproval on her lovely face.

Baliniri looked her in the eye and suddenly laughed, a big warm hearty laugh that brought an even more puzzled look to Mereet's face. "Don't blame Ayla," Baliniri said. "It's my fault." He took the girl's hand and held it close to his chest. "I like her very much, and for a moment I forgot myself." He released Ayla's hand now and spoke directly to Mereet. "Please. Come sit down here. I have something you'll want to hear."

Leaning on Ayla, he left Mereet standing by the window, looking ostensibly out onto the grounds . . . but in fact looking at nothing, through eyes focused inward. There was a strange expression on her face.

"Leave her to her thoughts and memories," Baliniri said. "Take me to Kirakos's room."

"It's over here," Ayla said, guiding him gently. "But I don't guarantee he will be awake." It was all she could do to keep her voice from quavering, to keep her body from shivering with ecstasy at his touch. Her mind had begun to fabricate fantasies in which he was the hero, and she was . . . She was not sure just what she was, when she came to think of it. Could she be his lover?

"I recognize it now," he said. His hand, no longer resting the weight of his big arm on her shoulder, ran down her back and paused for a moment, deliciously, at her waist before leaving her body. He stood erect, wincing a little, and went inside. "Kirakos?" he asked. "Kirakos, are you awake?"

Only the eyes moved in the inert face; she could see them by the light of the overhead torches, looking at Baliniri. "Come in," the old man called hoarsely. "I've been waiting for you."

Baliniri watched Ayla withdraw, a smile on his lips. How like Tuya she seemed, from the odd angle here and there! And there was the same strange mixture of innocence and shy sexuality about her, and the same warmth and sweetness.

"Come closer," Kirakos requested. "My voice isn't what it was." He chuckled humorlessly. "Neither is anything else. Never mind. I'm glad fortune brought you to me. Sit down here beside me."

Baliniri joined him, looking down into the strangely alive eyes in an all-but-dead face. "The girl," he said, "reminds me of someone very dear to me. Someone I've lost forever." Suddenly he realized what he was saying. "That was what drew you to Mereet, wasn't it?"

"Yes," Kirakos replied softly, almost wistfully. "She reminds me of my dear wife. These damnable resemblances force us to fall in love with these women even before we've any idea of their own merits. In both cases, however, they're considerable—Mereet and Ayla. I have taken steps to see that both women are well provided for in my will. They're both free, you know. As of yesterday. So is the whole household."

He sighed. "Ayla deserves a good man."

Baliniri let the sentence hang there. There was a thoughtful note in Kirakos's words.

"I want to talk to you about your plans," Kirakos said. His voice was weaker now; Baliniri had to lean down to hear him. "Listen to me. The kingdom of the delta needs you, as do all the nations that will shortly come to depend upon it for provender, once the famine has begun."

"Then you believe—"

"Young Joseph? Yes, he's real enough. But he's young and inexperienced and very much alone at court. Salitis is dangerously mad, and he leans harder on the lad daily. Joseph needs a strong friend at court, so he can guide Salitis. He can't do it by himself. And he knows about you, and Salitis remembers you and is still impressed—you were the only one who ever said no to him, and a man like that is always impressed by such a person."

"I said no and I meant no."

"Change your mind. Please. Without support at court, Joseph will weaken and let this madman ruin not only the delta but the whole region." He had begun to breathe rapidly, and now his words came more haltingly. Baliniri felt his wrist. The pulse was abnormally fast, and his flesh was hot to the touch. "We need you. All of us. The w-world needs you."

"Don't talk. Lie still."

"No. I haven't m-much time. Settle here. You'll do well here. You fancy Ayla, and she'll come well dowered."

Baliniri's mind raced. What good would he be in Lisht? His presence would only embarrass Tuya and pain him every time he saw her . . . providing, of course, that she was still alive. And he would be wasted in Nubia. Akhilleus, according to the messages that had come north by messenger, had already won his war. But here, organizing the army in such a way as to ensure its independence from the mad Salitis, he could find a fit use for his political skills. When he and Tuya were together he had already begun to feel dissatisfied with his rootless life. "Ayla," he said thoughtfully. "If I could—"

But when he looked back at Kirakos, the eyes were staring upward, unseeing. "Kirakos!" he said. "Kirakos! Come back! Come back! Please! Kirakos!"

# IV

The day after Kirakos was interred, amid little public ceremony, according to the rites of the Hai, Joseph and Asenath returned to the capital. A special honor guard had been sent by Salitis from the palace to accompany the young vizier and his lovely new wife, and Joseph used this occasion to make a formal entrance into the city. He sat high on a carrying chair with Asenath and waved with her to the onlookers in the streets as their party progressed through three of the four quarters of the city before being delivered to their palatial home, where Salitis himself welcomed the couple from the steps, embracing them with ostentatious pleasure. Music was played, dancers danced, and Petephres himself led the ceremony consecrating their new home and welcoming the newlyweds, however belatedly. Joseph, ever mindful of the faith of his people, kept a stony face through the whole ceremony, but thanked the priest graciously before going inside. This was the first clear view most of the city had had of the young pair, and the obvious signs of affection between them quelled rumors that had begun to circulate regarding their supposed incompatibility.

Afterward they appeared at an upstairs window, hand in hand, and were cheered by the crowd that had gathered in the street below. Then Joseph embraced Asenath, and she went off to supervise the feast the staff had already begun to prepare to welcome them back.

It was not a moment Joseph had looked forward to; he was now alone with Salitis, and he had not yet managed to read the king's mood. "Sire," he said, trying to think of what to say. "It's good to be back." The king's expression remained unreadable. "I gather you have, of course, had no trouble running the affairs of the kingdom without my small help."

The bantering tone turned out to be the best approach; Salitis beamed. "Everything's splendidly in order," he said. "Although I confess I'm fatigued, doing everything for myself. It'll be good to have you helping out again. I've missed you. And it appears that you and Asenath are pleased with your marriage. . . ."

It was not a subject Joseph wanted to talk about. "Yes, sire. I heard that Kirakos died."

"Yes. He should have passed away a long time ago. He was long past his prime. Nevertheless, I've ordered proper observances of his passing."

"And wisely, too, sire. He did still have friends in army circles—friends whose support we'll need in time to come. On the whole they all seem to have supported that surprise inspection trip of his, the one that hastened his death."

"Yes. The army has in truth gone lax. Before he died, Kirakos sent me someone we'll have use for. Remember the Mesopotamian general who stayed with him a while back? Baliniri?"

"Yes, sire. I thought he'd gone to Nubia."

"Yes, but . . . well, it's a long story. Suffice it to say he came back, and Kirakos talked him into coming to court and talking to me." Salitis was back to his pacing; Joseph watched him with apprehension, but he showed little sign of returning to his erratic behavior yet. "What do you think? I'd like to put him to work reorganizing the army. He apparently did this for Hammurabi after Mari fell."

"Sire, I can't imagine a better thing to do."

"Good. He's ready to get to work. He's even thinking of marrying. Kirakos freed his slaves before he died, and settled a fat dower on one of them. Baliniri seems to have taken a fancy to her—"

"Which one, sire?" Joseph asked, startled.

"A girl named Ayla, I think. She's quite rich now. He was very liberal with her. . . ."

"Well, it all sounds ideal. I got a very good impression of him in the brief time he was here, and he's young enough to be around a while—that's something we need. Part of the problem was that the generals were all, well, much older men."

"An excellent point. New ideas. New blood. New faces. Yes, yes." Salitis looked Joseph full in the eye for the first time. The king grinned now, and the mad glint was still there, if for no more than the blink of an eye, and Joseph's heart sank.

A panicky thought ran through Joseph's mind: a picture of the madness stretching on for years. Years of the horrible crushing headaches and the wild fits and the falling sickness. Years of incoherent rages and sudden blackouts. Years of sudden disaffections, orders for undeserved executions, years of brutality and tyranny and an ever-widening divorce from reality.

"I don't understand," Mereet said, stunned. "You can't mean this."

The scribe threw his hands up lightly in an expressive gesture. "It's all signed and witnessed," he affirmed. "The document couldn't possibly be clearer." The midday sun suddenly broke through the clouds and shone on his bald head. "In all modesty, I have to say with some pride that under the existing laws of the Hai, this will cannot be broken or even successfully challenged."

"I'm sorry," she whispered, sitting down. "I just can't seem to grasp the enormity of it. Nothing like this has ever happened to me before. You say that the full extent of the remaining estate, after the portions given the freed slaves—"

"An exact figure would be premature, ma'am. Suffice it to say that after tax has been paid and our fees settled, you will by the terms of your late mas—" He stopped and corrected himself. "Of the late Kirakos's will, you will now be, after the Lord of Two Lands and the grand vizier, unquestionably the richest person in the delta."

"I had no idea he had such wealth . . . And I thought I was running all his affairs."

"You were running his estates. The lord Kirakos was a man who did not let his right hand know what the left was doing. Not even his advocate knew the full extent of his holdings. And he had wisely converted his agricultural holdings just before the state announced the new order with regard to these matters. He made an immense profit at the time."

"I . . . I can't get my breath. I'll have to give all of this some thought."

"Of course, my lady. And in the meantime—"

"In the meantime I will continue to require your services, Pet-Osiris, and those of the advocate and the other scribes. All of you. You have served the lord Kirakos well. I trust you will continue to serve me with the same loyalty and efficiency."

"Why, yes, my lady! With the greatest of pl—"

"And to ensure your further devotion as well as repay in some small way your past devotion to my late master and friend, I'd like to—but please. Your brushes, your papyruses. Let's make this thanks official."

"Yes, my lady!" In the blink of an eye the materials were spread out before him on the long table beside her.

"Very well. The southern properties, on the point, where the river divides, from the double palm all the way to the point—do I need to be more specific than that?"

"No, no. All of that is high ground. You don't even need to specify. The property ends at the waterline."

"Very well. Sell it to the lord Ersu. He's coveted it for years. Get a stiff price out of him, the stiffest you can." He nodded, writing furiously. "Pay tax on the sale. Then, my loyal Pet-Osiris, you and the other scribes and advocates will share the remainder equally."

He looked up, staring, stunned. "My lady—"

"I'm of quite sound mind," she said firmly. "And it's all mine to dispose of as I see fit, isn't it?"

"Why, yes. But—"

"Enough," she said firmly. "It was well earned. Enjoy it in good health. If I can count on future service—prompt, efficient, and loyal—if you obey my will unquestioningly and execute my wishes with documents that cannot be contravened under Hai law, there will be future bonuses of comparable liberality."

"Then there'll be further dispositions of property?"

"Enough to deplete the papyrus marshes all the way to Sais."

"Yes, my lady! At your service, my lady!"

When Pet-Osiris left Kirakos's house, Mereet found Baliniri waiting for her, sitting on the ledge of the little pool in the inner court. "Captain!" she said. "How kind of you to come."

"How could I refuse you?" he asked. "You've been so kind to Ayla, and—"

"I'm happy she has found a friend," Mereet said. "And I'm glad to hear that you are accepting the position at court. As Kirakos said, Joseph will need a strong friend there." She took his hand now, pressing it warmly. "I suppose that as much as anything, I asked for you because I wanted to hear more about my loved ones."

"I'm sorry," he said. "I'd wanted to have only good news. But—"

"I've heard already. Our spies from across the border reported to me, in Kirakos's absence. I've heard. The coup against Dedmose and Madir failed. My husband"—here her voice faltered for the first time—"has taken ill, and of course I must go to him. That's part of why I wanted to talk to you. When I go, can you arrange my passage at the border?"

"I think so. There's a sort of lull in things up that way now. We exchange prisoners peacefully now and then. I can get a note through to Baka. . . ." He paused, started to say something, stopped, and finally forced himself to speak. "You know, of course, that he's very much in love with you. The way he speaks your name . . . He told me that he wanted to kill Shobai, but the first thing Shobai spoke of was his concern for you." He sighed. "They've become friends, united as much by their pain of loss as anything."

Mereet forced herself to remain calm. Her grave eyes regarded him neutrally. "I, too, have lost much," she said. "I will go to Shobai, as quickly as I can. I'm trying to dispose of these unwanted riches I have been left, here in the delta, and the story you told of Tuya, of her early life, has given me an idea."

A shadow passed over Baliniri's face. "I've never hurt so

much inside in my life," he said a little hoarsely. "But the only thing to do is avoid looking back. That's what got you through all this time, wasn't it? All these months away from husband and children?"

"Yes," she said gently. "That, and attending to the present. In a way it's been good for me. I could have come to hate Kirakos for keeping me from them. It could have poisoned my life." Now it was her turn to sigh. "I say this so easily. But when I think of how Shobai must have suffered . . . when I think of Teti and Ketan . . ."

"I didn't get to know the boy. But the little girl is enchanting, adorable. Ten years from now she'll be breaking the hearts of kings and princes."

Mereet closed her eyes, brushed away a stray tear. She fought to regain control. "You told me," she said, "of Tuya, of her hard life in the streets of Avaris."

"Yes. Baka told me. It was heartbreaking. When he'd finished, I loved her all the more. She's back with her husband. And she's pregnant."

Mereet's eyes opened wide. "Oh?"

He caught her meaning. "Oh, no. I don't think so. There wasn't time. It would have to be his. That was, I think, why she broke it off between us. She has a sense of honor, a—" He could not go on for a moment. He coughed.

"Rest easy," Mereet said, touching his hand lightly. "You happened along at a time when she needed someone very badly. You're a good man, Captain: a kind and decent man, with a good heart. Now make Ayla happy the same way." He nodded, still unable to speak, and she went on in a calm voice. "Baka's tales of the suffering in the streets touched my heart as they did yours. You see, I know more than most what a persuasive man Baka is."

"He's the vizier of Egypt now," Baliniri said. "He's succeeding Madir. Did you hear?" She nodded. "That's why I think I will have no trouble getting you across the border."

"Strange," she said, "I wonder if he and I will even recognize each other now. Well, that wasn't why I wanted to talk to you. You'll be staying here. If you can help my scribes and advocates dispose of my property and make sure no one alters my requests, you'll be doing me—and Tuya—a great favor." She looked him in the eye, still holding his hand.

"What do you mean?"

"I'm putting the entire property up for sale."

"The entire— Are you sure you want to?"

"Oh, yes. The vultures are already beginning to descend on the estate, sure a mere woman will be easy game for them. There's a priest named Petephres and his brother-in-law Ersu and a miserable little opportunist and social climber named Ameni, who has attached himself to the two of them and hopes to rise by buying when they buy and selling when they sell."

"Yes?"

"I'm going to teach them a lesson. My advocate is going to plant in their minds the notion that once I've sold out and have only gold, not lands, that they'll be able to swindle my money from me. My advocate will sell them land at high rates. They'll borrow heavily to buy it, thinking that once they divest me of my lands, it'll be easy to swindle me out of the rest. What they don't know is that all the land I'm selling them is due to be seized by the crown. Petephres, Ersu, and Ameni will think twice before they attempt another get-rich-quick scheme at someone else's expense, and my estate will end up with the gold."

"But you can't take the gold across the border with you."

"I've no intention of doing so."

"Then what . . . ?"

"I'm leaving it," she said in a voice full of firm resolve, "to the poor of Avaris. To all the failures and paupers and orphans, the sick and the hopeless and the forgotten. To the beggars and cripples and elderly. Above all, to the homeless children. If my advocates and scribes can write the documents in strong enough language, there'll never be another Tuya in the streets and alleys of Avaris, wandering cold and hungry, not knowing where she's going to sleep. There'll be a place for all of them to go. A simple shelter, but one with food and a roof."

He stared, unable to speak. She smiled, patted his hand, withdrew hers gently. "Now," she said, "I've got to get ready to leave soon. I have my own life to live, my own dear ones to care for, as I cared for Kirakos while he lived. My time here is done. Yours is just beginning. I can count on you, can't I, to watch over this project when I'm gone? See that no one alters it?"

Baliniri, deeply touched, cleared his throat, nodded vigorously, and spoke in a voice that was hardly more than a croak. "Of course you can. And bless you. Bless you."

# CHAPTER NINETEEN

## Lisht

### I

For quite some time Musuri, clinging against all evidence to the last sliver of hope, nourished the notion that Shobai might somehow recover. But as the days marched on and Shobai's flesh fell away from his great body and his face grew thinner, more hollow-cheeked, even Musuri had to accept the truth.

The change occurred one morning when Musuri came to visit Shobai and, after half an hour of vain attempts to communicate with him, left the blind man's room wiping his eyes. Gently Heket called after him: "Musuri! I know you haven't had anything to eat yet. Now come here and have some melon." He did not respond, but stood, sightless, staring at the wall with streaming eyes. "Musuri?" she said in a softer voice. She put the melon down on the table and came to his side. "What's the matter?" she asked. "Has he taken a turn for the worse?"

Musuri stood inert as Heket's soft arms went around him. "He didn't know me," he said. "He's gone off into some world of his own."

"Sit down, my dear," she said, and guided him to the table, where she took a seat beside him and took his hands in hers. "People who are dying prepare themselves by going back over their past and trying to sort it all out. After a time,

378

what happened twenty, thirty years ago seems to be more real to them than what's happening now or what happened last week. I think they're going back to when they were most alive, most receptive to the things around them." But as she said this her own mind started to turn over the events of Shobai's life. "Ah, poor man. I suppose that was also when he saw the most suffering."

"It would be the time when he could *see*," Musuri said bitterly. "All the forward motion of his life ended when Reshef blinded him and then murdered Hadad. I talked once to one of the Shepherds who was fleeing the rumors of plague that Hadad had planted among them. The soldier painted a picture for me of Shobai, standing there blinded, the blood running in rivers down his face, waiting for someone to lead him away, as, far across the deserted compound, he heard Reshef screaming, 'Shobai! I killed your brother!' "

Heket made a sign against evil and hastily patted his hand. "Now, don't think about that, my dearest. He's probably not remembering that at all. He's probably going back to happy memories."

Musuri wiped his eyes. "Happy memories? I wonder what—" He nodded slowly, and his shoulders relaxed. "You've got to be right. Heket, I hadn't told you this because I was waiting for confirmation, but we've had word that Mereet's alive."

"Alive! Where?"

"In the delta. She was the slave of a rich Shepherd, a man Shobai knew slightly before the Shepherds enslaved *him*. When the old man died, he freed her and left her his entire estates."

"You don't suppose she . . ."

"I don't know. From all reports she's still very beautiful. But the man was old and sick."

"But is she coming back?"

"That we haven't heard. But our informant said that another slave had a fat dowry settled upon her and plans to marry Baliniri."

Heket's mouth made a narrow O. "The one who—"

"The same. All the better, say I. He'd be an embarrassment—or temptation, I don't know which—to Tuya if he returned to the delta. Instead, he's taking a job with the Shepherd army, in the same way they want me to work for Baka—training duties."

Heket smiled and looked him in the eye. "And are you going to take the job they've offered you?"

He smiled back at her for the first time and squeezed her hand. "I think not. My soldiering days are done. I've invested a bit of money Akhilleus settled on me in city property. My—our—future is as secure as anybody's is in this unsettled time. You'll need help caring for Shobai's children. They'll have a lot of adjusting to do, and maybe I can help ease the pain for them."

Heket held his hand to her cheek. "Oh, I'm so happy," she said. "If I don't watch myself I'm going to start crying too."

"Don't," he said. "If it helps stop the tears to hear me say it, I'm happy too. Happier than I remember being, ever. Happier than I had any notion of being." He leaned over to kiss her, then sat back smiling. But the sadness returned to his face. "If only she could return to him before he dies."

"Does Akhilleus know about Shobai?" Heket asked.

"He sent a message back from Nubia, with gifts for the twins."

Heket stared. "I don't understand. He wouldn't come see his old friend on his deathbed? But—"

"I know it isn't like him. But you know Ebana's in her confinement now. They're expecting their own child soon. Ebana is not young anymore, and birthing is dangerous at her age. He'll want to be there. All the auguries, including Shobai's own vision, have indicated it'll be a prince for the line of Akhilleus!"

"But still—" she said.

"There's more," Musuri said. "Now, you *must* keep this a secret, my dear." He motioned her closer and whispered, "Akhilleus has big plans for that son of his."

Heket's brow rose. "Well, of course he has. He's king of Nubia, and his son—"

He shook his head, but did not raise his voice. "His plans extend *beyond* Nubia." He paused to let that sink in. "Everything he's done since he landed in Egypt has had an air of destiny about it. And he hates the Shepherds and wants them out of the delta."

"But—you can't drive the Shepherds out of the delta while you're up in Nubia. . . ." Her words trailed off as she realized what she'd said. She sat for a moment staring at him. "You mean—"

He smiled. "At the source of the Nile he turned down a great kingdom, one he was born to, in the most beautiful land I have ever seen. The only thing that could have prompted him to refuse was a higher, greater ambition. One," he said with emphasis, "greater than a petty kingdom in Nubia."

"But at his age . . ."

"Precisely. He's too old to reign, and he knows it. But a son . . ." He smiled and let his words take root. "A son who, bearing his blood and trained by him, might in time unify the two halves of Upper Egypt and all the Red Lands and drive the Shepherds into the sea forever!"

"Then . . ."

"Akhilleus will never reenter the domain of Dedmose . . . except at the head of a conquering army."

Heket blinked, sat silent.

"Except for Ebana, I've been closer to Akhilleus than anybody, and I've seen a dramatic change in him. He's gone from slave to tycoon to king, and there are times, Heket, when I can look at him and actually believe that some god animates him, conferring wisdom and power."

"But . . . a black pharaoh? There's the question of bloodlines. There's the state religion, which has to certify—"

"The state religion will certify anyone who grabs the crown and holds it. As for bloodlines, that whole question was mooted when the widow of Amenemhet the Fourth married that commoner and touched off the civil wars. How many 'kings' have we had since then? How many of them could trace their ancestors farther back than their grandfather's time? Why, Dedmose himself— Gods! Someone has to tell Dedmose about why Akhilleus never came back to the pharaoh! Shobai was supposed to . . . Well, never mind that for now. I was telling you about Dedmose's ancestry—" But now he realized he was on dangerous ground. "You get my meaning. Stranger things have happened in this world. Who, a generation ago, could have predicted that thousands of years of Egyptian rule would suddenly have been disrupted by a crazy migration of nomads, vagrants, from the gods alone knew where? That a bunch of sheep drovers could come in and take over the greatest kingdom that the world had ever known? That—"

A noise in the garden caught Heket's attention, and she pulled away. "Excuse me. I thought I heard the children—"

Her words were interrupted by Teti's lurching entrance.

The child, howling, cried, "Ketan's hurt! He fell down! He hurt his arm!" She rushed into Musuri's arms, and Heket went out into the garden. "Oh, it hurts so much! So much!"

Musuri hugged the little girl. "There, now! There, now, sweetheart! It'll be all right!" He stood and looked out the window. He could see Heket holding the little boy, examining his arm; as he watched, she turned his way and nodded, as if to say *Don't worry. It isn't serious.* He bent and picked up Teti, pointed out the window. "See? He'll be all right! It probably doesn't even hurt as much as it did, eh?"

"No, it doesn't," she said, wiping her eyes. "I was so scared." She rubbed her own arm. "It's much better now."

Musuri stared. "I thought he hurt *his* arm," he said. "You mean yours hurts too?" He couldn't believe it. "When he hurts, you hurt also?"

"Yes. The same when I hurt myself. Ketan cries."

"I'll be damned," he muttered to himself. He spoke to the child now. "But you're not very much alike, for all I can see. You're a little stronger than Ketan, aren't you? And you look out for him. Heket told me that when another little boy hits Ketan, you protect your brother. You rush right in and drive the other boy away."

"Yes! It is mean to hurt my brother!" Her little chin stuck out defiantly. "I tell the bullies that if they ever come back, I'll tell Baliniri, and he'll come and give them spankings."

"Baliniri, eh? Is he a friend of yours, then?"

"Yes!" the little girl said, beaming. "He's my best friend in the whole world. I'm going to make him a new sword, the best one in the world. Uncle Ben-Hadad's going to show me how. Baliniri went away. But it isn't the way Father is going away. Baliniri will come back. I know he will. He's just gone for a while, and Father is going away forever."

Musuri stared. The child had such a serious look on her face as she spoke. He wondered how much of what she was saying she had really understood. "Teti," he said gently. "What if Baliniri couldn't come back? What if he wanted to, but couldn't?"

"Oh, he'll come back!" she said stubbornly. "He promised!" But the possibility seemed really to enter her little mind for the first time, and a cloud passed over her rosy face. "I'll make him come back! To get the sword I'll make for him! I'm going to marry him someday! He won't forget me!"

And now something in the child's half-broken dream

reached into Musuri's callused old heart and tugged, and he had a catch in his throat. He hugged the little girl close and rocked her. Her mother had disappeared, her father was dying, her friend Baliniri was gone. She *had* to believe in something, with all the tenacity of her child's soul. He did not have the heart to spoil her dream or even to say the harsh words that would amend it. "I'm sure you're right," he said, ruffling her hair with his wrinkled and scarred old warrior's hand. "He won't forget you. How could anyone forget you, ever?"

## II

Tros once again stopped by in the afternoon to look in on Shobai. He spent an hour in his patient's room with the door closed, and when he returned to the outer room, Tros's face was grim. "Musuri," he said, "I think the time has come to call his friends together to say good-bye."

The old soldier, feeling helpless, pounded one wrinkled fist into the other palm. "I should be taking this better, I know I should." His voice was hoarse and constricted. "If only Mereet could return before—"

"I know, I know," Tros replied sympathetically. "But she may not even want to come. It's been years, you know. And while it wouldn't seem like her to stay away from the children or Shobai—even if he weren't dying—who knows what changes she's undergone? She's spent so much time in slavery, maybe thinking her family has abandoned her. . . ."

Musuri looked to Heket, the pain showing on her expressive old face.

"She'll be here," Heket asserted. "I know she will."

"Well, she'll have to hurry," Tros said. "I tried to give him a draught to increase his strength, but he was so weak he could hardly hold his head up. And, his mind is wandering. Sometimes he's quite rational; sometimes I can't tell whether he's awake or dreaming. While I was talking with him, he drifted back to a time when he and his brother were children, playing in the streets of Haran. Someone was making fun of

Hadad's limp, and Shobai came to his defense." He shook his head. "At least this time it was a pleasant memory. He tends to dwell on all the times he let Hadad down."

"It must be terrible, carrying that much guilt." Musuri could barely hold back his tears. "Ah, look here." He craned his neck, looking out the open window. "Here's Tuya and Mekim, the fellow who helped us rescue her." He went to the door and opened it. "Tuya!" he said, brightening. "I was just going to send for you." He greeted Mekim with a smile. "Come in. I'm going after Baka. Heket, darling, could you find Ben-Hadad? Perhaps Tuya could mind the children."

When they had gone, Mekim fidgeted nervously. "I should go," he said.

"No, no," Tuya said. "I want to talk to you." She sighed, a little bitterly. "Stay, please." She sat down, one hand on the slightly more visible bulge of her belly. "I've heard the news about Baliniri, you know. About his wedding."

"Uh, yes." Mekim forced himself to look her in the eye. "I don't know what to make of it. It was on the rebound, so . . ." He swallowed. "Do you know how crazy he was about you? I've never seen anything affect him the way you did, and he and I were together for years. When Baka told him about you and your husband—" He gulped again. "Look, I shouldn't talk. I'm only making you uncomfortable, with my big mouth."

"I deserve to be made uncomfortable," Tuya said stoically. "All I did was make him unhappy, and myself, and—" She frowned; the frown was immediately replaced by a thoughtful look. "It'll be a bittersweet memory that will stay with me all my life. Now I have to devote myself to my marriage and baby. It could have been worse, I suppose," she went on, trying to assuage her misery with a joke. "Back where my husband comes from, an adulteress can be killed with impunity —killed with the child inside her."

Mekim looked at her now. "It doesn't have to poison your life if you don't want it to, you know. Baliniri's gone. I'll be gone. The reason I came here was to ask Musuri for an introduction to Akhilleus. I was thinking of heading south and asking him for work. Anyway, almost nobody else knows what passed between you and Baliniri. Heket and Musuri aren't the types to hold it against you, and neither is Baka."

"I know," she said miserably. "Baka treats us like his erring children, to be loved and forgiven." Her shoulders slumped. "Even Ben-Hadad is trying to forgive me. He has many of his father's qualities, it appears. He takes the whole responsibility upon his own shoulders. If he hadn't neglected me, he says . . ."

"Well, it's true, isn't it?" Mekim asked. "And let him feel that way. It'll make a better husband of him." Suddenly, he thought of something and asked without thinking, "The child is his, isn't it?" But immediately he was embarrassed at having said this. "I'm sorry. Damn it!"

"It's all right," Tuya said. The look she gave him was compassionate. "I've always tended to blurt out things, act precipitately. I don't think I'll ever be that way again, ever do anything spontaneously or talk without thinking. I've made such foolish mistakes because of it. But to answer your question, yes. I broke off with Baliniri the moment I realized I was pregnant by Ben-Hadad. Well, *almost* immediately," she said, with a sad little smile. "It was hard to give him up. Very hard." There was wistfulness in her tone. "He was such a lovely man. I hope he'll be happy. I hope he'll remember me now and then."

Her reverie ended hardly a moment too soon. The door opened, and Heket preceded Ben-Hadad into the room. His face, as always, mirrored his every thought, without artifice. "Tuya!" he said. He forced a smile, then looked at Mekim. "I'm glad to have run into you. I never quite got around to thanking you for your help, sir." The two men exchanged greetings, but Ben-Hadad's congeniality could not disguise the fact that a wall lay between them: There was suspicion in Ben-Hadad's eye.

Mekim caught the nuance very quickly. "I hadn't really realized how sick your uncle was," he said. "I'll just be in the way here. Please ask Musuri to get in touch with me. Good luck, both of you."

After he had left, husband and wife stood looking at each other, a little awkwardly. A tentative half smile lingered for a moment on Tuya's lips until the more severe, confused look on Ben-Hadad's face drove it away. "I wish he hadn't come here," he said. "You know who he is?"

"Yes," Tuya said. "But we'd never met until the day at Sitra's house." Miserable that she'd lied to her husband, she came forth and put a hand on his arm. "Please, my dear. This is no time for thoughts like—"

He pulled away, his face set and strained. "I begin to see

that there isn't ever going to be any time when we can talk about it." He took a deep breath and tried to calm himself. "Tuya, I don't express myself easily. When I was a child I used to have a terrible stammer. I didn't begin to get over it until I came to Egypt. I still have a hard time saying what is on my mind." A self-mocking smile, with no humor in it at all, came over his face. "Particularly when I'm not sure what *is* on my mind. I can't sort anything out. My uncle turns me away and tells me he won't teach me, the only relative he has in the world, the secret of forging the black metal. I hurry from Nubia supposedly to be on Akhilleus's diplomatic delegation, then Baka says it was just a ruse of Akhilleus's to get me away from Nubia once he'd assumed power there. Nobody will give me any straight answers. They move me around like a token in a game of senet. And while I'm gone, my wife . . ." He let the words trail off, as if afraid of saying too much, too harshly. He closed his eyes. His face was twisted with anguish. "Why, Tuya? *Why!* I know I neglected you, but—"

His loud voice brought Heket in from the other room. "Please!" she said. "The doctor said no loud talk. Shobai's very weak. And you, sir—Tros especially forbids anyone to go pestering Shobai with questions he's in no condition to answer. If you can't control yourself, please go outside until you can do so." She looked from Ben-Hadad to Tuya, appealing to the calmer of the two. "Please, Tuya. My master is barely hanging on."

"I'm all right," Ben-Hadad said in a strangled voice. "I'll restrain myself. You can go about your affairs." The words came out just short of sounding like an order; Heket was still technically a servant, a person of another caste, although it was universally assumed that she and Musuri were bespoken. She glared at Ben-Hadad, but went out, closing the door behind her.

Ben-Hadad let out his breath through pursed lips and leaned back against the wall wearily. "I'm sorry. I haven't slept in . . . I don't know how long."

"Two days at least," Tuya said. "If you'd only relax and let me tell you—"

"I can't eat. I gag on food. If I get any down, it comes back again." He closed his eyes and wiped his sweaty face with both hands. When he recovered and opened his eyes, it was to change the subject abruptly. "I think I've lost all sense of purpose. I just learned that my friend Joseph is now the vizier to Salitis. He's a rich and powerful man—and he was a slave six months ago, maybe less. I should be happy for him, happy that I don't have to find him, after all. But the funny thing is, I didn't really care. I'd stopped caring that that was why I came here. Oh, I kept trying to remind myself, but it didn't mean anything. Just as the notion of writing to Mother, to Jacob, occurred to me from time to time . . . and I never did anything about it."

"You didn't write to me, either," Tuya said softly. "Perhaps if you had . . ."

"I know. *I know!*" He made an effort to lower his voice. "And I know I have no one but myself to blame. But even as I tell myself this, the thought tears at my heart. My uncle has turned me away. My wife . . ." He wiped his eyes now. His face bore a terrible expression. "You're sure? About the child?" His eyes went to her belly.

"There's not the slightest doubt."

His eye was cold and distant. His voice had a curiously hollow ring to it now. "If you only knew how much I want to believe that." He pushed away from the wall and went to the window. "Here comes Baka," he said. "Musuri's with him, and a couple of guardsmen. Now that Madir's power has been formally transferred to him, Baka's going to have to stop going through the streets without more protection. He forgets what an important man he's become."

"He'll probably resist being isolated from the people," Tuya said. "He's still Baka. He's the same person who led us in the delta. He'll never change."

"Don't count on it," Ben-Hadad responded bitterly. "People change. Shobai changed. You changed. For all I know, Joseph has changed beyond recognition and wouldn't speak to me if I were to see him again." He shook his head.

"Oh, I see," Tuya said, a slight edge on her voice. "Only the bad part doesn't change, eh? Is that what you're saying? People's good qualities change, and the bad part stays the same." She snorted softly. "For the first time I'm beginning to grow angry with you. If you're going to let this embitter you—"

He shot her an angry glance. "Of course," he replied sarcastically, "I should take it all lightly. I should pretend it never happened and forgive. I should—"

"That's exactly what you should do," she interrupted. "If you don't, it'll poison your life for you, forever. Well, I have a child in my body, dependent upon me for everything. You can poison your own life if you want to, but you're not going to poison mine or my baby's." Her eyes flashed as the anger grew in her. "It's your child, too, you know. And it has a right to be born into a house full of love."

He closed his eyes again. His mouth worked for a moment before he mastered himself. He opened his eyes and looked at her, his face full of pain. "I'm trying," he said hoarsely. "Please. I'm trying. I'm doing my best. But . . . it's just that . . ."

Baka's entrance broke into his struggle. The general looked from the one to the other and misread their anguish. "Let's control ourselves," he said. "Musuri says we only have a little time left with Shobai. If he sees us grieving over him—"

Ben-Hadad bit his lip and recovered. "You're right." He straightened his back and forced a smile onto his face. He even managed to look Tuya in the eye before looking back at Baka. "Is there any word about Mereet?"

"A runner came from the border," Baka answered. "Her party is on the way upriver. I hope she gets here in time." He sighed. "She'll feel terrible if she arrives too late." He shook his head slowly. "Listen to me, speaking for her as if I still knew her. Do you know how many years it's been since I've even seen her at all? Since she's seen me?"

"Don't worry," Tuya said. "It'll be all right."

Musuri entered the house and, without speaking, went directly to Shobai's room.

Baka turned to Tuya, and his face seemed vulnerable, much younger than it ever had before—yet much older too. "When she saw me last, I was a thin, bookish young scholar with his head in the clouds. Then the Shepherds came, and there was no one to lead the people in their fight against the invader. Believe me, if there had been, I'd have been the first to fall in behind him. But there was no one to lead the people; I had to do it. After I was pressed into service, I kept meaning to get back to Mereet, to take a weekend to see her . . . but the war kept intervening. And then I was captured and imprisoned, and when I was released, she had found Shobai and made her way across the border to safety."

There was a noise outside of the guardsmen speaking to someone. Baka ignored it and went on. "Now look at me," he said. "Once I was a scribe pretending to be a warrior, now

I'm a warrior pretending to be a vizier. Heads bow to me; knees bend. I issue an order, and a dozen men jump to attention and scurry about to do my bidding. I have to look resolute, knowing. But beyond the administrator, the warrior, is still the same confused young scribe who—"

The door opened. Baka looked up, nodded acknowledgment, and looked back at his friends, prepared to finish his thoughts. The handsome, richly dressed young matron who had entered, preceded by a servant, he took to be a neighbor of Shobai's, coming by to pay her last respects. She looked at him and then at the others.

She looked at Baka again, face to face. Recognition dawned, slowly at first, then with a stunning suddenness, on both of them. Neither seemed able to speak.

Baka was the first to recover. "Mereet!" he said, coming forward to take her hand. "Thank heaven you've come!"

# III

In the back room, under the coverlet on the narrow bed, the blind man stirred feebly, his huge, once-powerful hands aimlessly picking at the cloth that covered him. He hovered unsteadily between sleep and wakefulness, slipping uneasily from the one to the other. The visions, the dreams, kept changing, changing. . . .

But now, amid the sea of half-remembered faces and scenes, a single figure began to draw his attention. The figure was that of a young man, small, round-faced, curly-haired, and smiling. And as the face came gradually into sharp focus, the background began to fade little by little, and the figure stood out in bold relief against a backdrop of featureless gray, the gray of Shobai's sightless life.

Slowly the figure limped toward him, favoring a crippled leg that stood out at a grotesque angle. The awkward, slow gait forced upon the young man an odd posture in which the shoulders hunched alternately. Yet, for all the inherent ugliness of the cripple's distorted body, to Shobai there was a beauty and grace to his movements. Shobai's heart raced; he tried to take in every detail as if he would never see it again. And the details that stood out now overshadowed the unnatural angle at which the leg protruded and the strange, angular gait. Shobai's mind's eye focused instead on other details. First, the hands: beautiful, tapered, sensitive hands, the hands of an artist. Then came the eyes, kind, smiling, forgiving.

"Hadad," said Shobai. He found he did not have to speak aloud; his mind spoke for him, silently, easily, and the cripple heard every word as clearly as if he had spoken. "Hadad. Brother."

He could say no more. What was there to say? How could he apologize for the suffering he had caused his brother so many years ago, for the terrible loneliness, the cruelty, of the death Hadad had met trying to protect him that awful day north of Haran, in the encampment of the Shepherds, when Reshef the Snake had blinded him and murdered gentle Hadad? How could he—

Hadad smiled. *"Apologize? Shobai, suffering has come and gone for me, as it will soon pass away for you. In the blink of an eye you'll wonder why you held on to the pain of this world of yours as long as you did. We'll be together forever, where there's no suffering and no fear."*

And somehow, Shobai found himself whole again: tall and strong and sighted, standing before his brother, and weeping as he had not wept for years, weeping from emotions he could not define at all. *"Hadad . . . I finished your son's apprenticeship for him, but did not teach him the secret Father brought back from the Islands. Ben-Hadad thinks I've wronged him as terribly as I wronged you."*

*"Don't explain,"* Hadad said, *"I see it all. Perhaps it'll be the making of him. Perhaps he'll be driven to learn the secret for himself. Or perhaps the son he's going to have—* He smiled that old sweet smile, good-natured, untroubled. *"Yes, it'll be another Child of the Lion—perhaps this son will carry it through to completion."*

*"I thought that if he had to learn it for himself, he might learn how dangerous a secret it is. If I'd known it too young, fool that I was, I'd have given it to the Shepherds."*

Hadad shrugged easily, grinning. *"Perhaps. Perhaps not. In a moment or two, it won't make any difference. We sometimes fooled ourselves into thinking we controlled our surroundings, our lives. In a few minutes that illusion will be gone. It was an illusion that your first years were spent big*

Mereet, sitting on the edge of the bed, let out a long sobbing breath, and her shoulders slumped. "He's gone," she said in a low voice. "I'll cry, I know I will, but now, in a way I'm glad it's all over for him. All the suffering, all the—" But she could not go on. Tuya stepped forward to hold her close, but Mereet stiffened and looked up at Baka. Her eyes were full of unreadable emotions.

Baka found he could not easily meet her eye. He felt utterly ill at ease, as he had felt from the moment she had entered the house and thrown his thoughts completely out of kilter. He tried to smile, but it came out badly. He coughed behind his hand and stepped back a step. As he did, Heket moved to the bed to pull the coverlet up over Shobai's head. But she hesitated and looked around the room before she did. "I'm sorry," she said. "I didn't mean to be hasty. If you want me to wait . . ."

"No, no," Mereet said. "It's all right. He's gone. The part that was Shobai is gone." She turned back toward Baka, but found to her surprise that he had left the room. She rose slowly, with the weary motions of a woman twice her age, and tried to smile comfortingly at Ben-Hadad and Tuya; but they were looking at each other gravely and did not even notice her. She moved into the outer room. Baka stood with his back to her, looking out of the open window, his stance tense. "Baka," she said gently.

He did not turn at first. When he did his posture remained formal, soldierly. His face was under control now, and his voice was modulated, carefully neutral. "Pardon me," he said. "I had no intention of . . . of, well, asserting my 'rights' back there, or even of letting Shobai assert them for me. It was very awkward for me. But I couldn't upset him in his last moments." He took a deep breath. "He had become a good friend, although there was, to the end, a sort of barrier between us." His eye was serious and his tone thoughtful when he looked at her. "When I learned you two had married, I had thought to kill him. I suppose there's no use apologizing for that."

"Nor any need," she said gently.

"No. But when I came to murder him, the first thing he did was talk about losing you." Now the breath came out of him in one long shudder, but he recovered instantly. "His first thought was of you. Before his own life." A spasm of self-loathing shook him. Again he recovered, retreated behind the soldier's mask. "I knew him for a better man than I. You might imagine how *that* affected me, with my scholar's vanity. Since then I've made much effort to locate you . . . not for me, but for him, for your children." His back straightened pridefully. "Have you seen them yet?"

"I looked in on them. It might have been a bad time to wake them. I think Shobai had already said good-bye to them in his own way. They're as prepared for his death as they can be, Heket says." She shook her head, a little confused. "I've just been through another death, my master's, in the delta. He was a bad man who learned how to be better in his old age. In his last days he reminded me of my father, I think, although they really weren't much alike."

"You don't have to talk," Baka said.

"I do remember," she said, smiling sadly, "that you always tried to be fair and thoughtful. Oh, Baka, we don't know each other at all anymore, do we? You don't even look the same, you know. You've matured."

"I had to." He shrugged, embarrassed a bit. "You know me. I always did what had to be done. I gave high priority to being responsible. I suppose you suffered for it." He stiffened again and added, "My apologies, of course. I have much to apologize for." He waved off her attempt to disagree. "No. I know myself. And I know when I've failed the people close to me. But there always seemed to be an overriding reason for me to do as I did. I say this knowing it's a poor excuse."

"What you're doing is defining what it is that has made you vizier to the king," Mereet said as gently as she knew how. "Don't undervalue yourself. You know better than that. You're a very good man, Baka. That much I carry with me always. That much I know from seeing you again. I suspect you've really changed much less than I have." Her shoulders fell again, resigned. "I feel a million years old, older than the mountains, older than the river itself. Look at me. My husband has just died, and I haven't shed a single tear. I feel nothing, nothing at all."

"It's just delayed reaction," he said. "Many people feel that way immediately after a great stress."

"Or else everything has been burned out of me. Passions. Feelings. The capacity to care." She passed her hand over her face, composed her features, forced herself to look him directly in the eye. "No, that's not quite true. I care that you've stayed behind and helped me like this. It's kind of you. I can't begin to think what your feelings must be toward me. I gave you up for dead, married another man, had children by him. All while you were suffering in prison. I'm sure I don't deserve your kindness." Now it was her turn to wave his expostulations away. "No. Let's be honest with each other. It's all we have left."

"I wonder," he said. "I'd like there to be a friendship between us, even if nothing else develops. I stand ready to do Shobai's bidding at any time, to look after the three of you. No, don't refuse. You have no idea what power I have here. I can keep trouble away from you." A little stiffly he added, "I can look out for you and the children so discreetly, you won't even know you're being protected."

"Thank you," she said. "And . . . I'd be pleased if, some time soon, you could call on us. You know, from time to time." She held out her hand very formally; but when he took it equally formally, there was something unusual, something charged with meaning, and emotion, in the very touch of hand to hand, and their eyes locked for a moment, a moment of confused and unfocused feelings neither of them could have sorted out.

Mereet was the first to recover. She withdrew her hand and tried to smile, but the smile only mirrored her confusion. "Now I've got to get to my children. My babies! They're so big! I hope they'll remember me after all this time. I'll have to get to know them a little at a time."

Baka bowed formally. "Give them my best," he said. "Perhaps I can be of help. I know the children quite well." But there was something in his voice that gave promise of more. He turned with a soldier's economical motions and went away.

Mereet sighed and went back to the children's room. As she entered she could see Ketan sleeping, mouth wide open, the covers kicked down to his ankles; but Teti sat up looking at her, eyes wide open. There was no sign of recognition at all on the little face at first. Then the eyes blinked, once, twice. "M-mother?" the child said.

Mereet tried to catch her breath. And suddenly, making a lie of her earlier words, she learned how few emotions had been burned out of her by her experiences, and she found that, yes, indeed, she still remembered how to weep. Teti, tousle-haired, naked, warm from sleep, dashed headlong into her arms, and her heart opened, and all the joy and pain of living rushed into her soul again.

# CHAPTER
# TWENTY

## Ezion-Geber

Rumors of a coming drought had begun to drift about the entire land of Canaan—indeed, about all the lands between far Elam in the east and the Great Sea in the west. For the most part the rumors were dismissed by the villages' elders as irresponsible, based on superstition. In Canaan, for example, snowmelt in the high mountains to the north continued to feed the network of streams that flowed into Lake Chinnereth, and the overflow from the lake fed the Jordan all the way to its eventual death in the dreadful sink of the Salt Sea, where earthquake had destroyed Sodom generations ago. Furthermore, the rainfall in these northern lands had remained normal through the seasons, and the crops continued their high yield.

But elsewhere, the transition to famine was already beginning. In the desolate, heaven-blasted lands of the Arabah, south of the destroyed cities of the plain, the rumors had more easily taken hold. There had been no rainfall for several years already, and the coastal lands below the hills that bordered the Gulf of Eilat, which in wetter days had become salt marsh every year in days of rain, now lay as parched as the hills above them. What had once been mud was now cracked sands and shingle. The sparse semidesert greenery had largely died, and the native fauna—the cheetah and honey badger, as well as smaller game—had become so scarce that the Shepherd overlords of the gulf region had forbidden further hunting, at least until the rains began again.

Indeed, there seemed little reason now for the very existence of the threadbare port town of Ezion-Geber. There was no trade; the port had been closed to foreign ships during the protracted war between the Shepherds and the native Egyptians. The town's food had to be brought in by ship from across the Red Sea by the Shepherd-controlled Egyptian vessels, and with the wells that served the town drying up one by one, there was talk of the water supply having to be replenished by ship as well. The only ships that put into the port were Shepherd vessels, which came to carry away ore and a few finished metal products from the Shepherd-owned mines at Timna.

The town itself had the desolate look of a place cursed by some god. Timna itself, once a metalworkers' center—it had for a time been home to the great Belsunu, who had armed the Canaanite patriarch Abraham for his war against the Four Kings—was now a slave-labor camp in which men were worked in the blazing sun until they dropped . . . a place where the guards themselves were men who had been sent to this ghastly duty for their own infractions of Shepherd laws. Guards who had good work records were allowed, once a month, to go into Ezion-Geber for a weekend's carouse, such as it was; but there was little joy, little diversion, even precious little dissipation, to be found in a starveling backwater like Ezion-Geber. The few remaining whores, male or female, were aging, cynical, and diseased, thoroughly unappetizing even to the desperate wretches who had earned overnight leave among them. There was little to do in the town but reach for the nearest drug, be it poisonous mushrooms bought from the sailors or the vile palm wine dispensed at the town's two miserable taverns.

Worst of all, there was no leaving the town once you had landed there, unless it was to return to Timna. The last caravan had called from the north six months before; after that, orders had come down from Avaris forbidding any further traffic with the Canaanite and Moabite communities. And, of course, it was quite impossible to leave the town by ship; no passengers were allowed aboard the ore-carrying ships, and even the galley slaves remained chained to the seats while the boats were in port. Leg-chained slaves from the mines loaded the ore onto the boats, which otherwise bore only skeleton crews: captain, mate, the drummer who gave the oarsmen the stroke, and a token guard brought along in case of mutiny.

During the most recent cruise, Apek, mate of the ore ship *Beloved of Osiris*, had made friends with Beon, leader of the ship's guard. When the ship docked, their duties were suspended for a day because the ore shipment from Timna had been delayed. They inspected the town's whores, decided against such "pleasures," took a meager meal at the tavern nearest the docks, and proceeded to test, one by one, the available beers and palm wines their surly host trotted out for their inspection.

After the third sample of the local beers had been served, Apek called for a plate of olives, tasted the cup of beer before him, and sent it back, calling disgustedly for palm wine, the stronger the better. Beon sat back, belched loudly, and watched with an increasingly jaundiced eye the gyrations of a skinny "dancing girl" hastily called in from the street, as she went through a dispirited and totally perfunctory dance to the accompaniment of drum and shawm. The girl had a cast to one eye that obviously bespoke her desire to be someplace else, and, to top things off, proved, once the last of her shabby veils was gone, to have a highly suspicious rash, unappetizingly placed. Beon yawned and turned back to his drinking, his manner showing visible distaste for the whole proceeding.

As he did, a man wearing a rag across his forehead detached himself from the small crowd at the other end of the room and made his way to their table. He waited until the music had stopped; then he spoke in a voice whose tone, at once unctuous and tense, aroused instant dislike in Apek. "Pardon me, sirs. I couldn't help noticing. The girl, she was not to your taste?"

Apek was about to shout "Be off!" But Beon, a cynical grin on his battered features, shook his head. Beon looked up at the stranger with a cold eye and said, "She was fit fodder for a really desperate baboon." Beon yawned again and said, "Perhaps you can offer alternate fare for a couple of lonely seamen, then?"

Again Apek was ready to protest, but Beon shushed him. The stranger looked nervously from the one to the other as if sizing them up. "Perhaps I can," he said. "Uh . . . perhaps a nice clean boy, sir? A friend of mine bought two fair-haired young fellows from the Moabites before the town was closed to trade. Very clean, sir. Sound in every limb. Guaranteed to please." Apek looked at the stranger's shifty eye, at his desperation, and began to understand Beon's amusement. "No, sir?" the stranger said. "Then, perhaps, a little girl, stolen from an Ishmaelite caravan six months back. Only eight years old. She's never known a man, sir, I guarantee it."

Apek scowled. This was beyond the limits of taste already, yet the fellow seemed ready to go further. "We're not interested," he said, ignoring Beon's silent protests. "Nothing today, thank you—"

The stranger's shifty eyes jumped from one to the other, and he evidently misread their distaste. "Oh, I didn't mean to insult a couple of refined gentlemen," he said. "It's just that . . ." His voice broke. "Please, sirs. Could I join you for a moment?" Beon shrugged; the man sat down opposite them at the big table, his eyes darting from one to the other. "It's so seldom one meets cultured people, people of sensitivity. One gets so lonely here. . . ."

"Here," Beon said, tossing him a coin. "Get us more palm wine. Bring a cup for yourself." When the stranger had gone off to get the wine, Beon leaned forward and whispered, "This one amuses me. He's really at the end of his rope. There's no limit to how much he'd abase himself for a coin. Most likely what he wants is to get out of here. They all do. He thinks that if he flatters us enough, we'll give him a berth on the boat back to Egypt. Let's let him jabber. It might be entertaining." Apek nodded and sat back, just as the stranger came back with his loaded tray.

Beon expertly led him on, pouring him cup after cup of the strong liquor. He was some sort of Canaanite or Damascene, from his accent, and his name was Shamir ben-Hashum; he had come here looking for a ship back before the port closed, and had found himself trapped in this desolate hole, unable to get away. It was not fair; he had done nothing wrong, and here he was, imprisoned in this pit of vipers through no fault of his own. If the kind captains could see fit to let him work his way to Egypt, he would be eternally grateful; he would show his gratitude in any way they chose to require of him. He said this as if he were a catamite; Beon stood, and behind the stranger's back, as he addressed Apek, Beon made a face like a man vomiting up his lunch. Apek tried to suppress a shudder; the very idea of touching this man in any way, or being touched by him, filled him with revulsion.

"Please, sirs," Shamir said, "it's so short a ride, and to get away from this horrid place I'd do anything." He made calf's eyes at each of them in turn. "*Anything.*" His hands, nervous, trembling, clawed the air; the liquor had managed somehow to bring out the underlying malice, the venality, in him, to give his voice an even more unpleasant edge than before. "Surely the great Kirakos wouldn't mind if just one poor refugee were to turn up on his shores. . . ."

"Kirakos?" Beon said sourly, returning to his seat. "Dead and forgotten. And a good thing, too, you slimy guttersnipe. If Kirakos were alive, he'd have orders posted in the garrison to have scum like you flayed for asking a soldier of his command to break his laws." He spat disgustedly on the floor and looked at Apek. "I'm tired of this game. Let's get rid of this parasite."

"Parasite, sir? But—" The leech's eyes went quickly from one face to the other. "But you said Kirakos was dead. Surely this means his harsh laws have been repealed. Who is the new vizier? Perhaps his regulations are more humane, more magnanimous."

"The new vizier is Joseph of Canaan," Beon said. "And you're right, bloodsucker. His laws are softer on slime like you. Where Kirakos would have you flayed, Joseph in his mercy commands only that you spend the next five years pounding rocks in Timna." As he looked up, three of his men came in, uniformed, armed. "Here! You three! Over here! Take this man into custody!"

For some odd reason Shamir made no move to get away. Instead he stood, eyes wide with a new kind of madness, staring. His motions were jerky; his hands clenched and unclenched. "Joseph of Canaan?" he said incredulously. "Is he a red-haired man? How long has he been in Egypt?"

"He *does* have red hair," Apek replied, interested. "Anyone knows that."

"Joseph?" the stranger said. His voice had changed. There was a glint of insane rage in his eye, and his balled fists shook with impotent anger. "*Joseph?* Vizier of *Egypt?* It's not fair! He can't be alive! The gods curse him, he has to be dead!"

One of the soldiers grabbed Shamir's arm; he shook it

loose and backed away. "But he was kidnapped for a slave! His brothers planned to sell him, but then he was kidnapped! I asked them! He can't be alive! He can't have risen like that, and me here rotting!"

"Come along, you!" the soldier said. He and his partners advanced, swords drawn, and in a moment had Shamir pinned against the wall, their swords at his throat and belly, pressing just hard enough to break the skin. "All right, tie his hands behind him! Nice and tight! Wrap the package up nice and pretty, boys, and we'll deliver him to the captain of the guard; he's making up a nice new shipment of rock breakers for the Timna pits right now, and he'll be delighted to see this new addition. They don't mind how ugly or stupid or vicious you are up at the mines, so long as you have a strong back. And this one looks strong enough. He ought to last two years before he has to be dumped in a hole!"

Beon and Apek got up to leave. They did not look back. This raised Shamir's anger to fever pitch again. "You bastards!" he screamed. "I'll get you for this, if it's the last thing I ever do! And I'll get Joseph, too! I'll be back, just you watch! I'll find my way to Egypt and have my revenge! I'll kill him! Just you wait! I'll cut his heart out!"

Apek, a step behind Beon, went out the door, hearing the threats, the wild screams, still echoing in his ear. He shuddered. There was something *about* the fellow. Something chilling, frightening. Madness might well sustain him through the horrors of working in the mines, might bring him on the trail of the men who, in his eyes, had wronged him . . . if he lived.

But that was quite impossible. He would never survive five years doing that kind of labor, in that broiling sun. And even if he did, Egypt was closed to him. It was impossible.

But somehow Apek's mind would not dismiss the thought. After all, he had seen the madness in Shamir's eyes. He had heard the harsh tone in the back of his throat, with its jackal's growl. He could not put the thought aside, and he knew it would come back to haunt him.

He shuddered and hurried down the shabby street after Beon, the hateful screams still ringing in his ears. It was silly of him, he knew. But all of a sudden he couldn't wait until the *Beloved of Osiris* once again pulled anchor and stood out to sea.

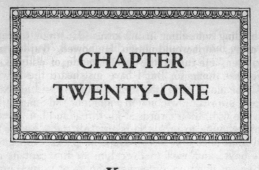

# CHAPTER
# TWENTY-ONE

## Kerma

Amenatu, commander of the Fourth Legion, walked briskly but unhurriedly up the long stairs to the west wing of the palace of Kerma. At the top of the stairs, two gigantic, perfectly matched warriors of Akhilleus's home tribe guarded the inner sanctum of the great king; but as the commander approached, they snapped smartly to attention and saluted him.

Amenatu returned the salute, but paused before entering the great door. "No one has announced the news formally," he said, "yet I would like to congratulate Akhilleus. Is the child born?"

"Yes, Captain." The Nubian language sat a little more easily on the lips of this soldier than was usual. "It was a boy-child." Saying this last, he could not suppress a proud grin.

"That's wonderful." Amenatu beamed. "Imagine, Akhilleus a father. And at his age."

"Akillu has no age," the soldier responded. "And he is the father of all men in Nubia. He is your father and mine."

"I couldn't agree more," Amenatu said. "Carry on." He kept the smile as he marched through the door, as he greeted the inner guards, as he was at last admitted to the inner room where Akhilleus, tall and big-boned, towered over a wide

402

bed, holding something in his arms. He tried to wipe the smile away, but it would not go. He bowed. "Pardon me, my father," he said, using the formal mode of address. "It is unseemly to smile so. But I have just heard the news." He bowed to Ebana, who lay propped up in the bed watching her husband cradle the tiny black infant in his mighty arms.

"You may well smile," Akhilleus said. "Look at this child! Already he has an arm of bronze. See how he pulls at my finger! Woman, you have done well."

"Give him to me," Ebana said. "He'll be getting hungry in a moment or two. I don't want you getting upset when he starts crying." She took the baby and held it to her breast. Akhilleus smiled at her and took Amenatu off into another room, moving with one great stride to Amenatu's two.

"Have you decided upon a name yet?" Amenatu asked as they came to the terrace, with its great sweeping view of the Nile's curve.

"Officially Amani," the old man said. "We decided to choose a Nubian name as a token of respect for the land and its people. But this boy will have another name as he grows, a name among the Egyptians, which will strike fear into their bones. He will have a name they will carve onto the stelae, which will remain forever. They will call him Nehsi—the Black One."

"Then rumor is also correct about, uh, certain ambitions our regime may have in the north?" the captain asked.

Akhilleus looked out over the river, his eyes mere slits, his face unreadable. "Ambitions?" he repeated slowly. A faint smile lingered on his lips. "Perhaps." He turned to Amenatu. "You've made a good name for yourself, Captain. I've followed your career since the fall of Kor. You're an able commander, and the men like and respect you."

"The respect and liking are mutual, sir," Amenatu said. "I never had any idea I would wind up holding brotherly feelings for black men a head taller than I."

"Life teaches us many things," the giant said. "One of these is that destiny is a thing to be trusted. I would never have believed where my own destiny would lead me. A slave on a galley. Commander of a pirate ship. A merchant prince. Turning down one kingdom to win another. Who would have believed it?" Now his voice changed. The philosophical turn of mind was replaced by a businesslike air. His voice became sharper, full of resolve. "Shall I give you a fleeting look at such ambitions as may lie ahead, Captain? Come, look."

He led Amenatu to a table, where a map of all the lands of Nubia and the two Egypts, Black and Red, had been drawn on sand in colored paints. "Here is the delta," he said, pointing. "Here is the domain of Dedmose. It ends just north of the forts, the Second Cataract. For now, that is."

"For *now*, sir?"

"Here to the north the cataracts end, and the Nile is clear sailing. Up this wadi here are valuable mines: copper, gold. Here are Khenu and Swenet—and Edfu. Here is Nekhen, on the west bank of the Nile, and Nekheb on the opposite side." He looked down at Amenatu and said in a measured voice, "With any luck, Captain, you will own a villa in Edfu by the time you are forty."

"A villa in—" Amenatu blinked. "But that's deep into Egyptian territory, sir!"

"Learn to think in other terms, Captain," Akhilleus said. "This son of mine . . . for his tenth birthday I will give him Thebes."

"Thebes, sir? Thebes?"

But Akhilleus's eyes were on the map again, and he seemed to be talking to himself. "I have put out the call to all the tribes of the south. To the west, the Kawahla. To the southwest, the Hamar and the Nuba and the Zande. To the south, the Nuer and the Mondari and the Lotuko and the mighty Dinka. I have appealed to the manhood of the young men of all the tribes and have invited them to join me in a great quest." He did look down at Amenatu now, and his smile was warm and his eyes no longer far away. "You'll like the Dinka, Captain. They're even taller than my own people, and they're afraid of nothing and nobody in all the world."

"This takes my breath away. I'd known you had plans, but I'd always thought they involved a gradual move on the borderlands, for the purpose of annexing those mines you mentioned. But Thebes?"

"Thebes," Akhilleus said, a hard glint in his eye. "Why not? Why not the Fayum? Why not Lisht? Why not—"

"Lisht, sir? But I thought Baka was your friend."

"Baka is a gallant soldier. So were the commanders of Semna and Kumma and Dorginarti. So were Kashta and Taharqa. I honor them, as I honor Baka." Akhilleus started to say something else, but stopped. He strode to the window and looked downriver, to the north. "Baka is a great soldier, but one who leads a weak army." He looked back at Amenatu now. "You know, of course, that Baka is now vizier of Egypt. Yes. That means his control over the army is now secondary. It seems to be under the actual command of a man named Anup. A good man, but no Baka."

His eyes blazed now with an inner fire. "Nothing, nothing at all, to the north is what it was. Baka is wise, but young. He is not Madir. He is armed by Ben-Hadad, not my old friend Shobai. That makes some difference right there." His voice grew thoughtful. "Now, if Ben-Hadad were to find the Nubian smith he was looking for—the one who works iron—that would be another matter. But he doesn't know where to find him, and, sad to say, neither do I, although I've had men looking for him ever since the fall of Kerma. When I first heard about him, I tricked Ben-Hadad into going back to Egypt, citing the will of Dedmose. I didn't want the lad finding him before I did." He sighed. "Perhaps the smith is dead. He might have died at the battle for Kerma. Nobody seems to know." His back straightened, and he shrugged it all off.

"But that's all speculation," he said. "I don't need iron weapons to take the Red Lands. I don't need them to take Lisht. And this son of mine won't need them to take—"

But now he turned and smiled. And the faraway look in his eyes was gone once and for all. "You can see," he said slowly, "where my thoughts are bending."

Amenatu bowed formally. "My compliments, sir. The Shepherds have been in the delta too long already. And from all the reports one hears from downriver, the Shepherds, too, are not what they were. Their Golden Pharaoh so little resembles his father, one can hardly believe they're of the same blood. Yet there *are* so very many of them, sir."

"Yes," Akhilleus said. "But they've kept busy putting down rebellion in their own lands. Salitis reigns with a heavy hand. Even the Shepherd soldiers are complaining of his tyranny. There have been small mutinies within their own ranks. The situation is so bad, he's had to hire a new general from Mesopotamia to reorganize his army." He smiled. "But it won't do any good in the long run. When they settled in one place the spirit went out of them. Put a nomad in a city and he begins to die before the first sunset."

"Forgive me, sir. I almost forgot why I came. The inspection, sir. The Fourth Legion is drawn up before the palace. You were to address them, I think, and award medals for valor."

"Right you are," Akhilleus said. "Come along. We'll do that right now."

But when at last the king and commander stood on the parapet looking down at the assembled troops of Amenatu's unit, Akhilleus found he could not maintain the air of high seriousness, of royal detachment, that the occasion demanded. He looked across at the sea of faces; these were men he had led and fought beside, men who had shed blood in his service, in the service of the cause he had not yet fully revealed to them. Try as he might, he could not distance himself from them, as another king might. Instead, he felt a wave of love, of pride, of kinship, go through him, and it was like a fresh surge of power, of youth, flowing into his battered and weather-worn old body as he stood there. And instead of the speech he had prepared, he found himself speaking the words in his heart.

Grinning, he held up his great arms like a magus bestowing his blessings. "I have a boy-child!" he cried in a great echoing voice that carried, ringing, over all the bright young faces before him, over the streets of the city, over the bazaars and squares and alleyways. "I have a son! A prince for Nubia!"

# Epilogue

The fire was all ashes now, and a chill wind sighed down from the mountains. Mothers cradled their young to their breasts and huddled against the cold. The old men pulled their robes more closely about them and shivered. Winter was coming, and its dreaded hand would lie on the land for months to come.

The Teller of Tales spoke, but a gust of cold wind blew his first words away. When he spoke again, his voice had a hollow, disembodied quality, and there was a doleful singsong to it that the listeners gathered before him had not heard before:

"Then came the winds of change," he said. "Winds that blew ruthlessly across all the lands of the Crescent, carrying away with them, once and forever, the ordered life the people of the lands beside the Great Sea had known since time immemorial; leaving in their wake a new and puzzling life from which the mere thought of surfeit, of plenty, was banned. The seven years of ripe harvests came and went, and the great famine began."

The wind sighed above; echoing it, there came a soft sigh from the rows of listeners, a low murmur of concern. The old man raised his voice.

"But as the ill winds blew and thousands starved in the

407

*northern steppes, a great power, Joseph, son of Jacob, had come to guide the hand of the Golden Pharaoh. Justice came for a time to the rich delta lands, which alone had survived the famine. With justice came a second great migration, as the hungry thousands staggered across the parched Sinai desert in search of food, of work, of a new life. And with justice came peace.*

*"But in the Southern lands, peace was brief. A new and powerful leader had arisen to contest the throne of Dedmose, king of kings, lord of the Red Lands. Tomorrow you shall hear—"*

*There came a low protest from the ranks before him, and the rising wind blew it away. Again he raised his voice: "Tomorrow you shall hear of the rise of Akhilleus, of the desperate search of Ben-Hadad for the lost secret of the working of the black metal, which alone could halt the forward surge of the invader and drive the Shepherd overlords from the shores of the Nile. Tomorrow you shall hear of the young son of Ben-Hadad and of the fatherless children of great Shobai and what fortune awaited them as they grew and took up the banner of the Children of the Lion in a changing land."*

*His voice boomed out now, and the wind howled. "You shall hear of how the sons of Jacob forsook the Land of Promise to go into peril in a foreign country. . . ." The winds shrieked and pulled at his tattered robes, and his voice faded. And as he withdrew, all they could hear over the roar of the wind was the one last, dying word:*

*"Tomorrow . . ."*

READ THIS THRILLING PREVIEW
OF A BOLD NEW SAGA
FROM THE CREATORS OF WAGONS WEST
AND CHILDREN OF THE LION

# AMERICA 2040

---

## BY EVAN INNES

As the author of the CHILDREN OF THE LION Series, my interest is writing about men and women whose faith and resourcefulness give them the drive and courage to do what they think is right in the face of adversity. These are the types of people you will find in Evan Innes's AMERICA 2040. This thrilling novel pits freedom-loving, upstanding men and women determined to continue the American way of life in face of a crazed Russian Premier determined to force the final nuclear confrontation.

I know every reader will be impressed by this exciting series as much as I was, as the power of good triumphs over the forces of evil.

Peter Danielson
Author of CHILDREN OF THE LION

To American President Dexter Hamilton, entering Greater Moscow in the spring of 2033 was a fifty-year leap into the past, an enigmatic separation from his familiar, changing, bustling world. The impressive modernity of Gagarin Airport, the city's newest civilian and military aviation facility, had not prepared him for the real Moscow.

There was snow in the city, grayed, trodden, piled. Along the motorcade route he and his entourage caught glimpses of real antiques: diesel-powered trucks spouting the contaminants of burning fossil fuel to cloud the chill air. People swaddled in animal furs. Drab, stern, slab-sided apartment buildings that had been built shortly after World War II.

Under a lowering, slate sky, the Kremlin loomed redly beyond the frozen Moskva River. To Hamilton, and to millions, the triangularly shaped fortress housed most of what was evil in the world. The relationship between Russia and the United States remained tense, hostile, suspicious, and dangerous, but Dexter Hamilton wanted to be the American President who halted the eternal arms race and delivered the world, forever, from the threat of nuclear incineration. To that end, he was to meet with the Soviet leader, Premier Yuri Kolchak.

The President was young to be serving in that office, only forty-six, having been born in 1987. His silvering hair—a tight, curled mass that clung to his well-formed head—seemed to be a tacit signal that, although young, here was a wise, experienced man.

Behind the smile-crinkled blue eyes, the classic nose, the upturned mouth, there was the strength that had given him the governorship of North Carolina, then a seat in the Senate, and finally the Oval Office.

When the limousine hummed through guarded gates, past heavily armed and stalwart men handpicked for Kremlin duty from the huge Red Army, Dexter Hamilton was guided from the car by a woman general. He walked with long, quick strides, eager to begin the summit meeting with Premier Yuri Kolchak.

Premier Kolchak was waiting for him behind a wide, gleaming table in a conference room. The Premier was a darkly handsome man, but there was something in his eyes that bothered Hamilton, a quality he'd seen before. Then the memory came back to him: When he was quite young he'd owned a little dog that had wandered into a field and been swept up in a tomato picker. The dying, mutilated dog lay stunned and shocked. In Kolchak's eyes were those same qualities—a pain that seemed to approach madness. Was there truth to the rumor that the Premier was seriously ill?

*Several minutes after the meeting has begun, Yuri Kolchak rises abruptly from his seat, obviously taken ill. He is led away hastily, without explanation or apology. Hamilton is escorted back to his suite, where, except for a serving girl bringing dinner, he is left alone for the night.*

The next morning there was a knock on the door of his luxurious suite in the Kremlin, and a smiling, dark-haired serving girl in livery appeared. Pleasant aromas of coffee, real eggs, and ham came from the serving cart she was standing behind. A great number of covered serving bowls were on the cart, certainly enough for more than one man.

Just then he heard a deep, resonant voice coming from behind the girl.

"Good morning, Mr. President. You slept well?"

Premier Kolchak was dressed informally in tunic, trousers. At forty-seven his slightly Slavic face was smooth, and his dark and bristly hair showed no hint of gray. He extended a hand. Hamilton took it. Each grip was firm.

"Forgive me for surprising you," Kolchak said as the serving girl disappeared out the door. "But if I had taken time to warn you that I was coming, we'd have to invite our aides and observe protocol." There was no explanation of the previous meeting's cancellation.

"I understand," Hamilton said. Kolchak took a seat and Hamilton sat across the table, and they began to eat.

"My people don't understand your real purpose here," the Premier said.

"Well, Yuri," Hamilton began, "you like straight talk, so here it is: I'm here to talk peace. I want to talk about what we have in common. We're all passengers on a small, increasingly overcrowded planet. It is time we took down the bombs from the space stations and junked the missiles and the space weapons. The men who bring peace to the world will be sung in history down through the ages. Let's make those men you and me."

"I could learn to like you," Kolchak said. "I will give you anything you want from this conference."

The statement seemed simple enough, direct enough, but there was something wrong.

"Because you see," Kolchak said, his dark, hard

eyes boring into Hamilton's, "whatever you achieve in this present conference does not matter." The Premier had finished eating. He leaned back, wiped his lips on a linen napkin, let it fall to his knee. "What matters is what you and I say here in this room." He smiled. "I hope you will be receptive and reasonable."

"I'll do my best."

"For centuries," Kolchak said, "elitist and imperialist countries have delayed the destiny of the masses. We can no longer allow that. Soon, Mr. President, the downtrodden of the world will be free to share in the fruits of their own labors. Within my lifetime, the revolution will be total." He paused. "With one single exception. We will allow the continued existence of the United States as a governmental entity. In time, with the rest of the world's workers freed from their masters and living in equality with their fellows, you will see reason and work with the rest of the civilized world." Ever since the use of the first atomic bomb on Japan, men had dreaded that someday, in some country, a madman would be in a position to push the button. This, Hamilton felt with a despair that made him want to strike out, was the man.

"Mr. Premier, this must be the first time in the history of my country that a President has been so threatened."

Kolchak shrugged. "We can no longer allow you to prevent the legitimate aspirations of the peoples of this world. We have liberated many countries. We will liberate more."

"Are you speaking of South America?"

"That, first."

South America was dominated by the emerging

imperialistic giant Brazil, whose armed forces had overwhelmed Cuba, ending Communist rule there. However, Communist insurgents continued to rebel against Brazilian authorities in the Caribbean and South America. An American fleet was stationed in the Pacific, but as of yet there had been no direct confrontation with the Russians.

"Are you declaring war?" Hamilton asked. "For we will fight you over that continent."

"There will be a war only if you choose to interfere. If both our countries let loose all our military power there will be little, if any, life left on Earth. But that doesn't really matter."

"What, in God's name, does matter?"

Kolchak leaned forward, his face pale, his lips twitching in obvious pain. "The triumph of right."

"Your brand of right, of course?"

"Of course. There is no other. Now will you pull out of South America and let events take their course?"

"No."

Kolchak leaned back, sighed. "Then, Mr. President, prepare yourself for some very difficult decisions."

"We've faced tough decisions before," Hamilton said. "I'll admit that you're scaring the living daylights out of me, but we won't stand aside and let you gobble up what's left."

Kolchak smiled. "Understand this, Mr. President. Before I die, the world will be Red or dead, and quite frankly I don't give a"—he used a Russian obscenity unfamiliar to Hamilton—"which it is."

Hamilton heard himself saying words, inane words. "May you have a long life, Mr. Premier."

"No, my friend, you will not escape the responsibility in that way."

"You *are* ill," Hamilton said softly.

Kolchak, with a cold smile, nodded.

"Perhaps we could help in some way. Our medical research—"

"Is no better than ours."

"How long?" Hamilton asked.

"Fewer than nine years."

"I'm sorry," Hamilton said. "But we have time to think about it, to talk. Yuri, there's no winning a war. My God, man, we've both got enough warheads in space to do the job twice over. If you push the button I'm dead, but I'll have time to push my own button and you're dead."

"But I'm dead regardless of what happens," Kolchak said. With a wicked gleam in his black eyes, he added, "All I care about is that the world is ours . . . or else it does not exist at all."

*President Hamilton returns to Washington, where he briefs the head of the CIA and orders him to make the assassination of Yuri Kolchak a top priority. Then Dexter Hamilton and his scientific advisor, Oscar Kost, explore other ways to avert annihilation of the American people and their way of life. Their search takes them to Vandenberg Air Force Base in California, to learn about Project Lightstep, a top-secret operation.*

Dexter Hamilton and Oscar Kost were introduced by a two-star general to Harry Shaw, a small, dark man, with a wide forehead and thin mouth that was, nevertheless, capable of a wide smile.

"This is a genuine pleasure, Mr. President, Mr. Kost," Shaw said.

"The pleasure is mutual," Hamilton said. "I have

to confess that I know absolutely nothing about this project. Please start at the beginning.''

"I'll try to make it brief," Shaw said. "When I was an undergraduate I worked with platinum metals and their ability to store heat and energy, but it wasn't until I got my hands on a supply of rhenium that I began to make any progress. I decided to hit a few molecules of rhenium with antimatter, and as a result we almost obliterated Los Angeles. The reaction was contained, but just barely," Shaw added.

Hamilton didn't see the significance. A bigger and better bomb would not make Yuri Kolchak take his finger off the button. Nuclear bombs could already destroy all life on Earth, so why bother with something else?

"Harry," Hamilton said, "just tell me rhenium's other applications."

"It's currently the energy source for an experimental space vehicle disguised as a simple planetary probe. It's out beyond Pluto right now. If we've succeeded, that vehicle, propelled by rhenium, has made a round trip to within a few million miles of the star closest to our system, Proxima Centauri. That's thirty trillion miles in a billionth of a second."

Hamilton felt a sudden surge of joy. He glanced at Kost. Oscar's hooded eyes were gleaming. For the first time since his meeting with Yuri Kolchak, Hamilton felt a swelling of hope in his breast. As the countdown clock jerked its second hand closer to the critical moment when the experimental space vehicle's computer-screen transmission would be received by Vandenberg, a fantastic and exciting dream grew inside Dexter Hamilton: If Yuri Kolchak sent the whole world up in smoke and dust and fire, there would be still one last hope for the human race.

"One minute and counting," an amplified voice said, breaking the tense silence.

Hamilton's eyes were on the clock.

"Thirty seconds . . . twenty—"

Screens came to life, flickered, were blank. There was an air of supreme tension in the room, a breathless hush except for the counting voice.

"—five, four, three, two, one—!"

A large screen flickered, static lines flowering, diminishing, and then the screen was filled with fire— harsh, golden, roiling, boiling fire.

"Oh, God, no," Hamilton said. Seen close up, a sun is an awesome furnace, the golden fires of thermonuclear reaction forming slowly roiling masses on its curved surface.

"Wait," Harry Shaw said, his voice cracking with excitement. "We're not on the scopes. We're on radio telemetry."

And slowly, slowly, the screen changed, the fire gradually becoming more distant.

"The camera is changing lenses!" Shaw yelled. "We were too close!"

A cheer went up.

"It worked! Thank God, it worked!" Harry Shaw yelled, doing a little dance. It worked! Man could travel faster than light. With some luck, and some tricky, very secret planning, there could be people, Americans, out there traveling through the far reaches of space.

Now there was hope. At least some would survive. Hamilton would see to that. He could not trust Yuri Kolchak to leave the United States alone. Kolchak would want total world domination, and Dexter would never bow down and live under Communism. There'd be a part of the United States of America alive, out there in space. And if the missiles began to lance down from the orbiting space stations, at least a seed stock of humankind, if the form of Americans, would be alive.

*The colossal rhenium-powered spaceship, secretly constructed under the Utah desert over a period of six years, is ready for lift-off. In the interim, Yuri Kolchak's health and the international political situation deteriorate. President Hamilton addresses the nation and the world, on the brink of nuclear war, disclosing at last history's best kept secret, the* Spirit of America.

From cameras outside, a view of the White House was flashed upward to satellites, and a band played the "Star Spangled Banner." The anthem was being fed to the sound monitors in the Oval Office. As the last notes of music died, the director stabbed a finger toward Hamilton, who sat immobile, his calm, kind, distinguished face in repose, his eyes looking directly into the cameras. At last his drawling voice broke the almost unbearable tension.

"My fellow Americans. Today, December 24, 2040, this great nation of ours is about to embark upon humankind's greatest adventure.

"Even as I speak, while hundreds of thousands of our servicemen and women are massed in South America because of that age-old curse of mankind— war—other brave men and women are preparing to leave behind family and loved ones, their homes, their native country, even the planet of their birth.

"Today, one thousand Americans will leave Earth to open a new frontier among the stars.

"We Americans have a history of facing and

overcoming the unknown. Our forefathers dared a great ocean and overcame great obstacles to establish this nation, under God, and in freedom. They came to face the fierceness of a raw, vast land, and they established a nation that is unique, a nation wherein each and every individual has equal rights.

"Today our freedom faces its gravest test. Even now, our avowed enemies in South America threaten to overwhelm us, and the largest battle fleet ever to be assembled is massing off the western coast of the South American continent.

"I cannot tell you, my fellow citizens, what tomorrow will bring. But I can tell you this: The spirit of America will not die. The force and the dream that made this country great will live on in those brave pioneers who today will leave Earth to venture into the unknown.

"America now offers hope to the billions of people, citizens of every country. For the great ship that will journey to the far stars can, with international cooperation, bring the blessing of plenty back to our wasted world. American science, American genius, and the American dream have opened up a vast new empire, which can provide us with badly needed living space, a safety valve for our overpopulation, a source of rich, new raw materials to quiet our hunger and restore to us, and to the world, the standard of living we once knew.

"As President of the United States and as your spokesman, I extend the hand of cooperation and friendship to our enemies. The destiny of humankind cannot continue in bitter warfare until there is nothing left but ashes and cinders. No, we have a higher destiny. Our destiny lies among the stars."

Hamilton's face was seemingly at peace, his eagle's eyes looking straight into the camera.

"And now, my fellow Americans, let us experience this great moment together."

The first view was from a distance. Desert. Low mounds in the background, and then, from a hovering helicopter, the first view of the ship. It looked like some fantastic toy buried in a round hole in the ground. Only when the airborne camera pulled back to a long shot and it was possible to see vehicles, antlike people, the temporary town, was it possible to gain an idea of the ship's vast size.

From the top it looked like a huge wheel and had been painted red, white, and blue. On a blank expanse of metal near the core were Old Glory and the words *UNITED STATES*. And on the outer wheel, proudly, in huge letters that gleamed in gold against white, *Spirit of America*.

It came to life slowly. First a billowing rush of smoke pouring up from the circular pit around its sides, obscuring it, and then tongues of flame.

Was it merely illusion or did that impossibly huge mass move?

Smoke. Flames. Rocketry had reached its zenith. Fuels of high mass-to-bulk ratio had been developed during the space-station-building epoch. Combustion times had been extended. But never before had such a mass been lifted from Earth's gravitational pull. Never before had so much fuel been expended in so short time.

The ship crawled upward, and the flames decreased, and *Spirit of America* emerged from them, huge, round, lifting slowly, slowly, and that sound familiar to all Americans was rumbling and roaring, the awesome power sound of bellowing rockets as it had never been heard in such intensity. And now it was accelerating slowly, slowly, too fantastic to be anything but trick photography, and yet it was real.

The ship bellowed straight up for long minutes, and then, as the cameramen began to switch to their long lenses, it tilted slowly and angled off toward the east. It was so big that the longest lenses could follow it into orbit. True, the ship was but a bright speck of reflected sunlight when, after the rockets had ceased firing, it swam through the darkness of near space, a bright star to be seen with the naked eye, but it was there, and after the long tension of watching the takeoff, a billion Americans cheered.